W9-AXG-386

SUNNY
MAKES A SPLASH

JENNIFER L. HOLM & MATTHEW HOLM
WITH COLOR BY LARK PIEN

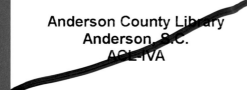

graphix

AN IMPRINT OF

■ SCHOLASTIC

Library of Congress data available

ISBN 978-1-338-23318-6 (hardcover)
ISBN 978-1-338-23317-9 (paperback)

10 9 8 7 6 5 4 3 2 1   21 22 23 24 25

Printed in China 62
First edition, September 2021
Edited by David Levithan
Lettering by Fawn Lau
Color by Lark Pien
Creative Director: Phil Falco
Publisher: David Saylor

For Jo

CHAPTER ONE: Yearbook

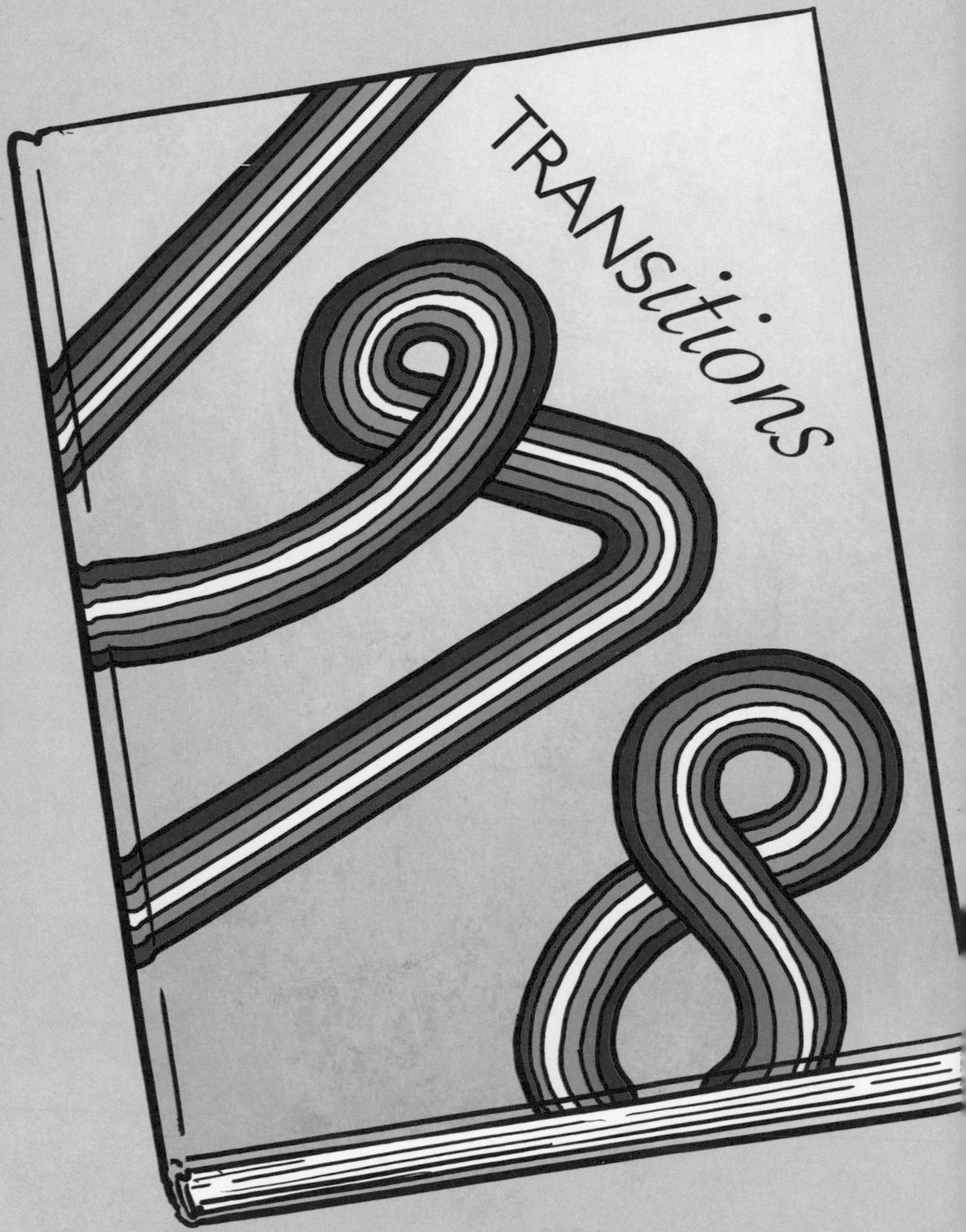
TRANSitions

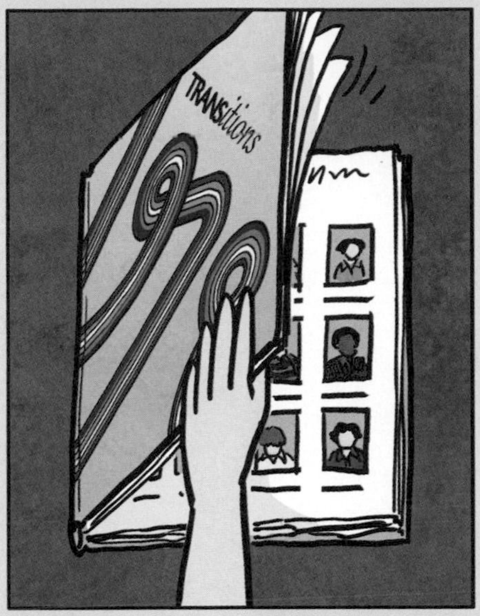
TRANSitions

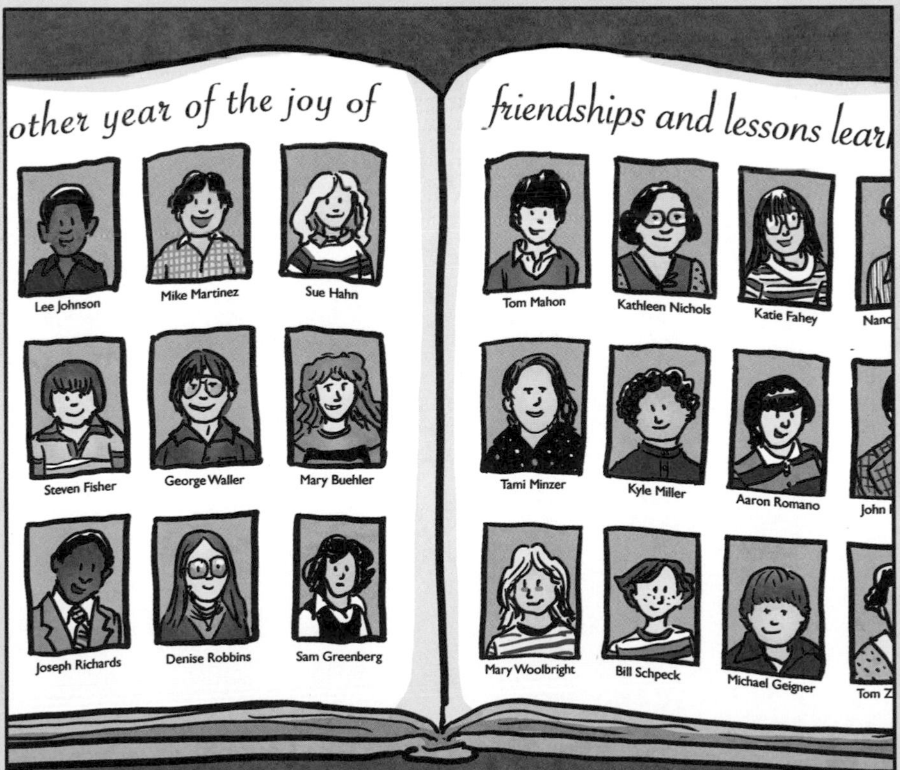
other year of the joy of
friendships and lessons
Lee Johnson
Mike Martinez
Sue Hahn
Steven Fisher
George Waller
Mary Buehler
Joseph Richards
Denise Robbins
Sam Greenberg
Tom Mahon
Kathleen Nichols
Katie Fahey
Tami Minzer
Kyle Miller
Aaron Romano
Mary Woolbright
Bill Schpeck
Michael Geigner

Thanks for the Memories!

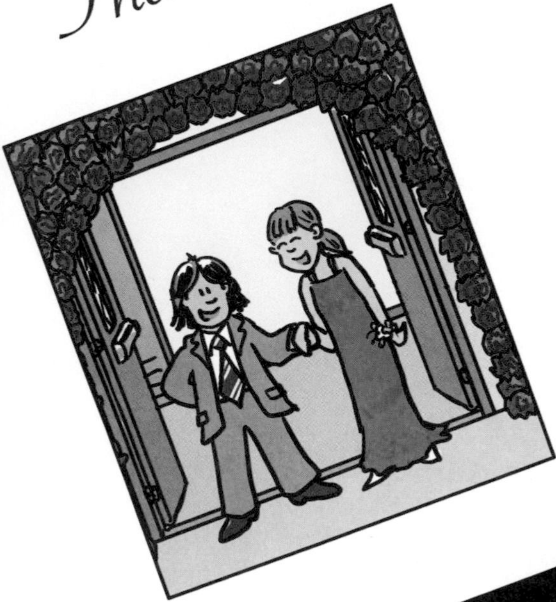

SPRIN
FLING!

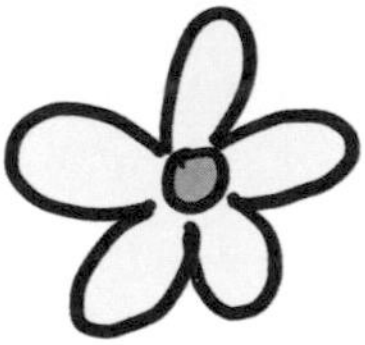

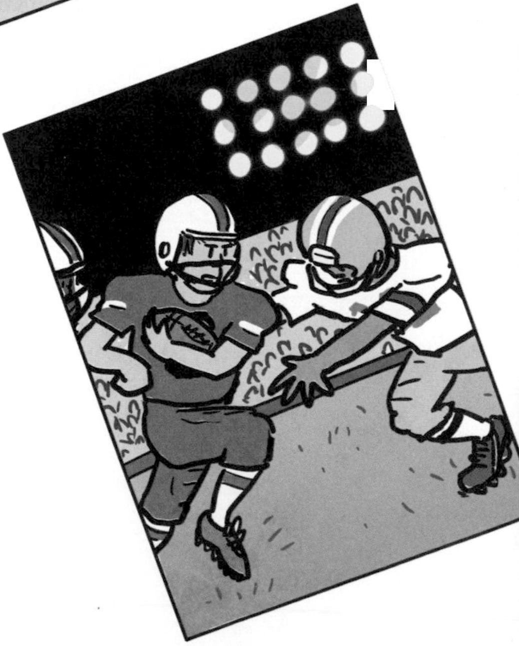

TOUCH
DOWN!

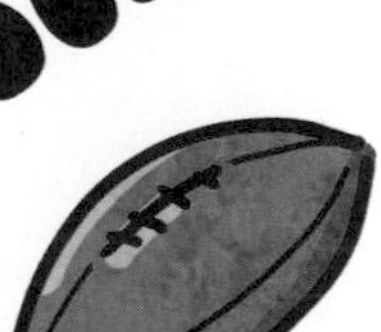

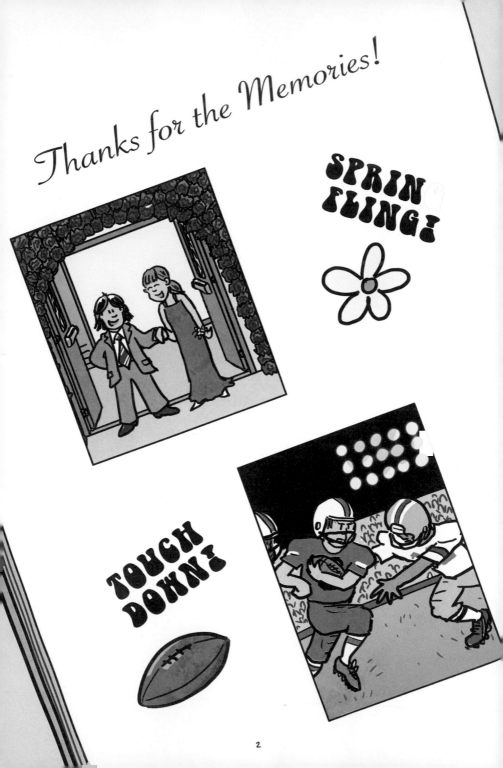

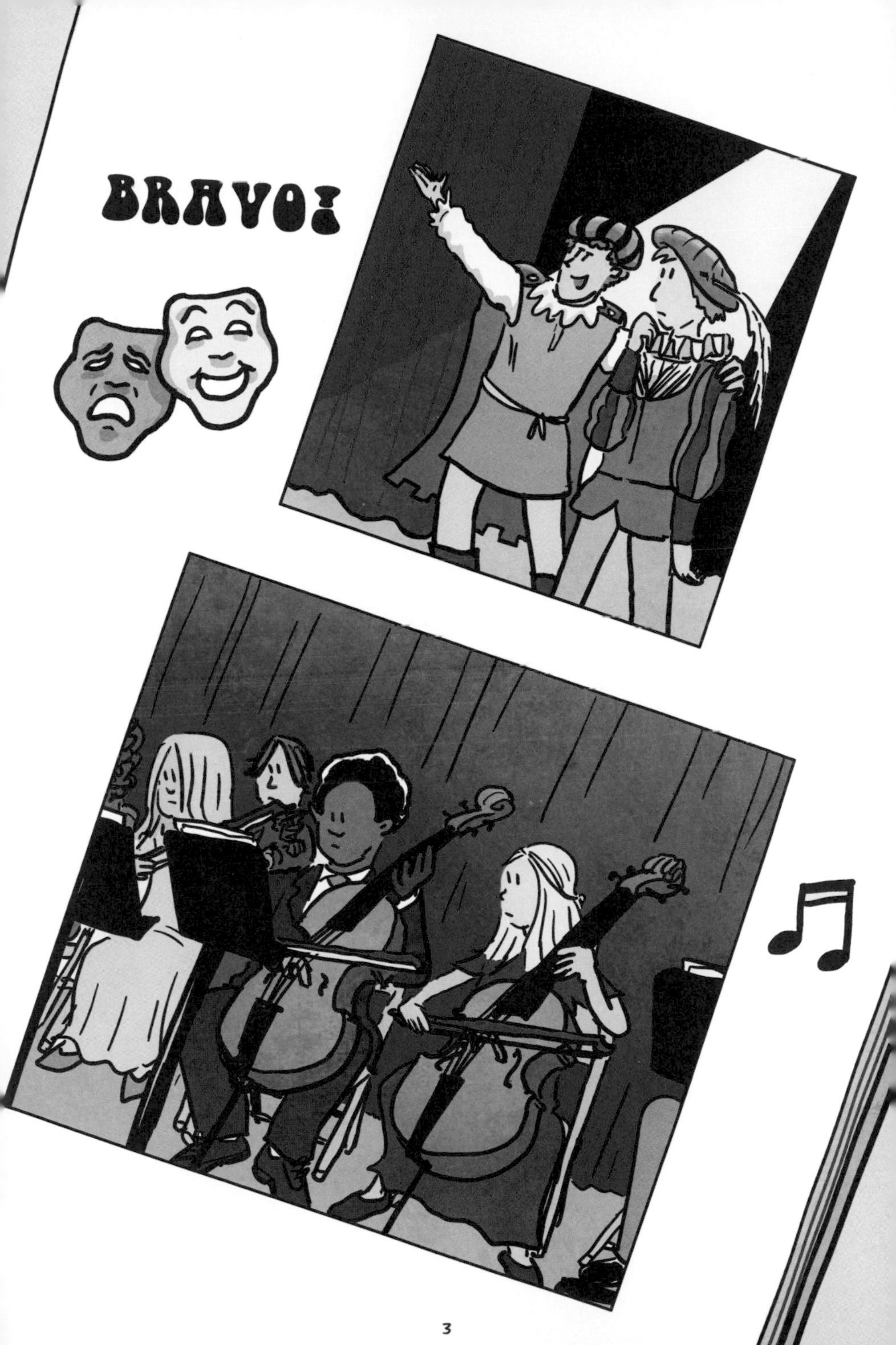
BRAVO!

 The **VOTES** are in...

Here are our favorites!

FRIENDLIEST

Brian

BEST HAIR

Deb

COOLEST GUY

Rob

SMARTEST

Arun

CLASS CLOWN

Dwayne

COOLEST GIRL

Lisa

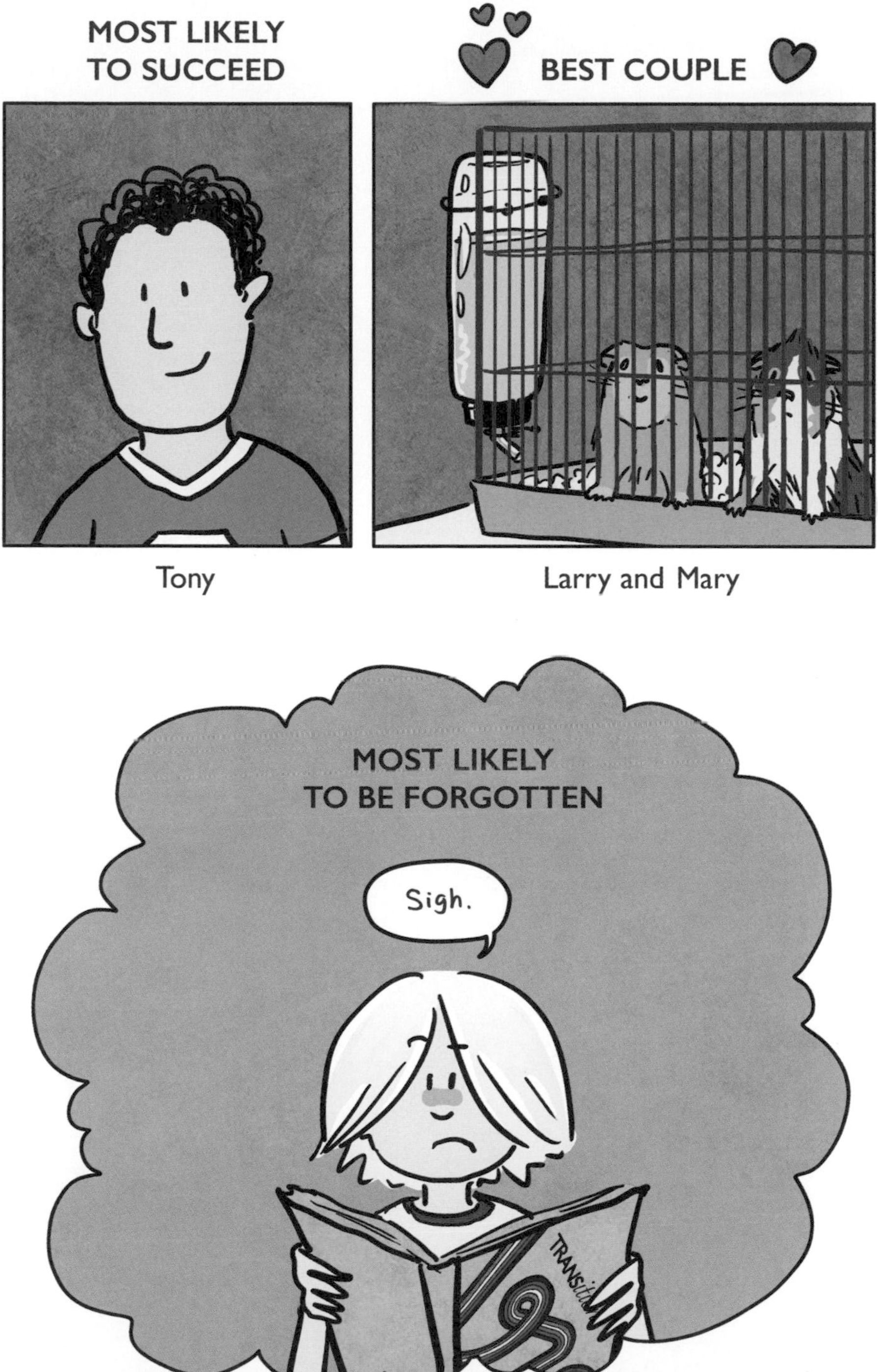
MOST LIKELY
TO SUCCEED
BEST COUPLE
Tony
Larry and Mary
MOST LIKELY
TO BE FORGOTTEN
Sigh.

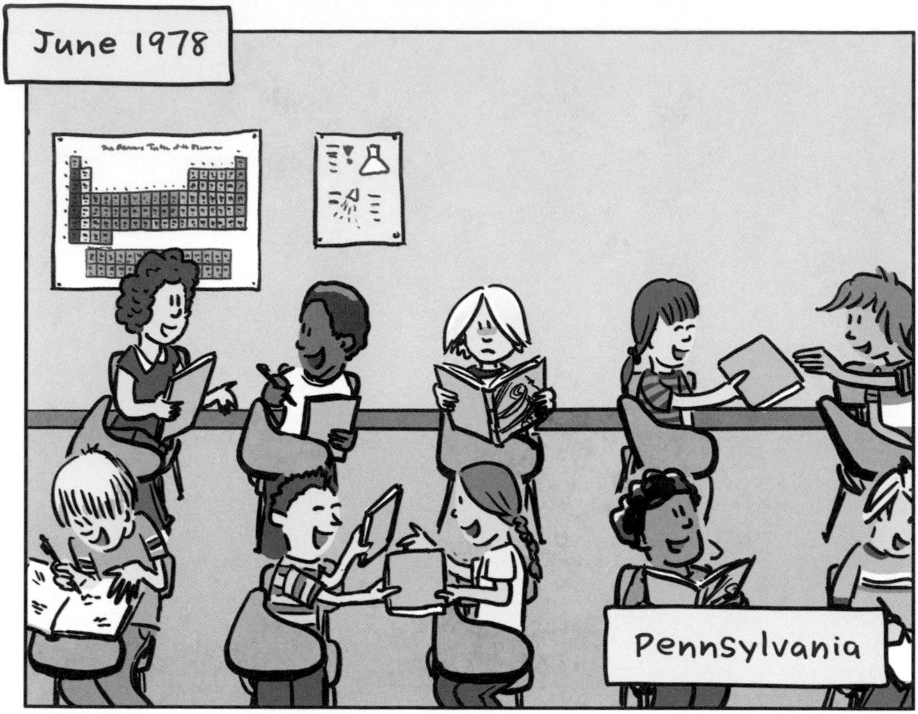
June 1978
Pennsylvania

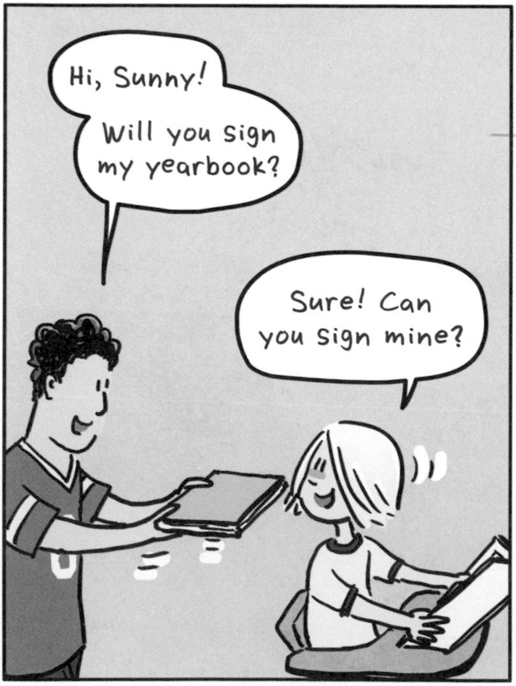
Hi, Sunny!
Will you sign my yearbook?
Sure! Can you sign mine?

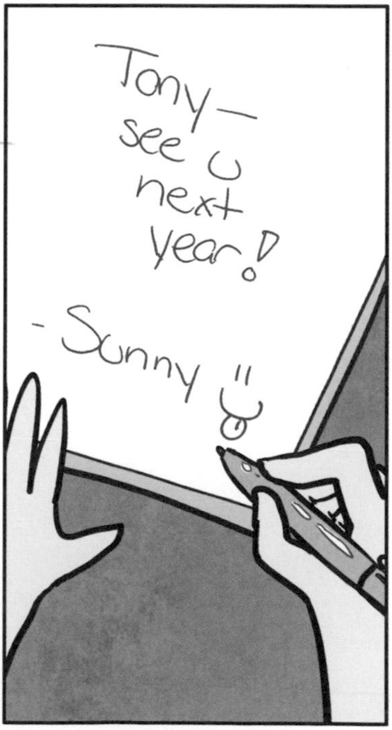
Tony— see u next year!
- Sunny

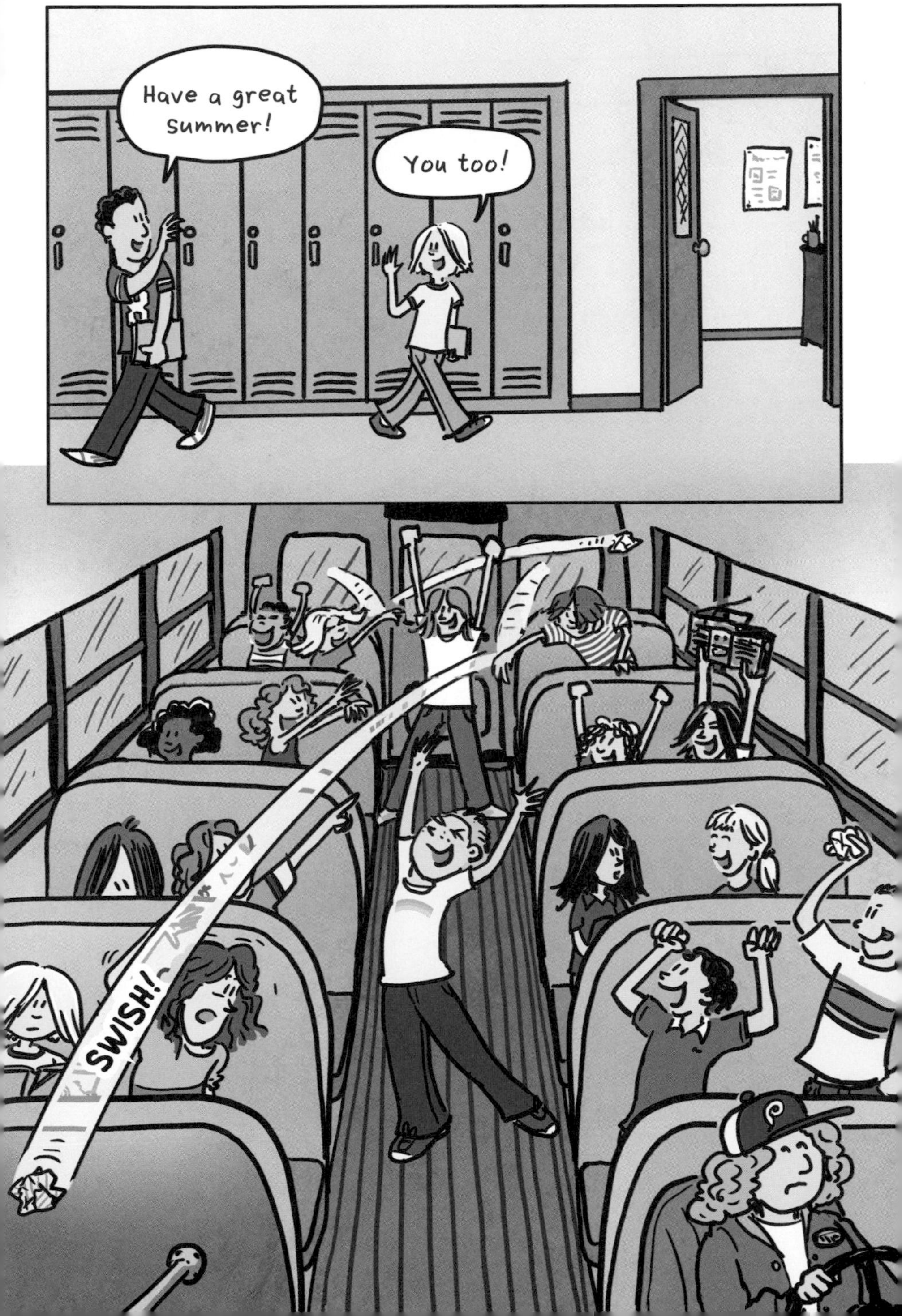

Have a great summer!
You too!
SWISH!

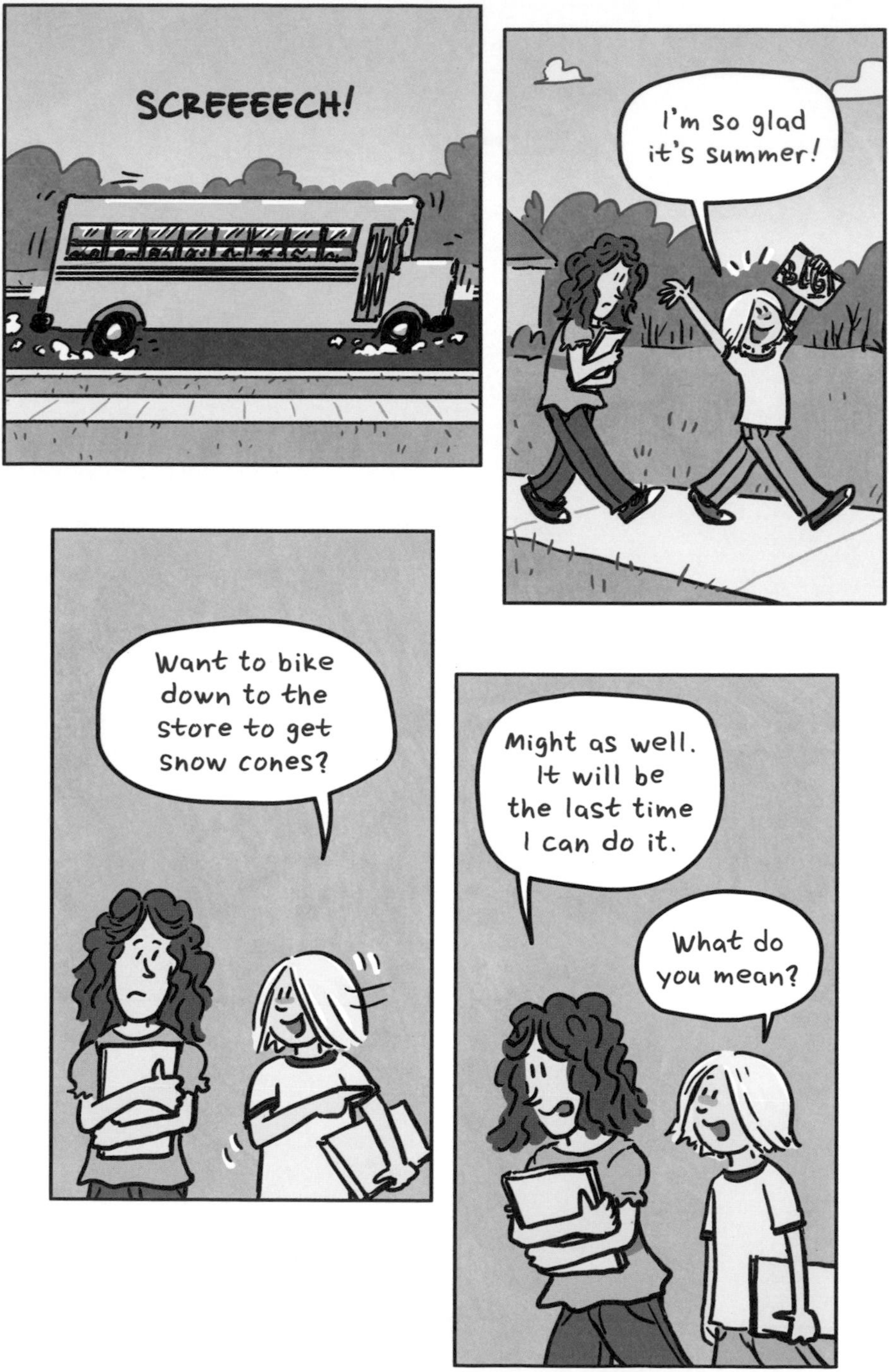
SCREEEECH!
I'm so glad it's summer!
Want to bike down to the store to get snow cones?
Might as well. It will be the last time I can do it.
What do you mean?

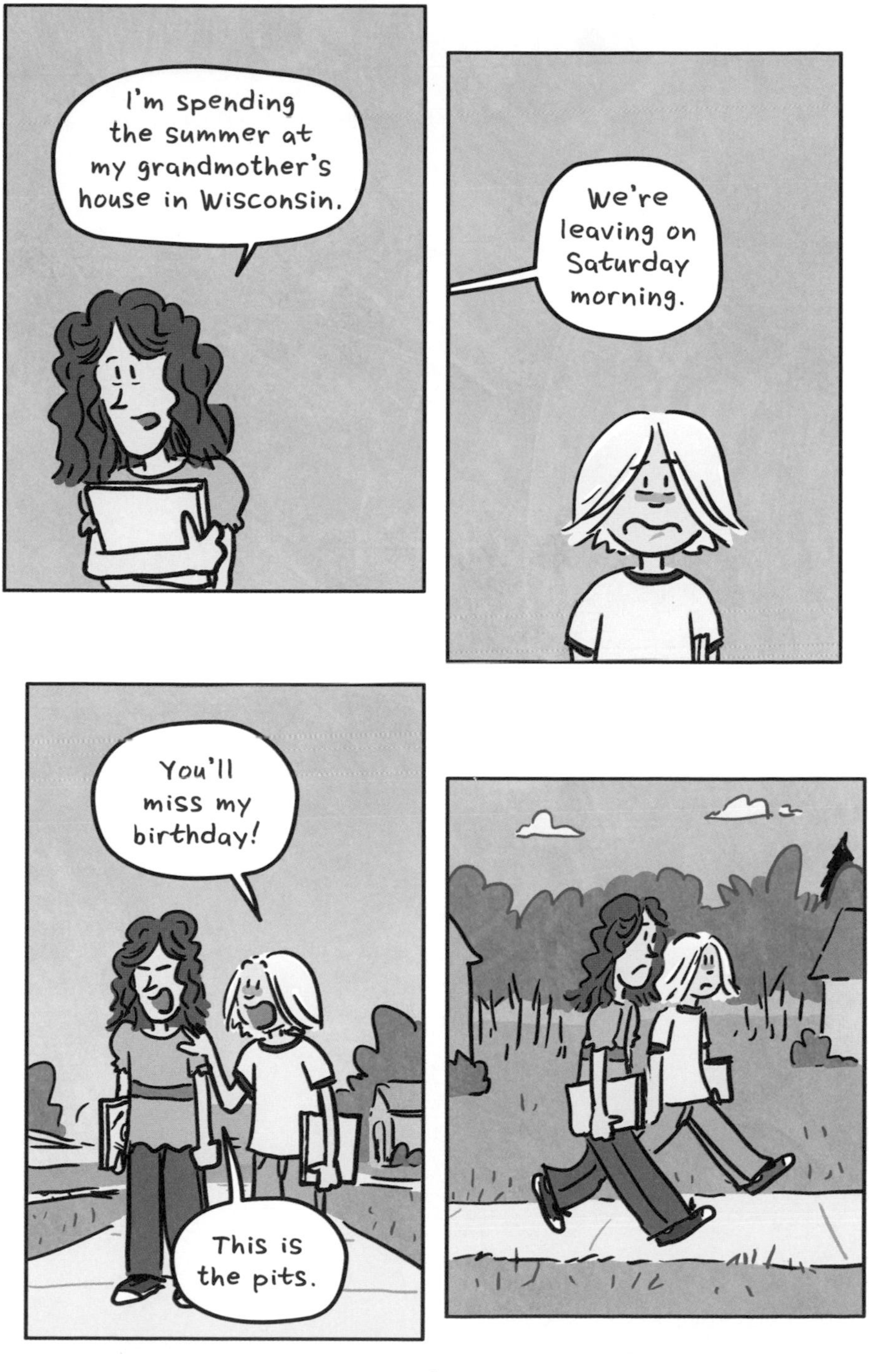
I'm spending the summer at my grandmother's house in Wisconsin.
We're leaving on Saturday morning.
You'll miss my birthday!
This is the pits.

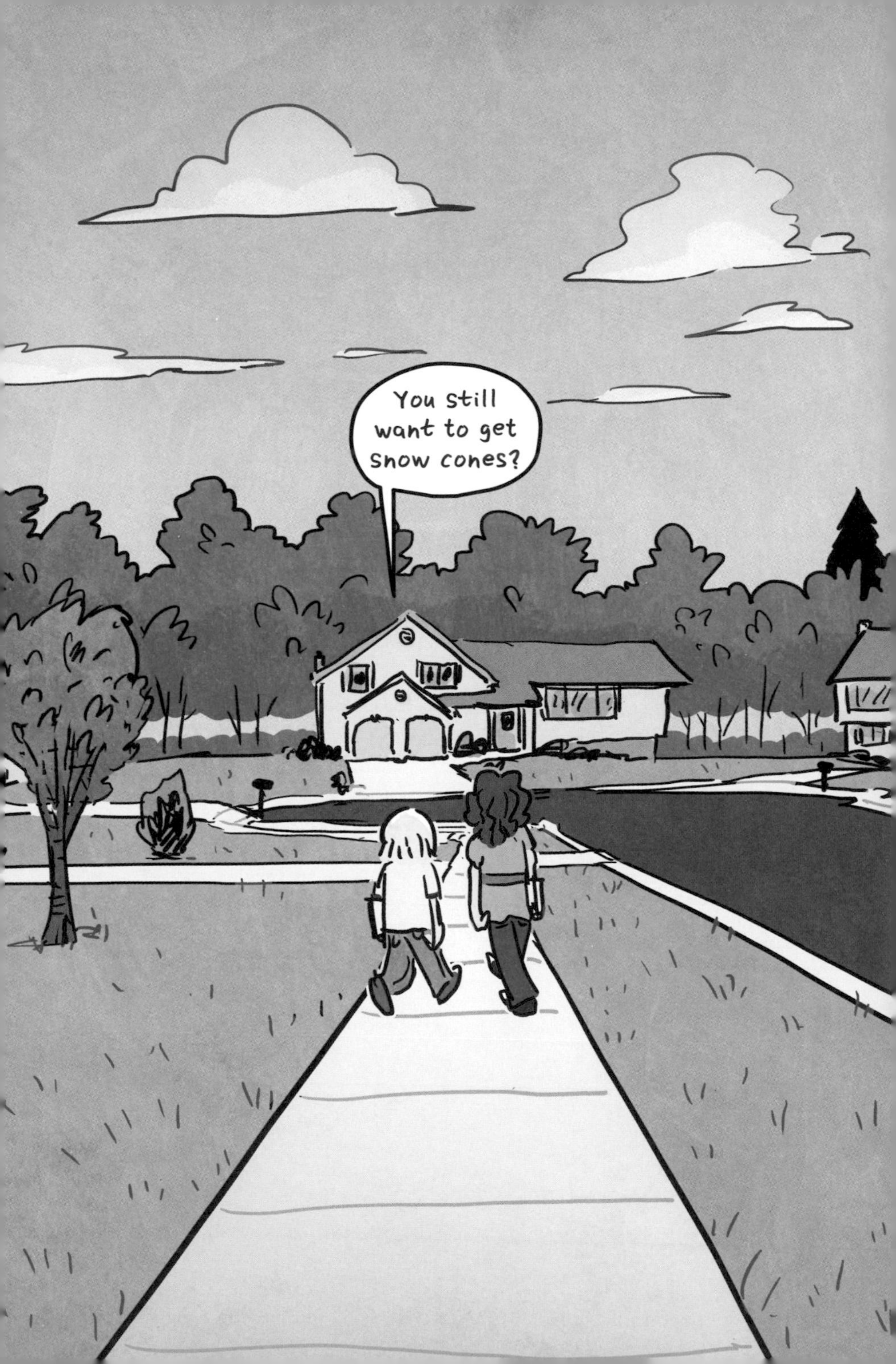
You still want to get snow cones?

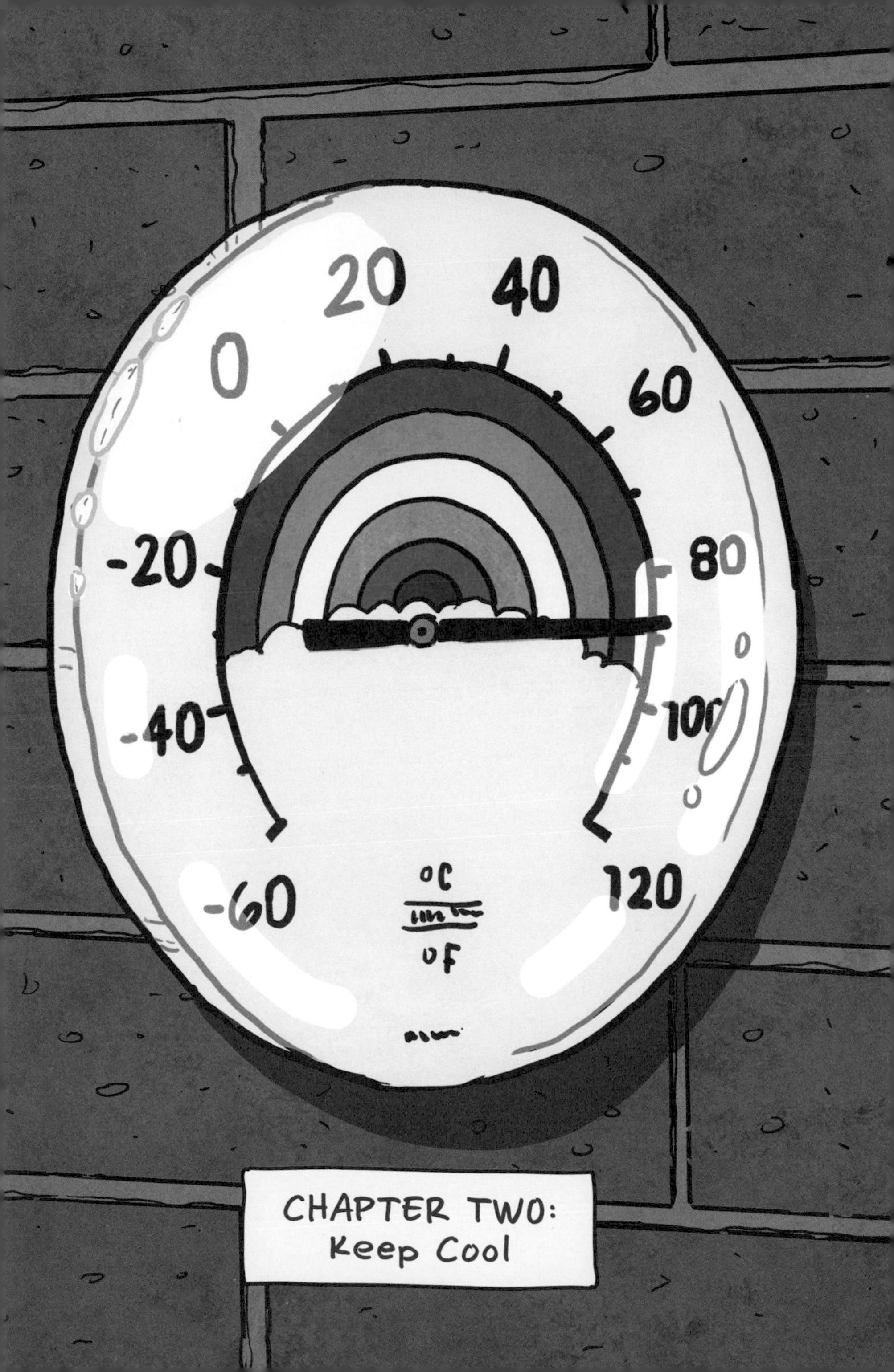
20
40
0
60
-20
80
-40
100
-60
120
°C
°F

CHAPTER TWO: Keep Cool

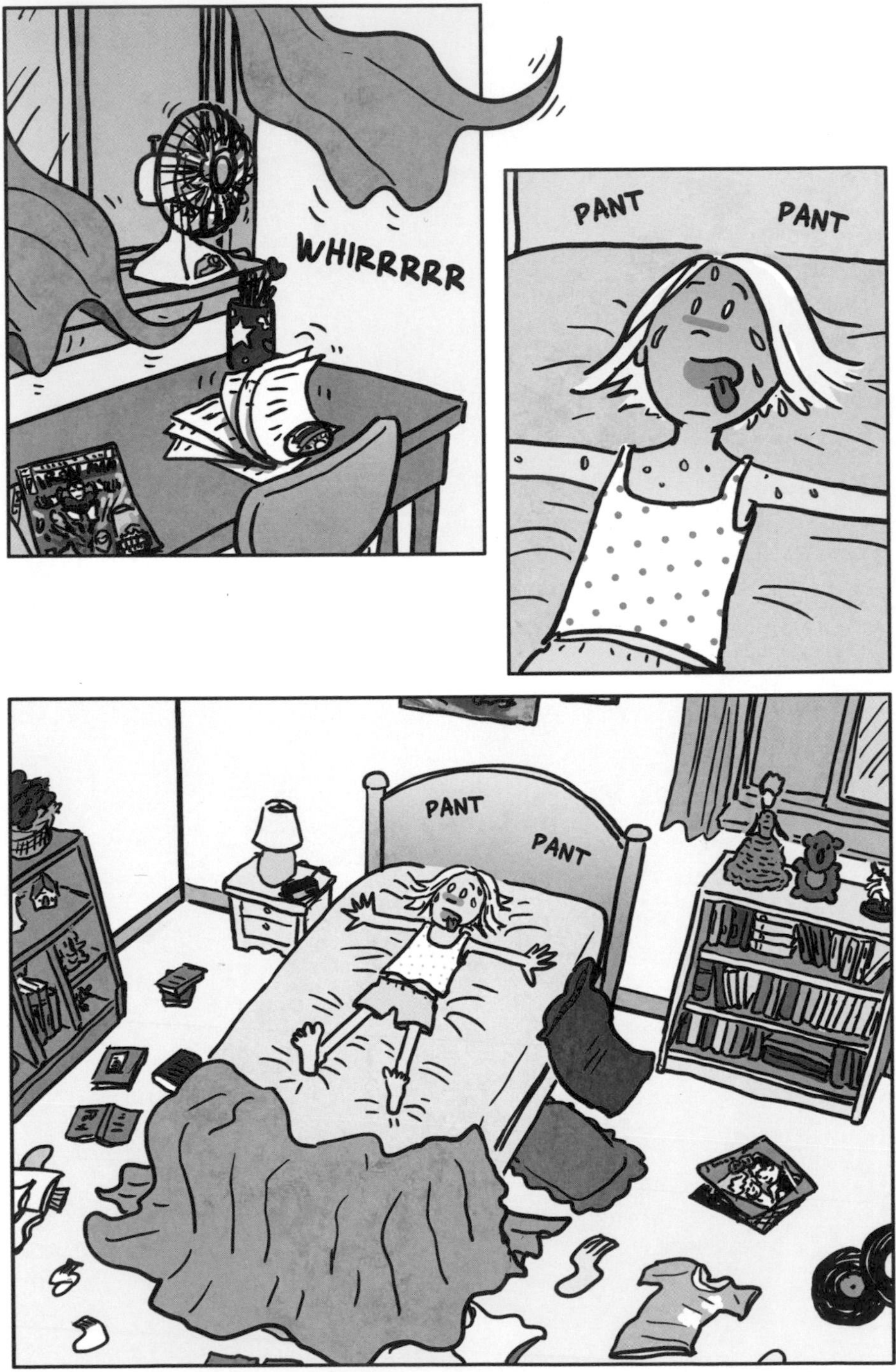
WHIRRRRR
PANT
PANT
PANT
PANT

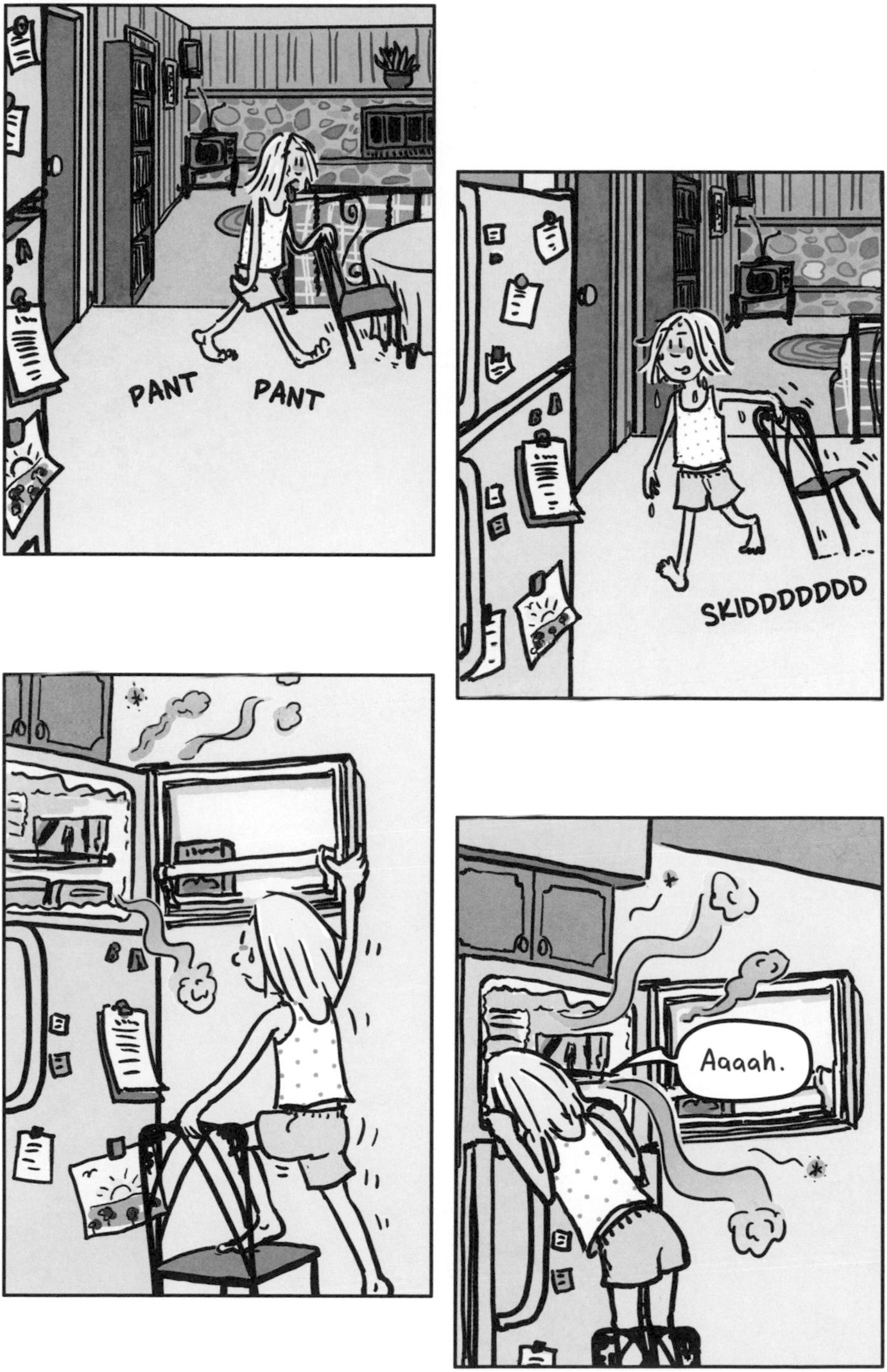
PANT PANT
SKIDDDDDDD
Aaaah.

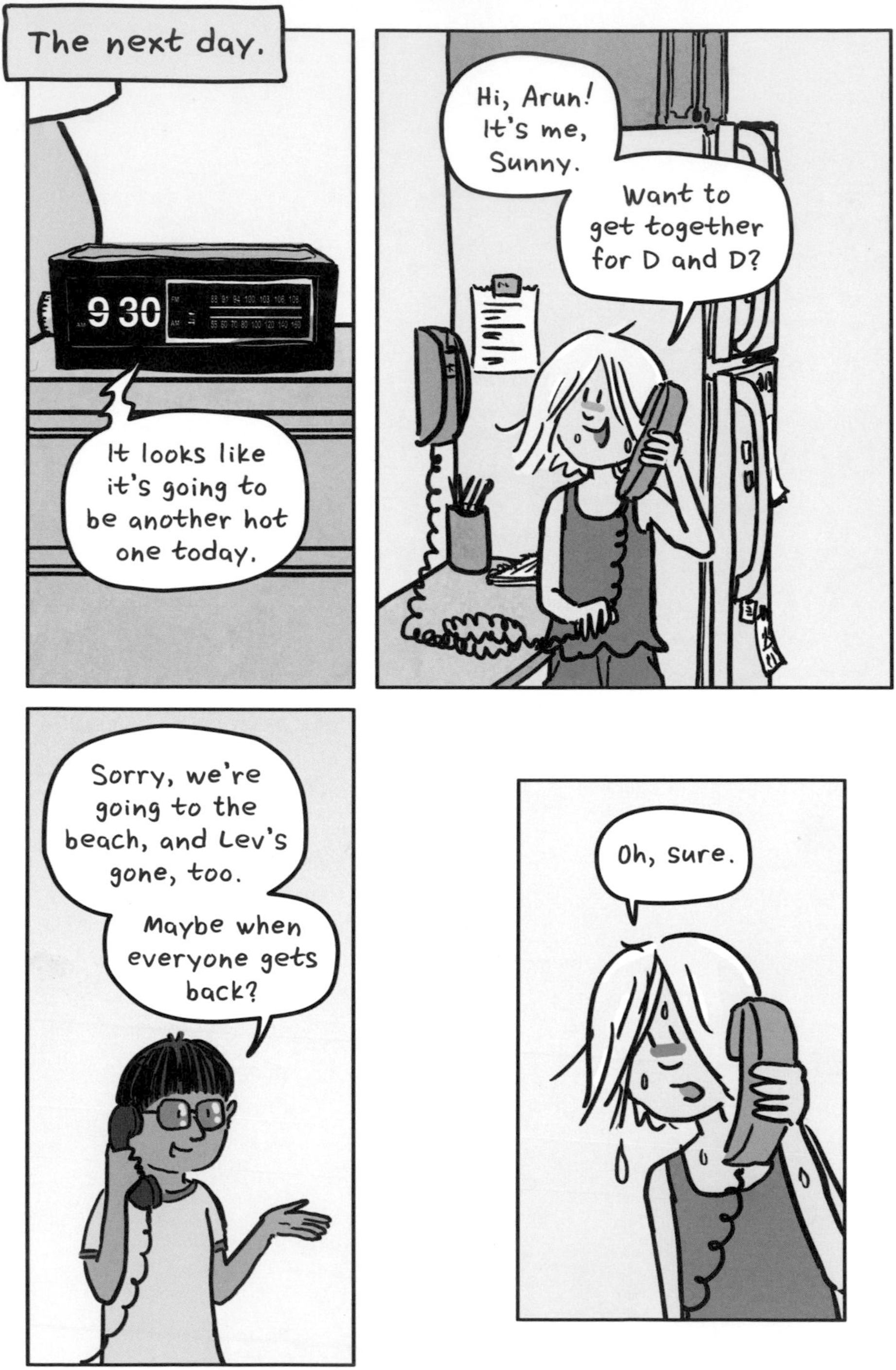
The next day.
It looks like it's going to be another hot one today.
Hi, Arun! It's me, Sunny.
Want to get together for D and D?
Sorry, we're going to the beach, and Lev's gone, too.
Maybe when everyone gets back?
Oh, sure.

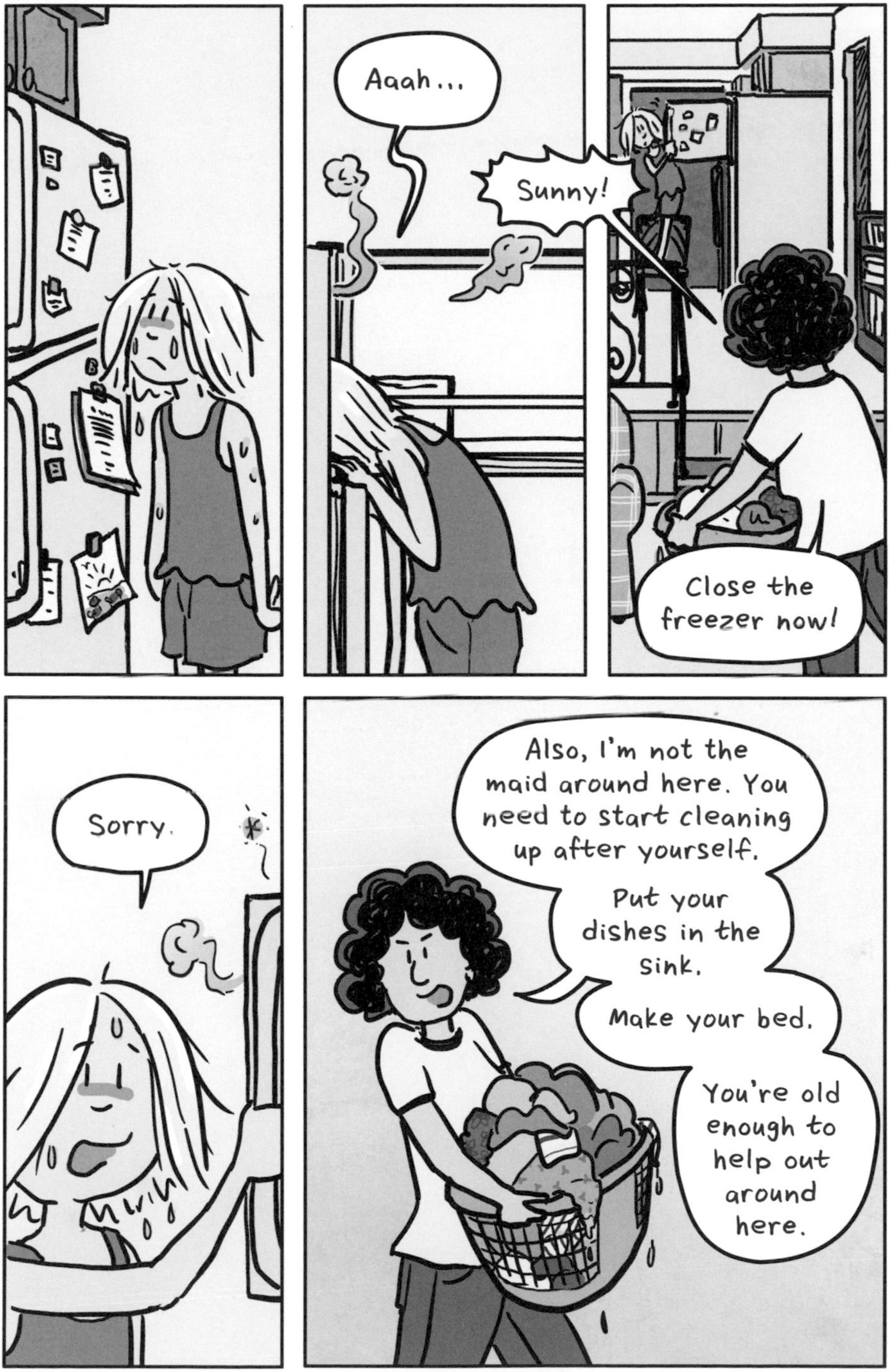
Aaah...
Sunny!
Close the freezer now!
Sorry.
Also, I'm not the maid around here. You need to start cleaning up after yourself.
Put your dishes in the sink.
Make your bed.
You're old enough to help out around here.

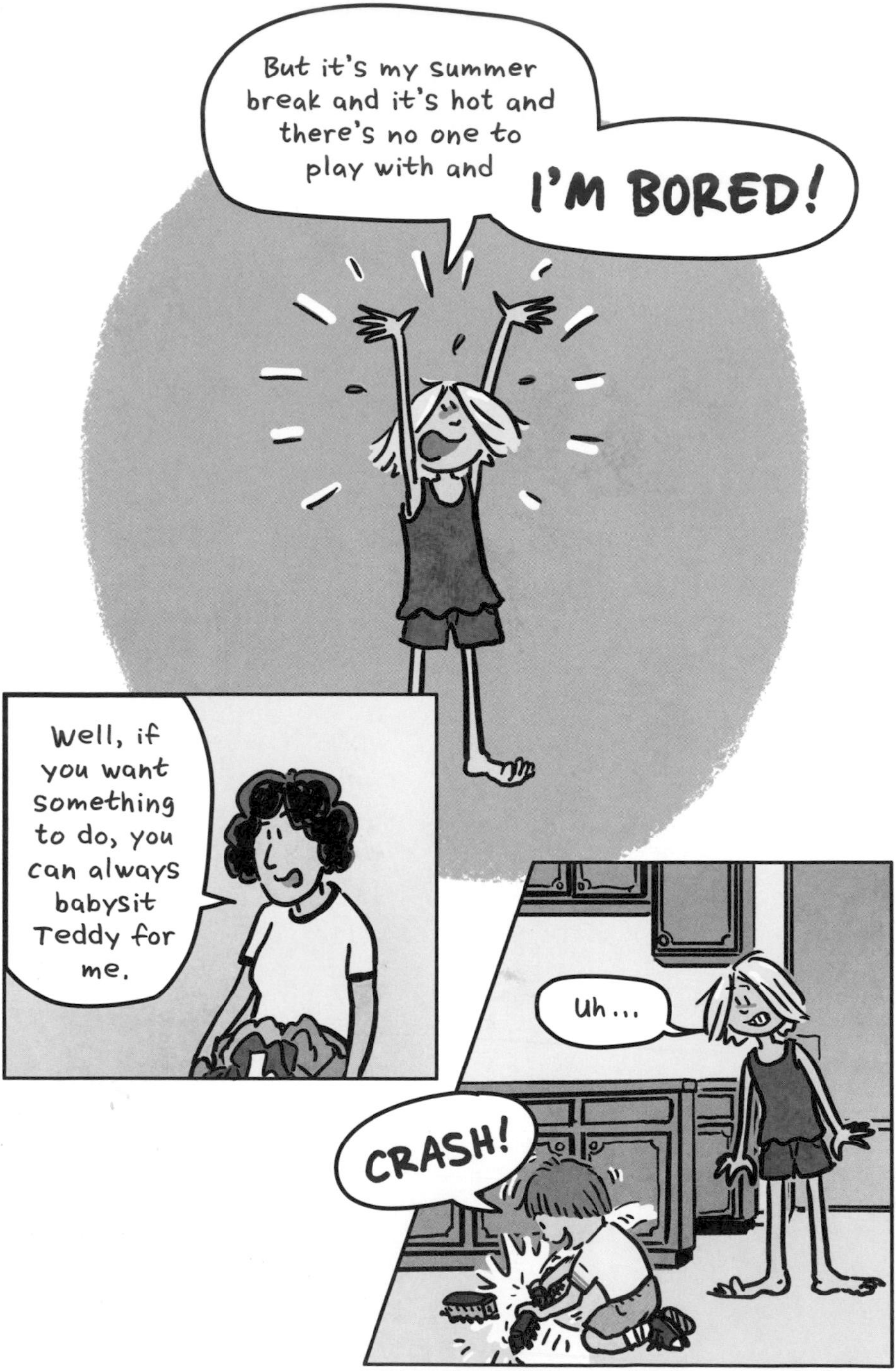
But it's my summer break and it's hot and there's no one to play with and
I'M BORED!
Well, if you want something to do, you can always babysit Teddy for me.
Uh...
CRASH!

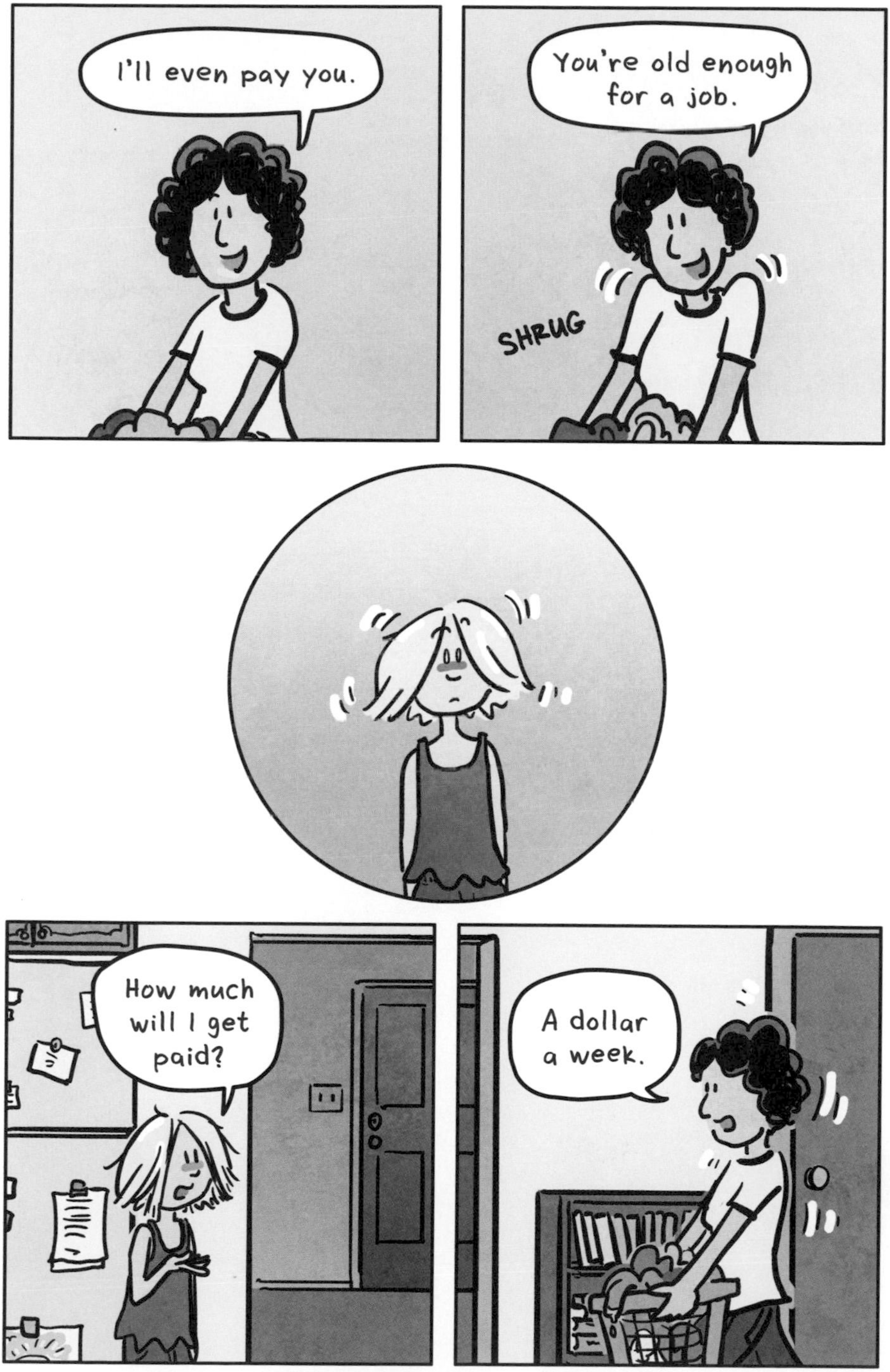
I'll even pay you.
You're old enough for a job.
SHRUG
How much will I get paid?
A dollar a week.

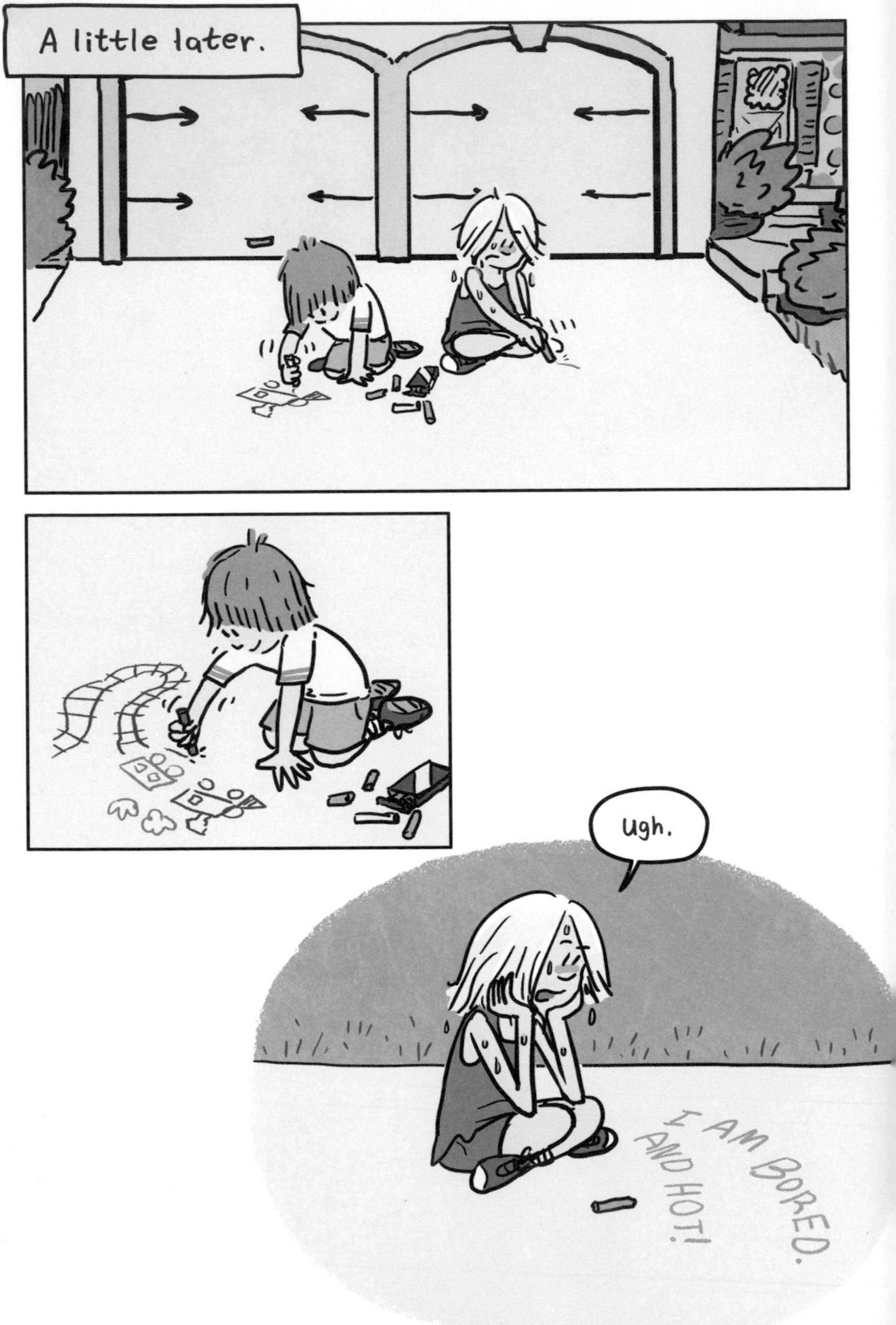
A little later.
Ugh.
I AM BORED.
AND HOT!

CHAPTER THREE: Splash

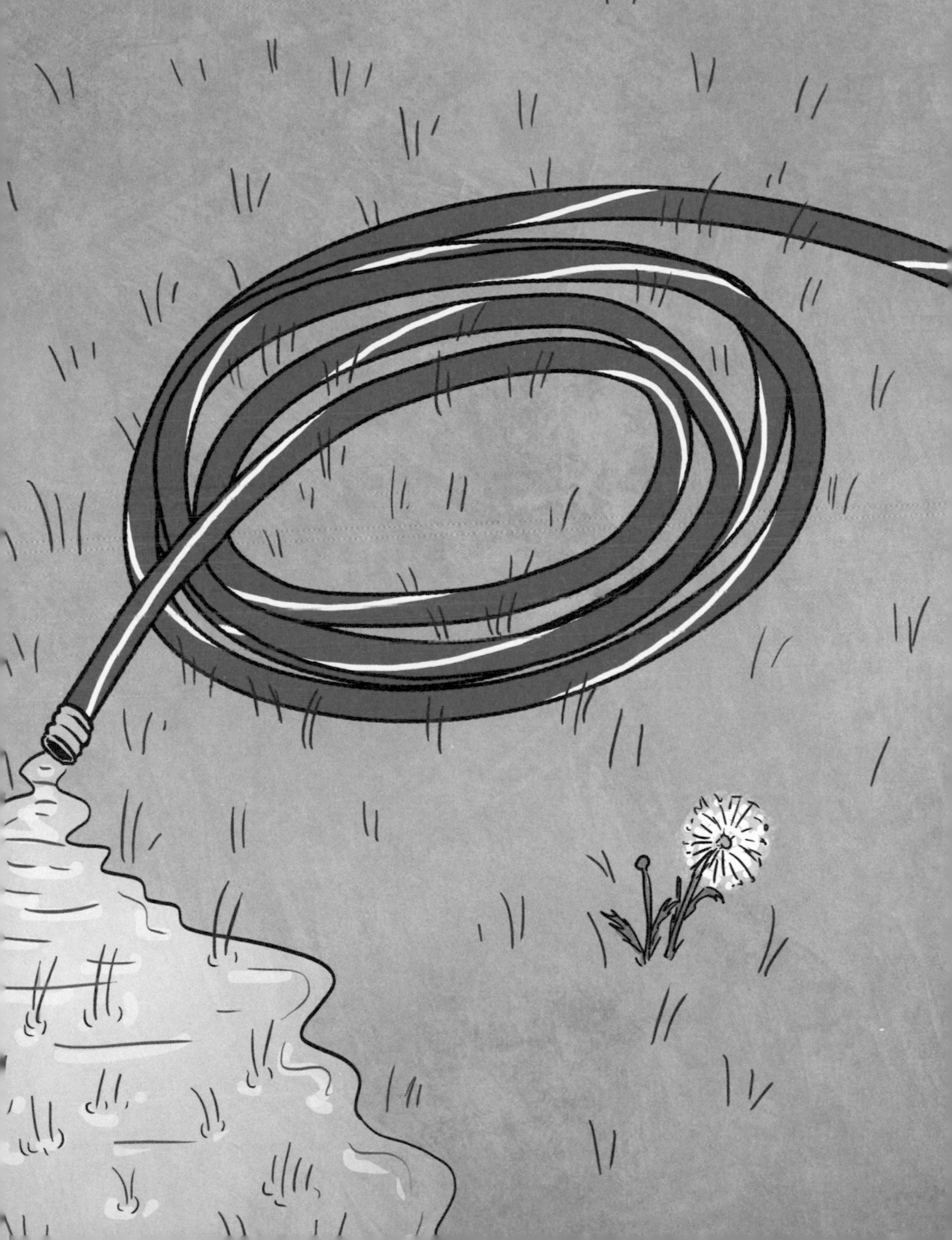

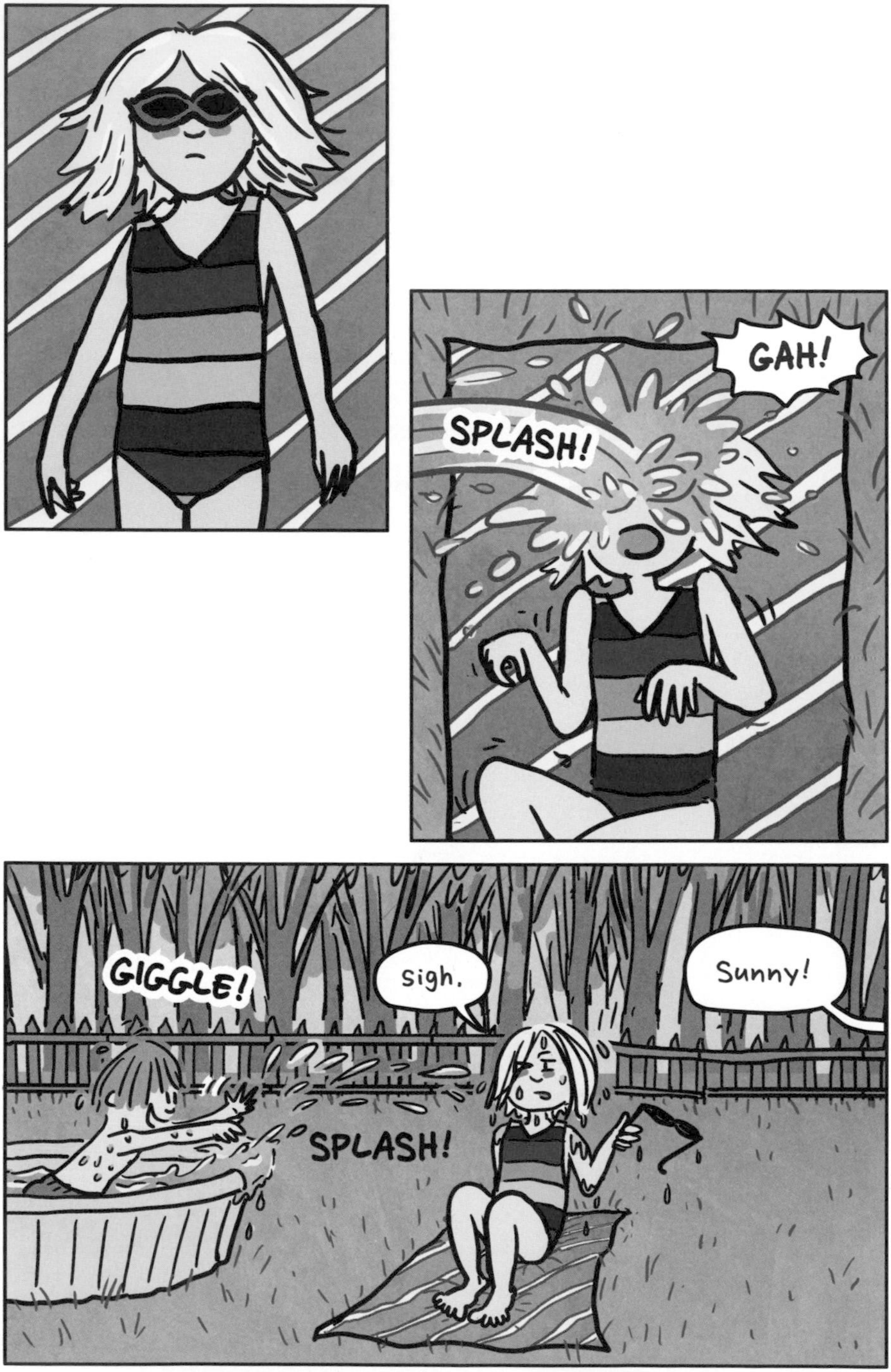
GAH!
SPLASH!
GIGGLE!
sigh.
Sunny!
SPLASH!

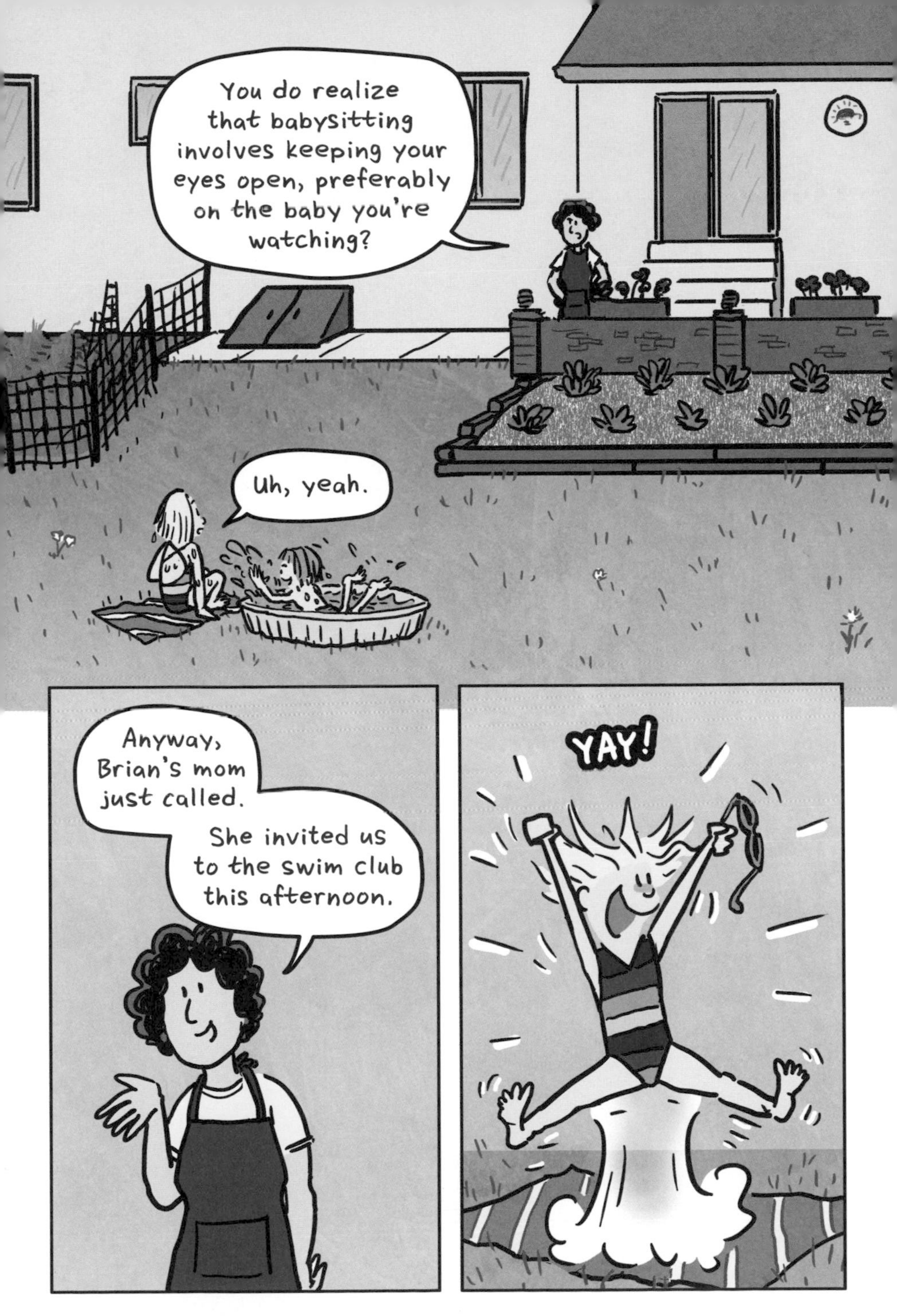
You do realize that babysitting involves keeping your eyes open, preferably on the baby you're watching?
Uh, yeah.
Anyway, Brian's mom just called.
She invited us to the swim club this afternoon.
YAY!

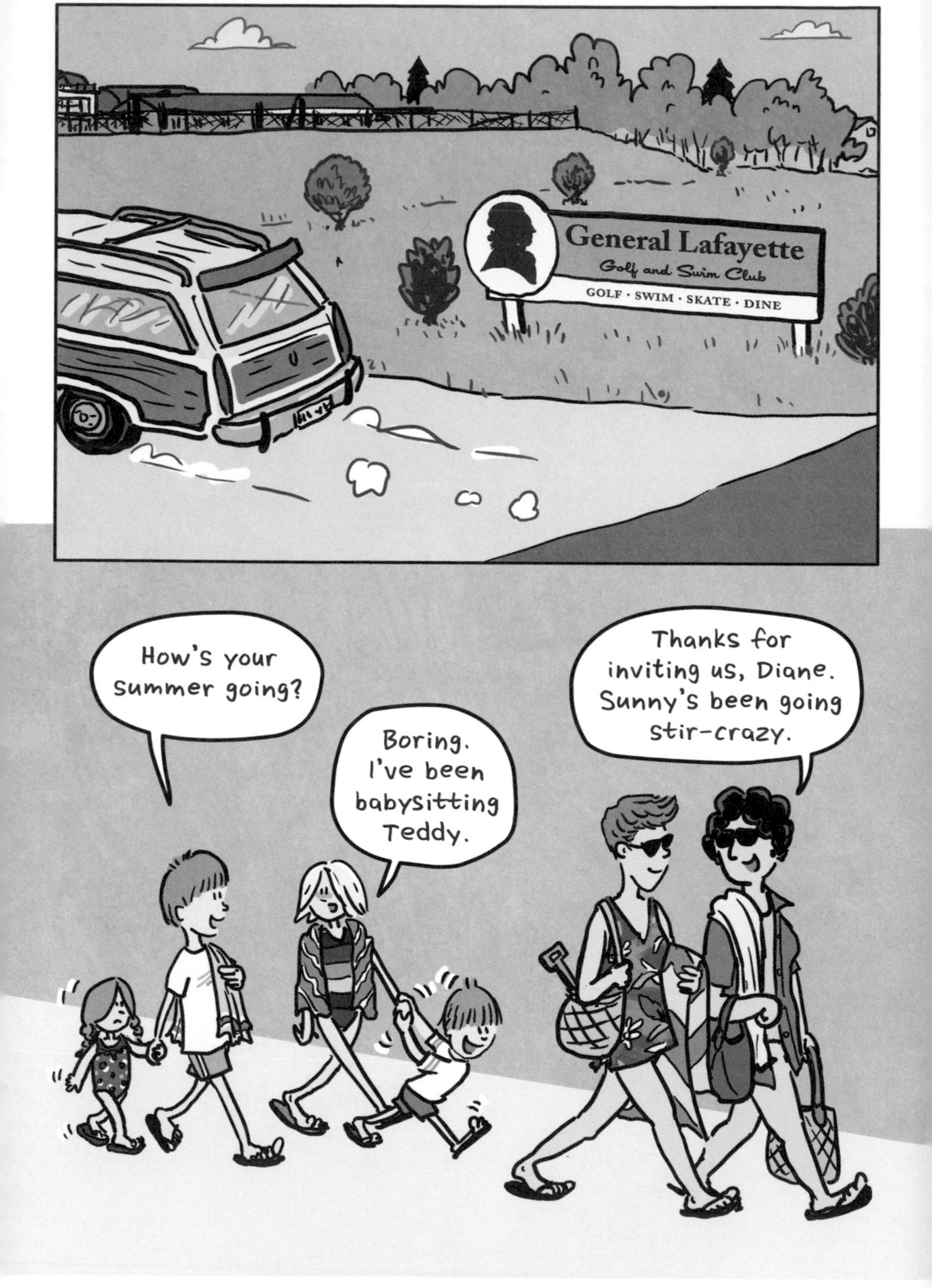
General Lafayette
Golf and Swim Club
GOLF · SWIM · SKATE · DINE
How's your summer going?
Boring. I've been babysitting Teddy.
Thanks for inviting us, Diane. Sunny's been going stir-crazy.

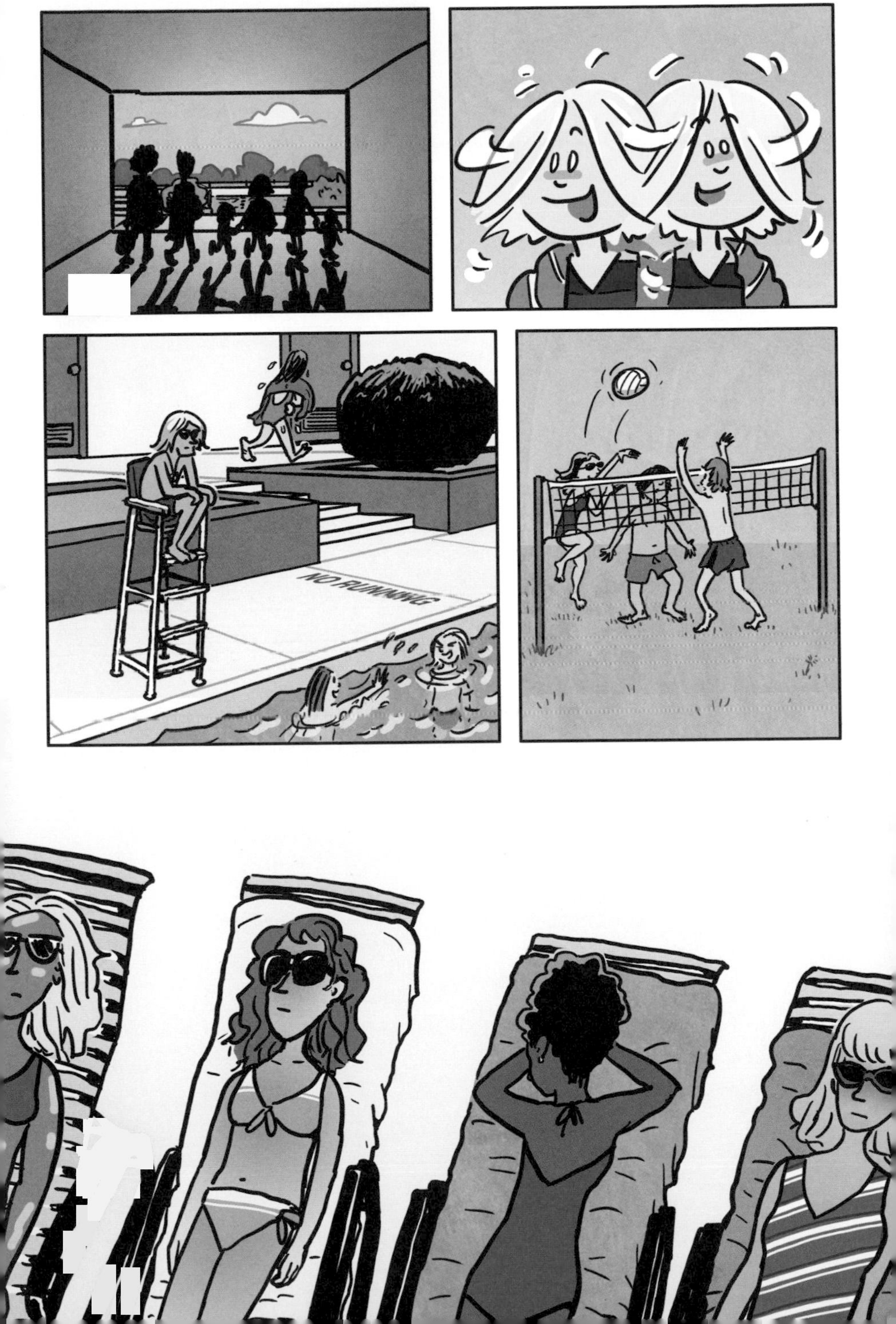
NO RUNNING

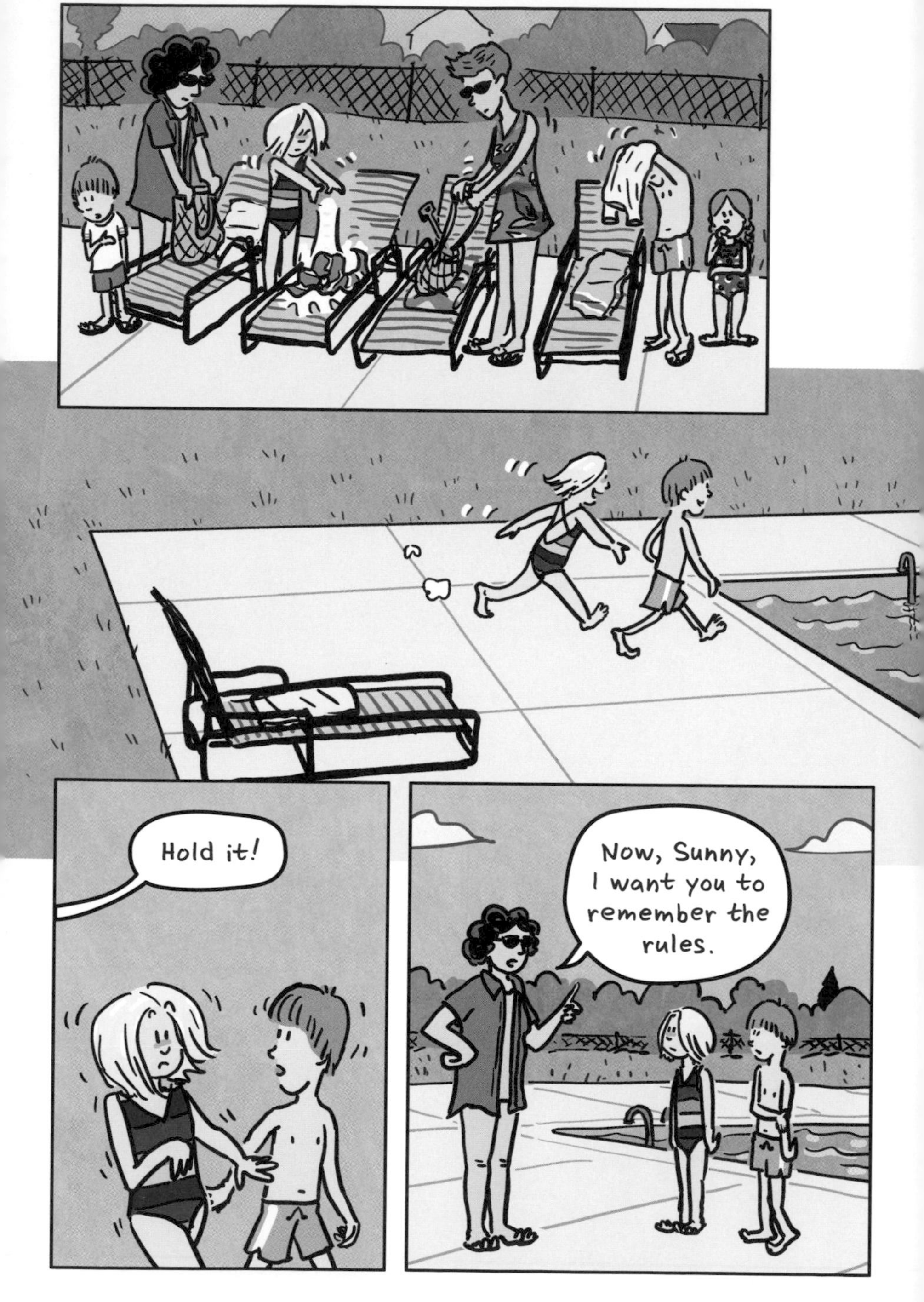
Hold it!
Now, Sunny, I want you to remember the rules.

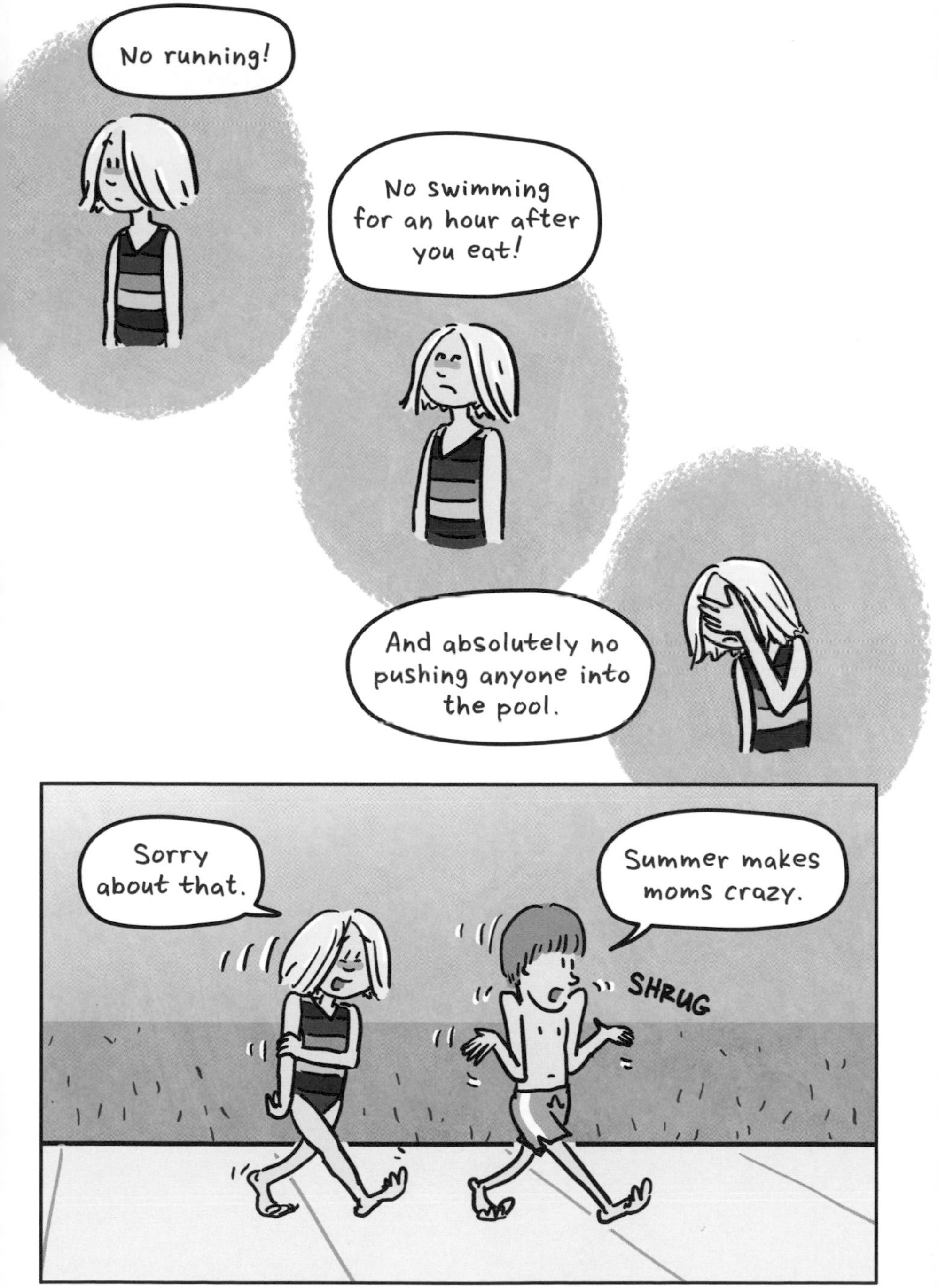
No running!
No swimming for an hour after you eat!
And absolutely no pushing anyone into the pool.
Sorry about that.
Summer makes moms crazy.
SHRUG

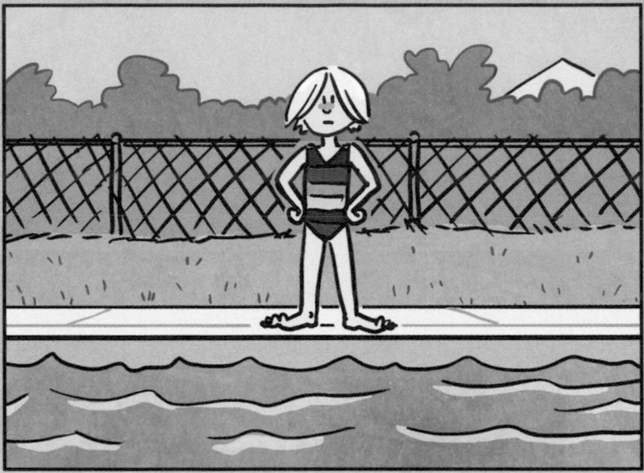

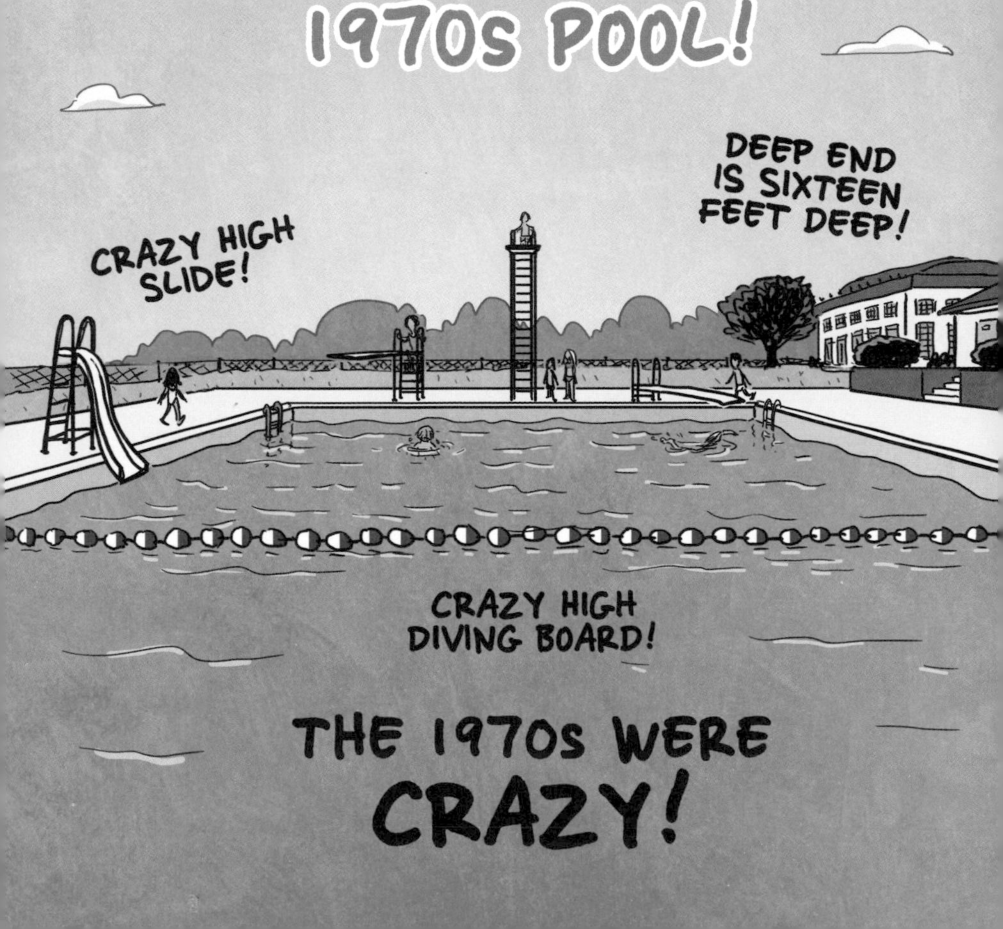
1970s POOL!
CRAZY HIGH SLIDE!
DEEP END IS SIXTEEN FEET DEEP!
CRAZY HIGH DIVING BOARD!
THE 1970s WERE
CRAZY!

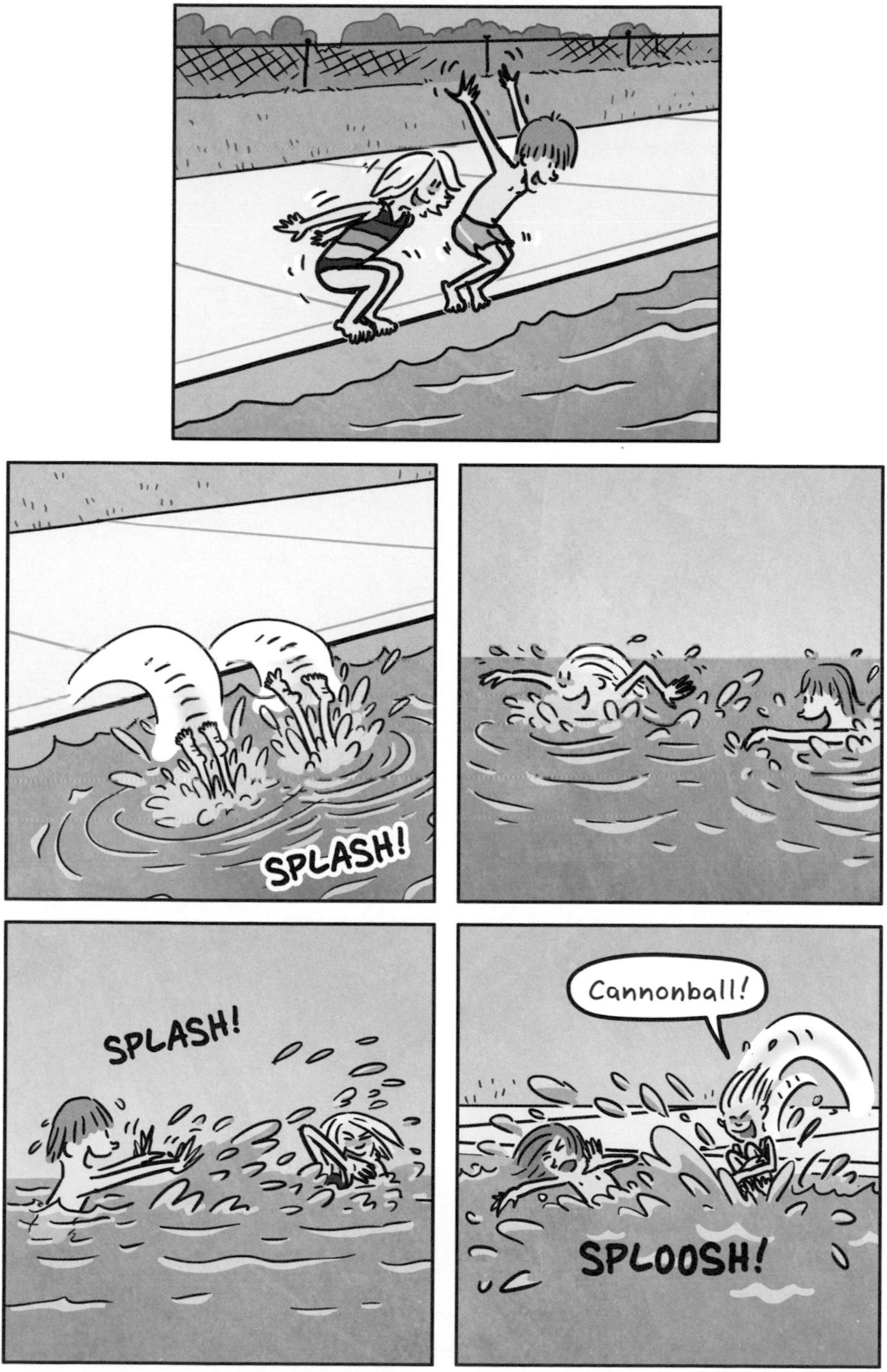
SPLASH!
SPLASH!
Cannonball!
SPLOOSH!

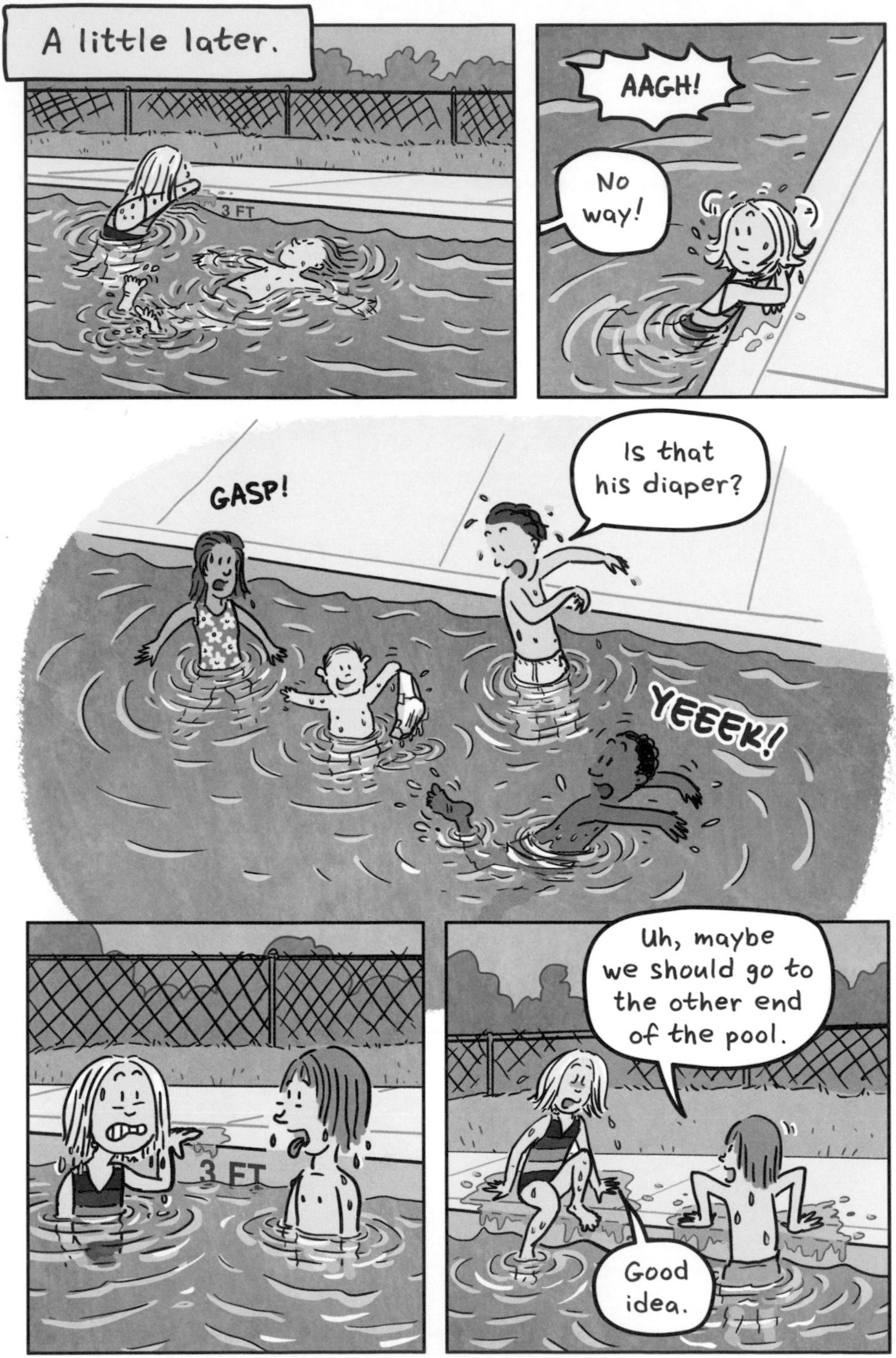
A little later.
AAGH!
No way!
GASP!
Is that his diaper?
YEEEK!
Uh, maybe we should go to the other end of the pool.
Good idea.

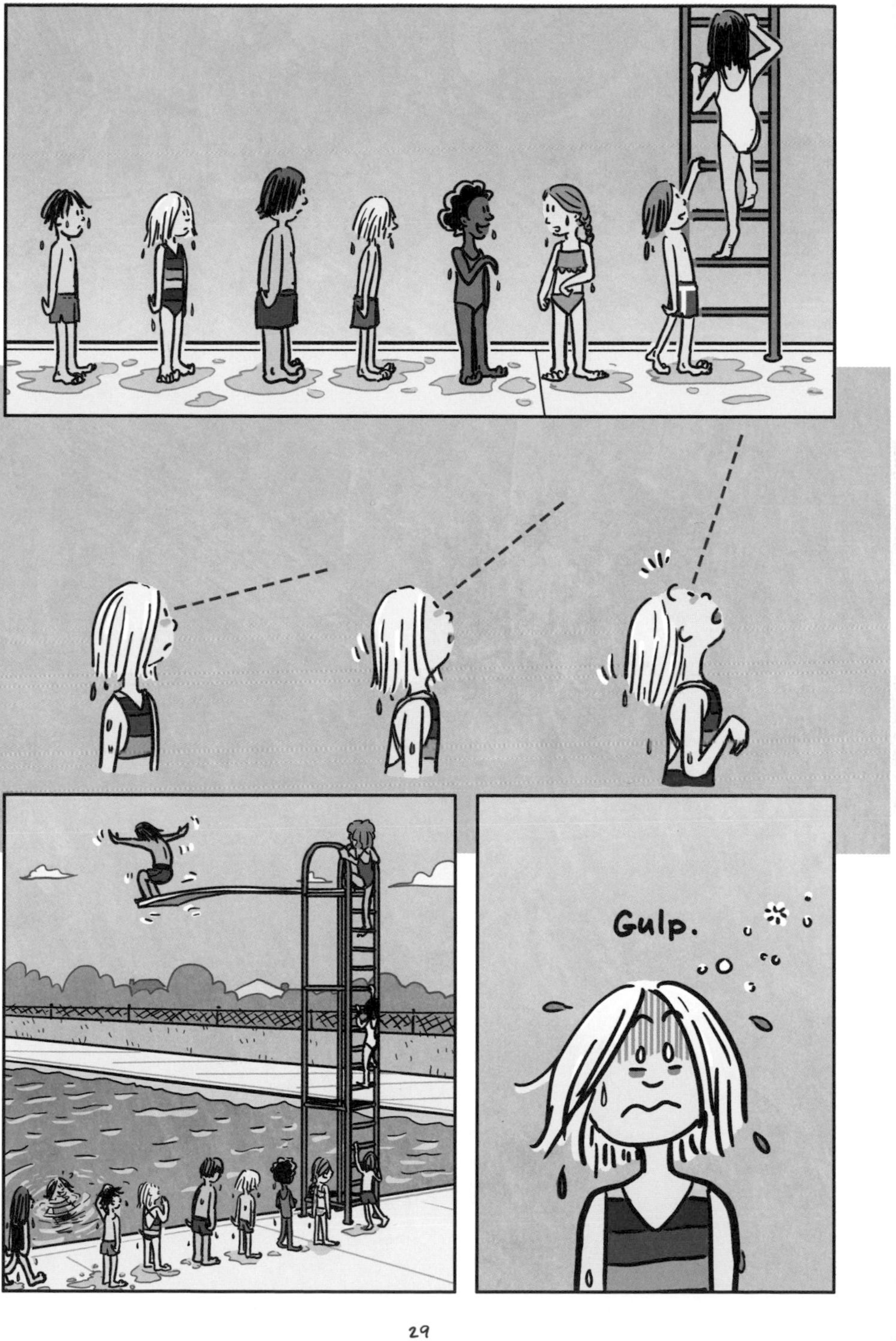
Gulp.

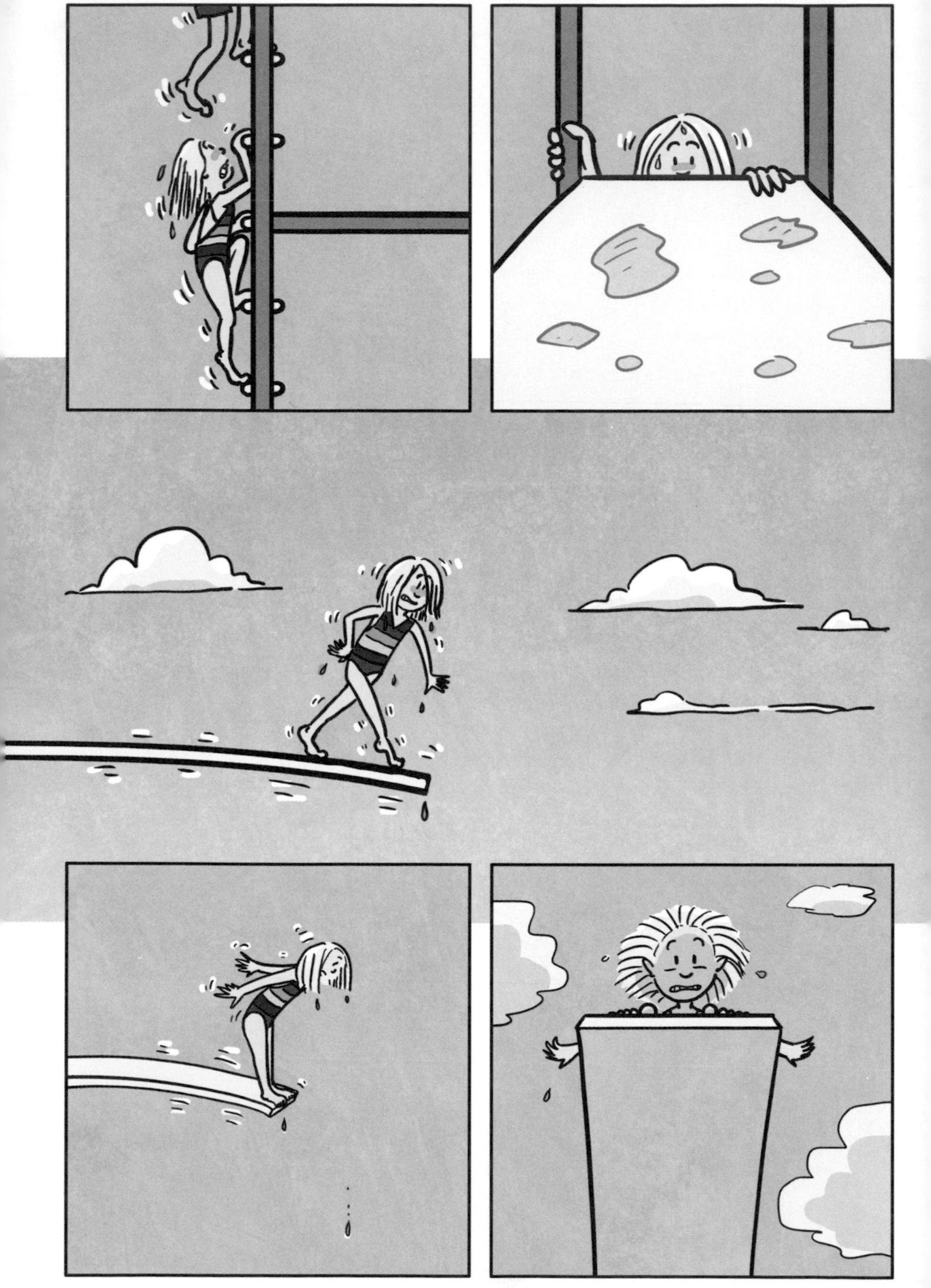

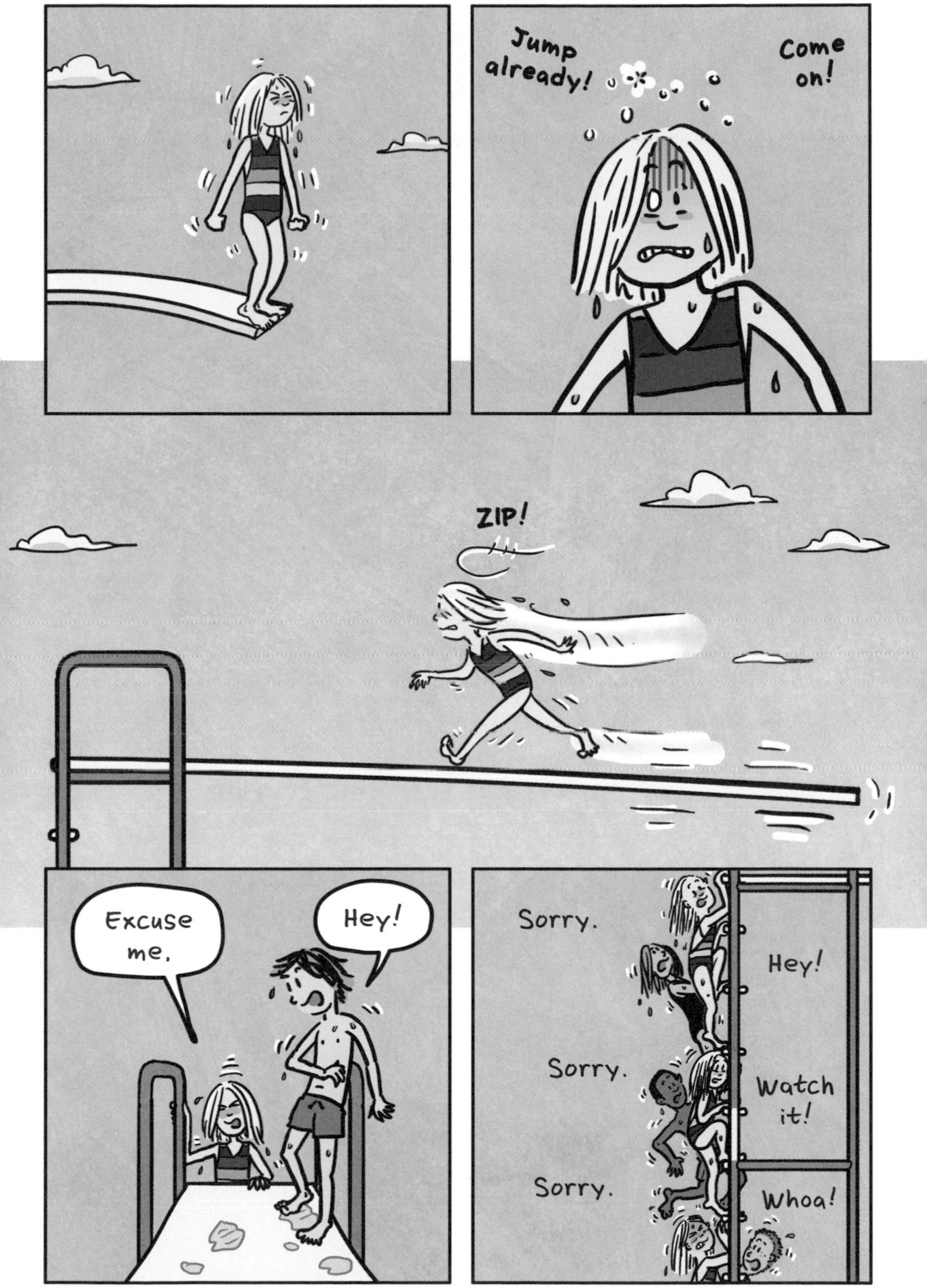
Jump already!
Come on!
ZIP!
Excuse me.
Hey!
Sorry.
Hey!
Sorry.
Watch it!
Sorry.
Whoa!

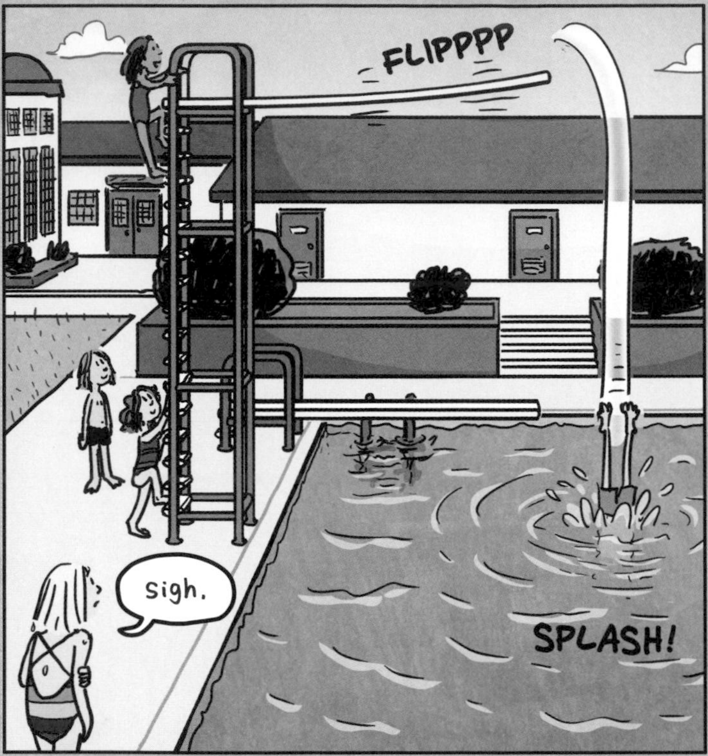
FLIPPPP
sigh.
SPLASH!

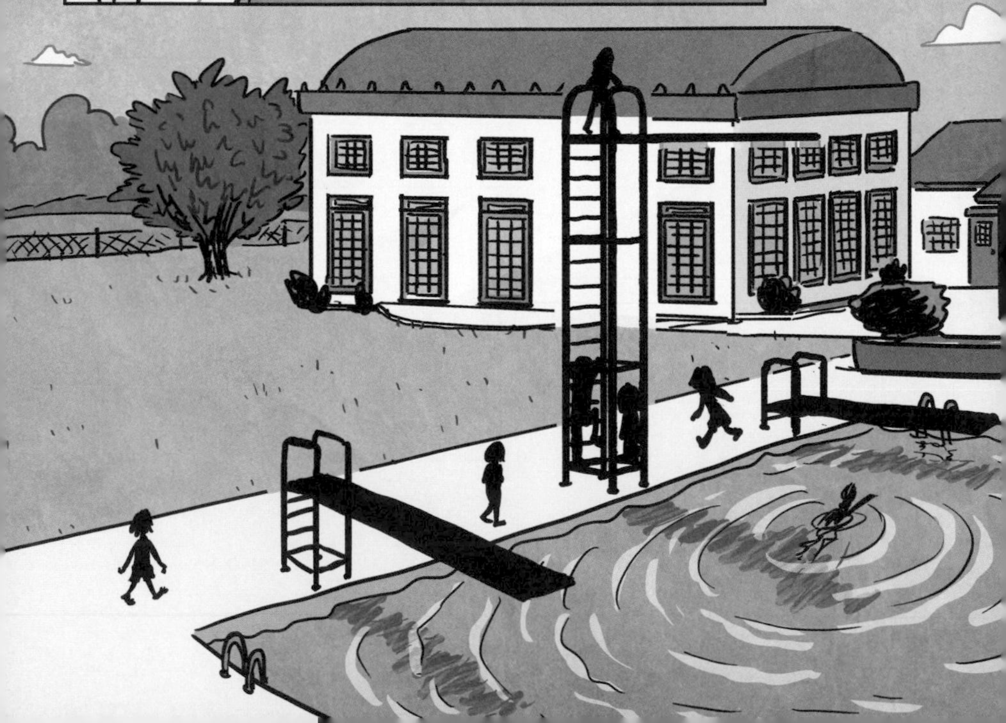

GENERAL LAFAYETTE
GOLF AND SWIM CLUB

GUEST
PASS

1978   POOL   00268

CHAPTER FOUR:
French Fries

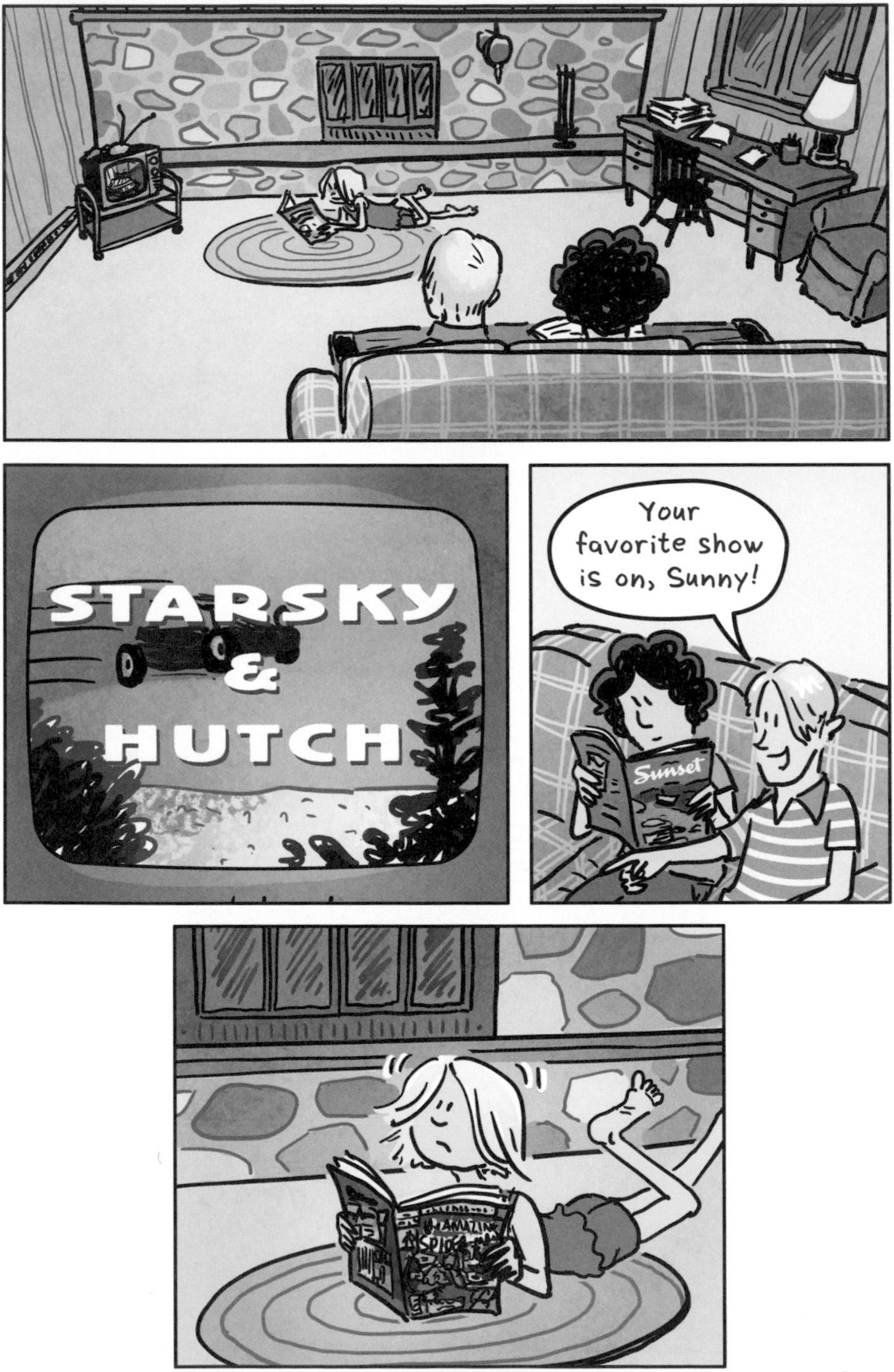
STARSKY & HUTCH
Your favorite show is on, Sunny!

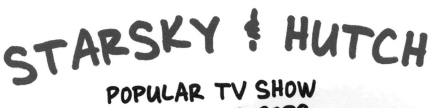

STARSKY & HUTCH

POPULAR TV SHOW
ABOUT TWO COPS

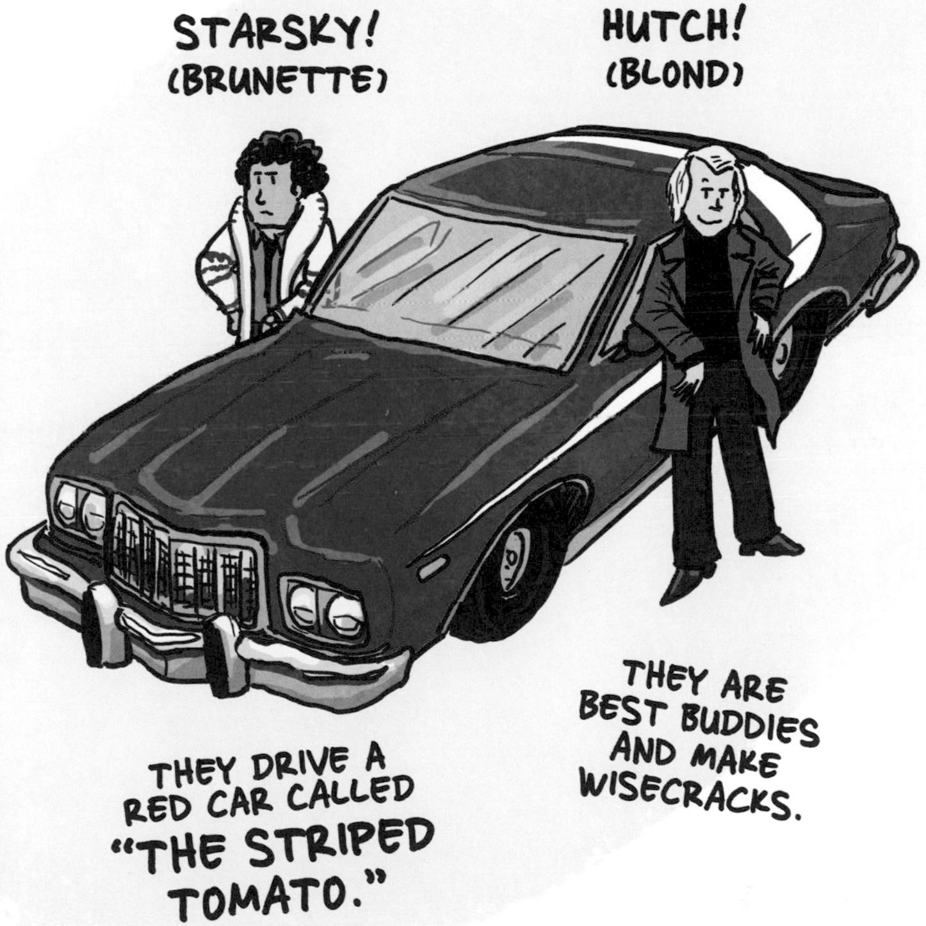
STARSKY!
(BRUNETTE)
HUTCH!
(BLOND)
THEY ARE
BEST BUDDIES
AND MAKE
WISECRACKS.
THEY DRIVE A
RED CAR CALLED
"THE STRIPED
TOMATO."

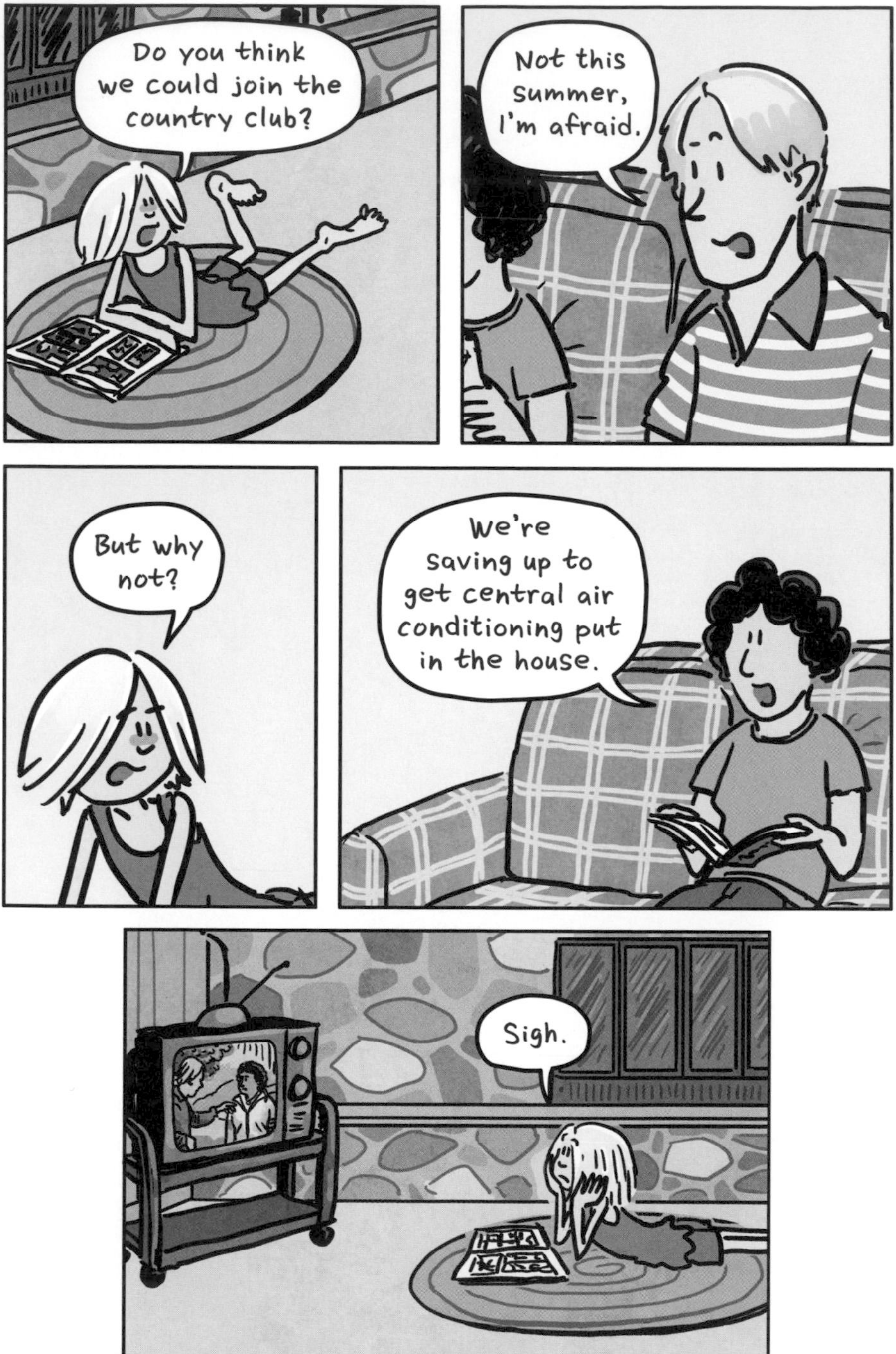
Do you think we could join the country club?
Not this summer, I'm afraid.
But why not?
We're saving up to get central air conditioning put in the house.
Sigh.

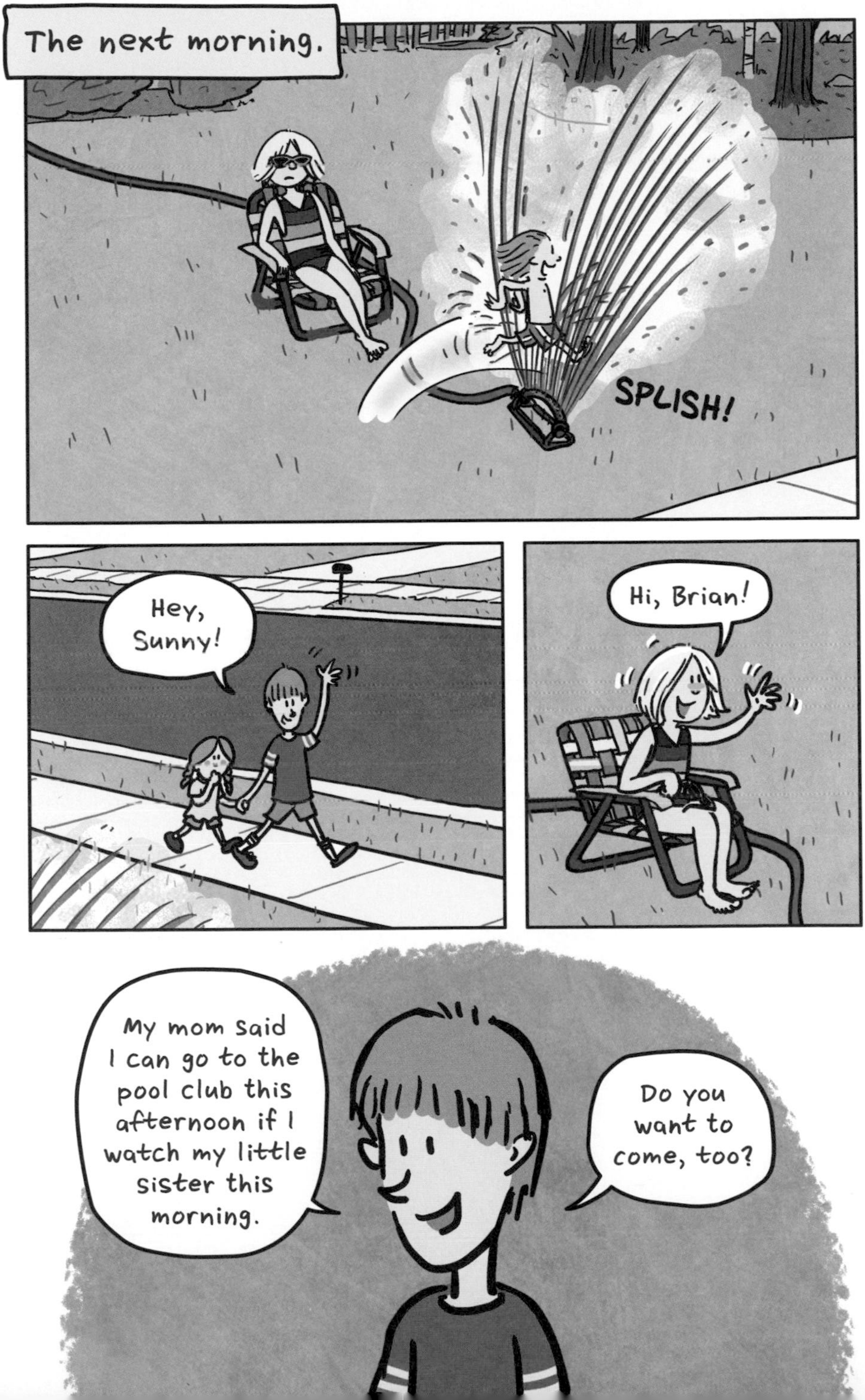
The next morning.
SPLISH!
Hey, Sunny!
Hi, Brian!
My mom said I can go to the pool club this afternoon if I watch my little sister this morning.
Do you want to come, too?

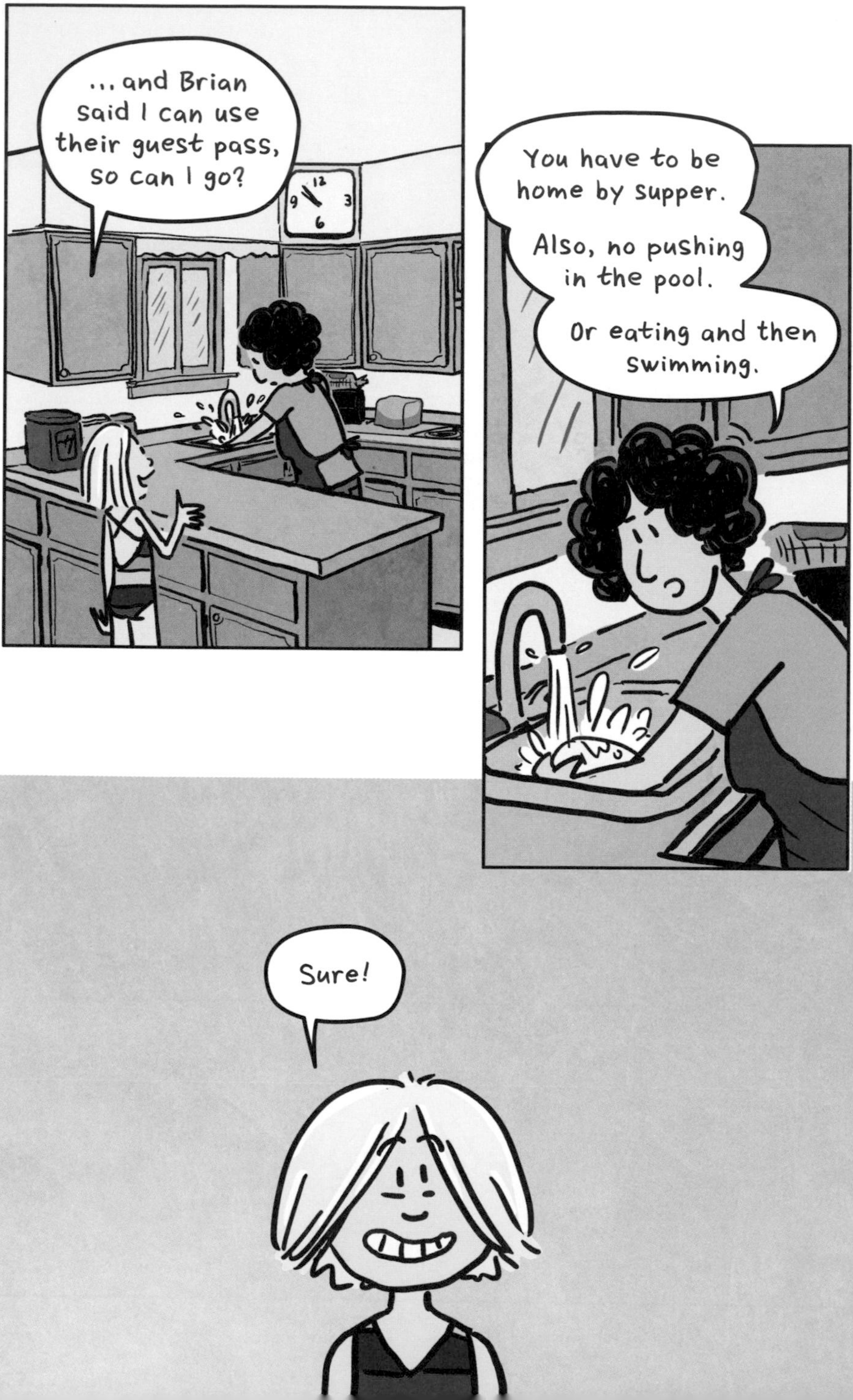

... and Brian said I can use their guest pass, so can I go?
You have to be home by supper.
Also, no pushing in the pool.
Or eating and then swimming.
Sure!

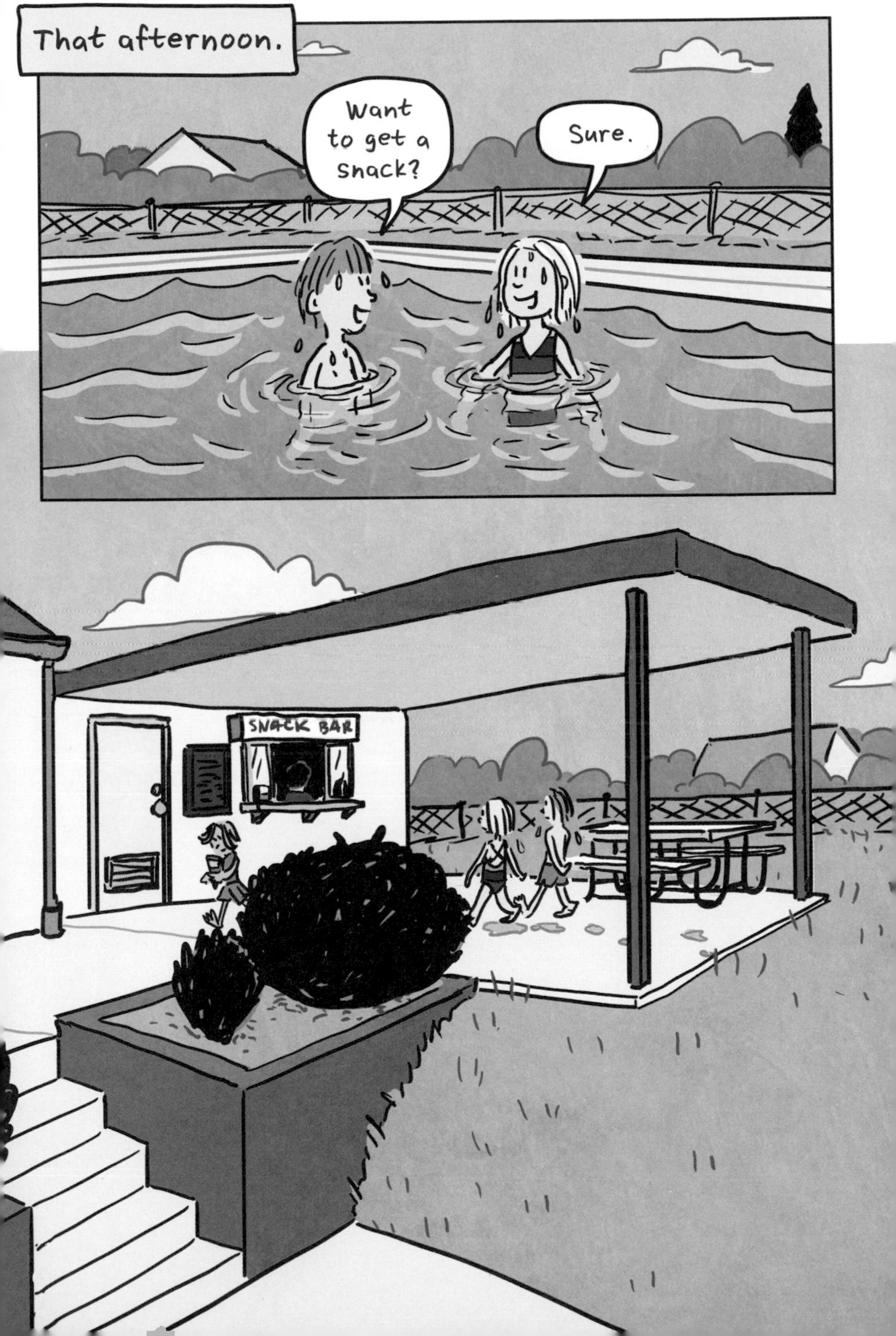
That afternoon.
Want to get a snack?
Sure.
SNACK BAR

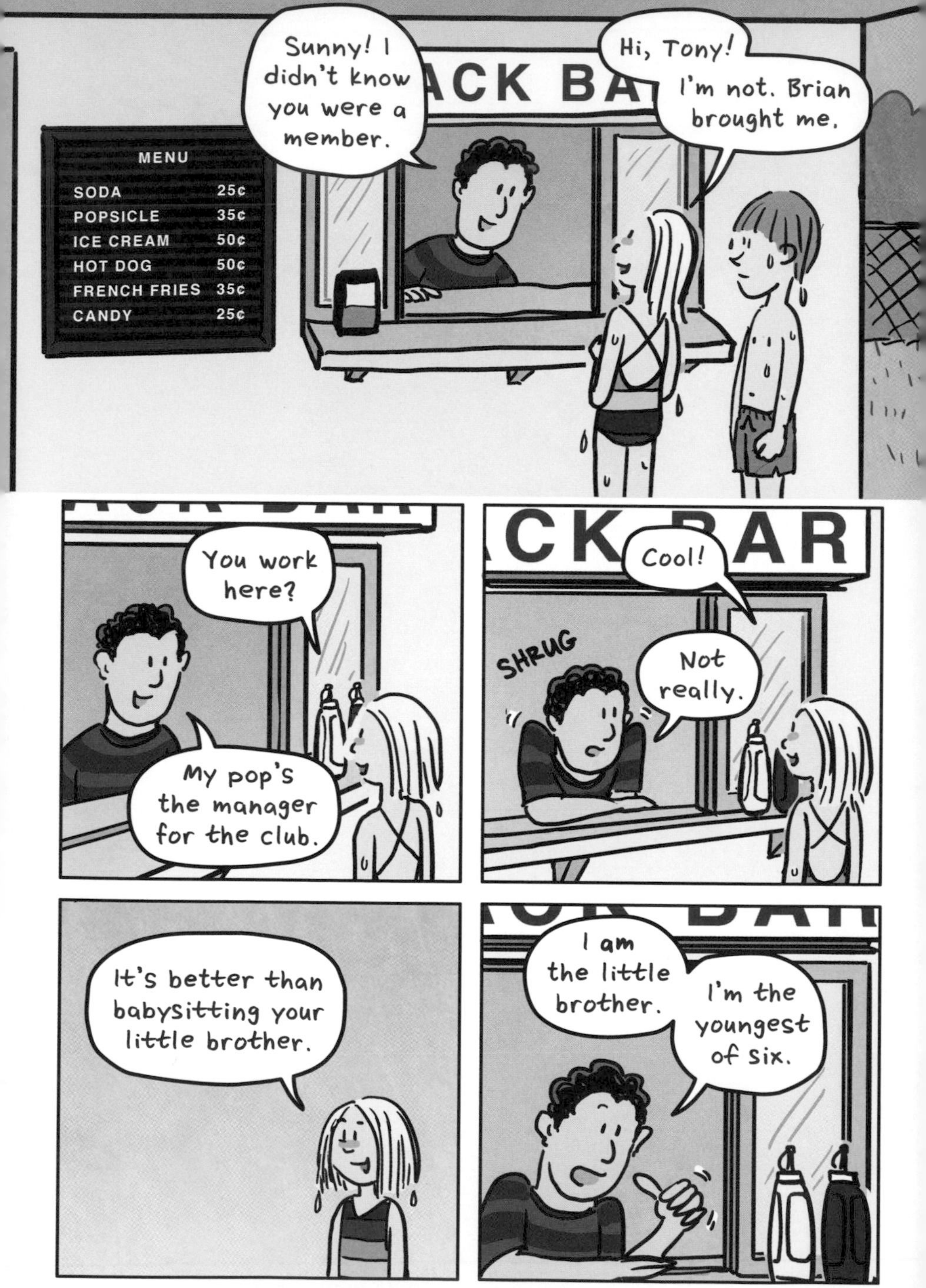
MENU
SODA 25¢
POPSICLE 35¢
ICE CREAM 50¢
HOT DOG 50¢
FRENCH FRIES 35¢
CANDY 25¢
ACK BA
Sunny! I didn't know you were a member.
Hi, Tony!
I'm not. Brian brought me.
You work here?
My pop's the manager for the club.
CK BAR
Cool!
SHRUG
Not really.
It's better than babysitting your little brother.
I am the little brother.
I'm the youngest of six.

SIX?!?

So what can I get you?

Popsicle.

I can't decide.

SNACK BAR

SODA
POPSICLE   35¢
ICE CREAM   35¢
HOT DOG   80¢
FRENCH FRIES 75¢
CANDY   35¢

I kind of want fries and a Popsicle, but I only have fifty cents.

The fries are on me.

Really?

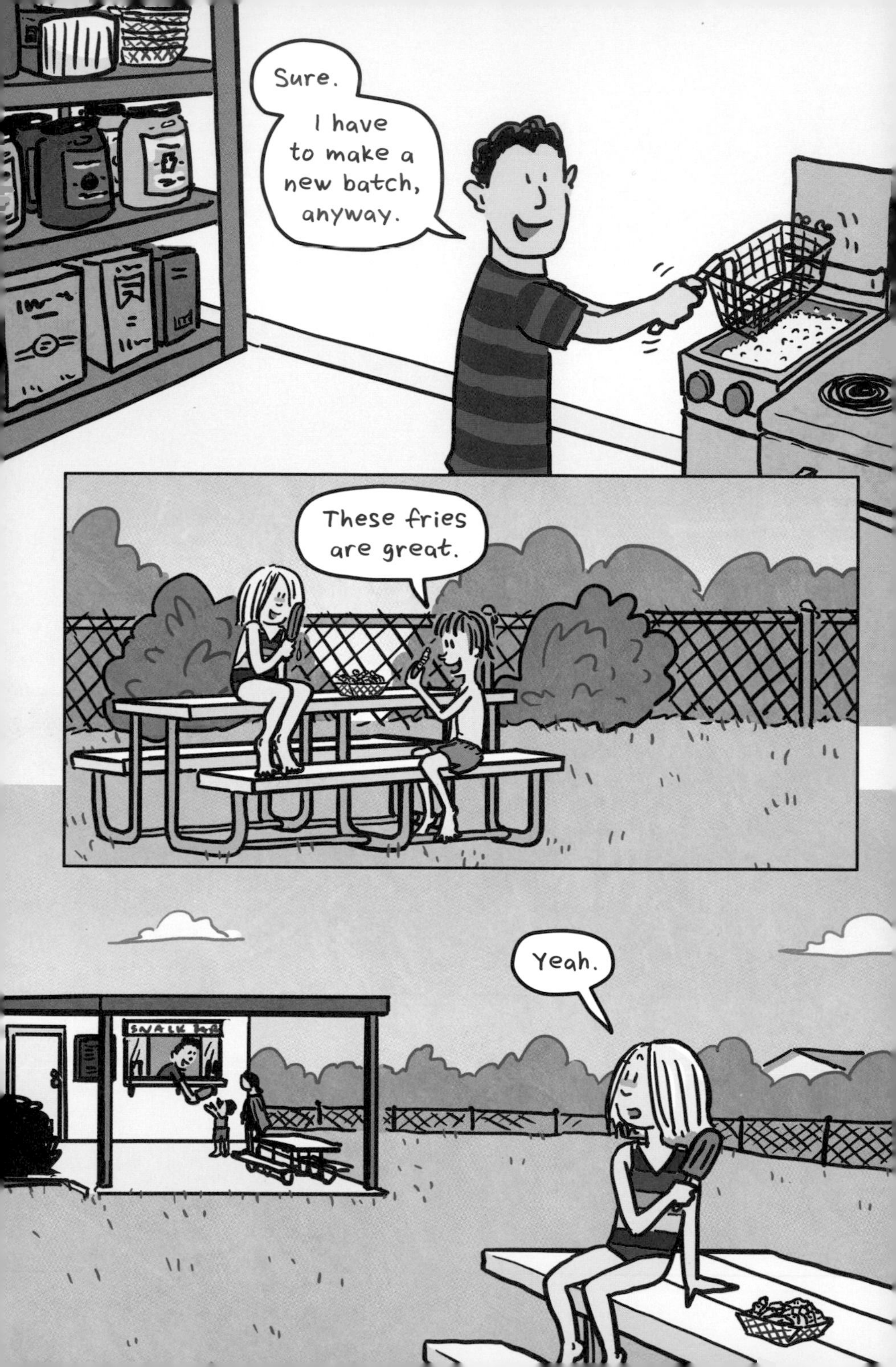
Sure.
I have to make a new batch, anyway.
These fries are great.
Yeah.

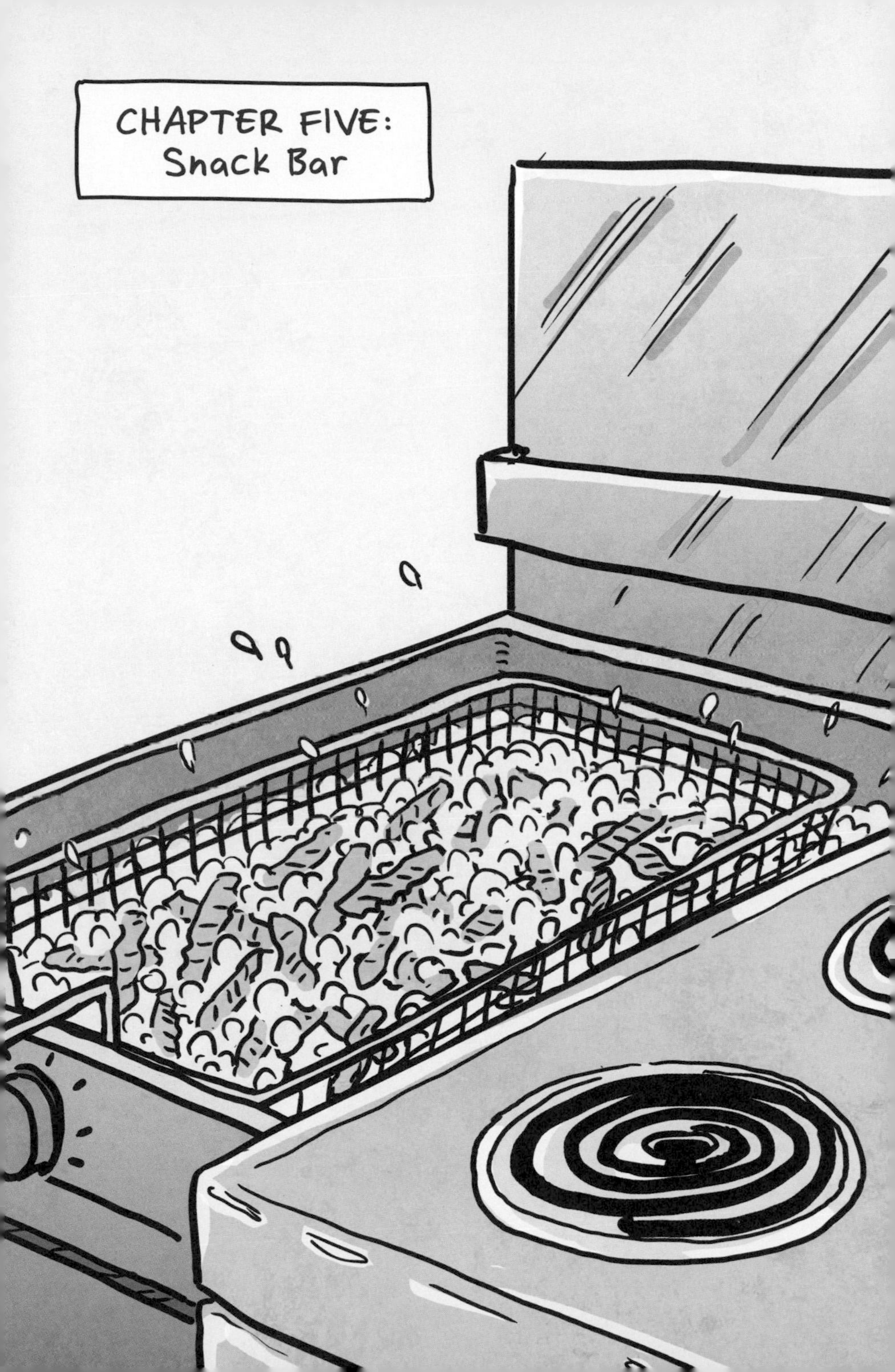
CHAPTER FIVE:
Snack Bar

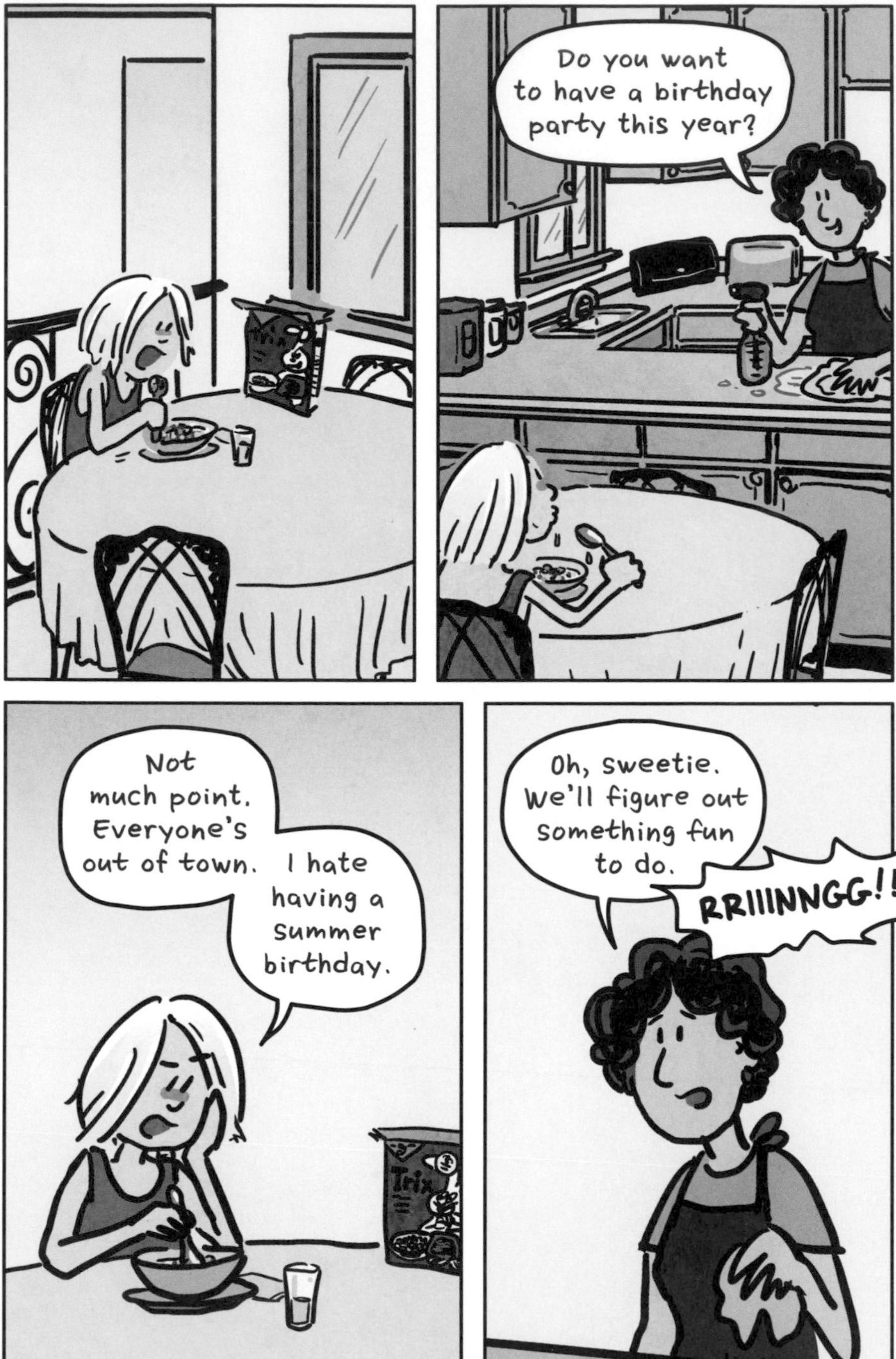
Do you want to have a birthday party this year?
Not much point. Everyone's out of town.
I hate having a summer birthday.
Oh, sweetie. We'll figure out something fun to do.
RRIIINNGG!!

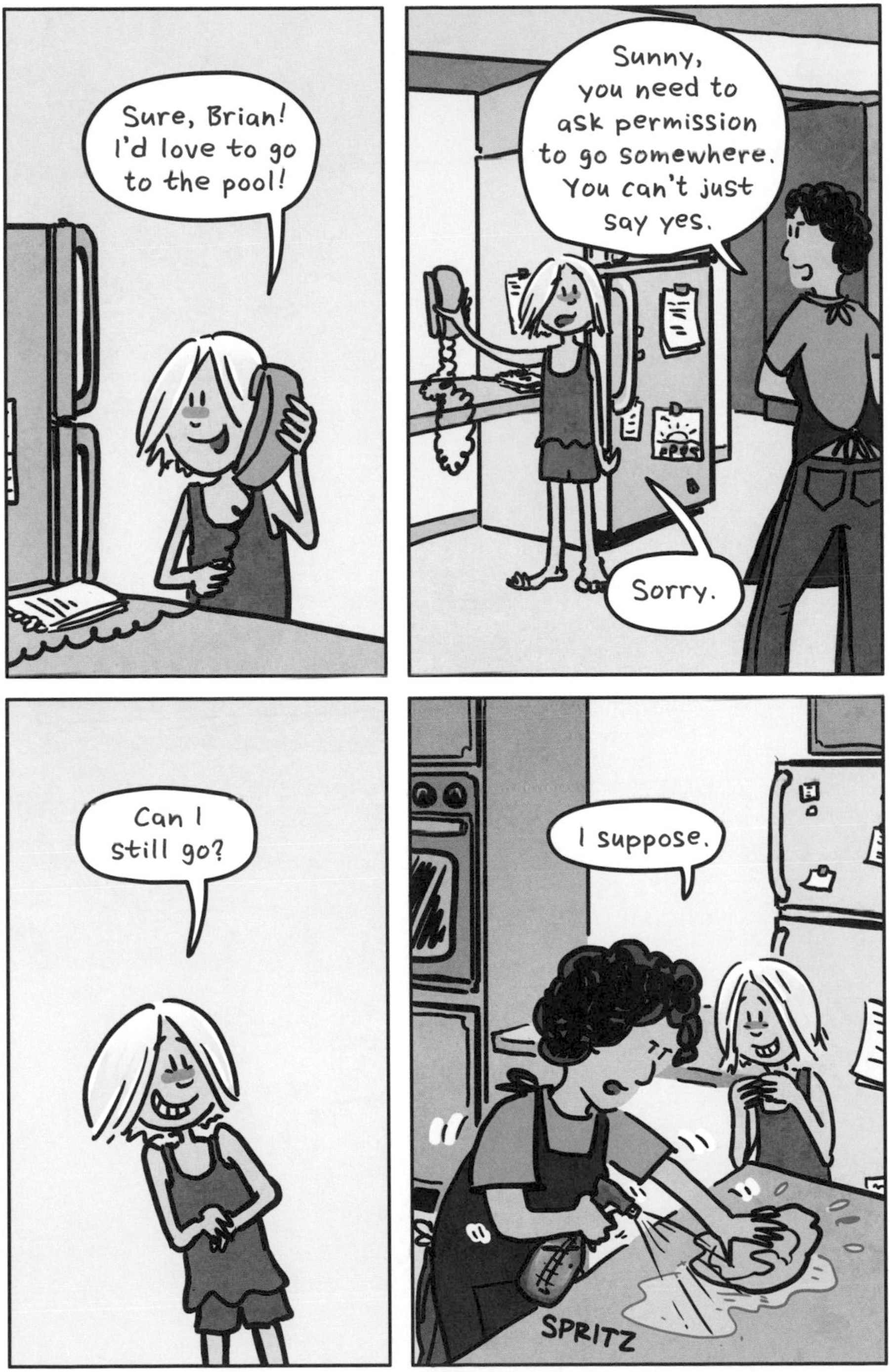

Sure, Brian! I'd love to go to the pool!
Sunny, you need to ask permission to go somewhere. You can't just say yes.
Sorry.
Can I still go?
I suppose.
SPRITZ

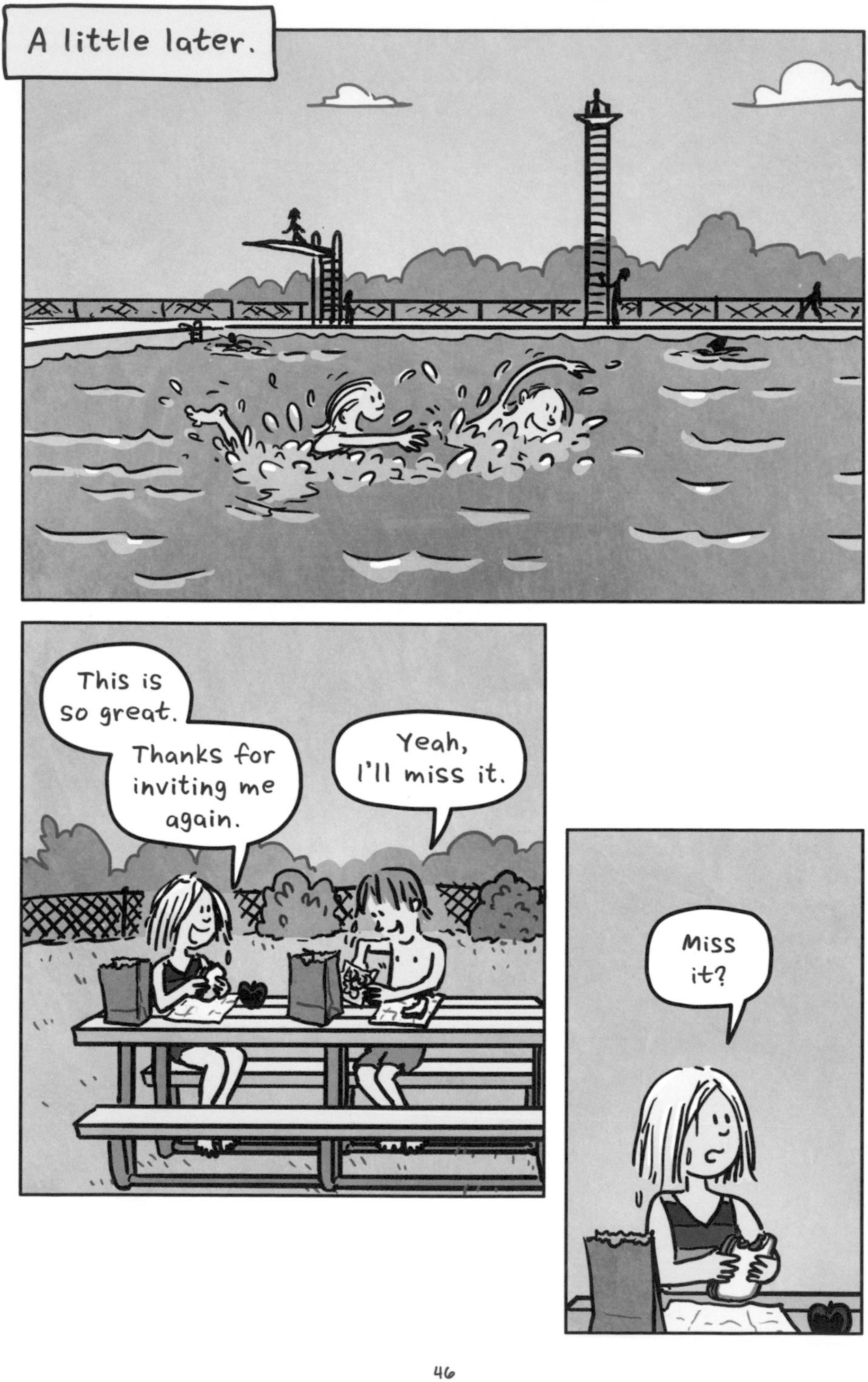
A little later.
This is so great.
Thanks for inviting me again.
Yeah, I'll miss it.
Miss it?

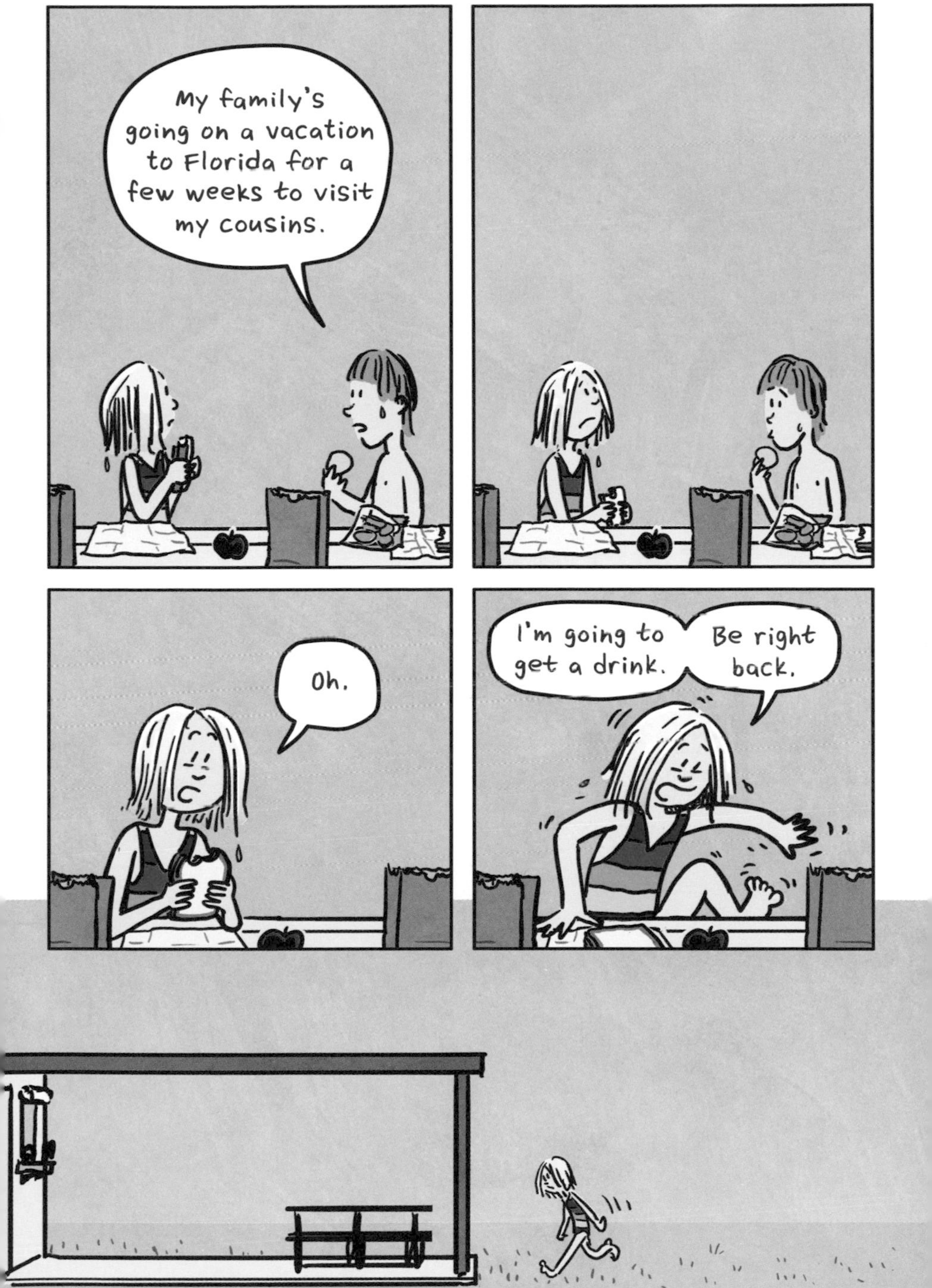
My family's going on a vacation to Florida for a few weeks to visit my cousins.
Oh.
I'm going to get a drink.
Be right back.

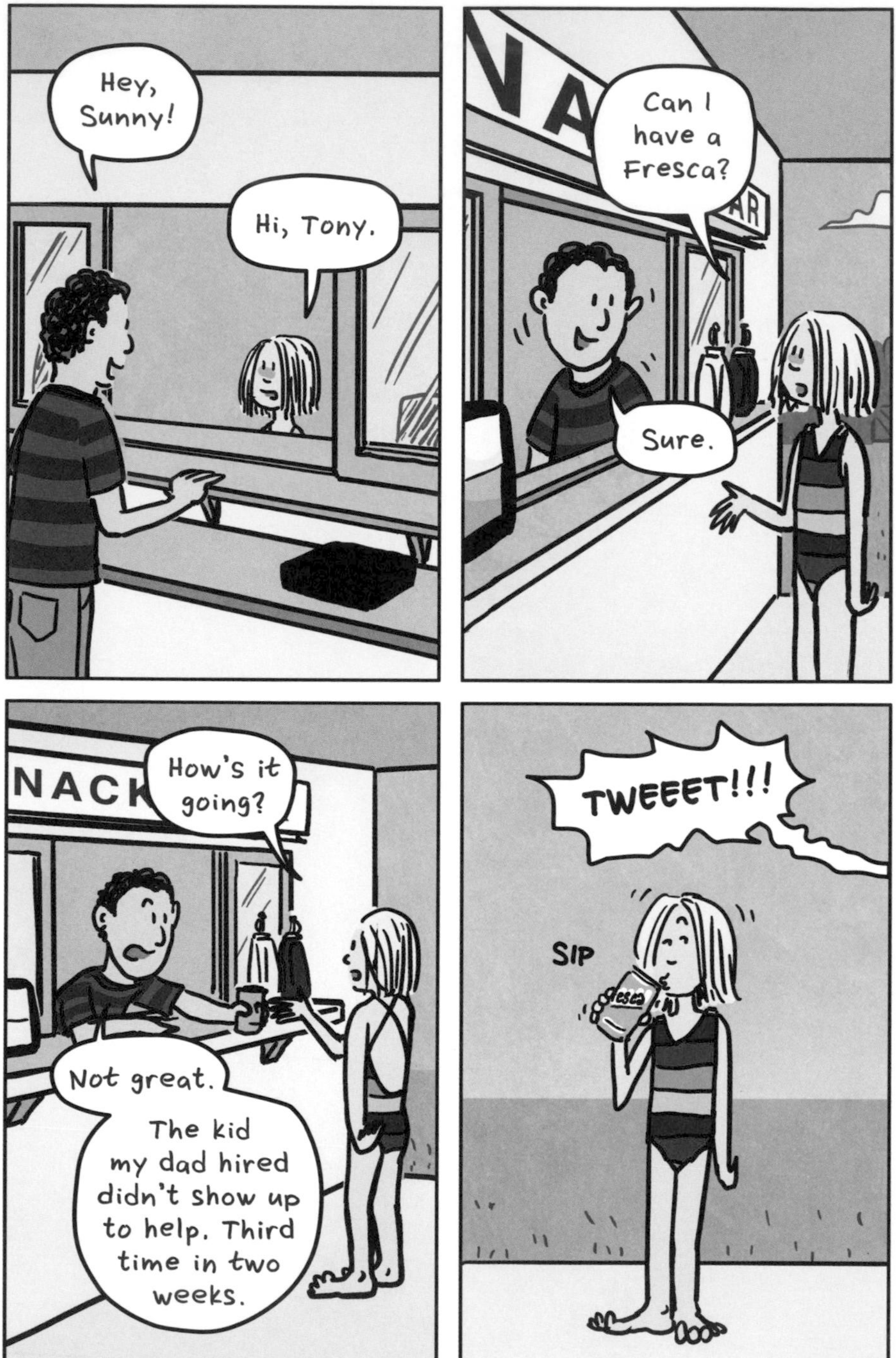
Hey, Sunny!
Hi, Tony.
Can I have a Fresca?
Sure.
How's it going?
Not great.
The kid my dad hired didn't show up to help. Third time in two weeks.
TWEEET!!!
SIP

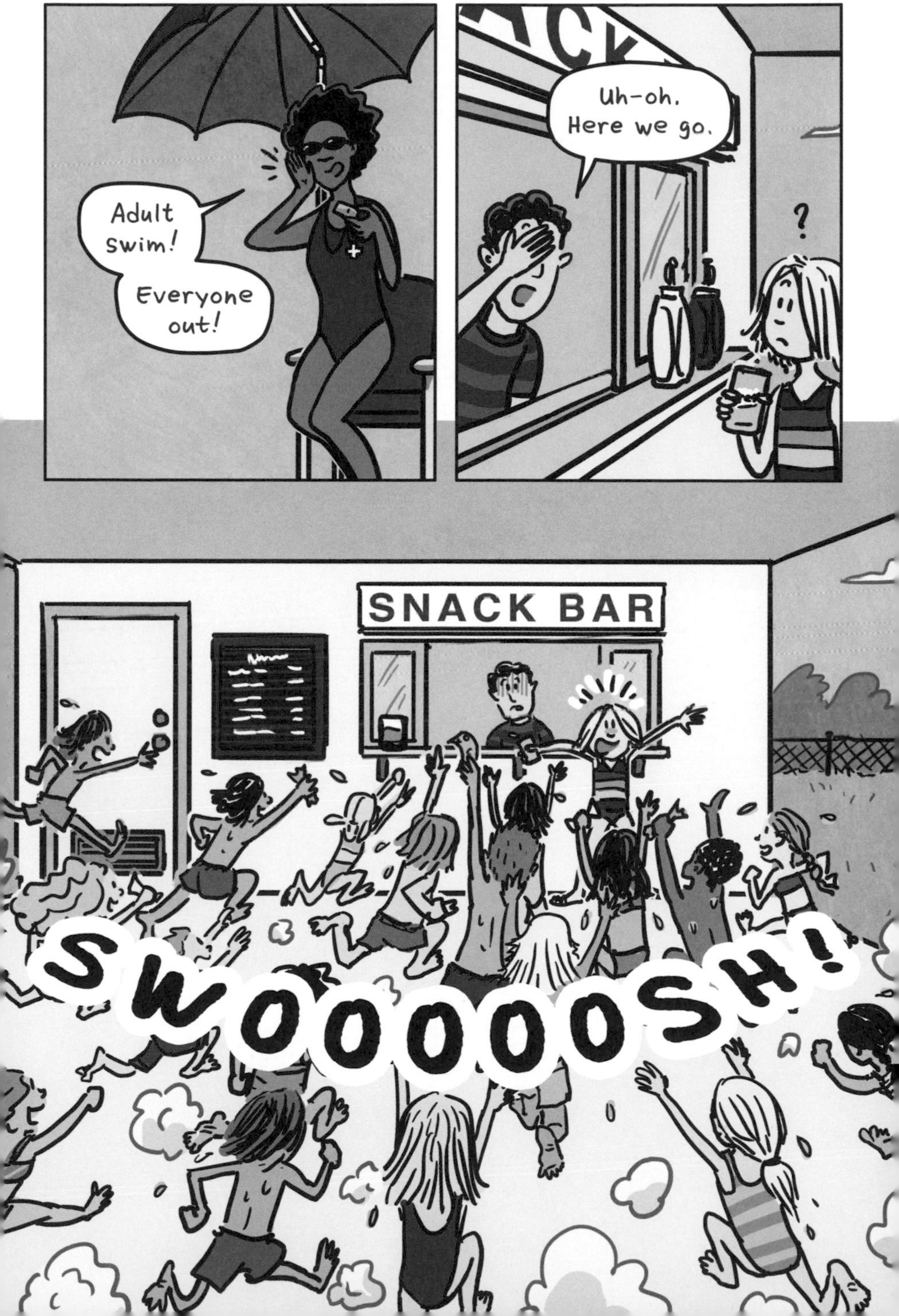
Adult swim!
Everyone out!
Uh-oh. Here we go.
?
SNACK BAR
SWOOOOOOSH!

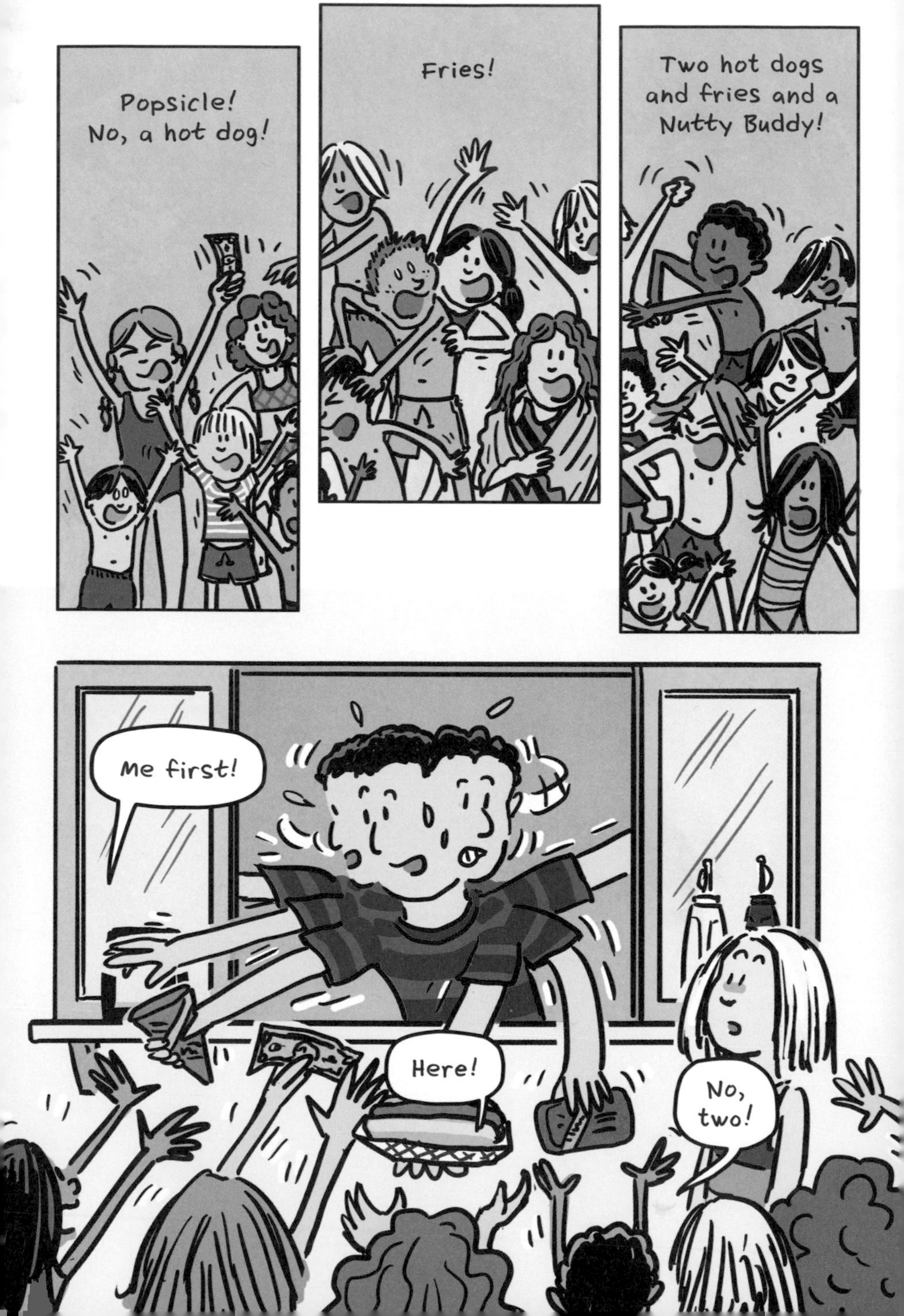
Popsicle! No, a hot dog!
Fries!
Two hot dogs and fries and a Nutty Buddy!
Me first!
Here!
No, two!

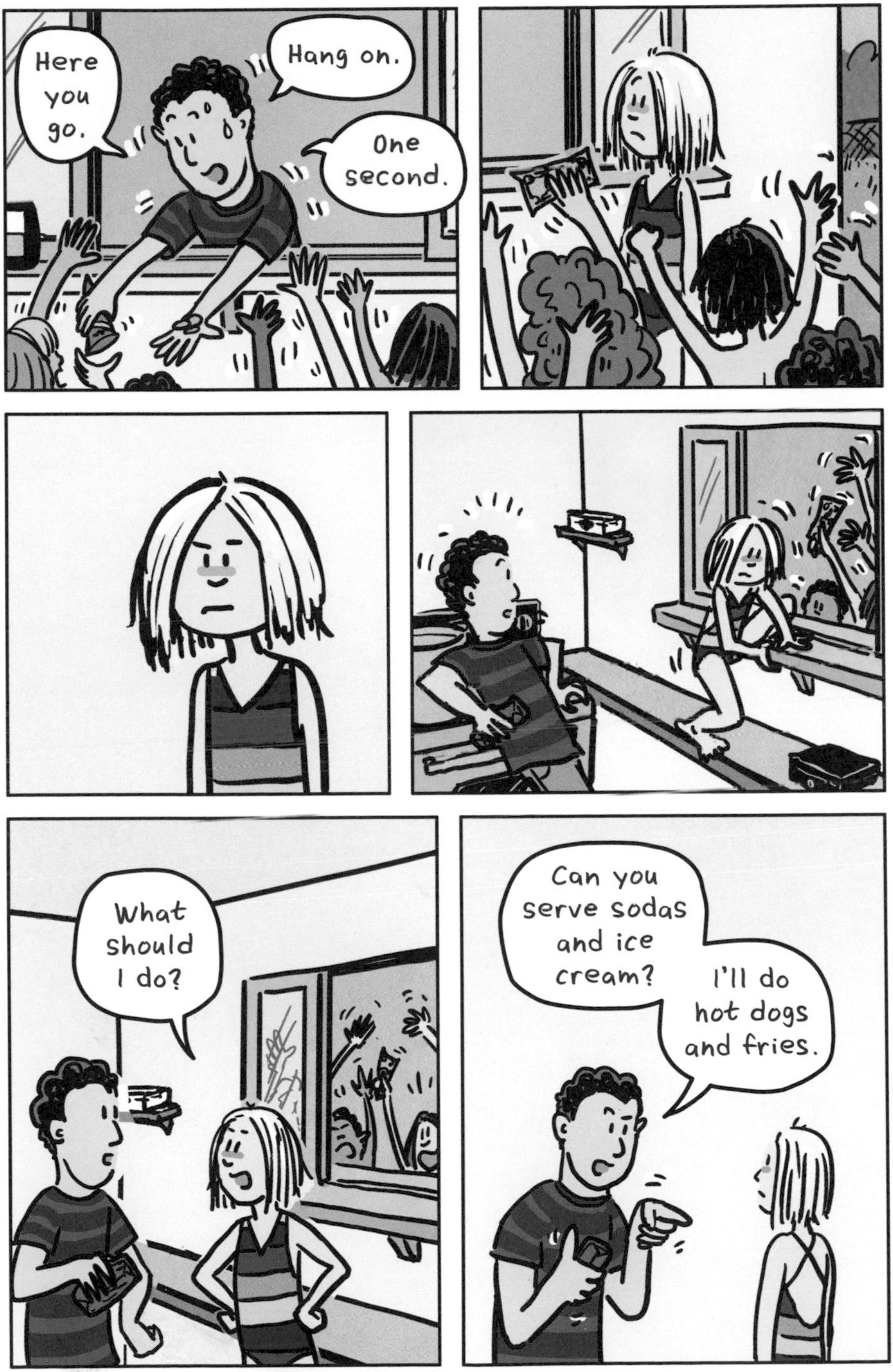
Here you go.
Hang on.
One second.
What should I do?
Can you serve sodas and ice cream?
I'll do hot dogs and fries.

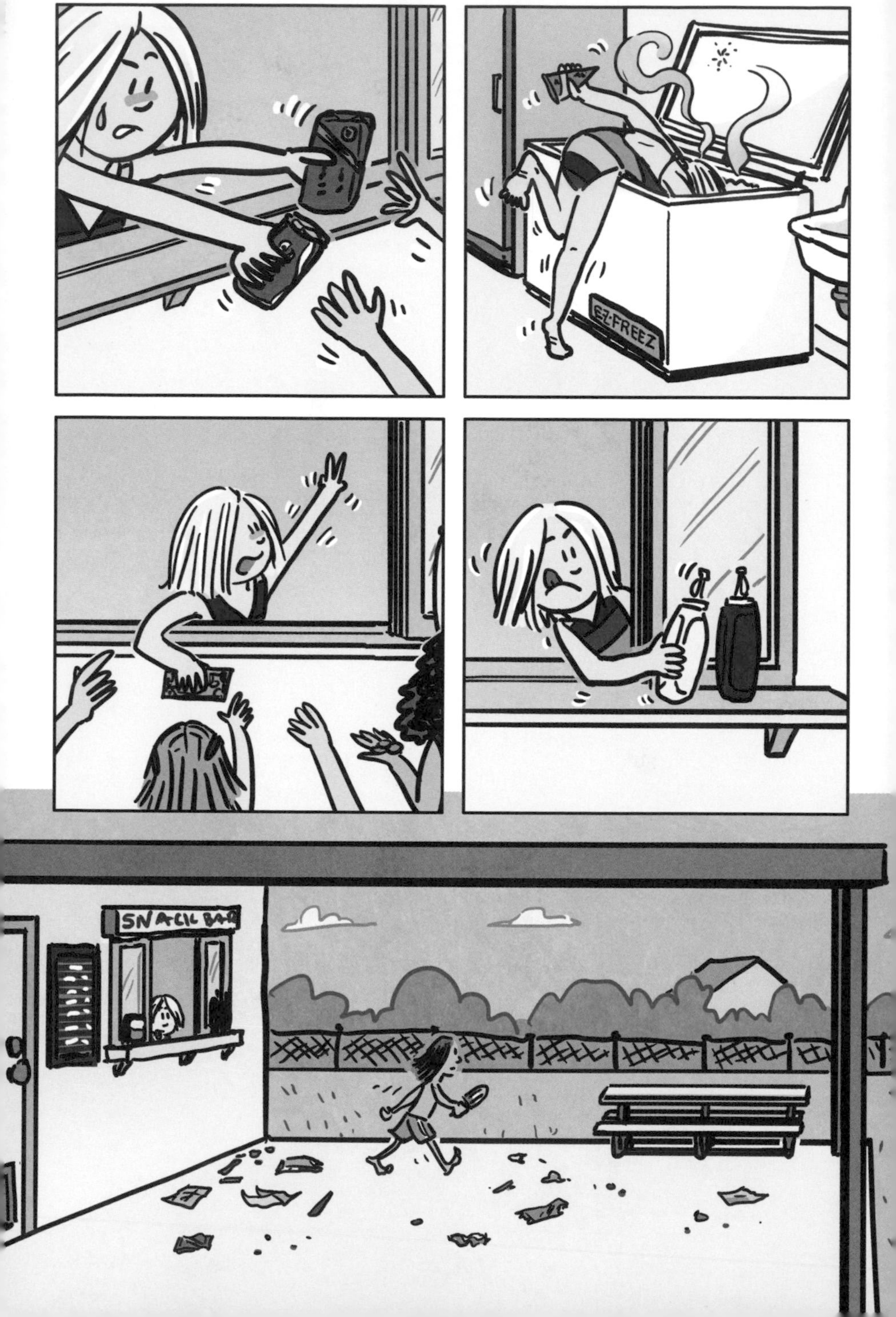
E-Z FREEZ
SNACK BAR

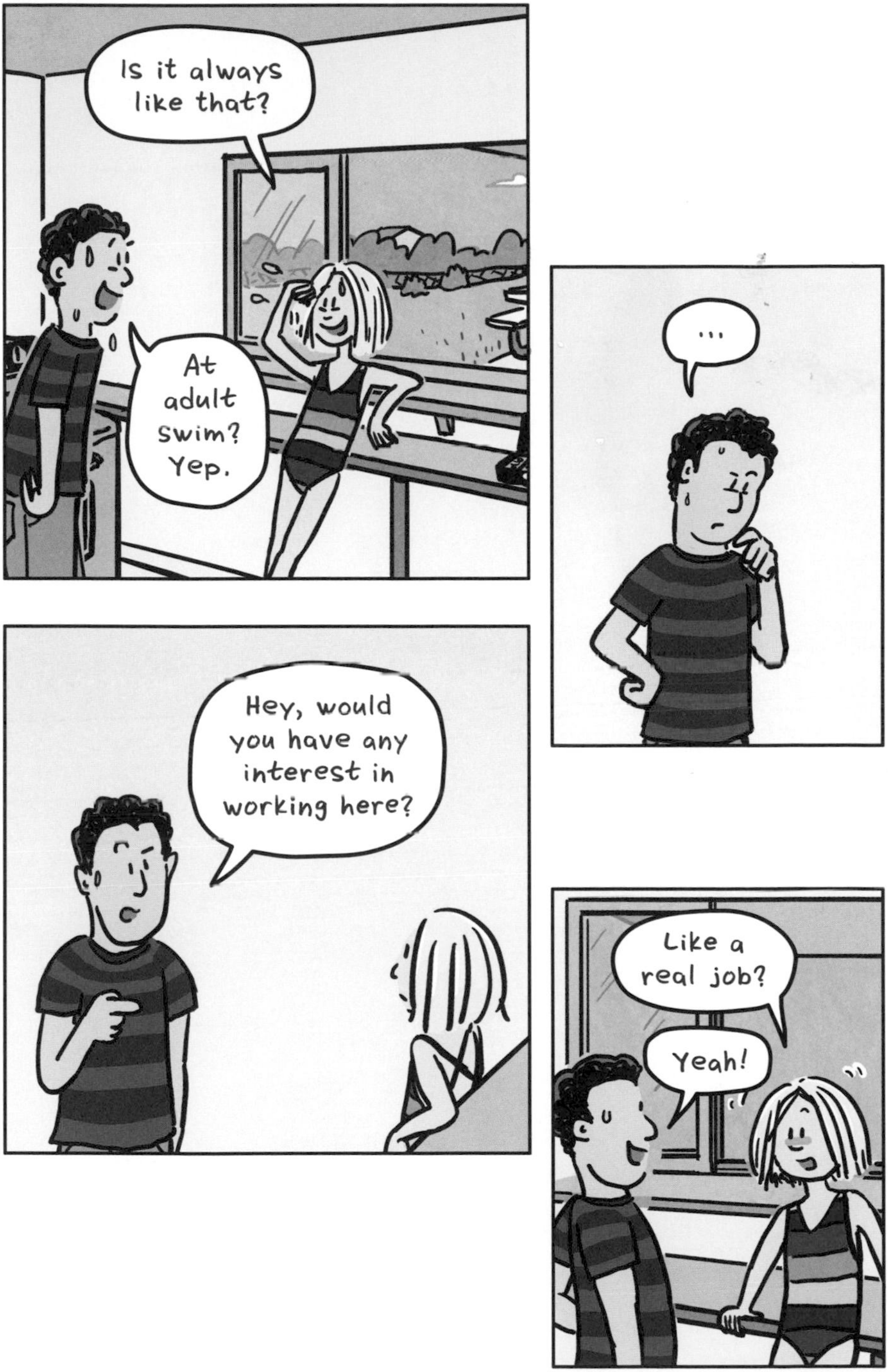
Is it always like that?
At adult swim? Yep.
...
Hey, would you have any interest in working here?
Like a real job?
Yeah!

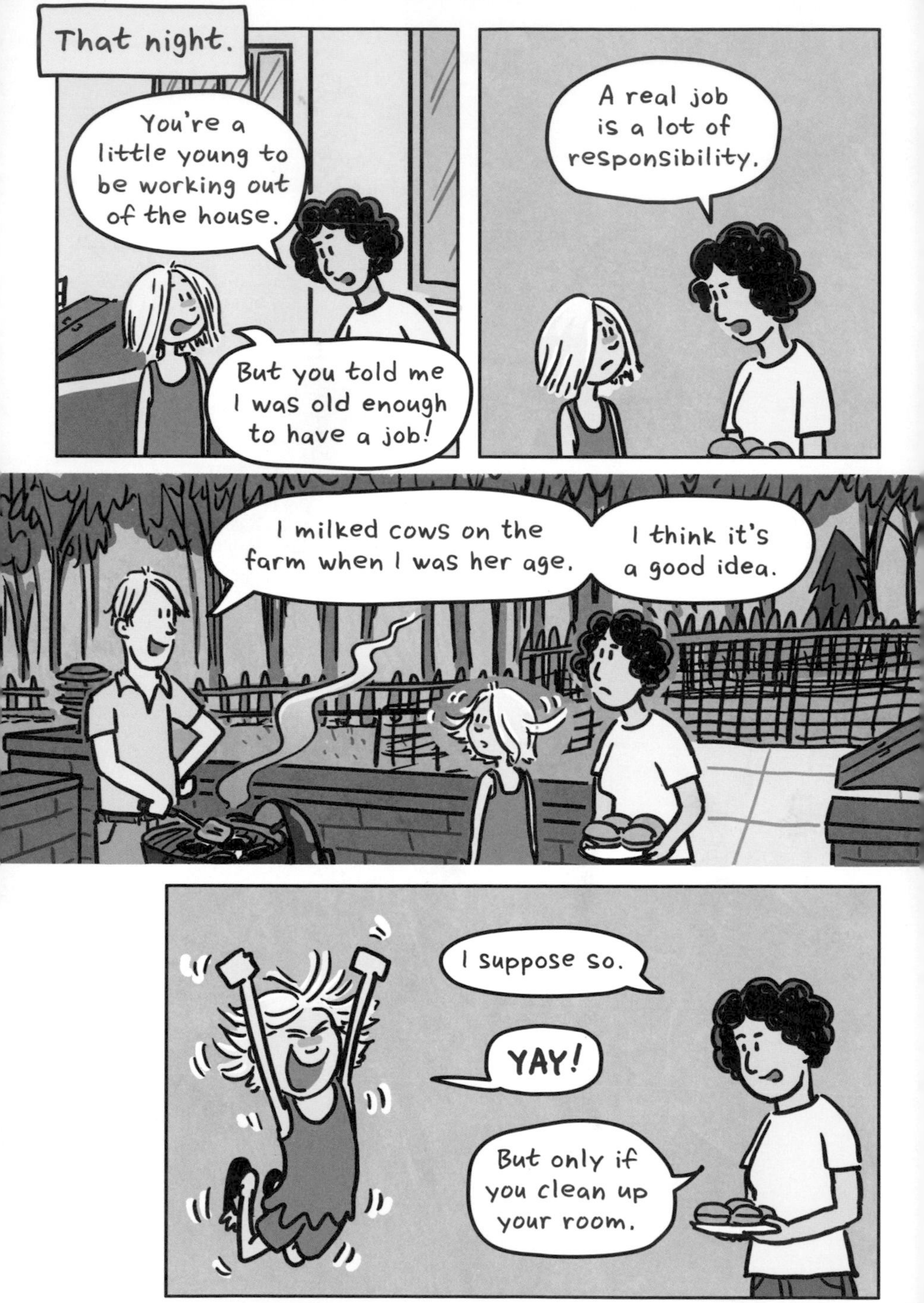
That night.
You're a little young to be working out of the house.
But you told me I was old enough to have a job!
A real job is a lot of responsibility.
I milked cows on the farm when I was her age.
I think it's a good idea.
I suppose so.
YAY!
But only if you clean up your room.

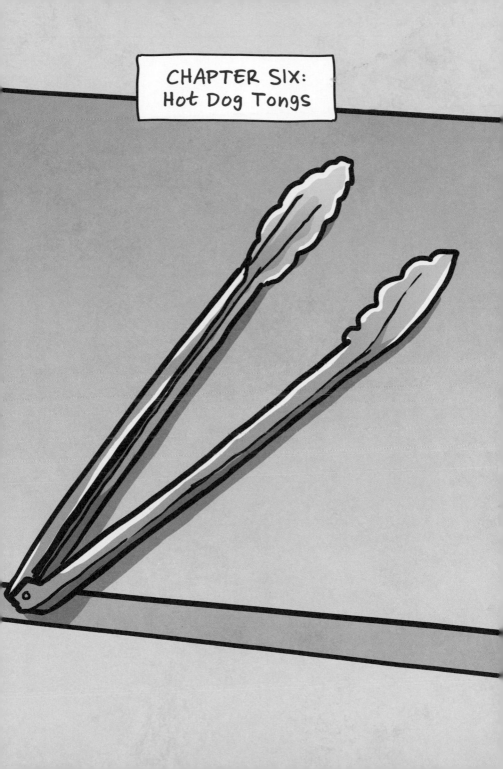

CHAPTER SIX:
Hot Dog Tongs

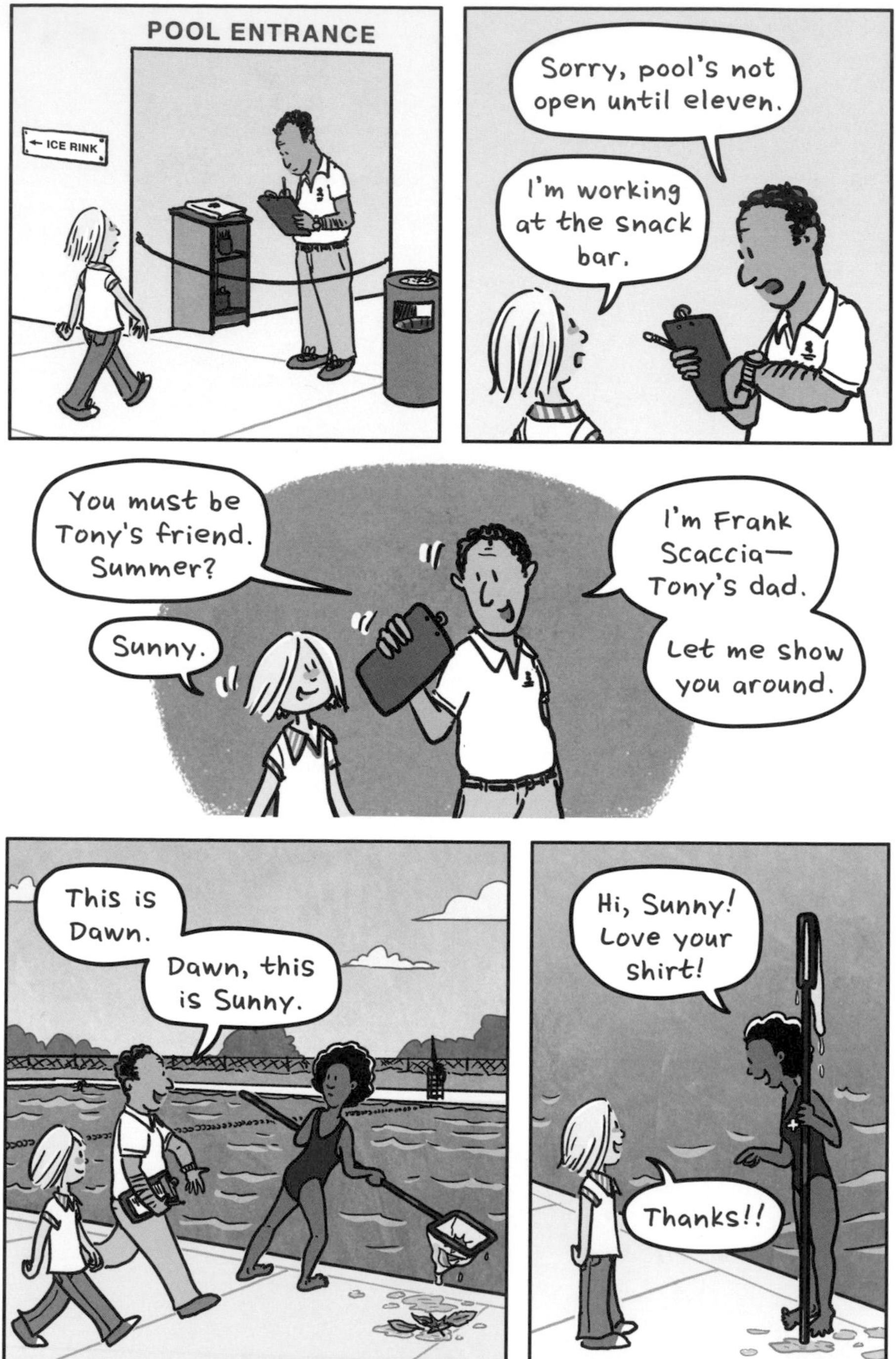
POOL ENTRANCE
ICE RINK
Sorry, pool's not open until eleven.
I'm working at the snack bar.
You must be Tony's friend. Summer?
Sunny.
I'm Frank Scaccia— Tony's dad.
Let me show you around.
This is Dawn.
Dawn, this is Sunny.
Hi, Sunny! Love your shirt!
Thanks!!

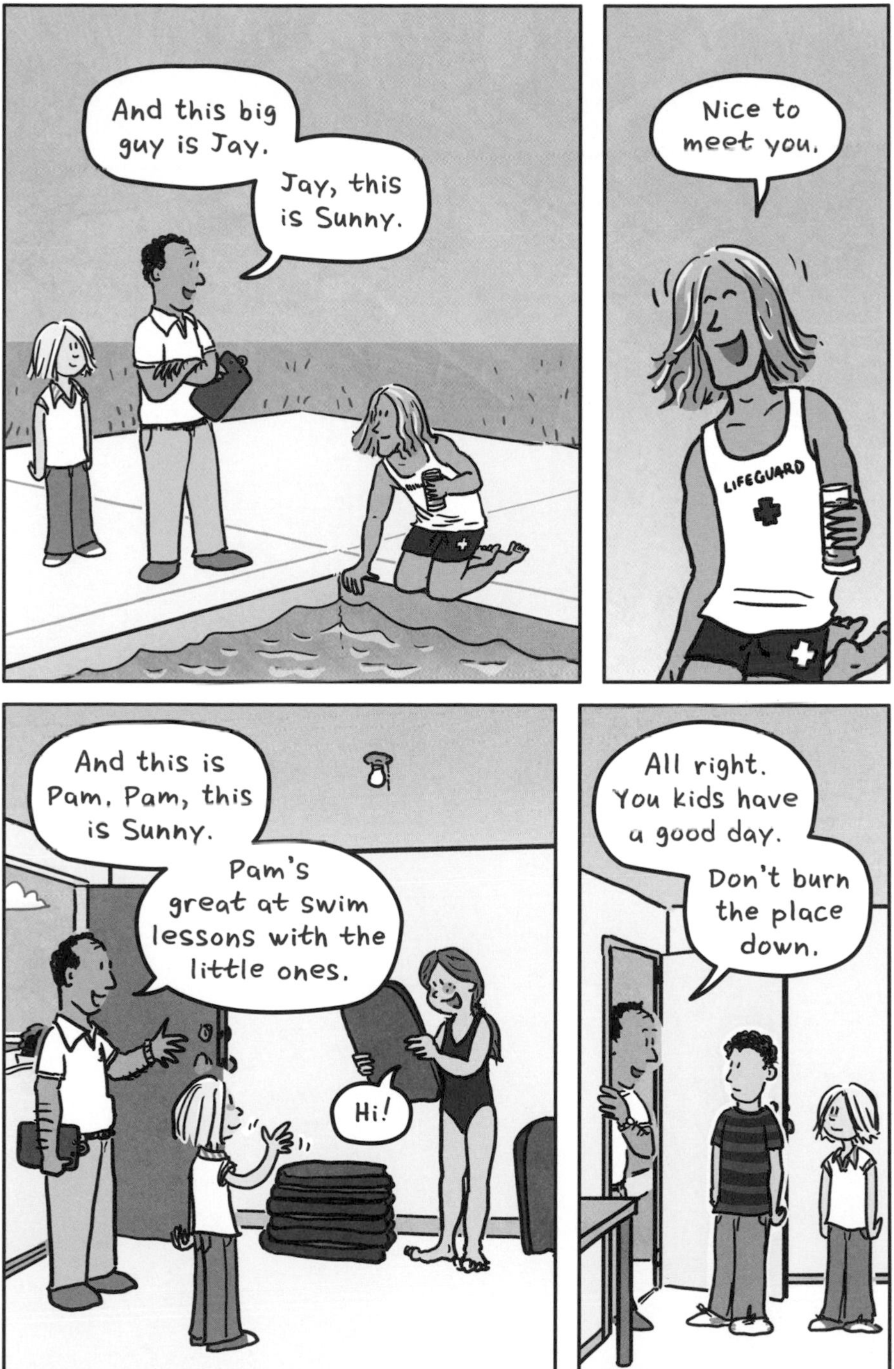
And this big guy is Jay.
Jay, this is Sunny.
Nice to meet you.
LIFEGUARD
And this is Pam. Pam, this is Sunny.
Pam's great at swim lessons with the little ones.
Hi!
All right. You kids have a good day.
Don't burn the place down.

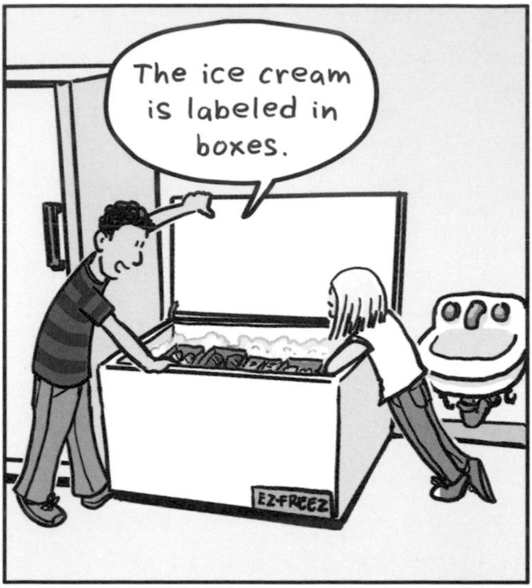
The ice cream is labeled in boxes.
EZ-FREEZ

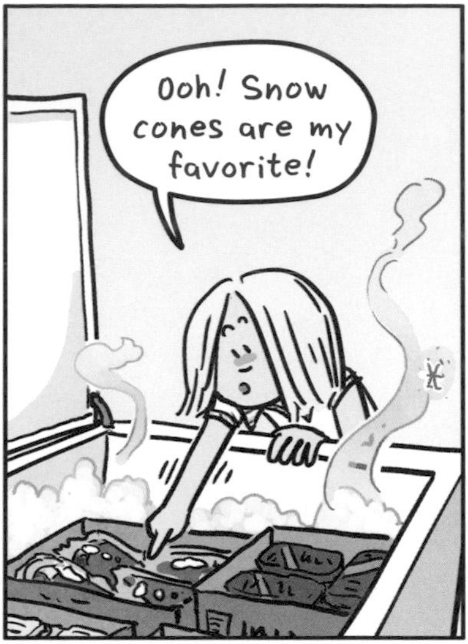
Ooh! Snow cones are my favorite!

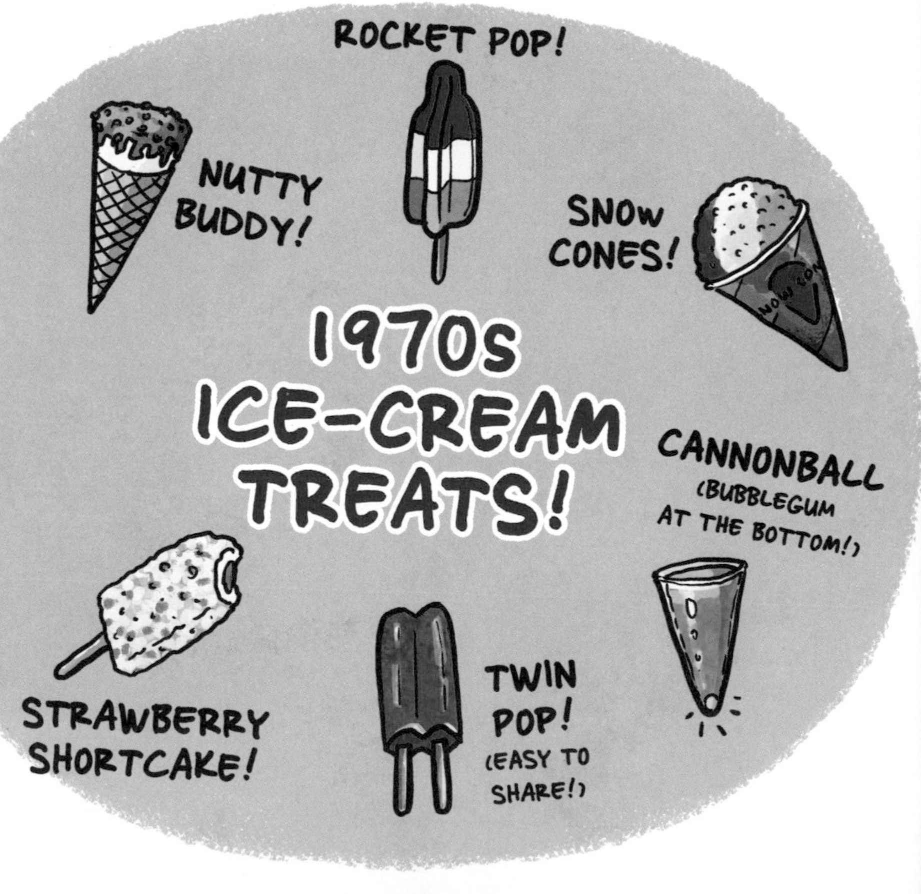
ROCKET POP!
NUTTY BUDDY!
SNOW CONES!
1970s ICE-CREAM TREATS!
CANNONBALL (BUBBLEGUM AT THE BOTTOM!)
STRAWBERRY SHORTCAKE!
TWIN POP! (EASY TO SHARE!)

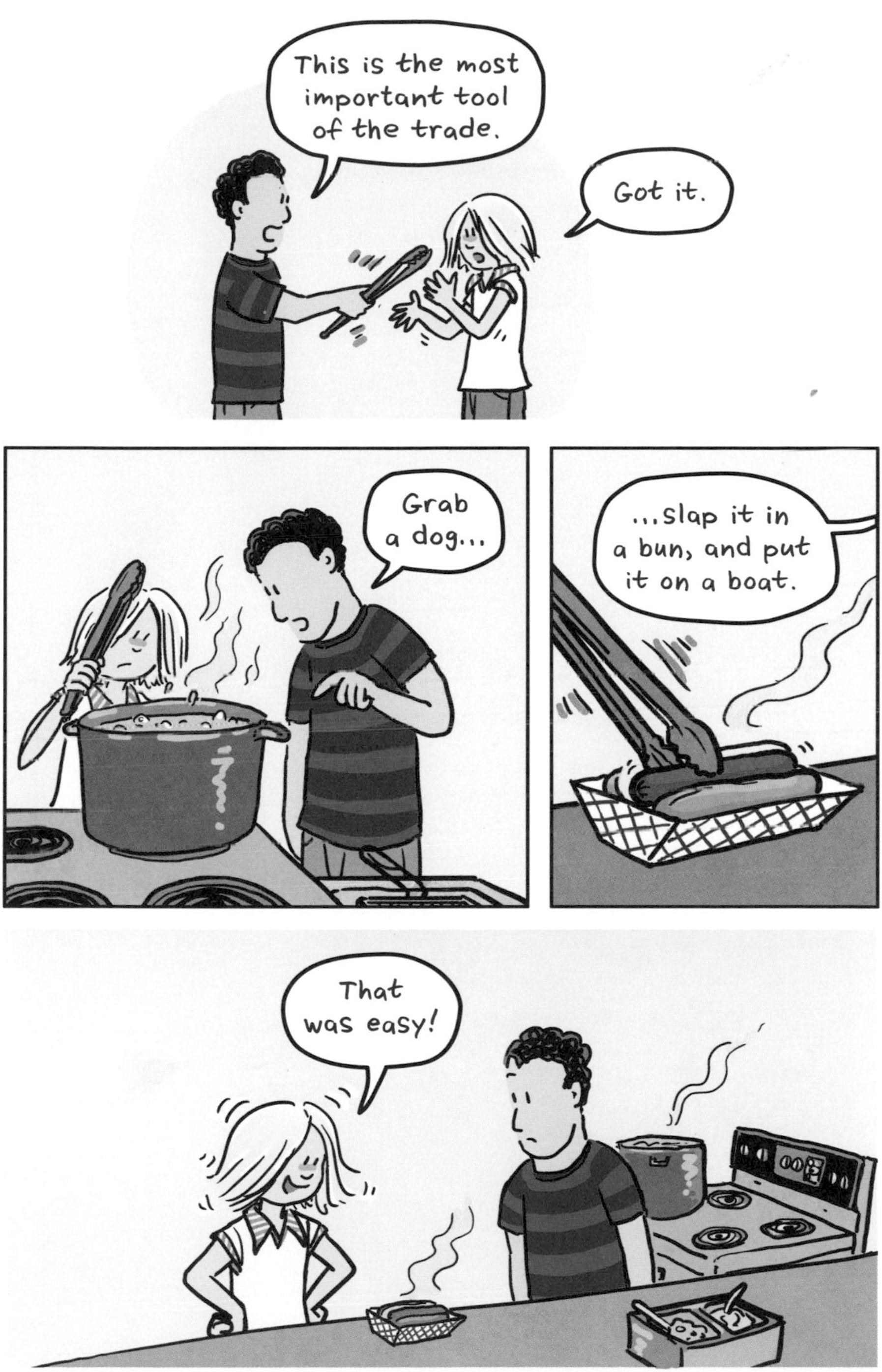
This is the most important tool of the trade.
Got it.
Grab a dog...
...Slap it in a bun, and put it on a boat.
That was easy!

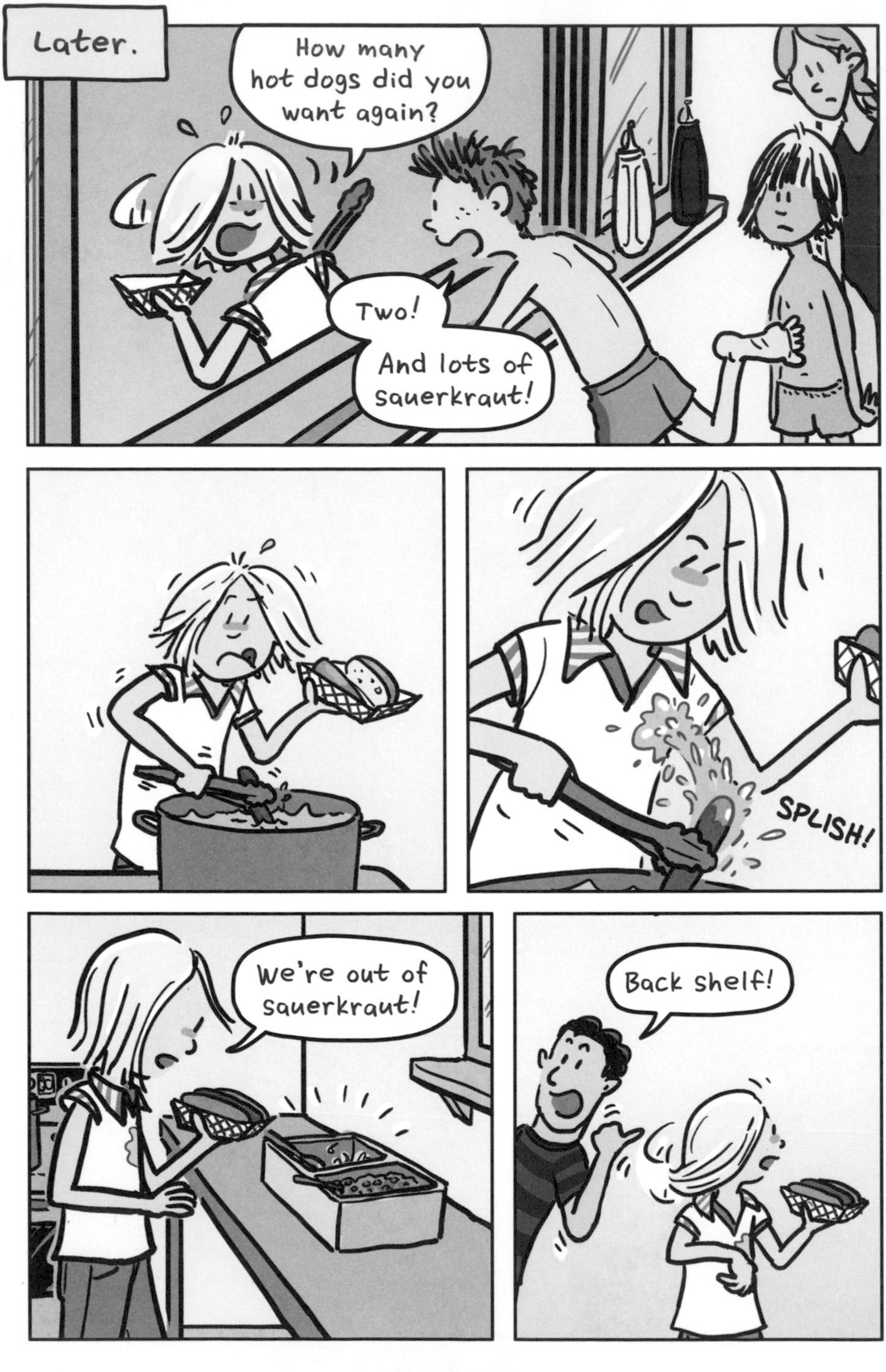
Later.
How many hot dogs did you want again?
Two!
And lots of sauerkraut!
SPLISH!
We're out of sauerkraut!
Back shelf!

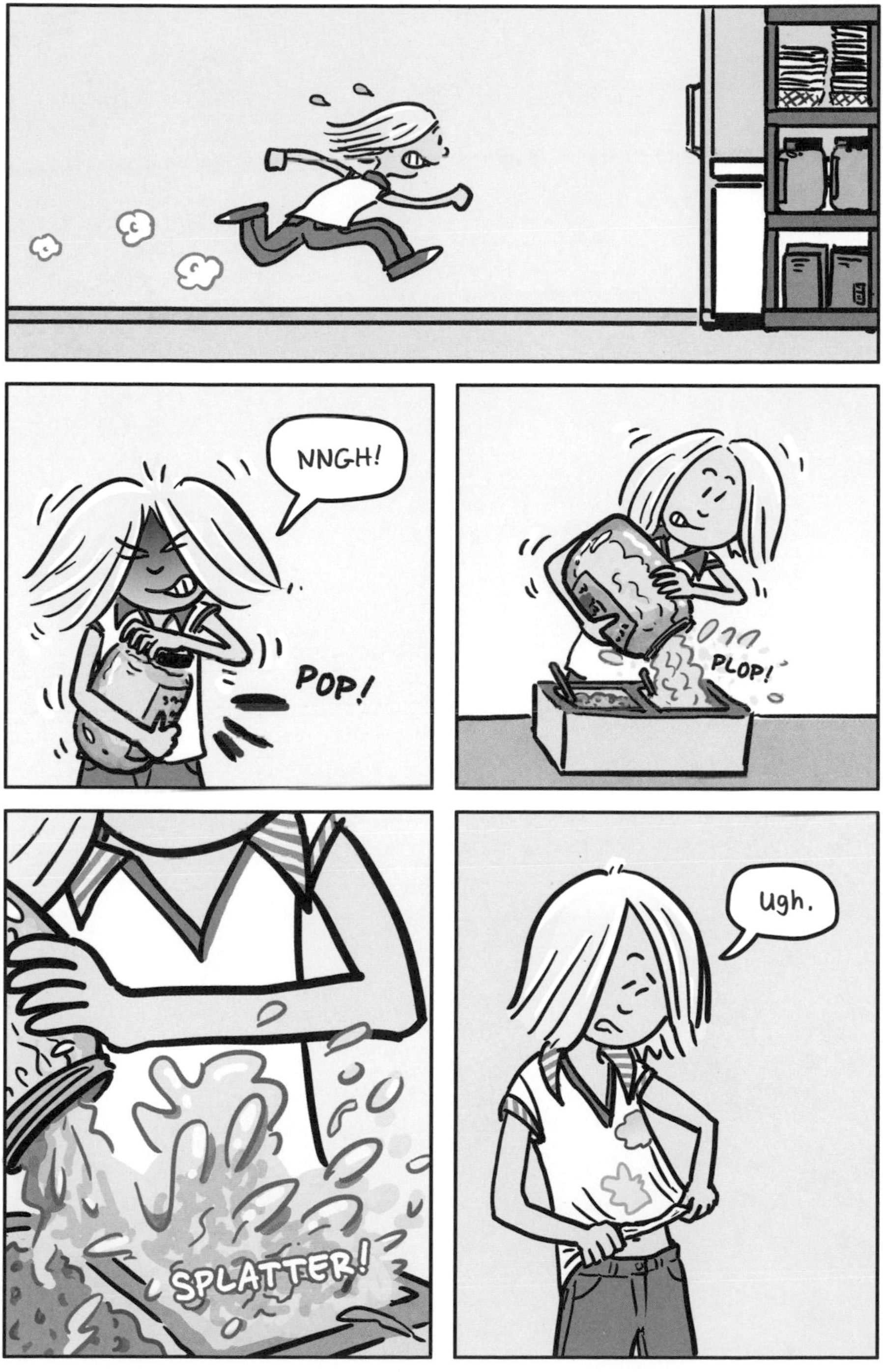
NNGH!
POP!
PLOP!
SPLATTER!
Ugh.

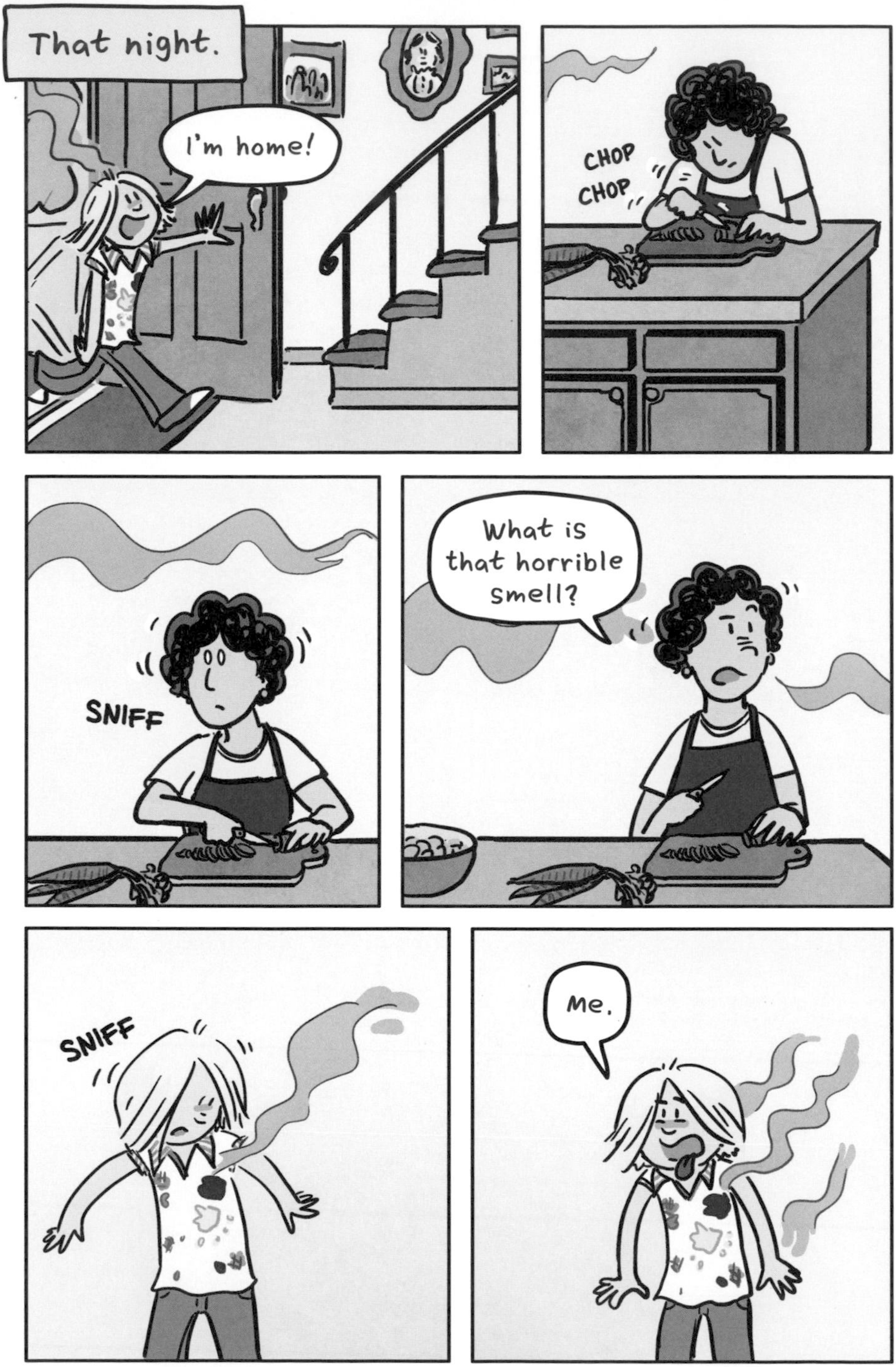
That night.
I'm home!
CHOP
CHOP
SNIFF
What is that horrible smell?
SNIFF
Me.

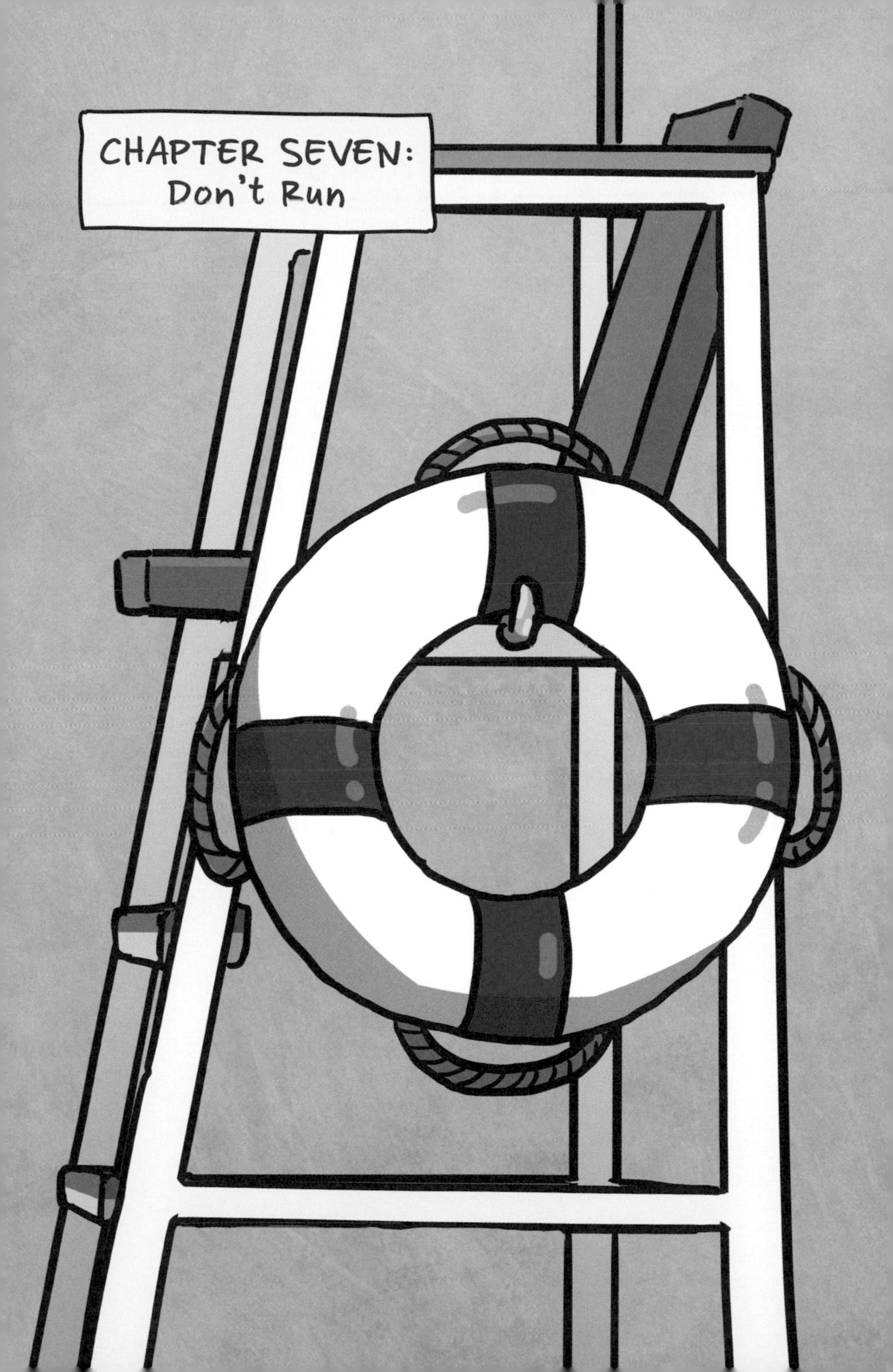
CHAPTER SEVEN:
Don't Run

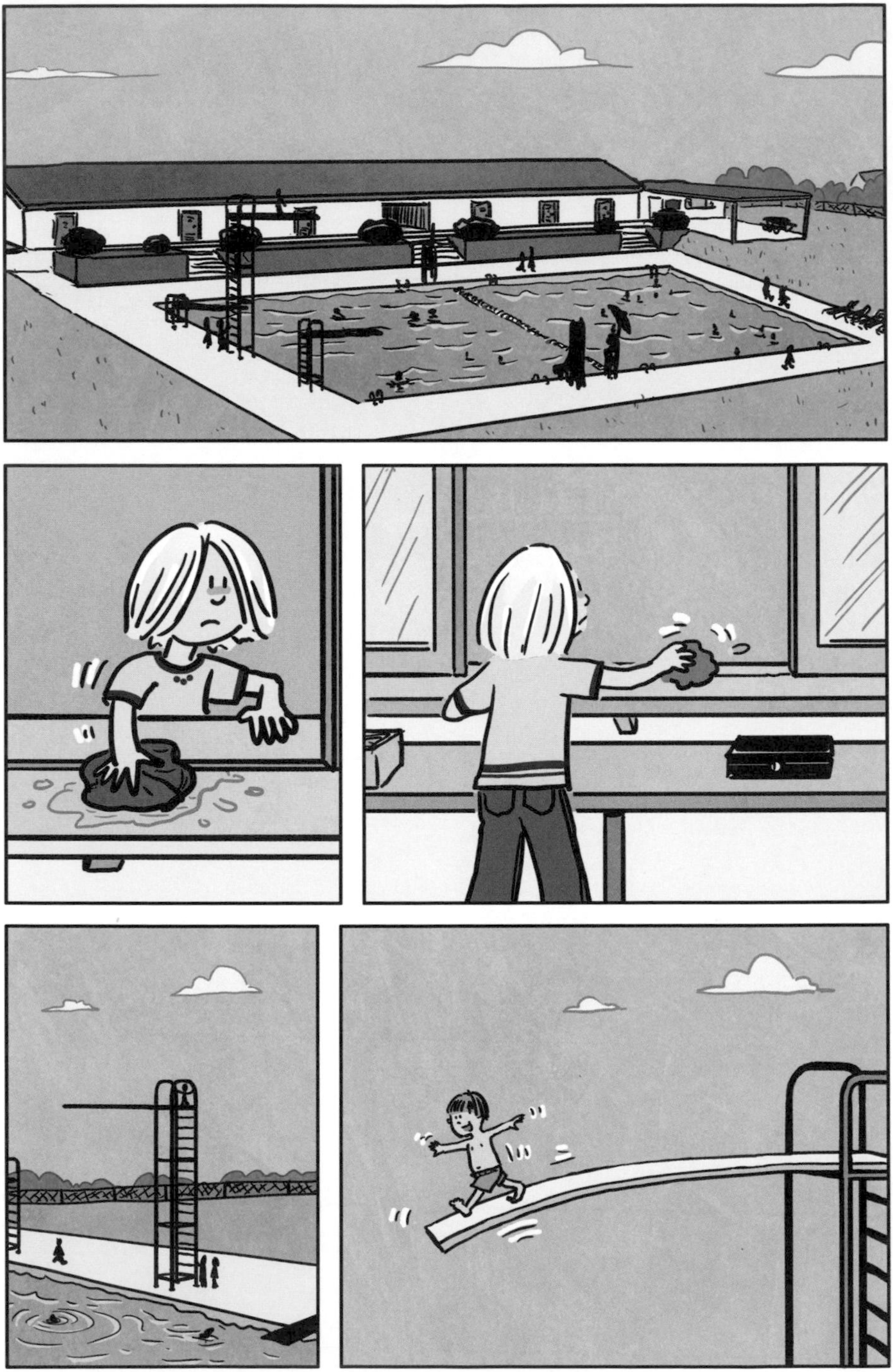

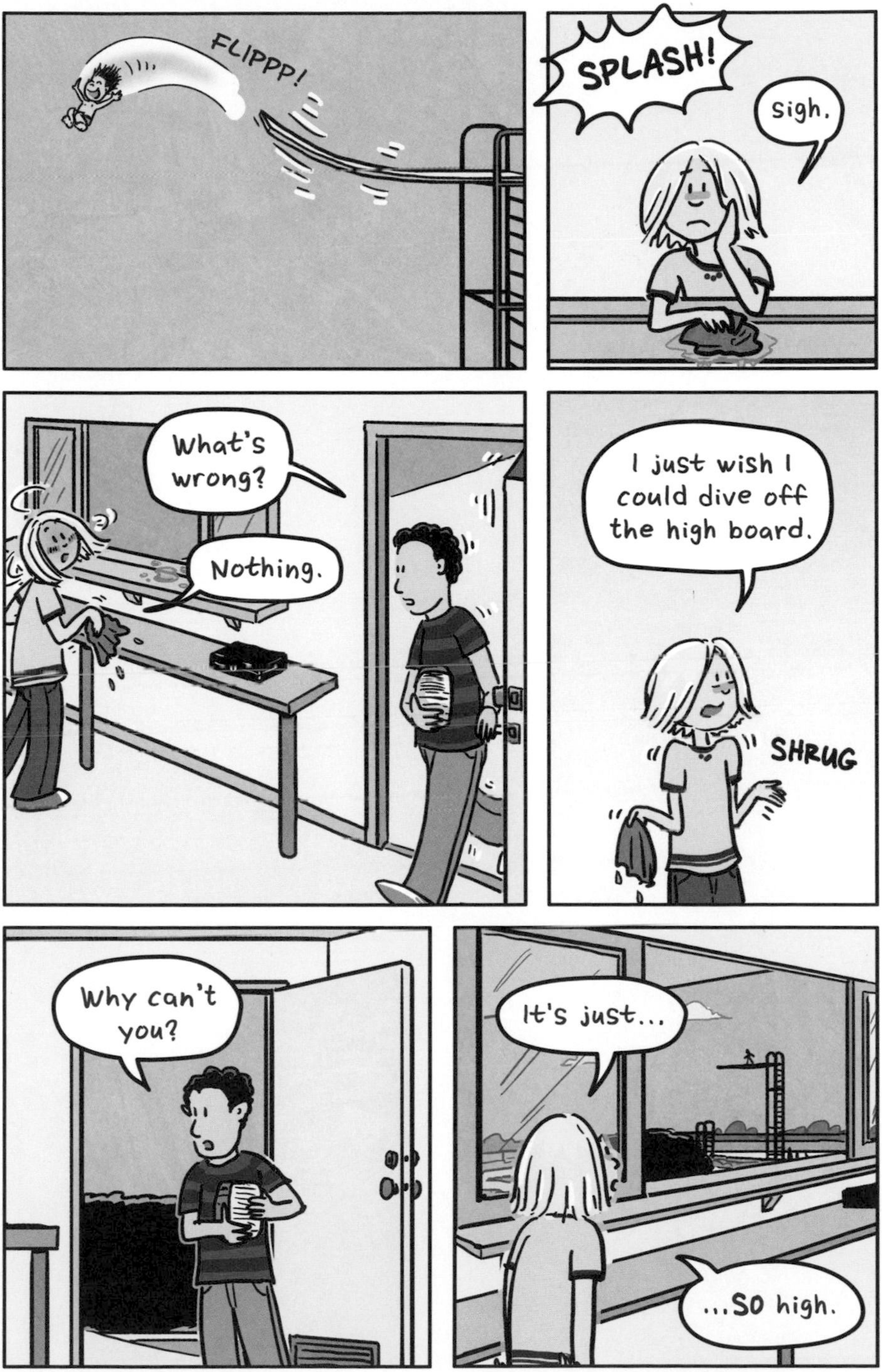
FLIPPP!
SPLASH!
Sigh.
What's wrong?
Nothing.
I just wish I could dive off the high board.
SHRUG
Why can't you?
It's just...
...SO high.

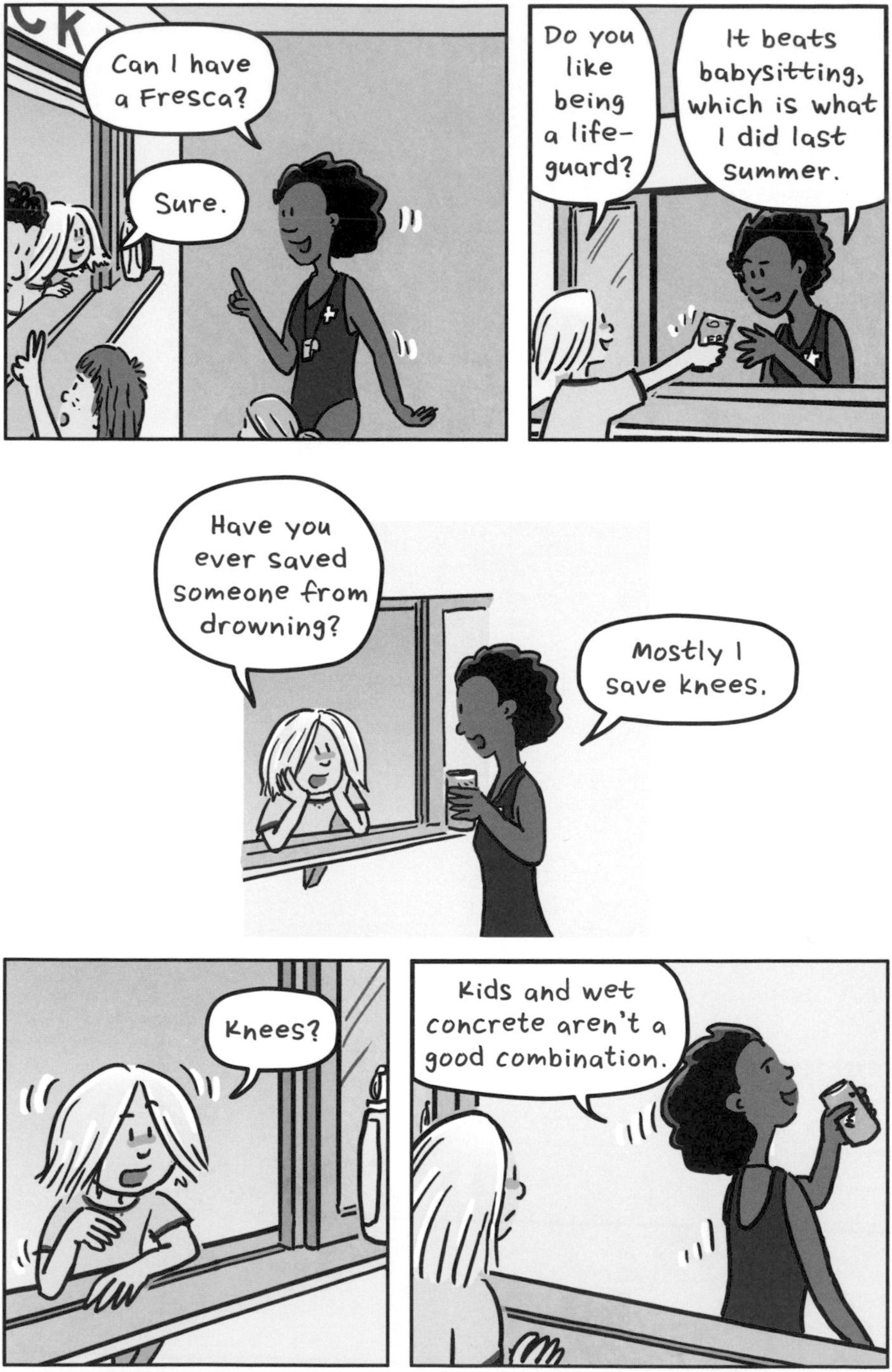
Can I have a Fresca?
Sure.
Do you like being a life-guard?
It beats babysitting, which is what I did last summer.
Have you ever saved someone from drowning?
Mostly I save knees.
Knees?
Kids and wet concrete aren't a good combination.

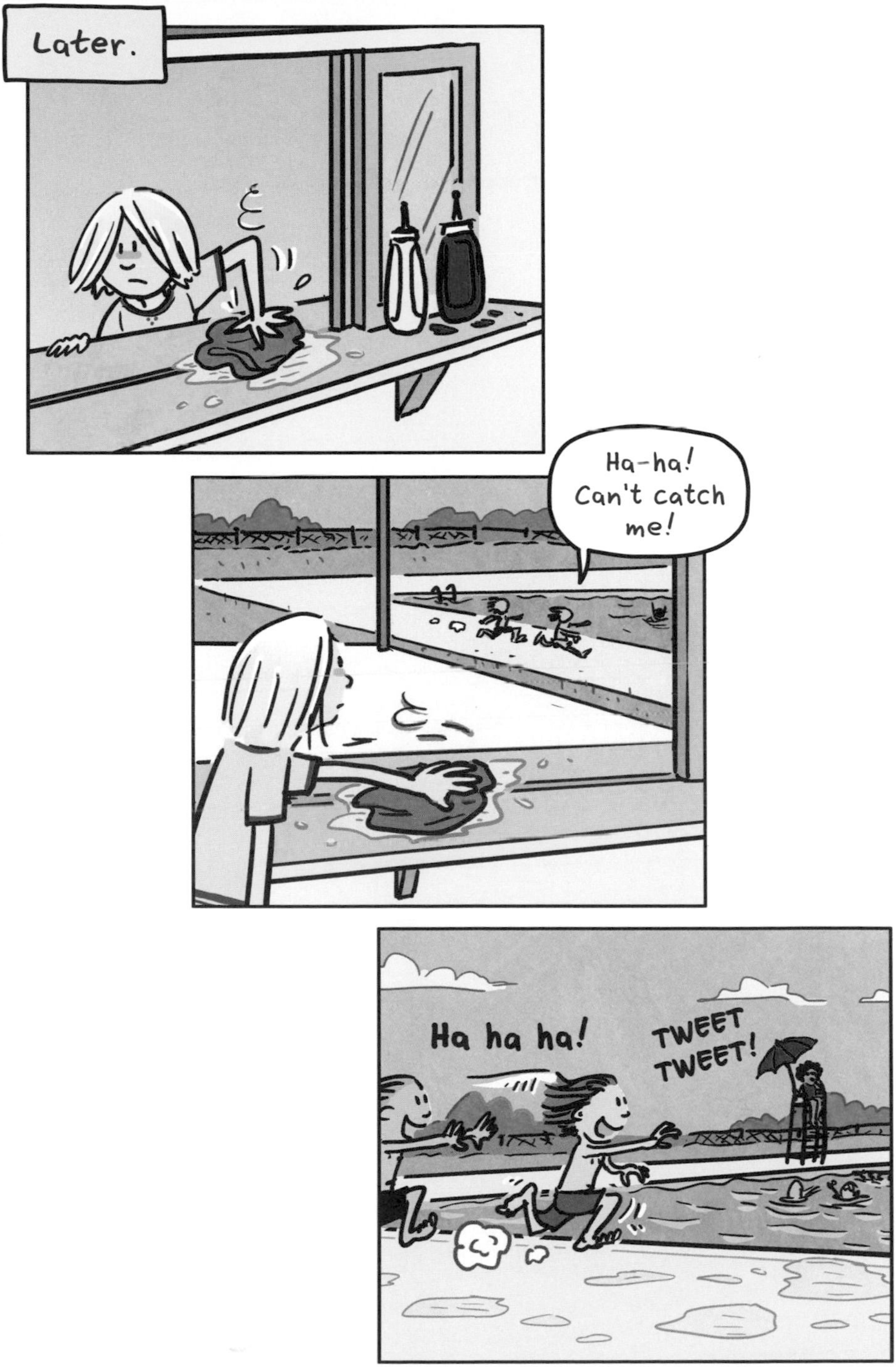
Later.
Ha-ha! Can't catch me!
Ha ha ha!
TWEET TWEET!

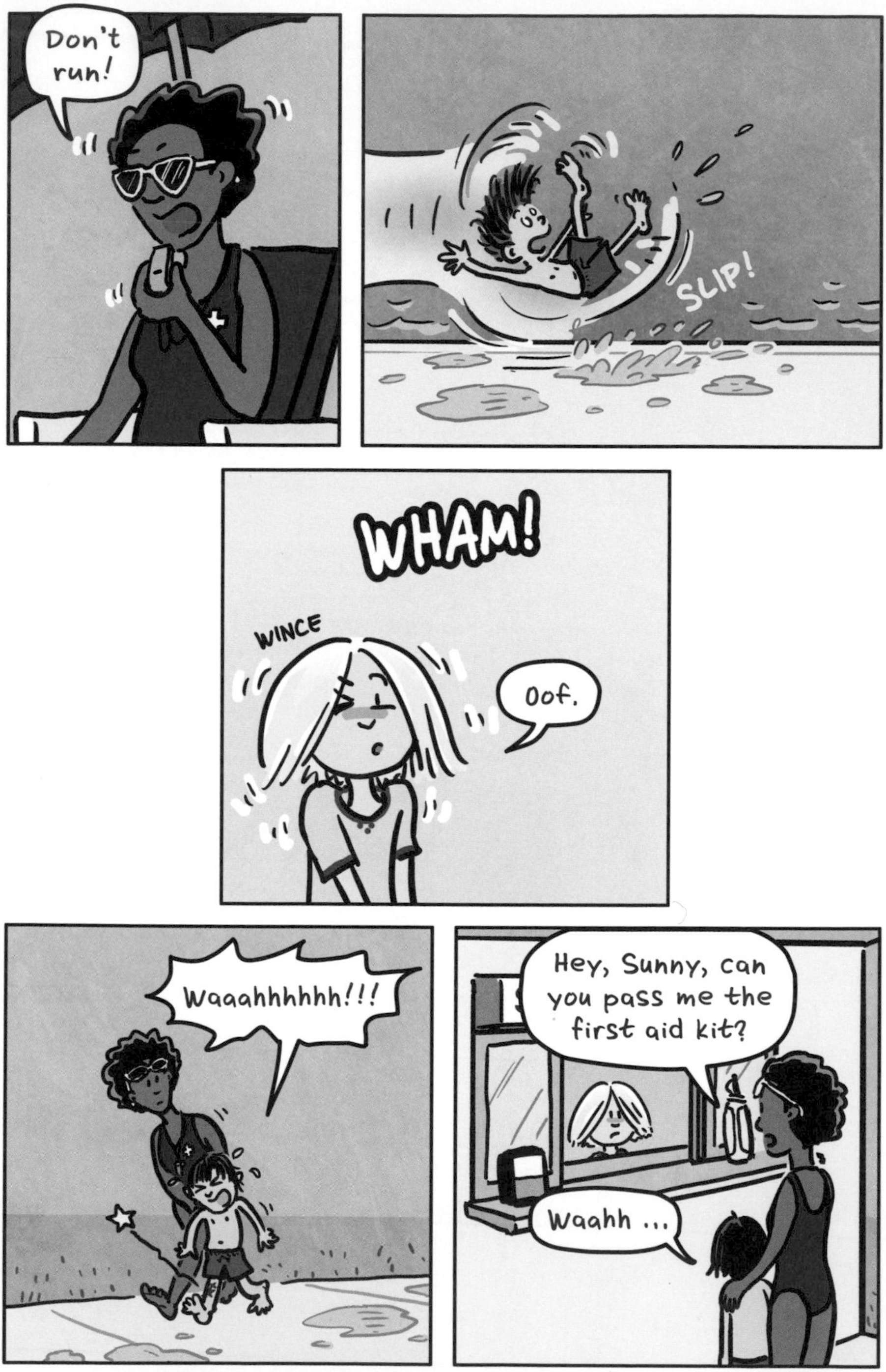
Don't run!
SLIP!
WHAM!
WINCE
Oof.
Waaahhhhhh!!!
Hey, Sunny, can you pass me the first aid kit?
Waahh ...

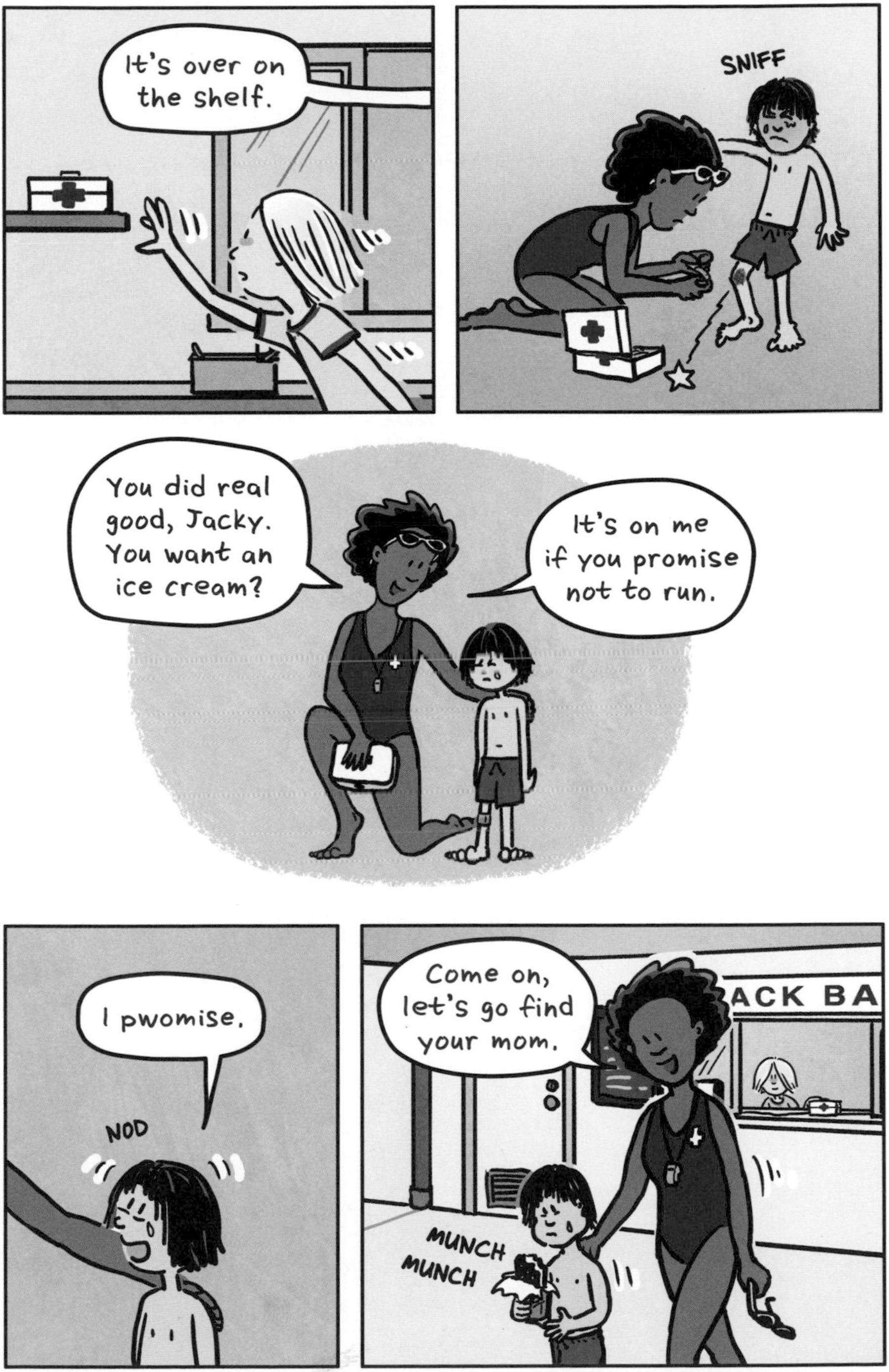
It's over on the shelf.
SNIFF
You did real good, Jacky. You want an ice cream?
It's on me if you promise not to run.
I pwomise.
NOD
Come on, let's go find your mom.
ACK BA
MUNCH
MUNCH

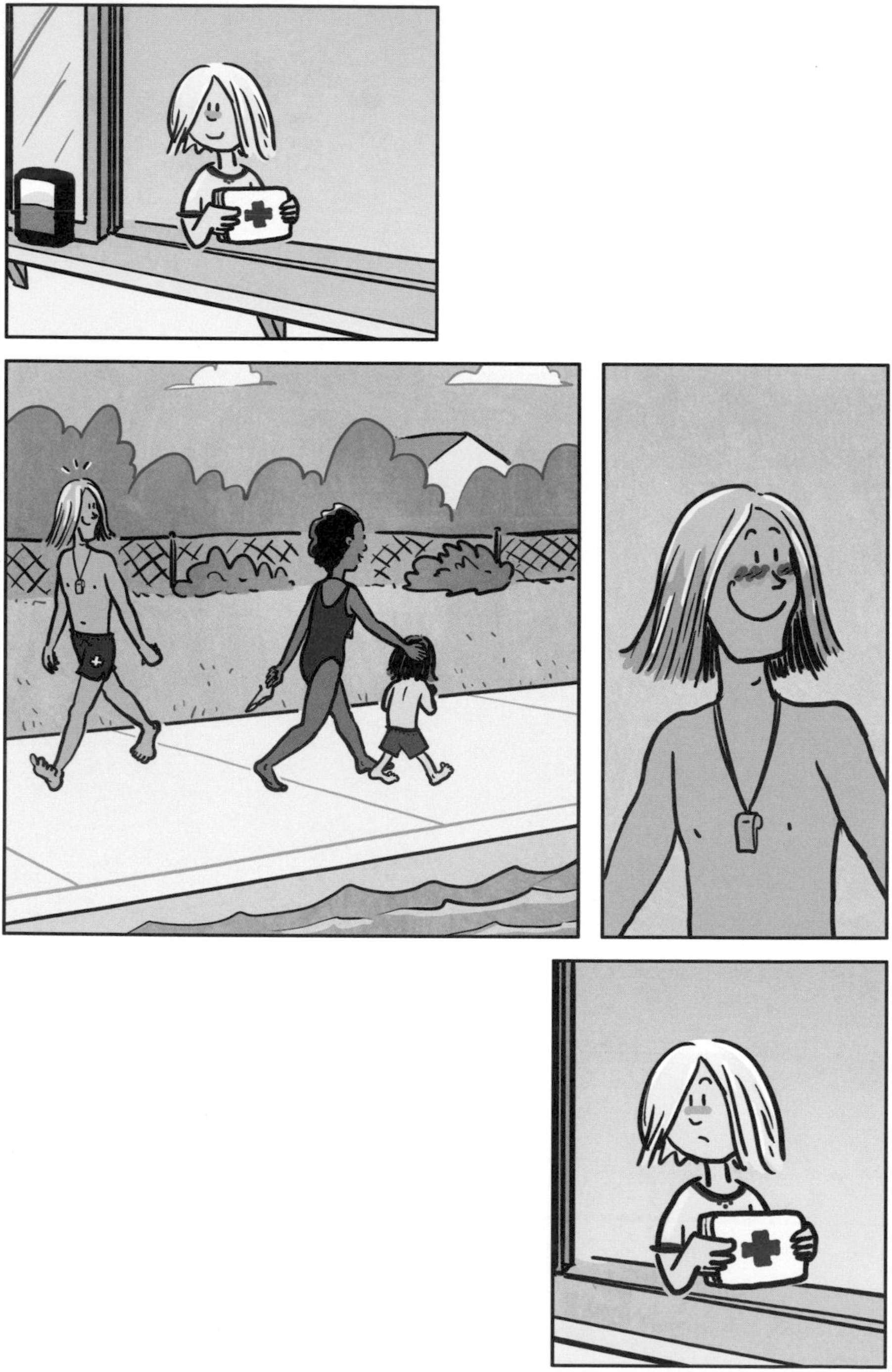

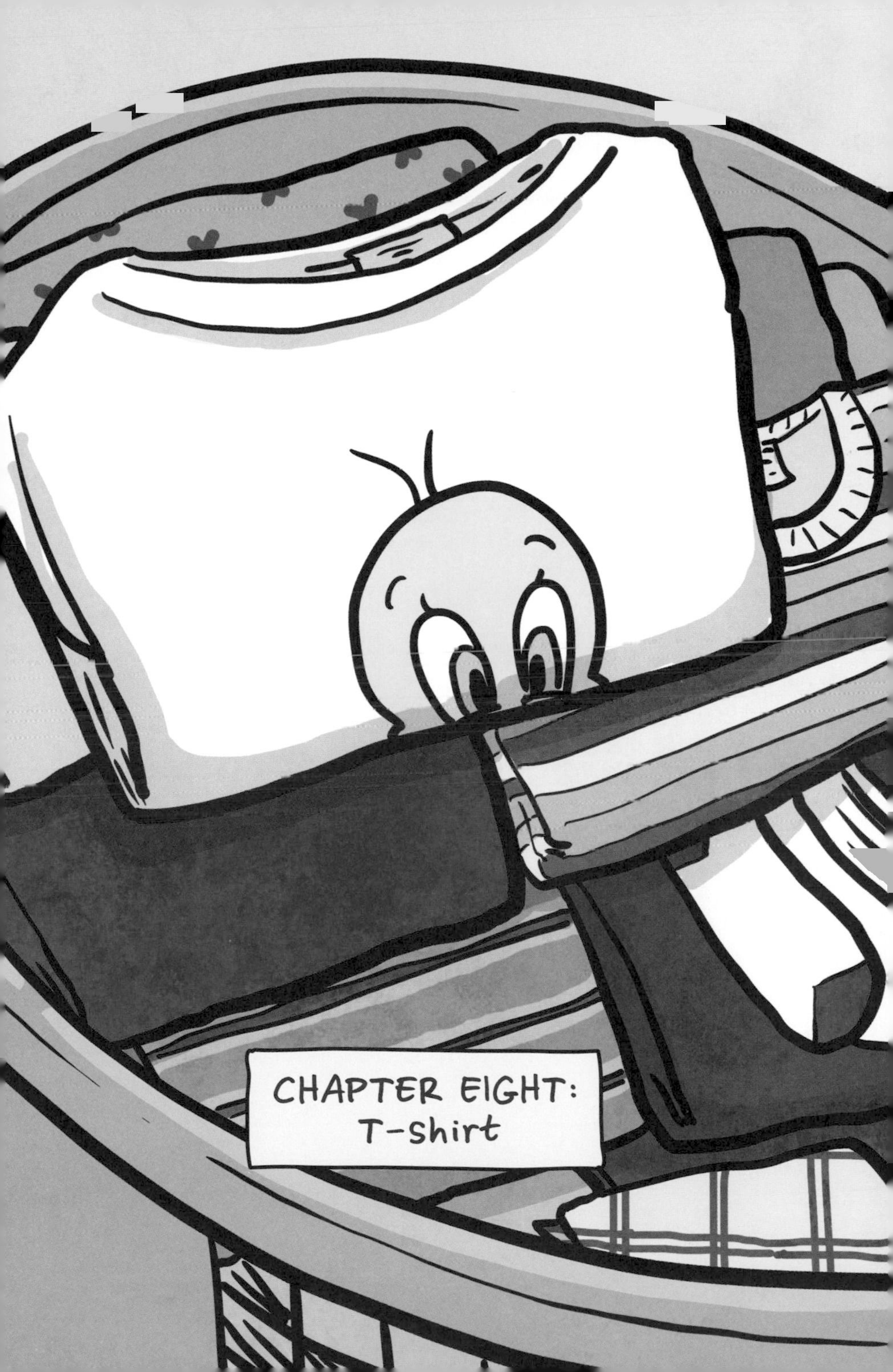
CHAPTER EIGHT:
T-shirt

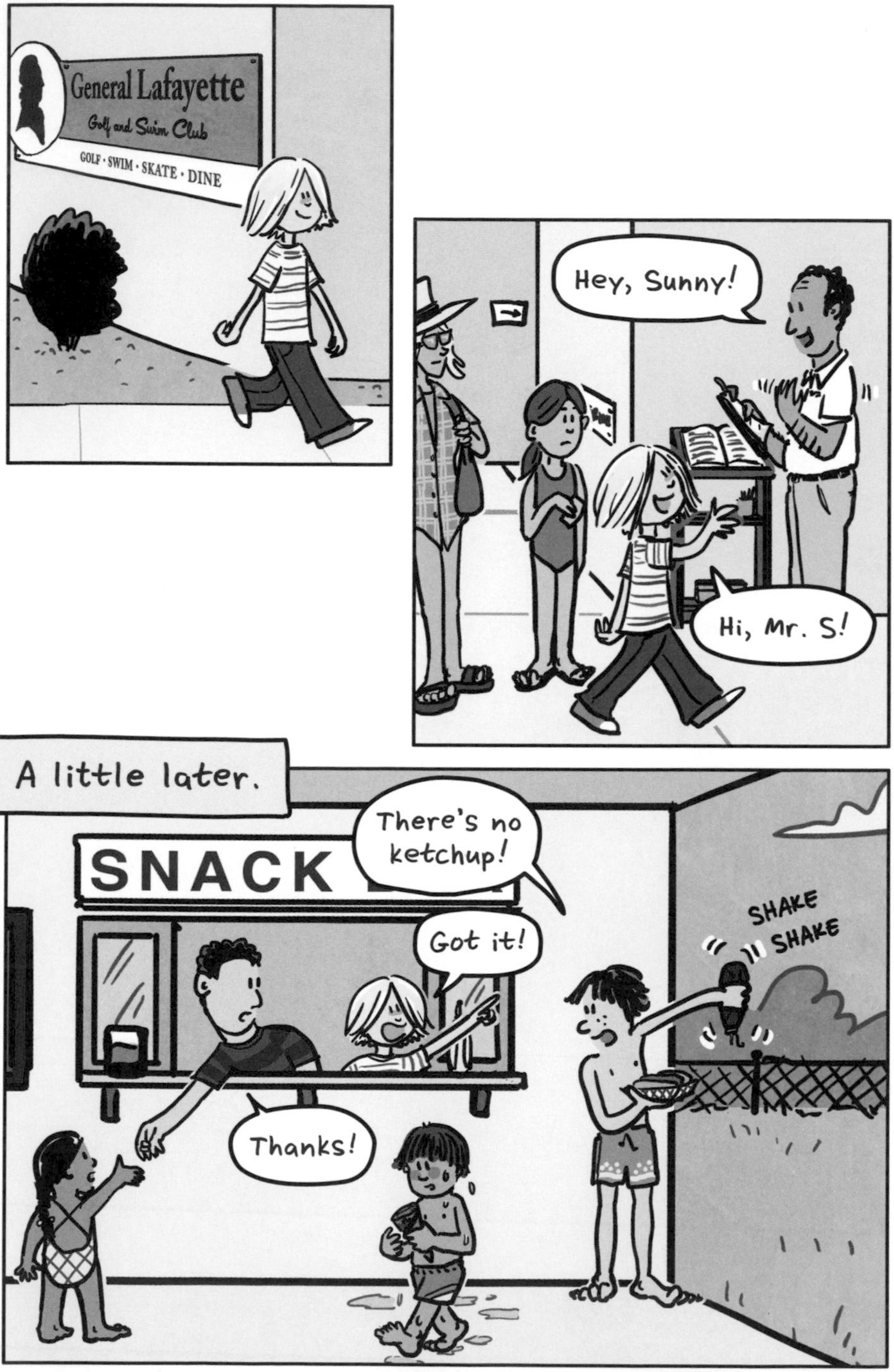
General Lafayette
Golf and Swim Club
GOLF · SWIM · SKATE · DINE
Hey, Sunny!
Hi, Mr. S!
A little later.
SNACK
There's no ketchup!
Got it!
SHAKE
SHAKE
Thanks!

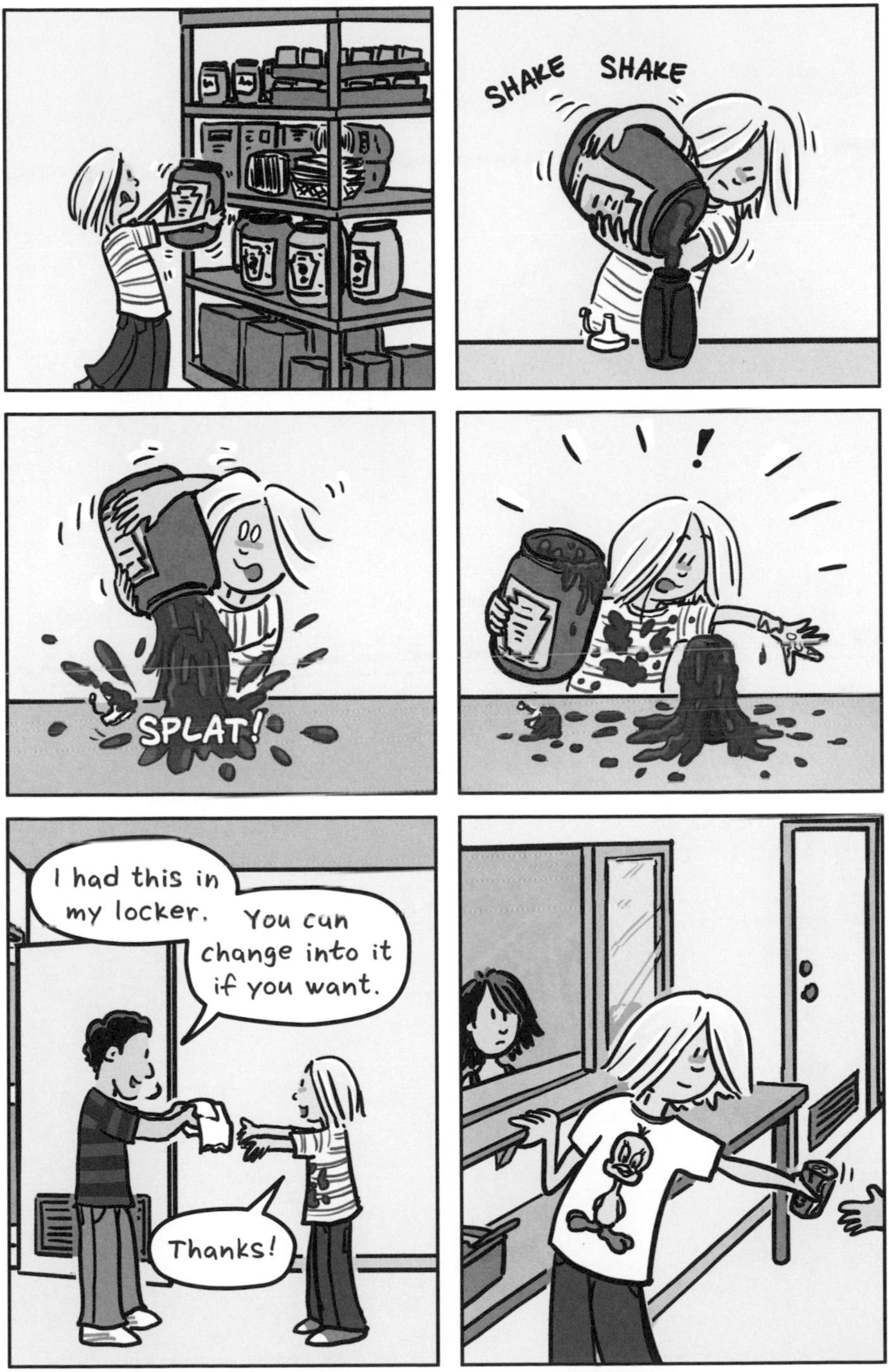
SHAKE SHAKE
!
SPLAT!
I had this in my locker.
You can change into it if you want.
Thanks!

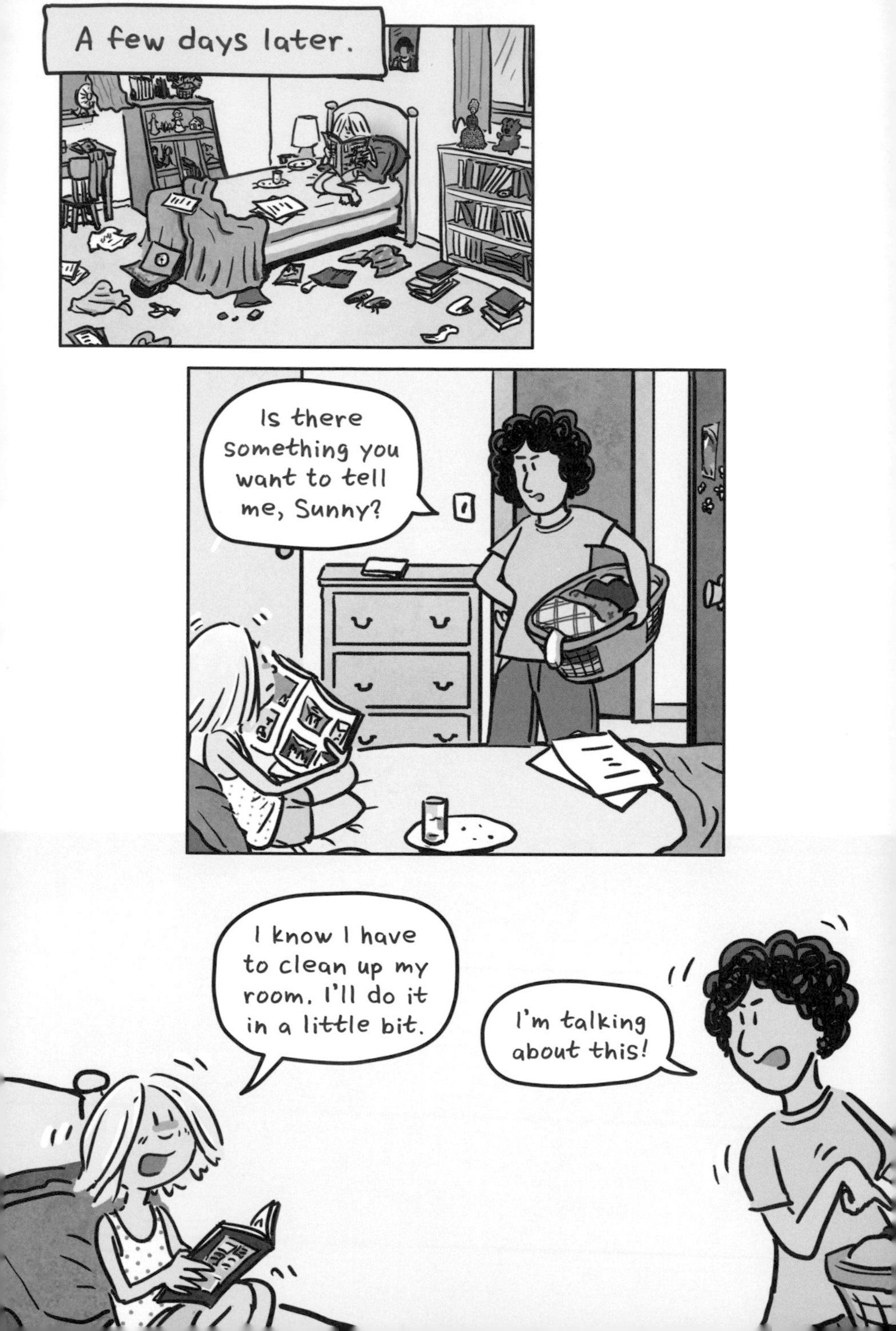
A few days later.
Is there something you want to tell me, Sunny?
I know I have to clean up my room. I'll do it in a little bit.
I'm talking about this!

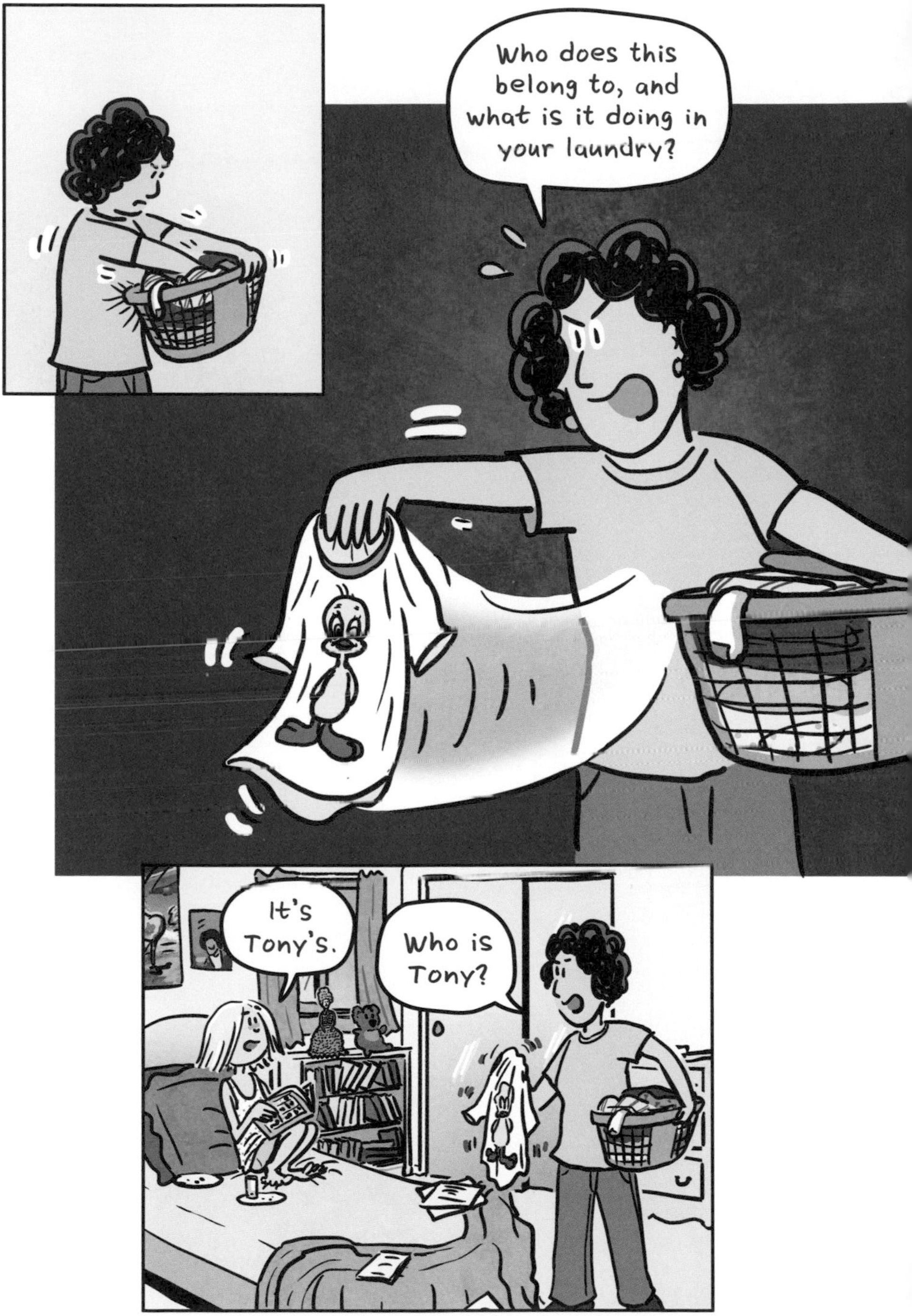
Who does this belong to, and what is it doing in your laundry?
It's Tony's.
Who is Tony?

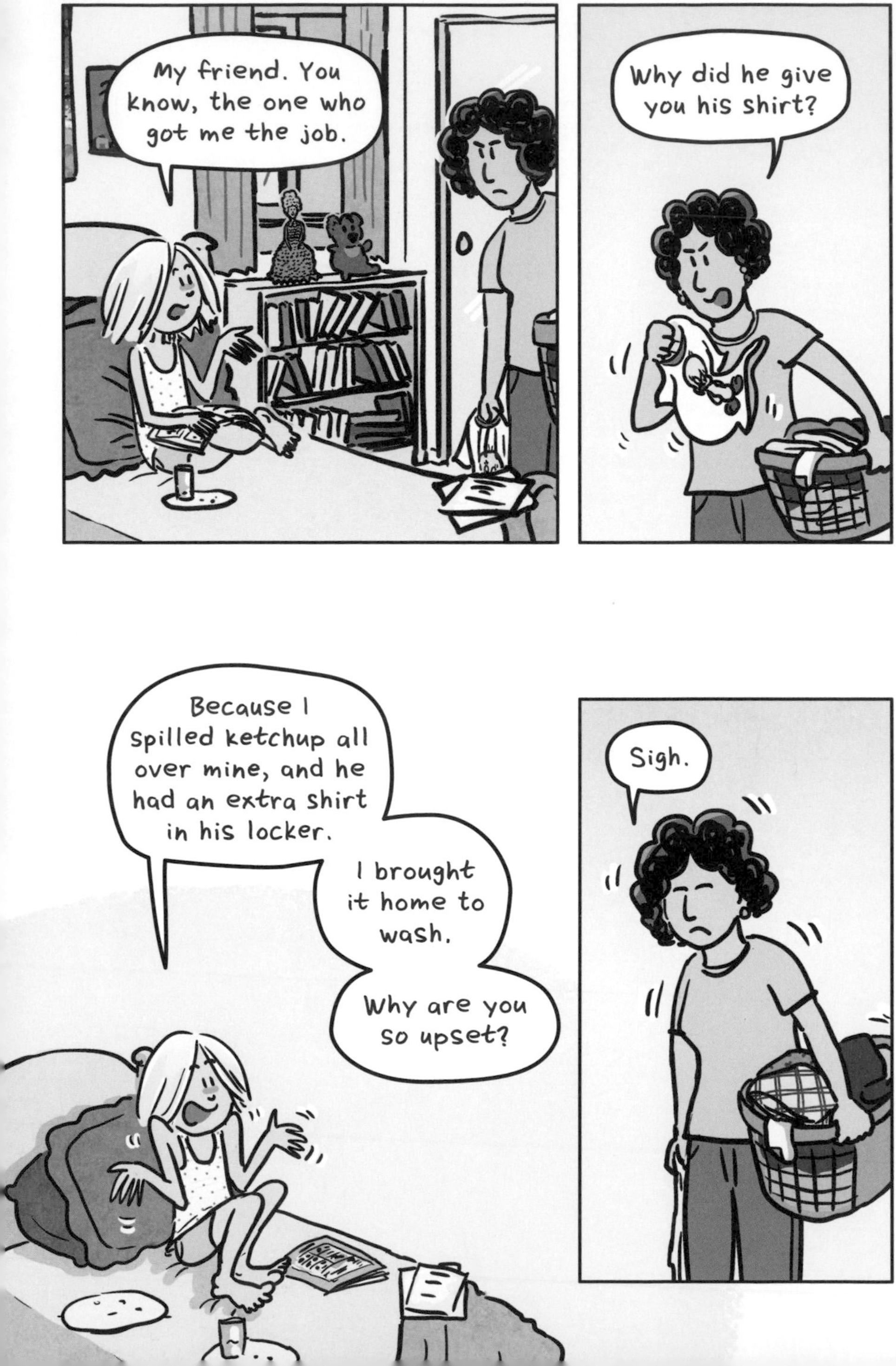
My friend. You know, the one who got me the job.
Why did he give you his shirt?
Because I spilled ketchup all over mine, and he had an extra shirt in his locker.
I brought it home to wash.
Why are you so upset?
Sigh.

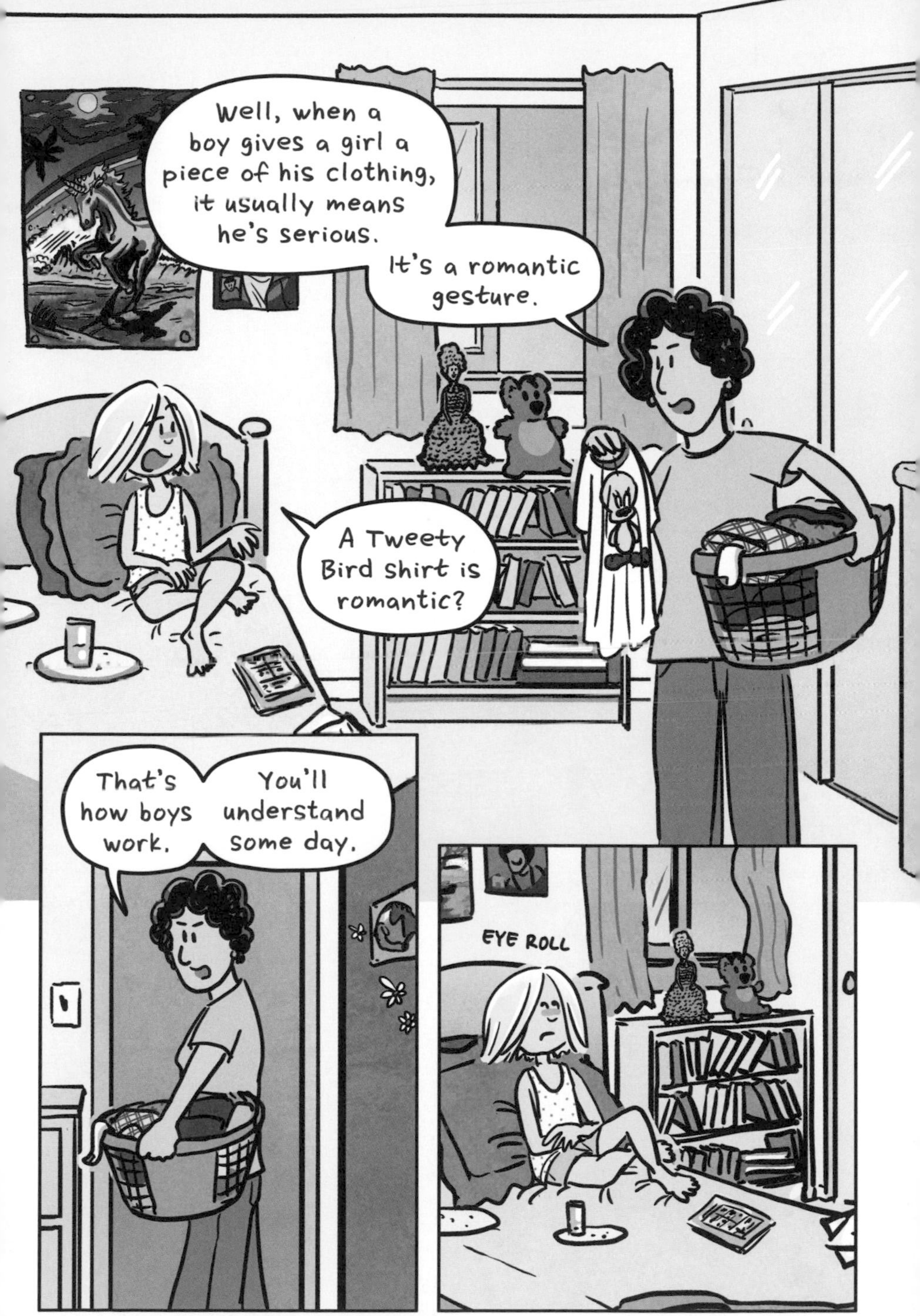
Well, when a boy gives a girl a piece of his clothing, it usually means he's serious.
It's a romantic gesture.
A Tweety Bird shirt is romantic?
That's how boys work.
You'll understand some day.
EYE ROLL

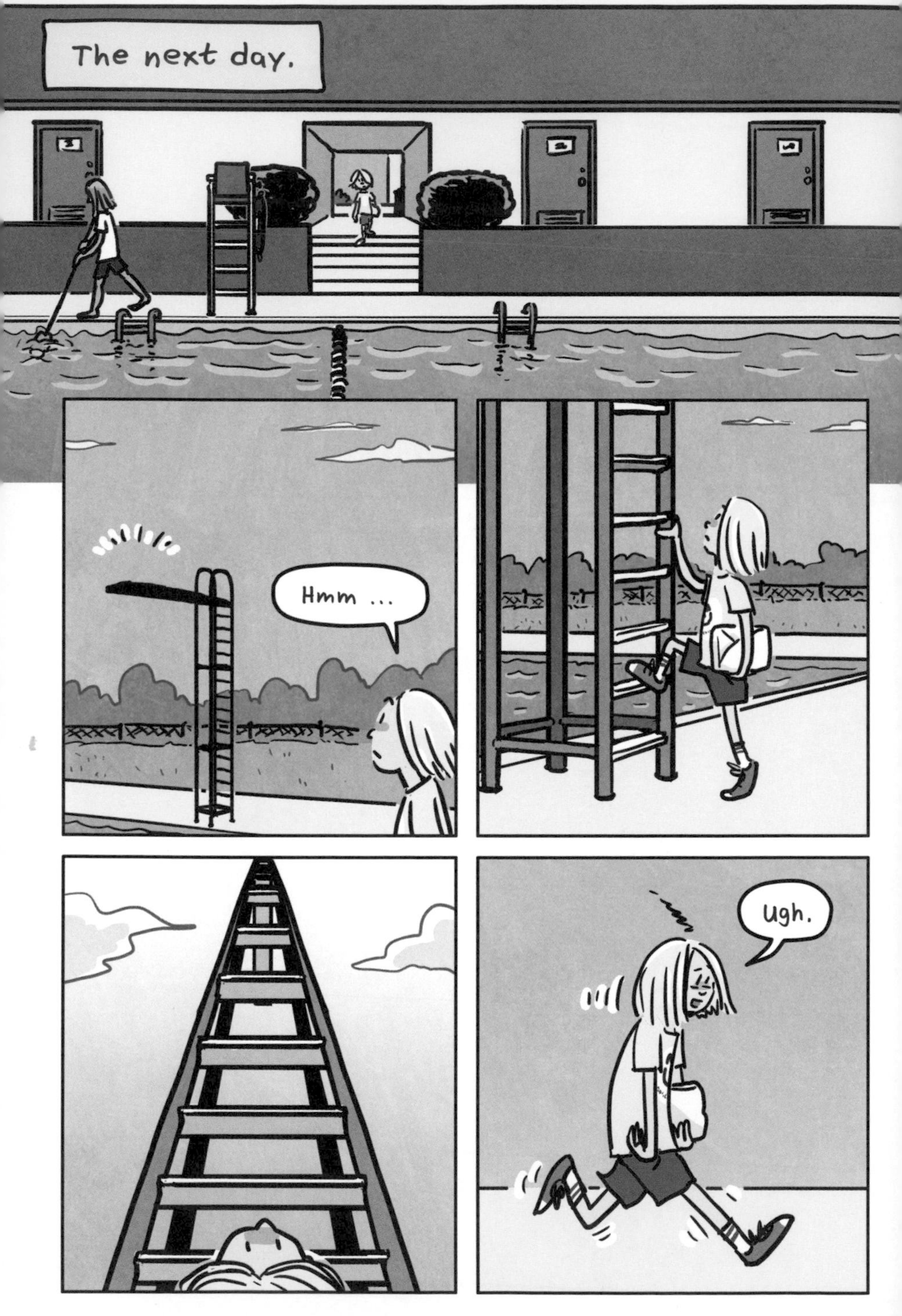
The next day.
Hmm ...
Ugh.

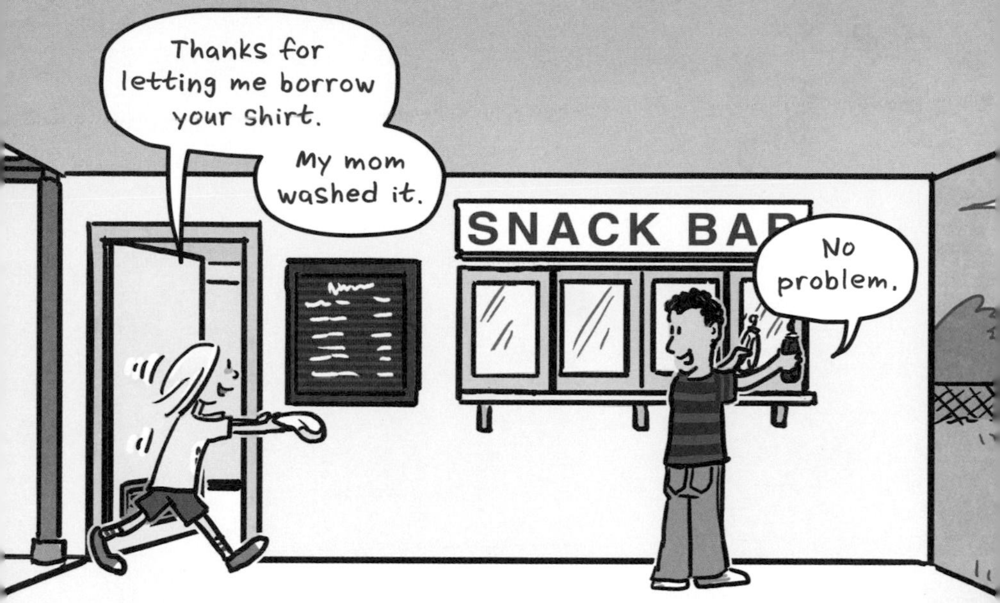
Thanks for letting me borrow your shirt.
My mom washed it.
SNACK BAR
No problem.

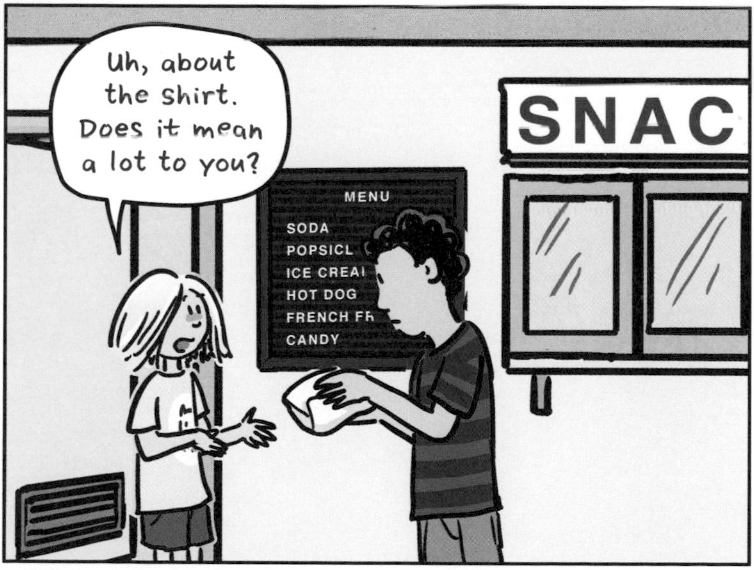
Uh, about the shirt. Does it mean a lot to you?
MENU
SODA
POPSICL
ICE CREAI
HOT DOG
FRENCH FR
CANDY
SNAC

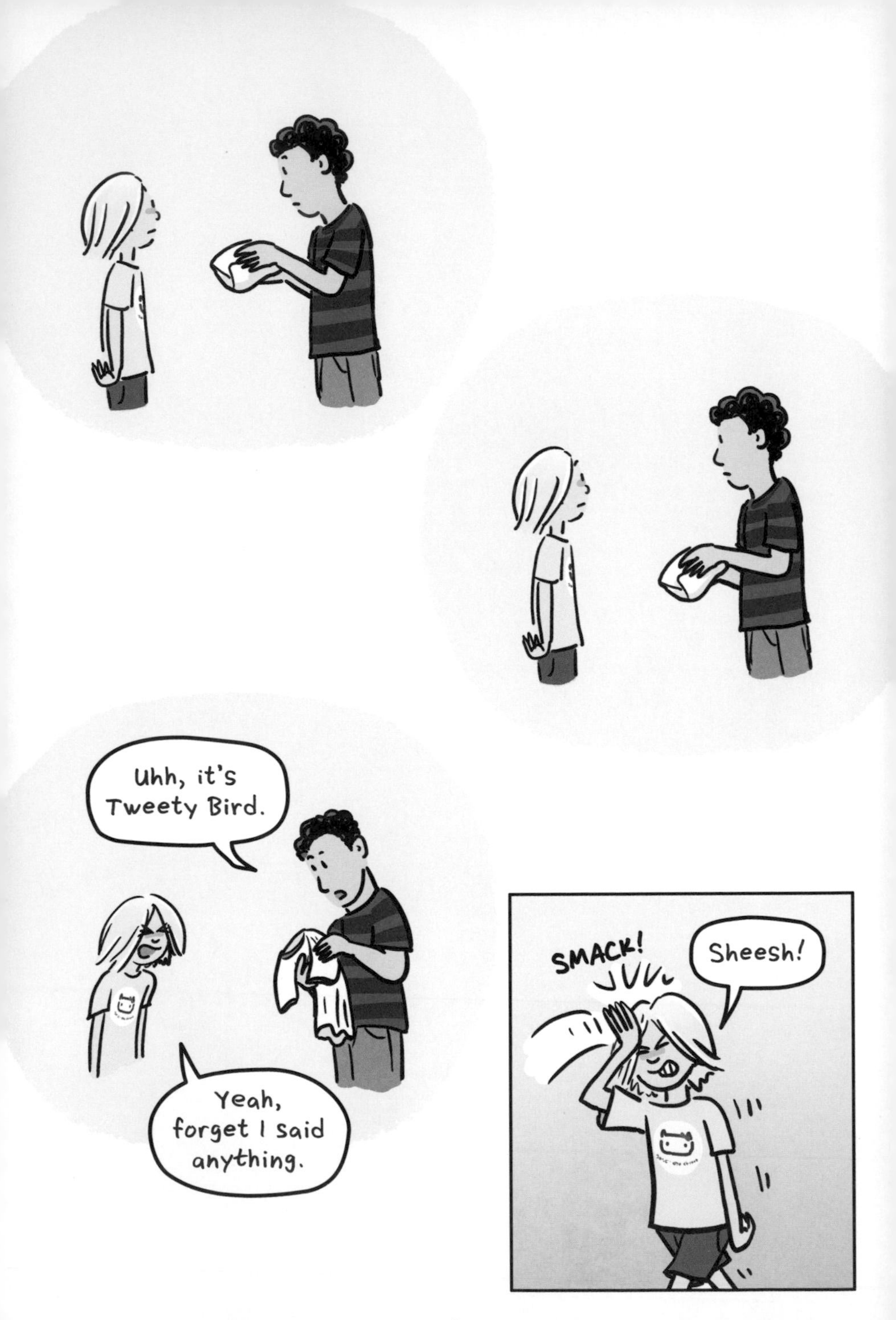
Uhh, it's Tweety Bird.
Yeah, forget I said anything.
SMACK!
Sheesh!

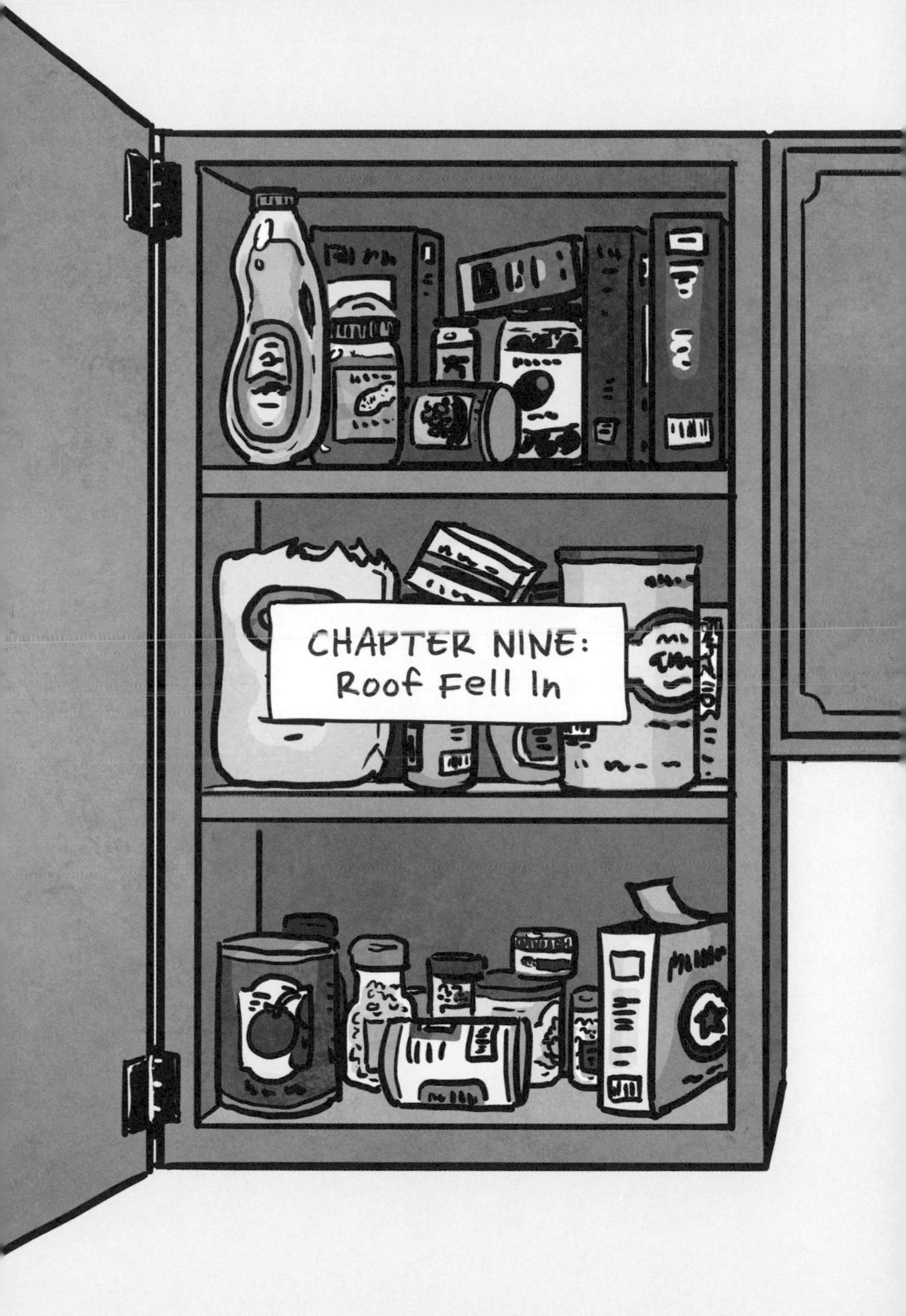
CHAPTER NINE:
Roof Fell In

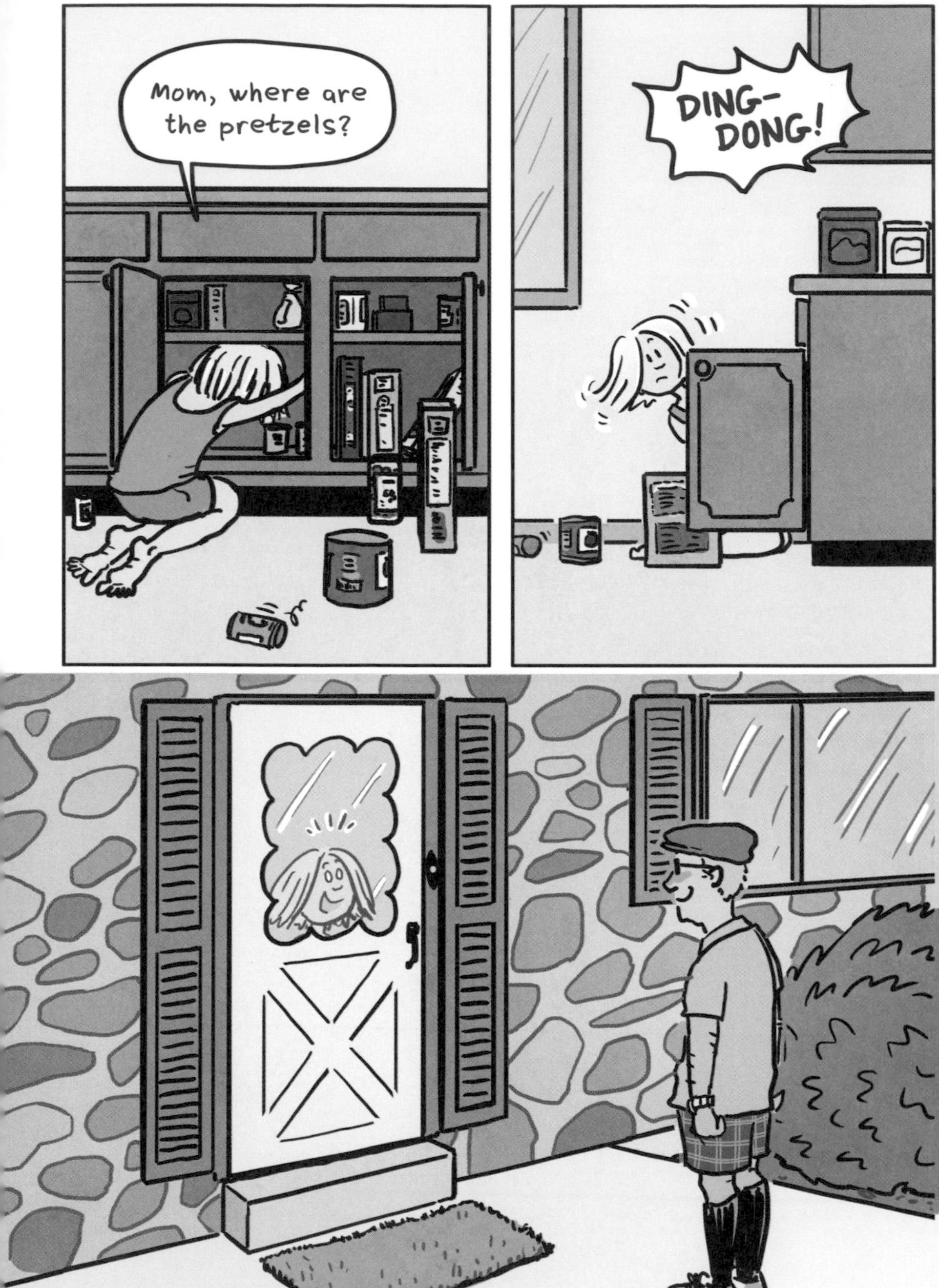
Mom, where are the pretzels?
DING-DONG!

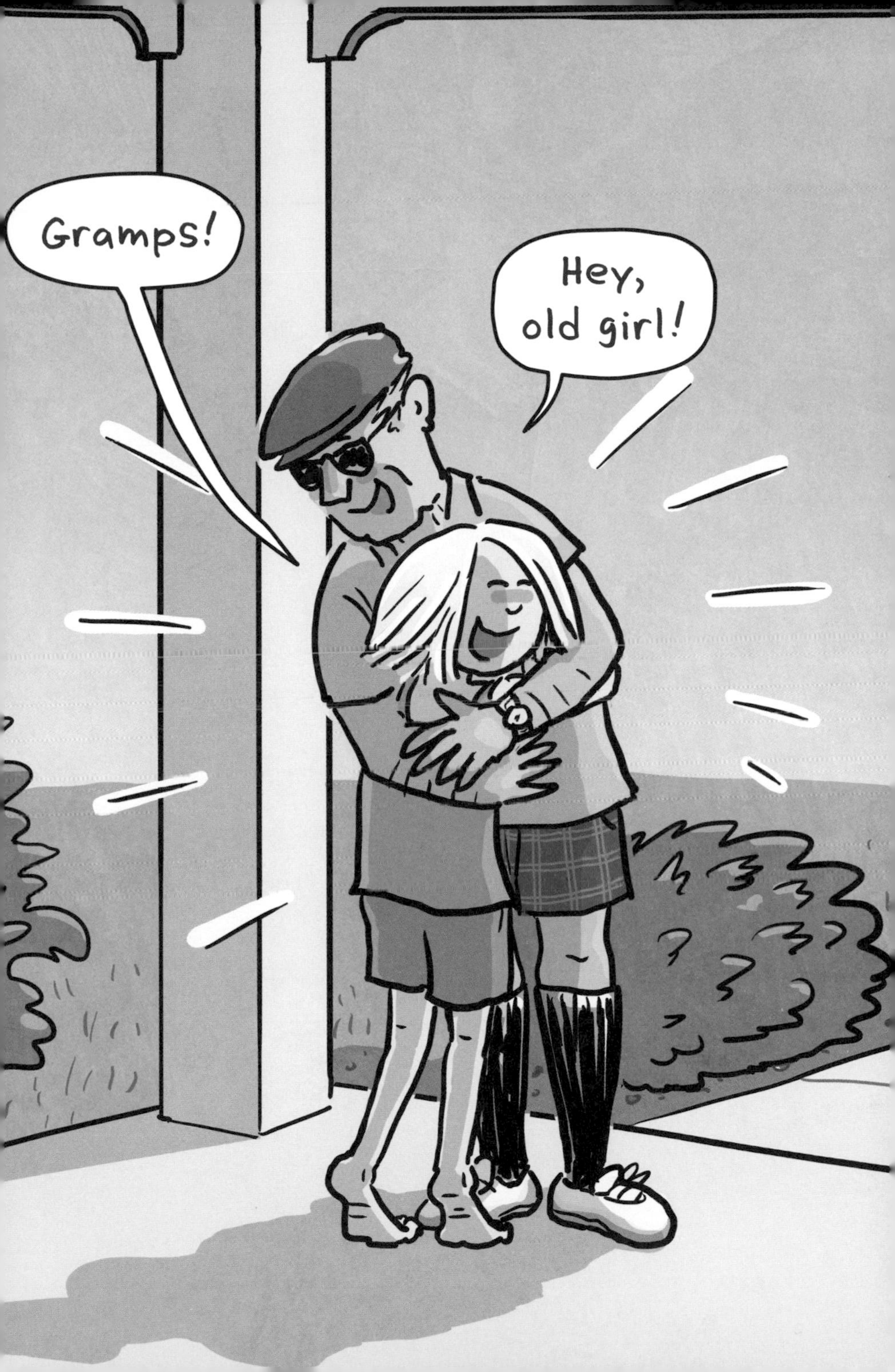
Gramps!
Hey, old girl!

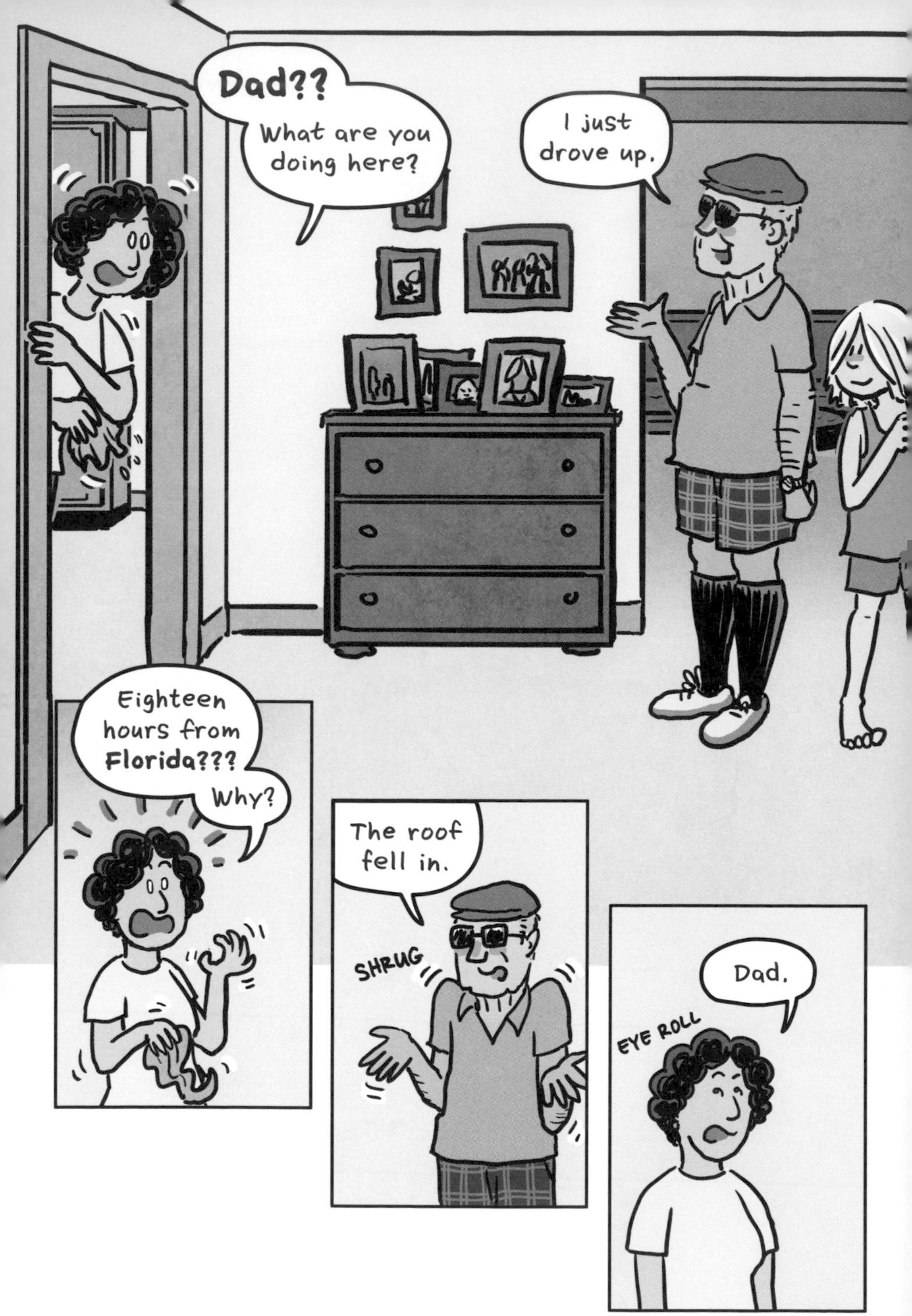
Dad??
What are you doing here?
I just drove up.
Eighteen hours from Florida???
Why?
The roof fell in.
SHRUG
EYE ROLL
Dad.

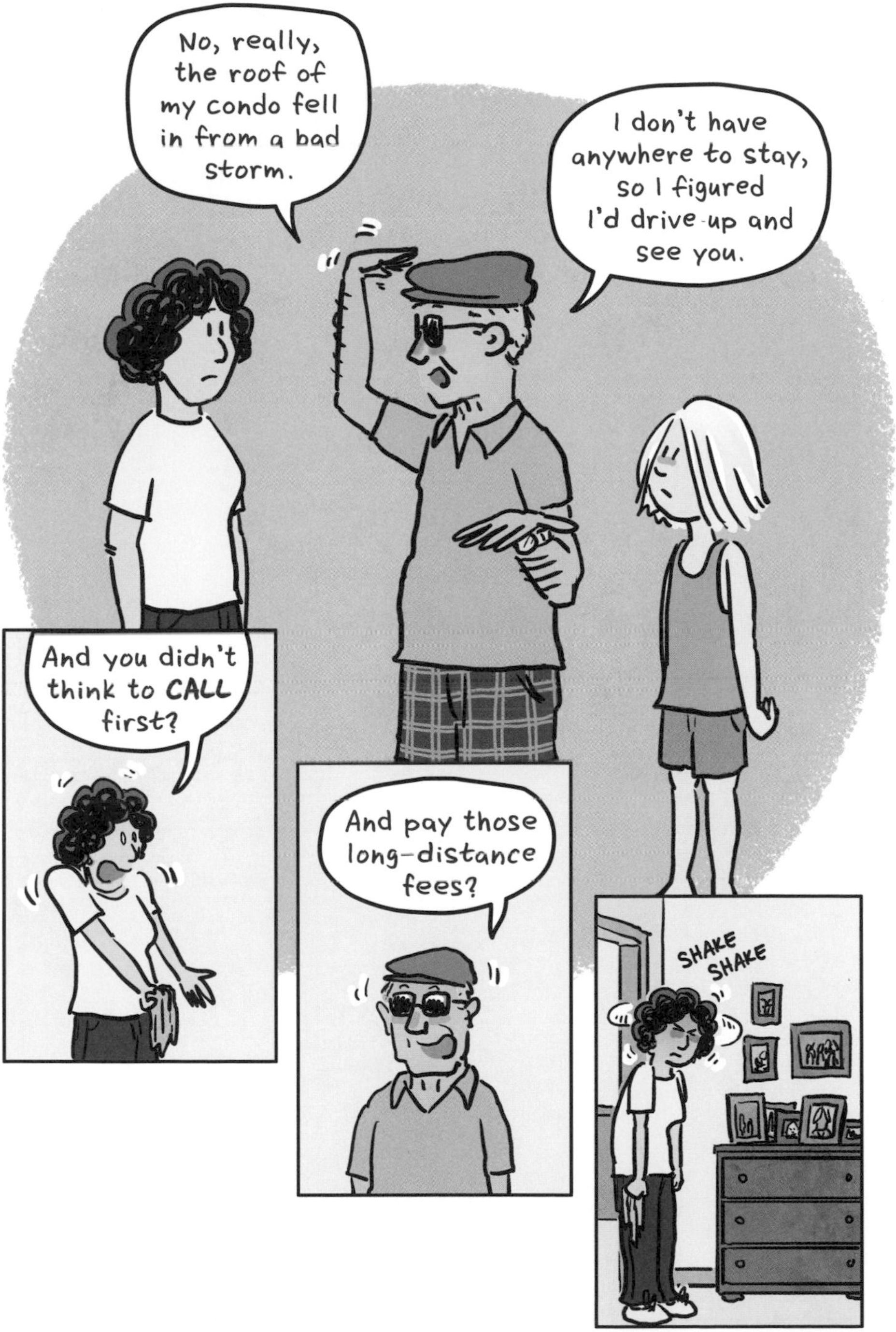
No, really, the roof of my condo fell in from a bad storm.
I don't have anywhere to stay, so I figured I'd drive up and see you.
And you didn't think to CALL first?
And pay those long-distance fees?
SHAKE SHAKE

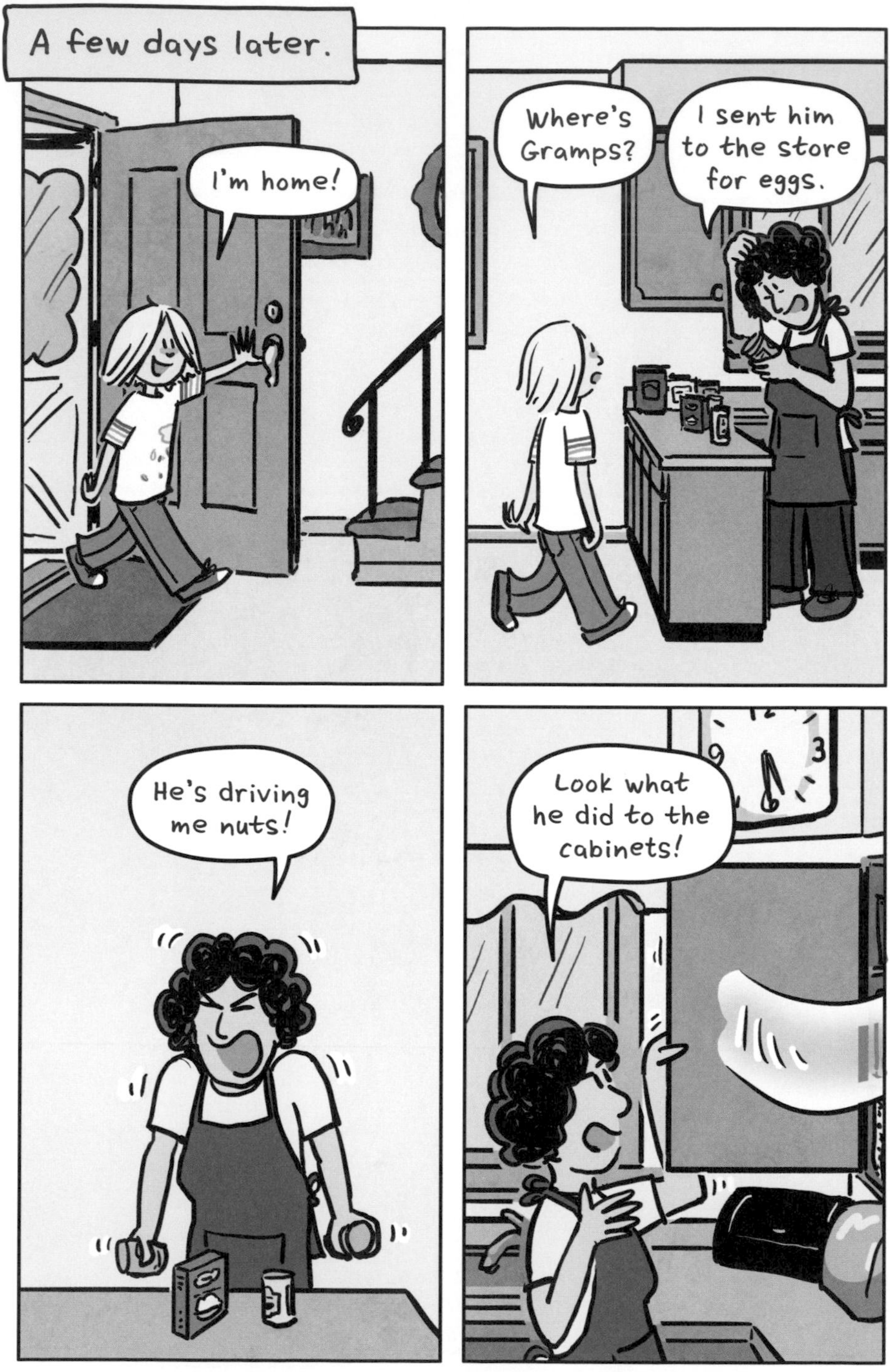
A few days later.
I'm home!
Where's Gramps?
I sent him to the store for eggs.
He's driving me nuts!
Look what he did to the cabinets!

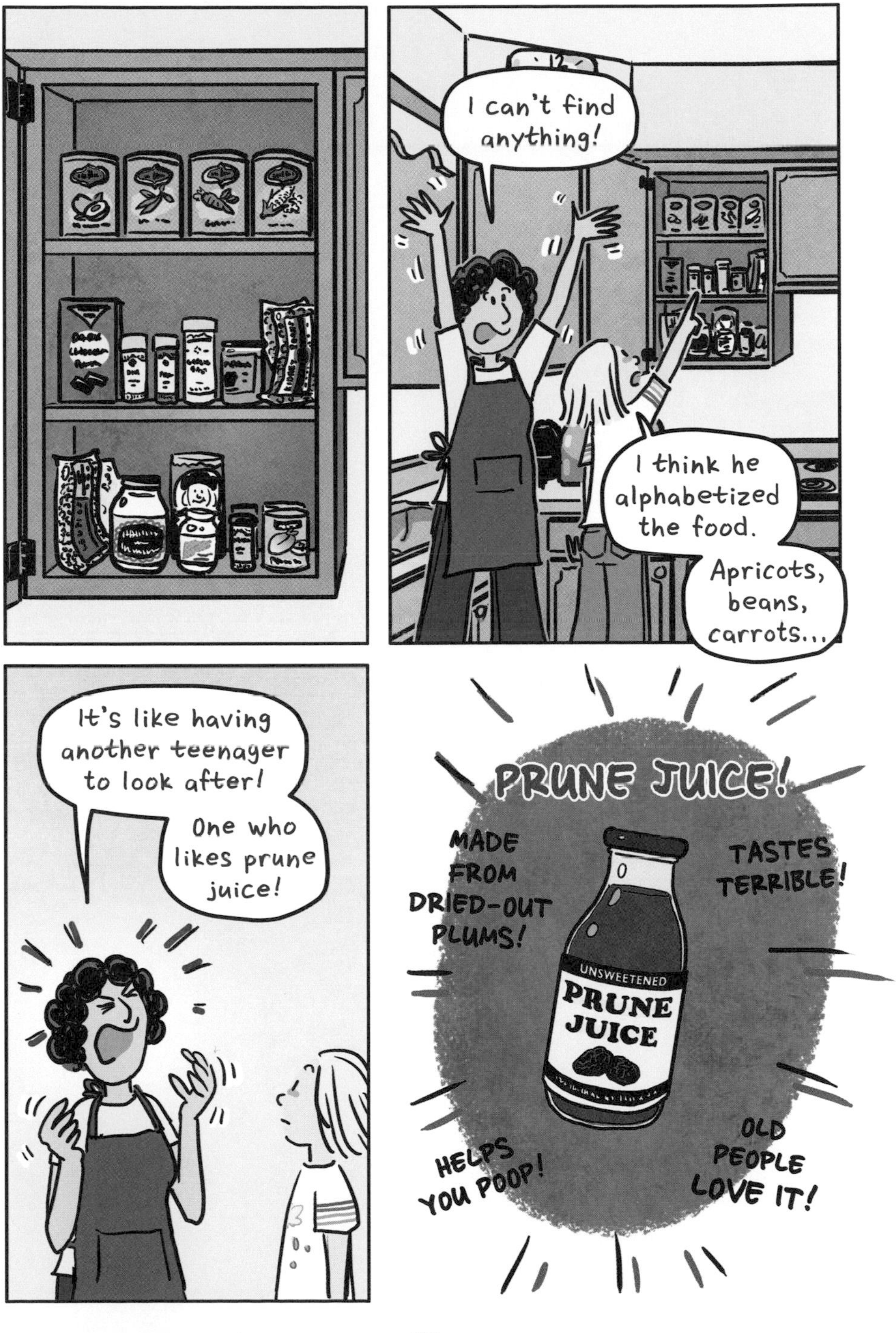
I can't find anything!
I think he alphabetized the food.
Apricots, beans, carrots...
It's like having another teenager to look after!
One who likes prune juice!
PRUNE JUICE!
MADE FROM DRIED-OUT PLUMS!
TASTES TERRIBLE!
UNSWEETENED
PRUNE JUICE
HELPS YOU POOP!
OLD PEOPLE LOVE IT!

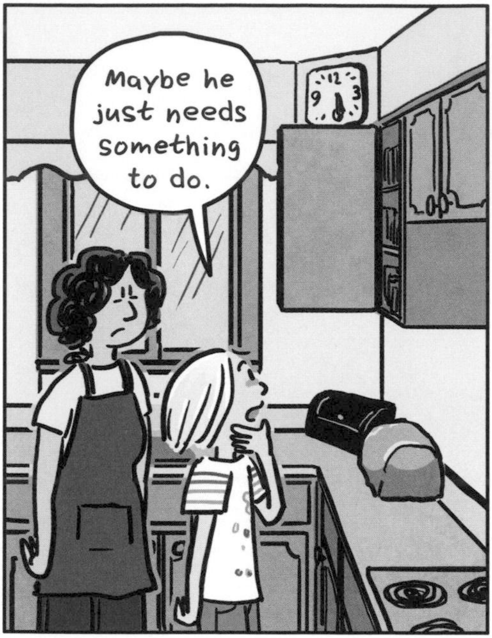
Maybe he just needs something to do.

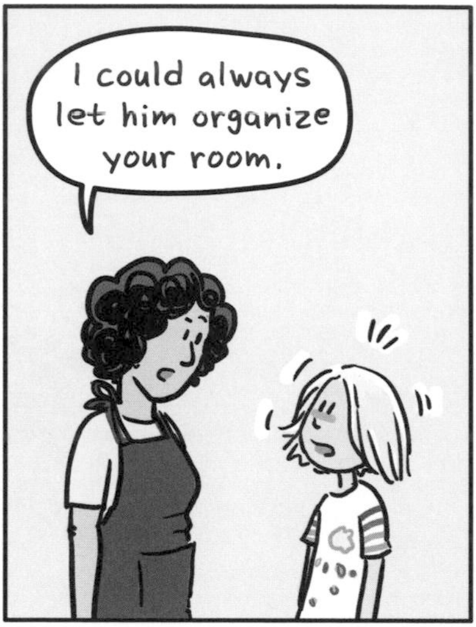
I could always let him organize your room.

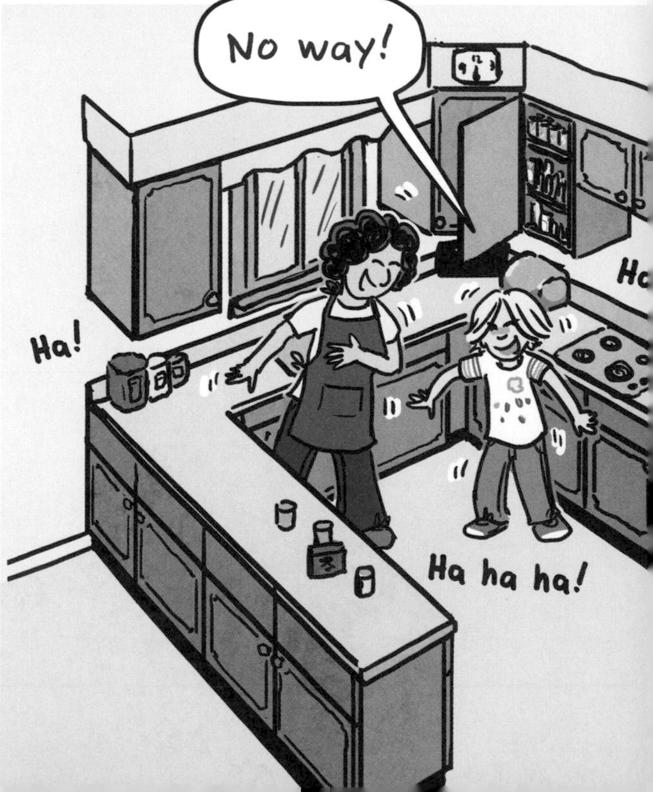
No way!
Ha!
Ha
Ha ha ha!

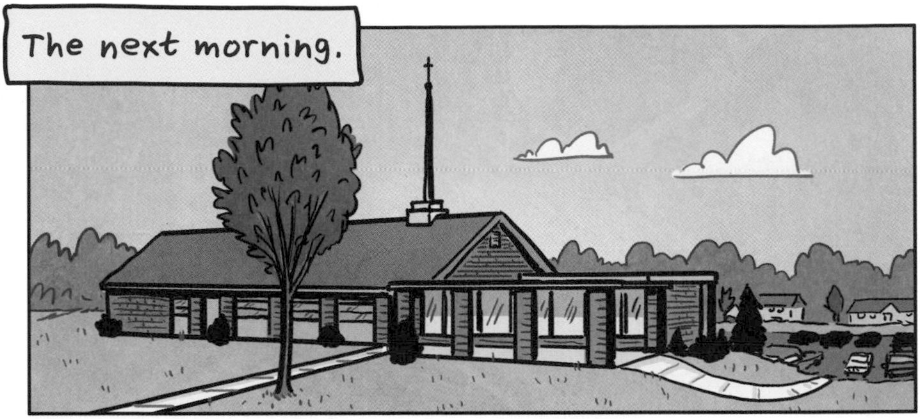
The next morning.

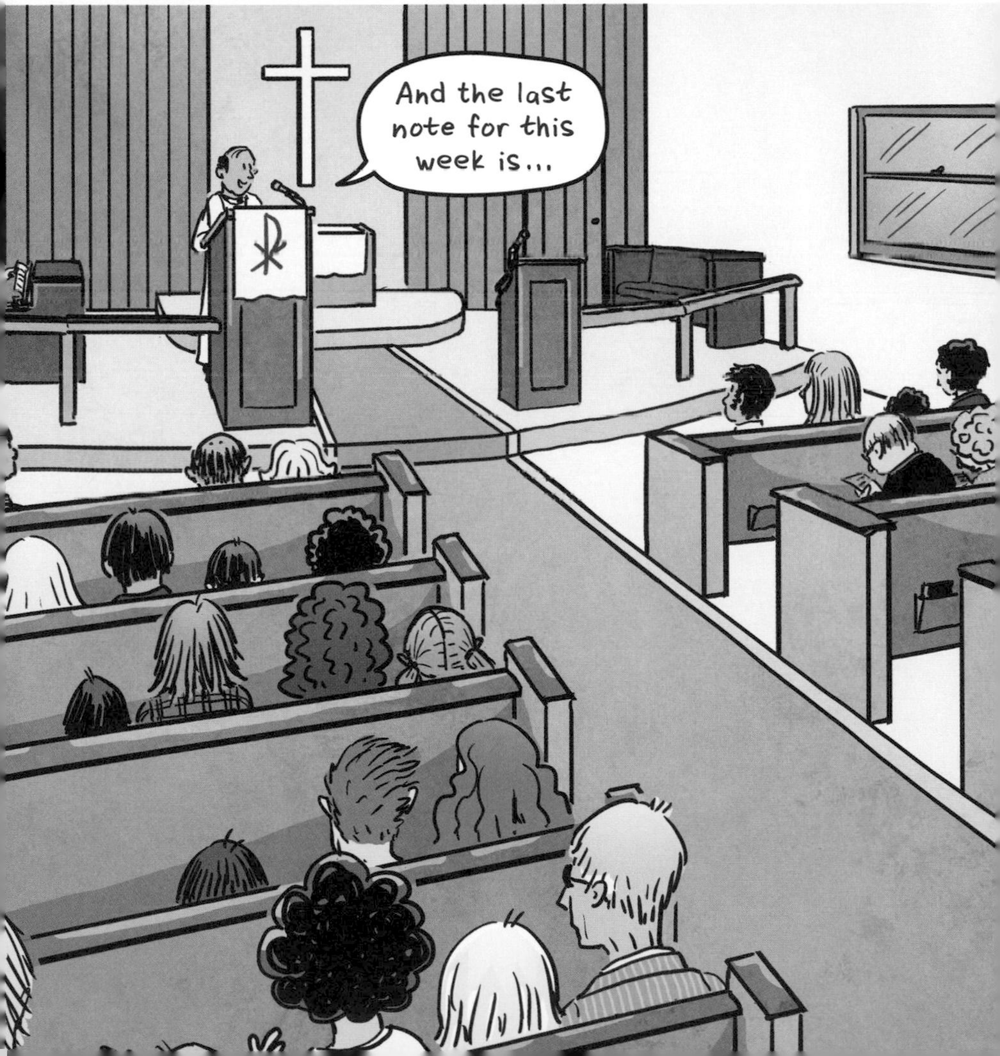
And the last note for this week is...

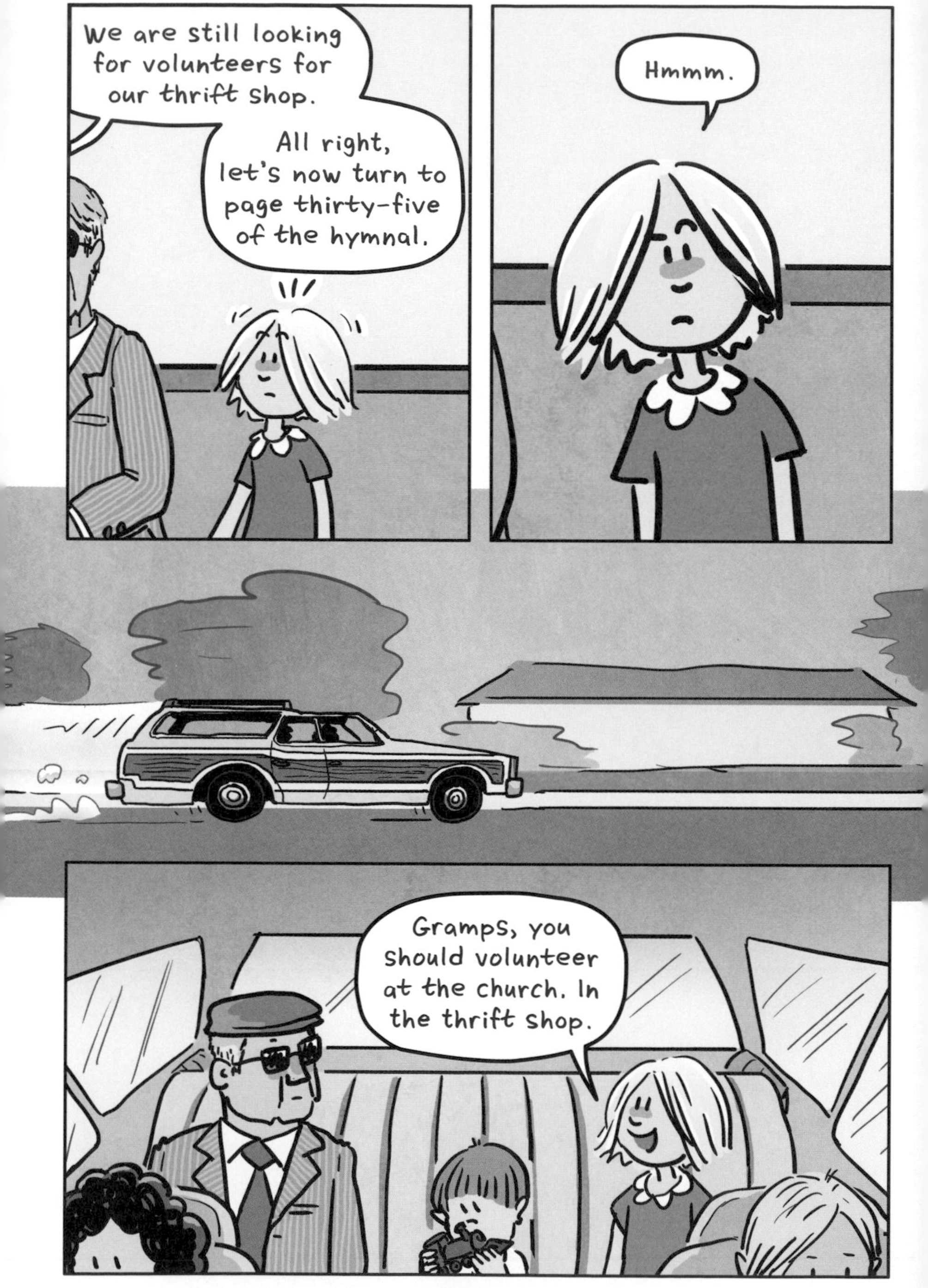
We are still looking for volunteers for our thrift shop.
All right, let's now turn to page thirty-five of the hymnal.
Hmmm.
Gramps, you should volunteer at the church. In the thrift shop.

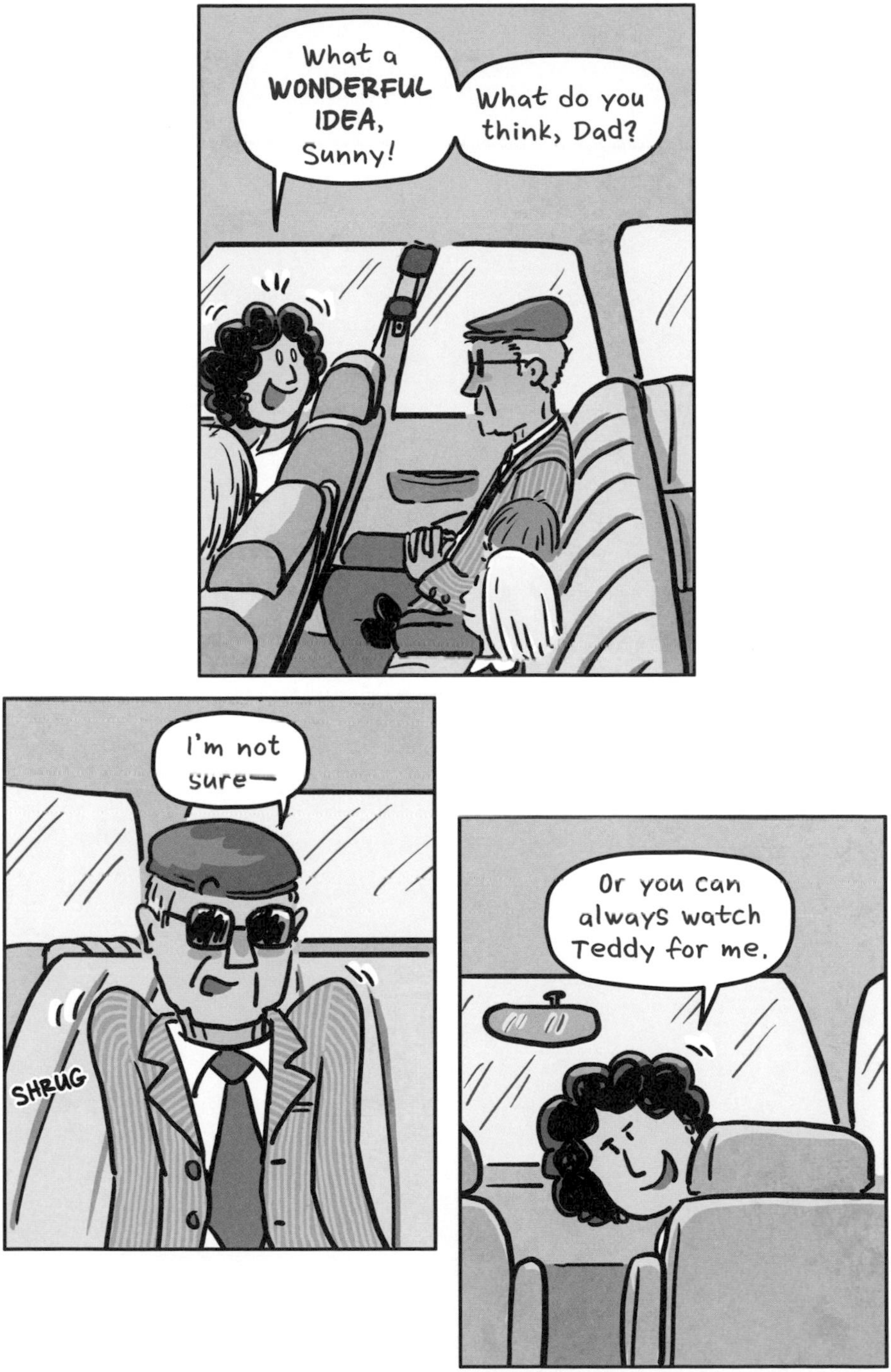
What a **WONDERFUL IDEA**, Sunny!
What do you think, Dad?
I'm not sure—
SHRUG
Or you can always watch Teddy for me.

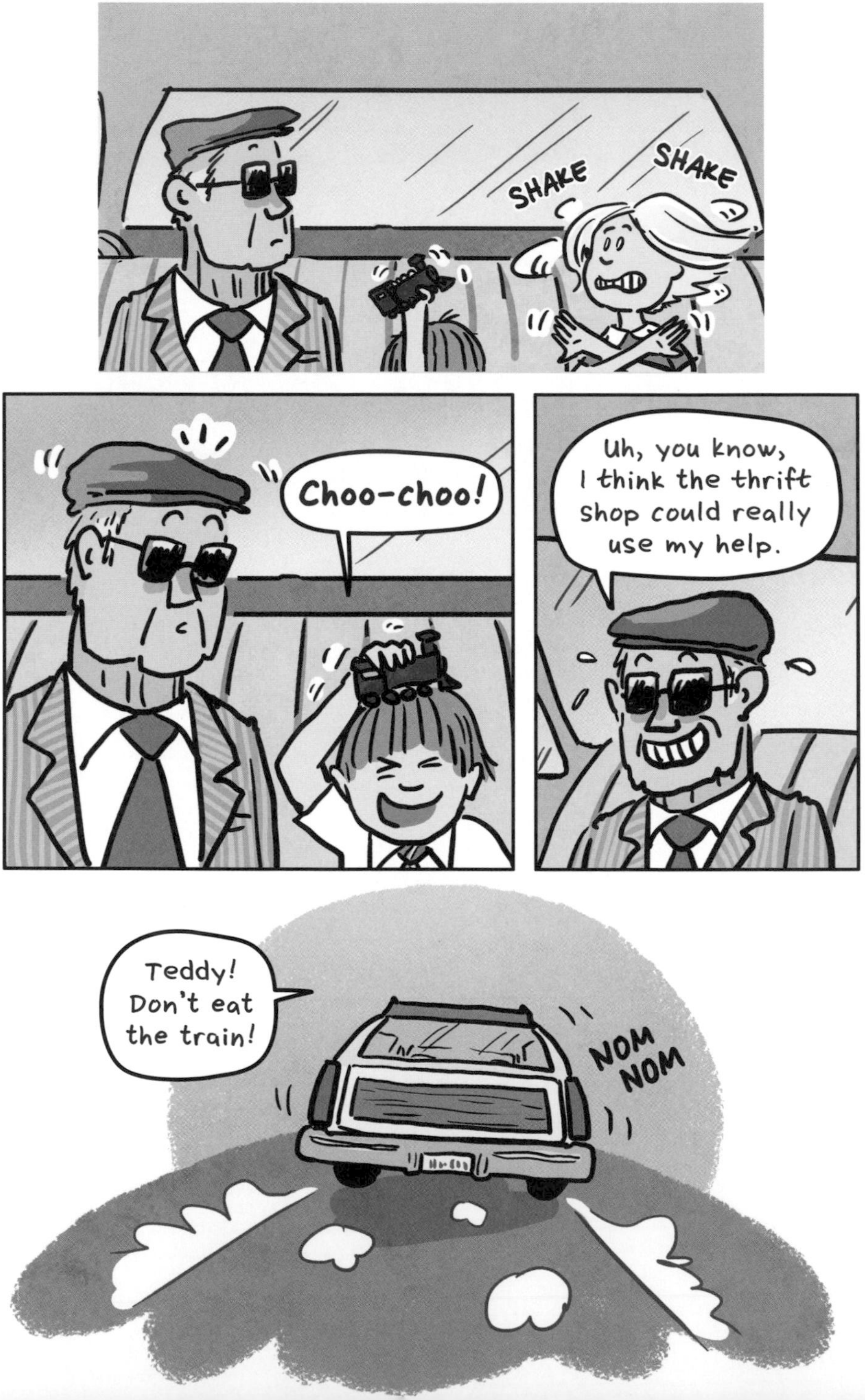
SHAKE
SHAKE
Choo-choo!
Uh, you know, I think the thrift shop could really use my help.
Teddy! Don't eat the train!
NOM NOM

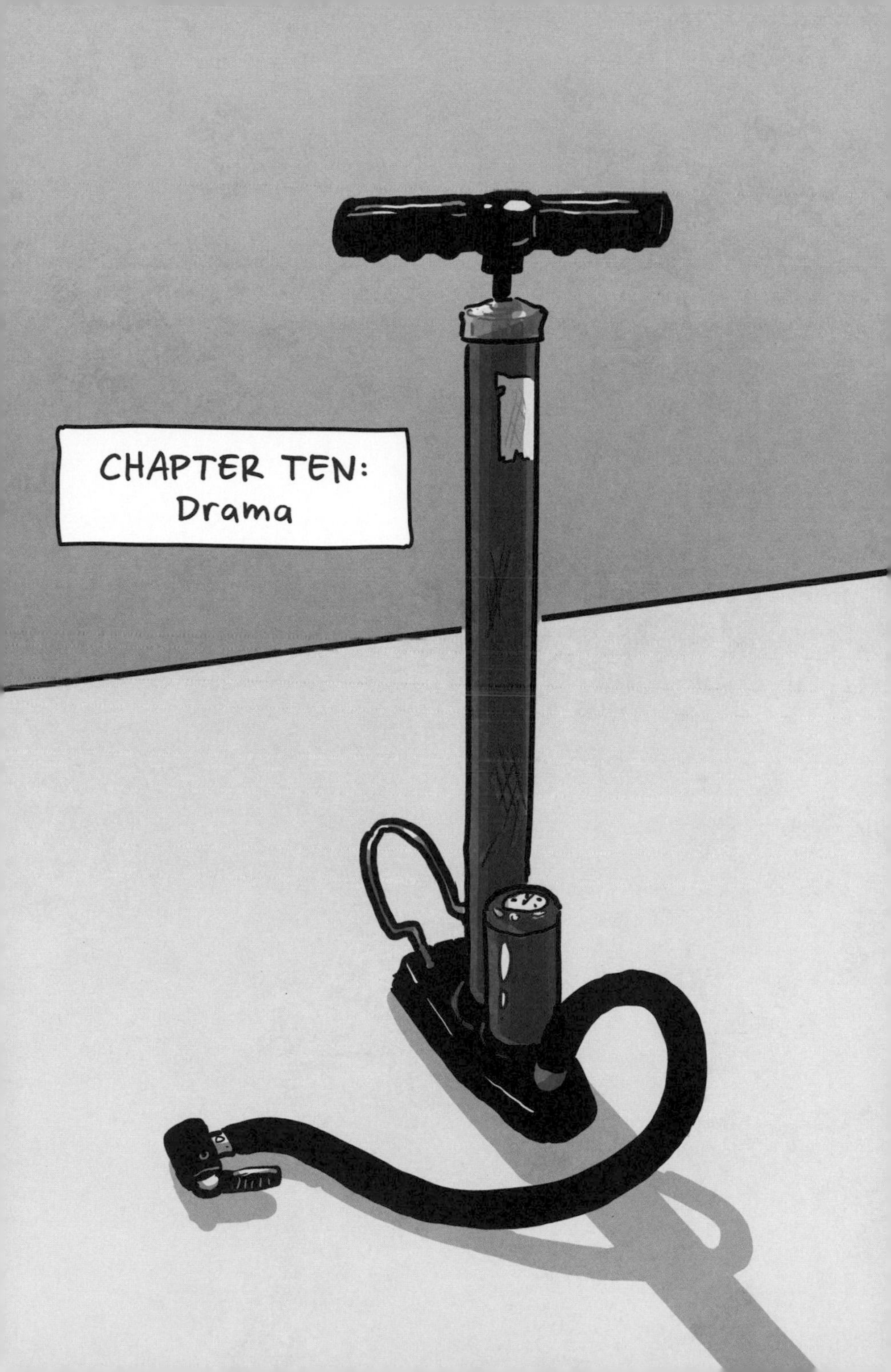
CHAPTER TEN:
Drama

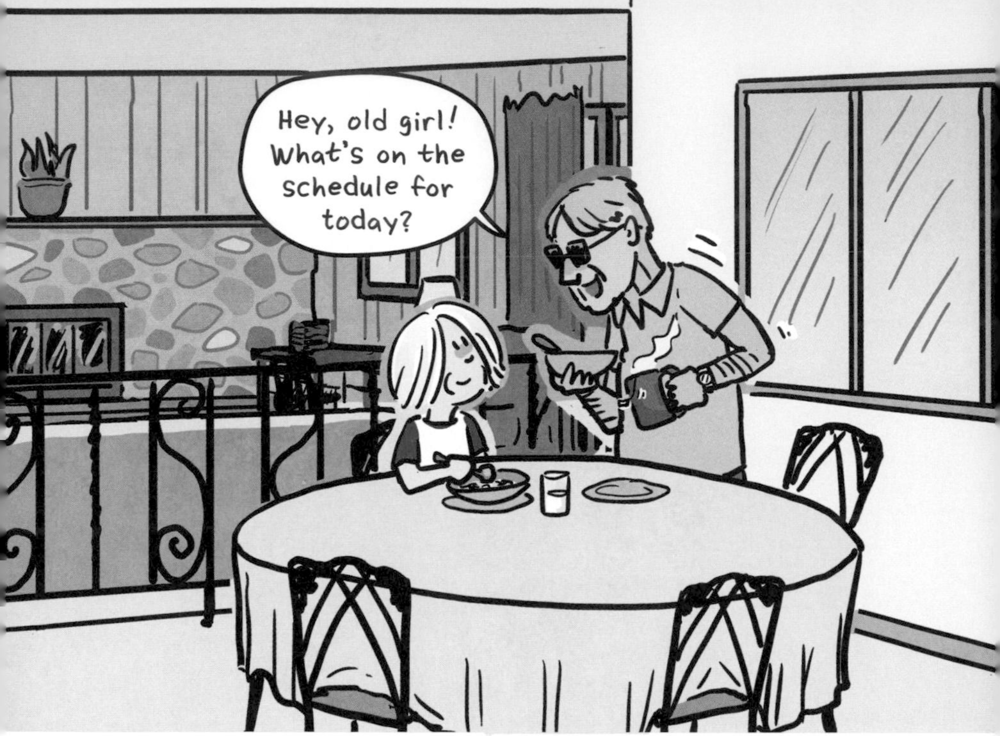
Hey, old girl! What's on the schedule for today?

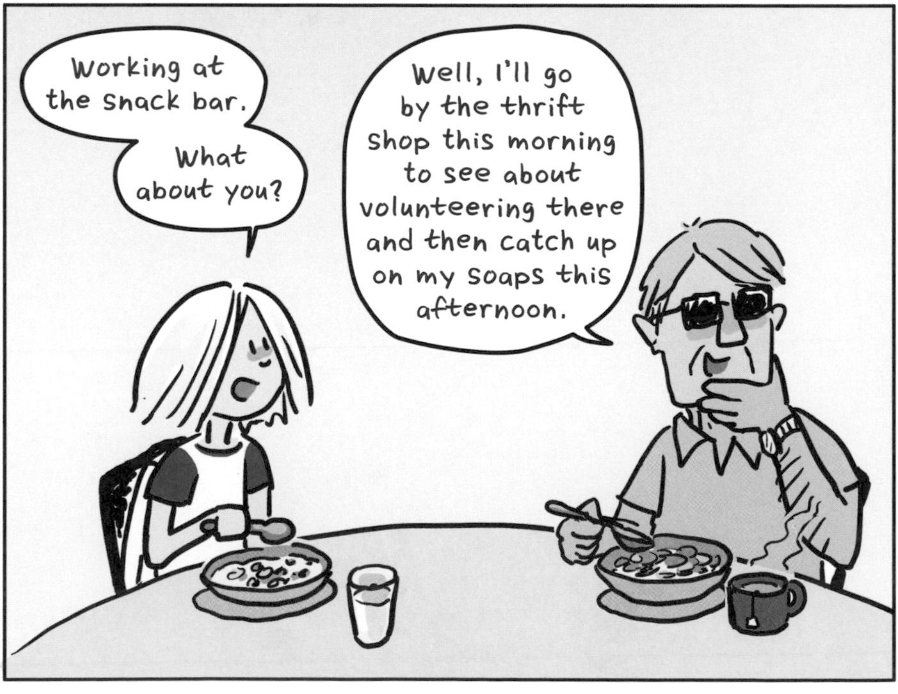
Working at the snack bar.
What about you?
Well, I'll go by the thrift shop this morning to see about volunteering there and then catch up on my soaps this afternoon.

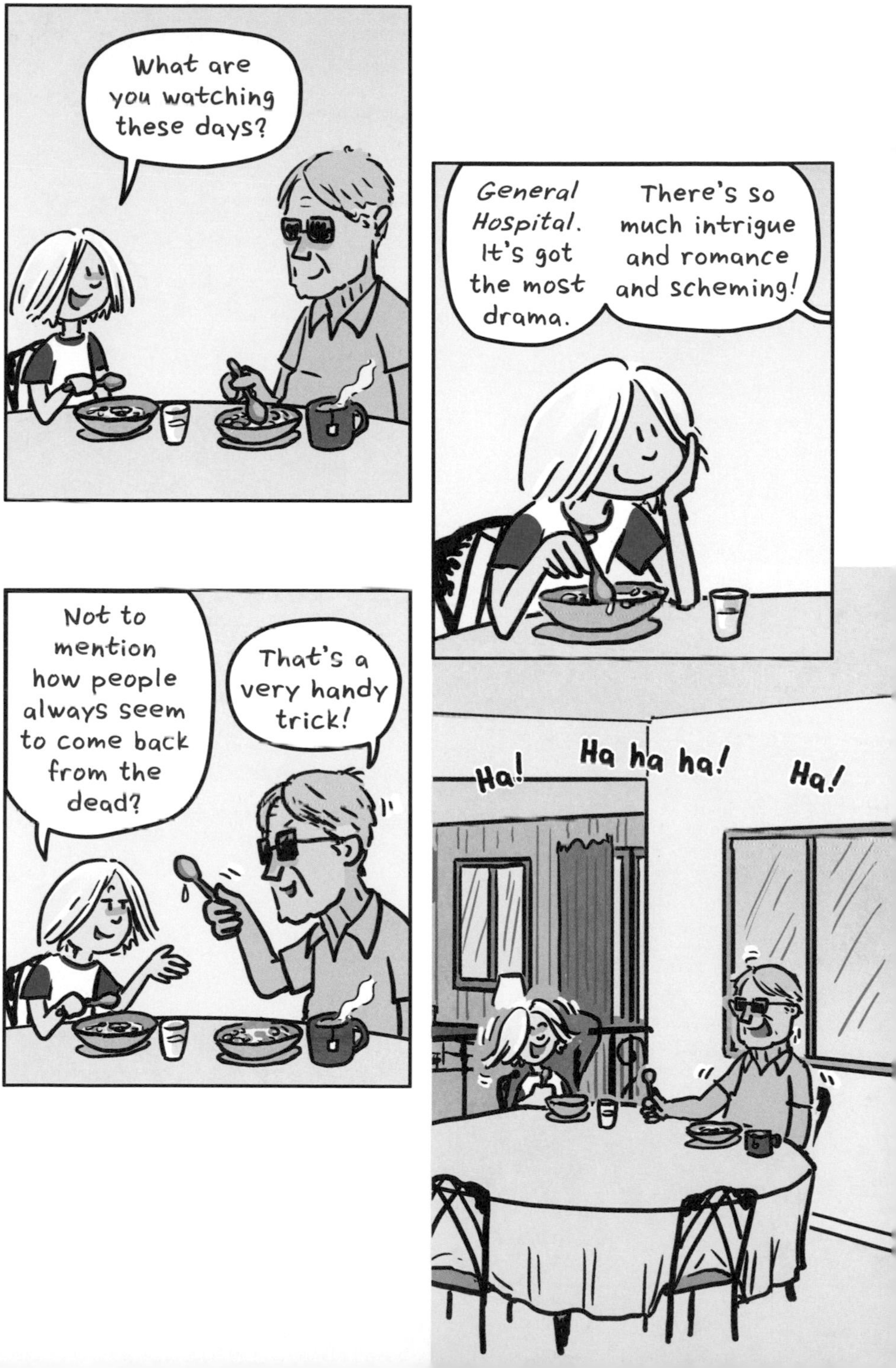

What are you watching these days?
General Hospital. It's got the most drama.
There's so much intrigue and romance and scheming!
Not to mention how people always seem to come back from the dead?
That's a very handy trick!
Ha!
Ha ha ha!
Ha!

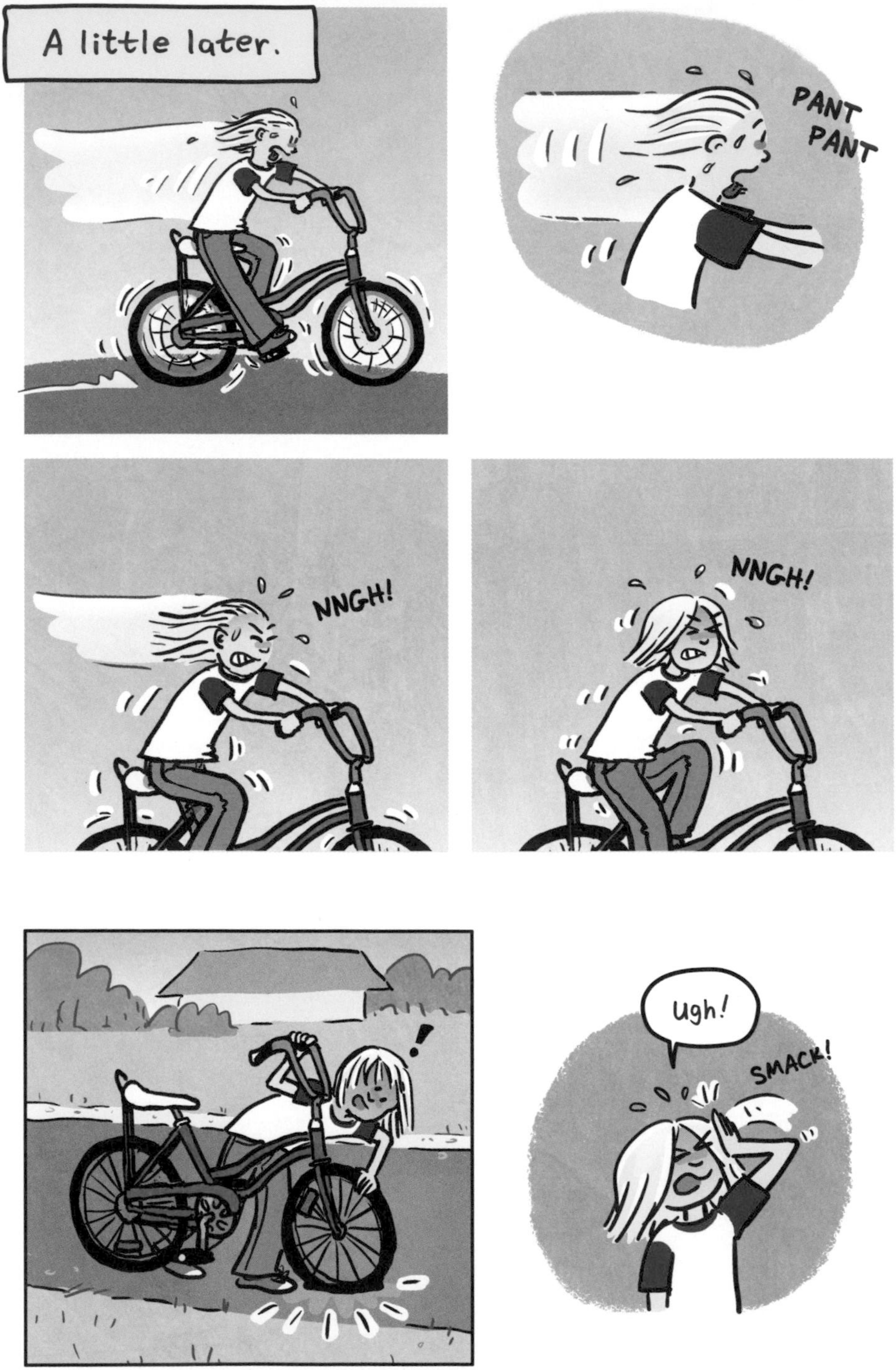
A little later.
PANT
PANT
NNGH!
NNGH!
!
Ugh!
SMACK!

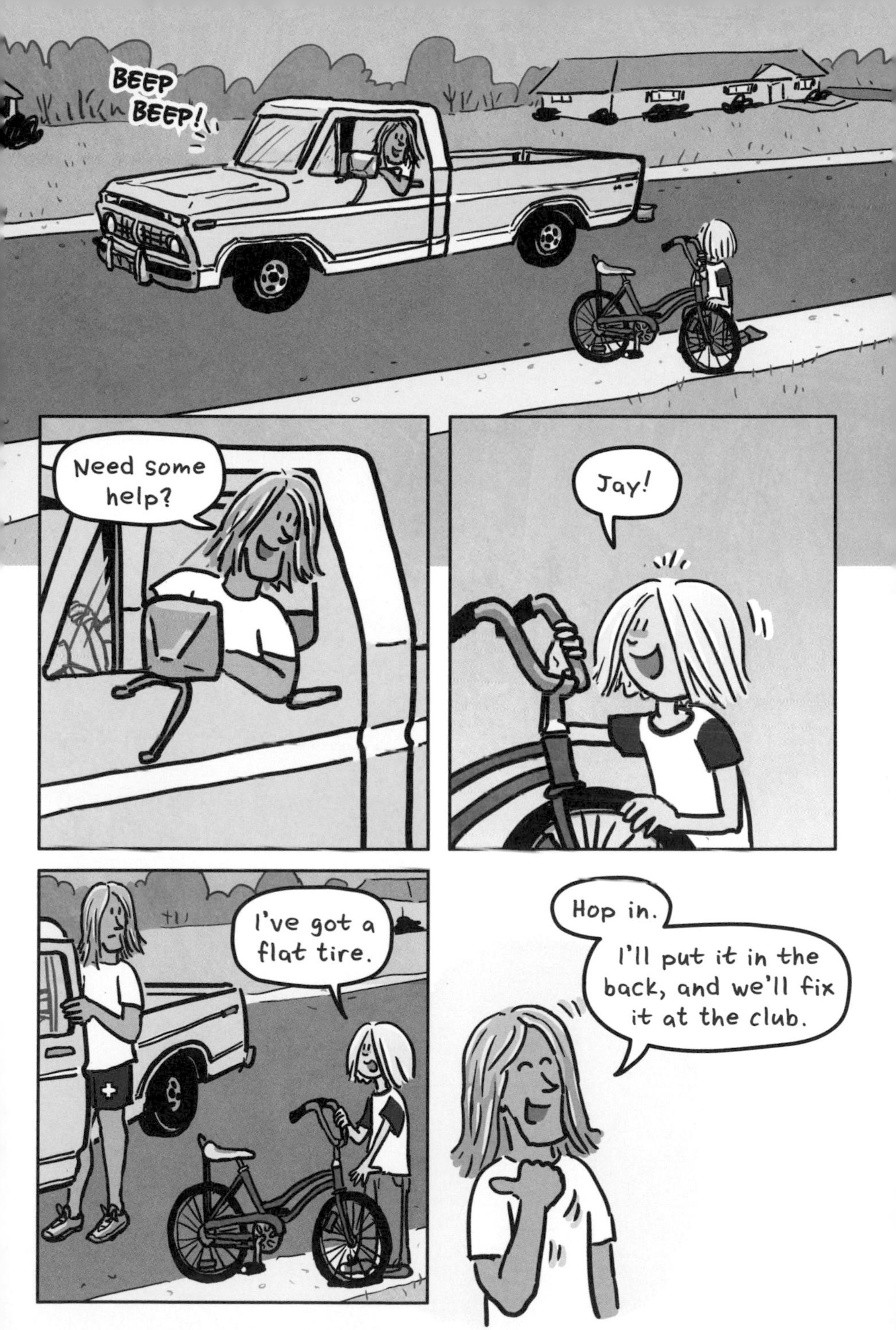
BEEP BEEP!
Need some help?
Jay!
I've got a flat tire.
Hop in.
I'll put it in the back, and we'll fix it at the club.

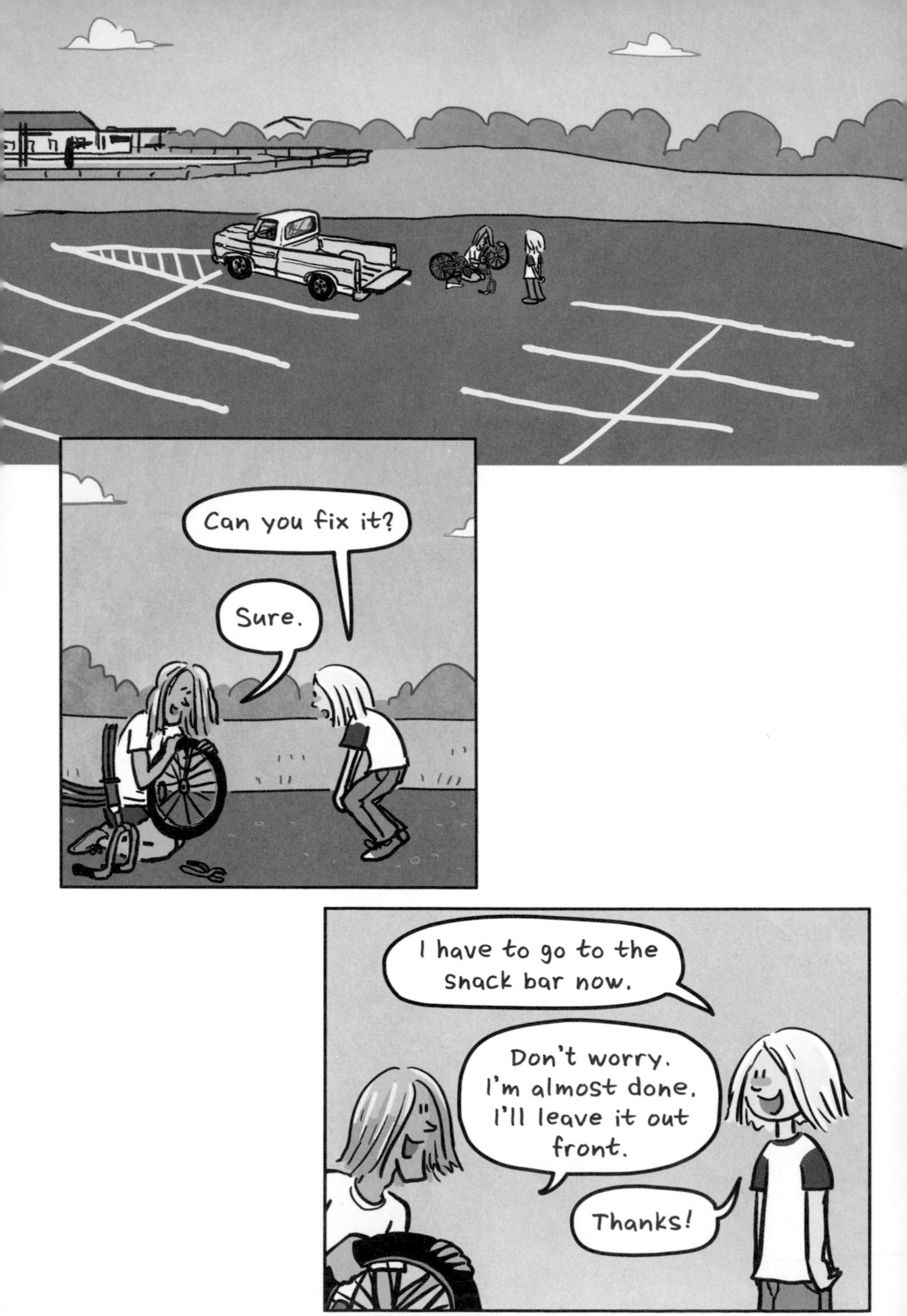
Can you fix it?
Sure.
I have to go to the snack bar now.
Don't worry. I'm almost done. I'll leave it out front.
Thanks!

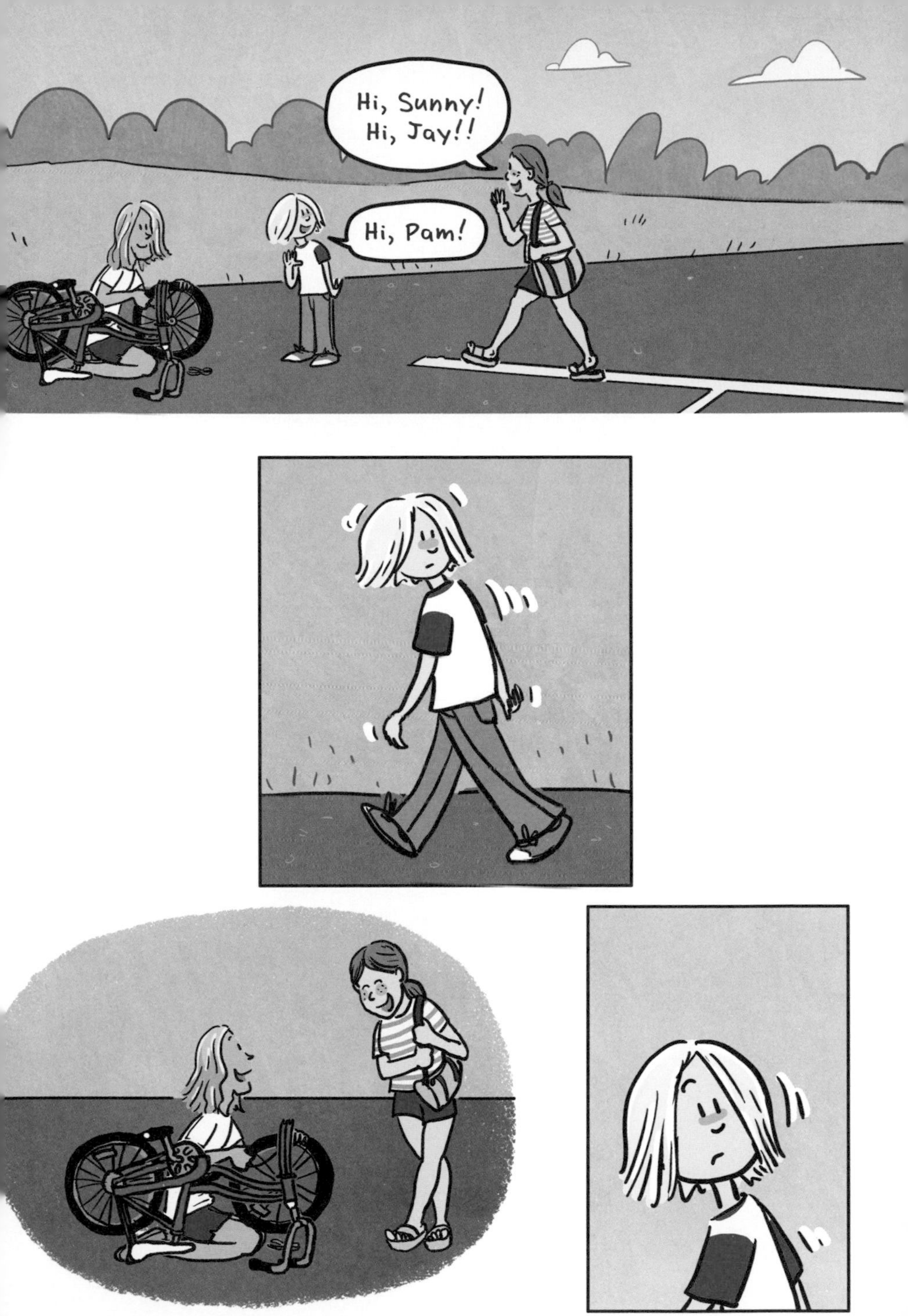
Hi, Sunny!
Hi, Jay!!
Hi, Pam!

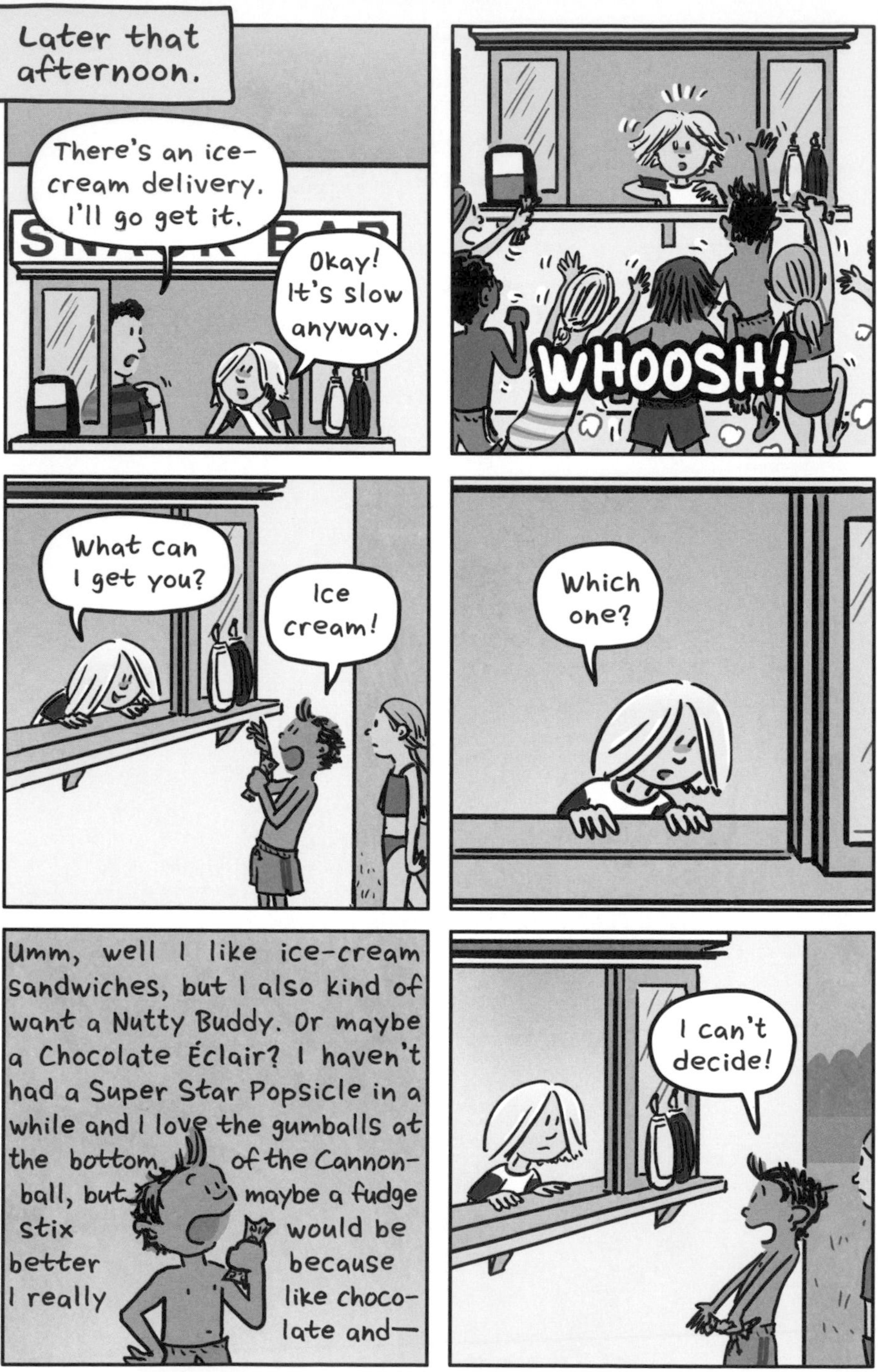
Later that afternoon.
There's an ice-cream delivery. I'll go get it.
SNACK BAR
Okay! It's slow anyway.
WHOOSH!
What can I get you?
Ice cream!
Which one?
Umm, well I like ice-cream sandwiches, but I also kind of want a Nutty Buddy. Or maybe a Chocolate Éclair? I haven't had a Super Star Popsicle in a while and I love the gumballs at the bottom of the Cannon-ball, but maybe a fudge stix would be better because I really like chocolate and—
I can't decide!

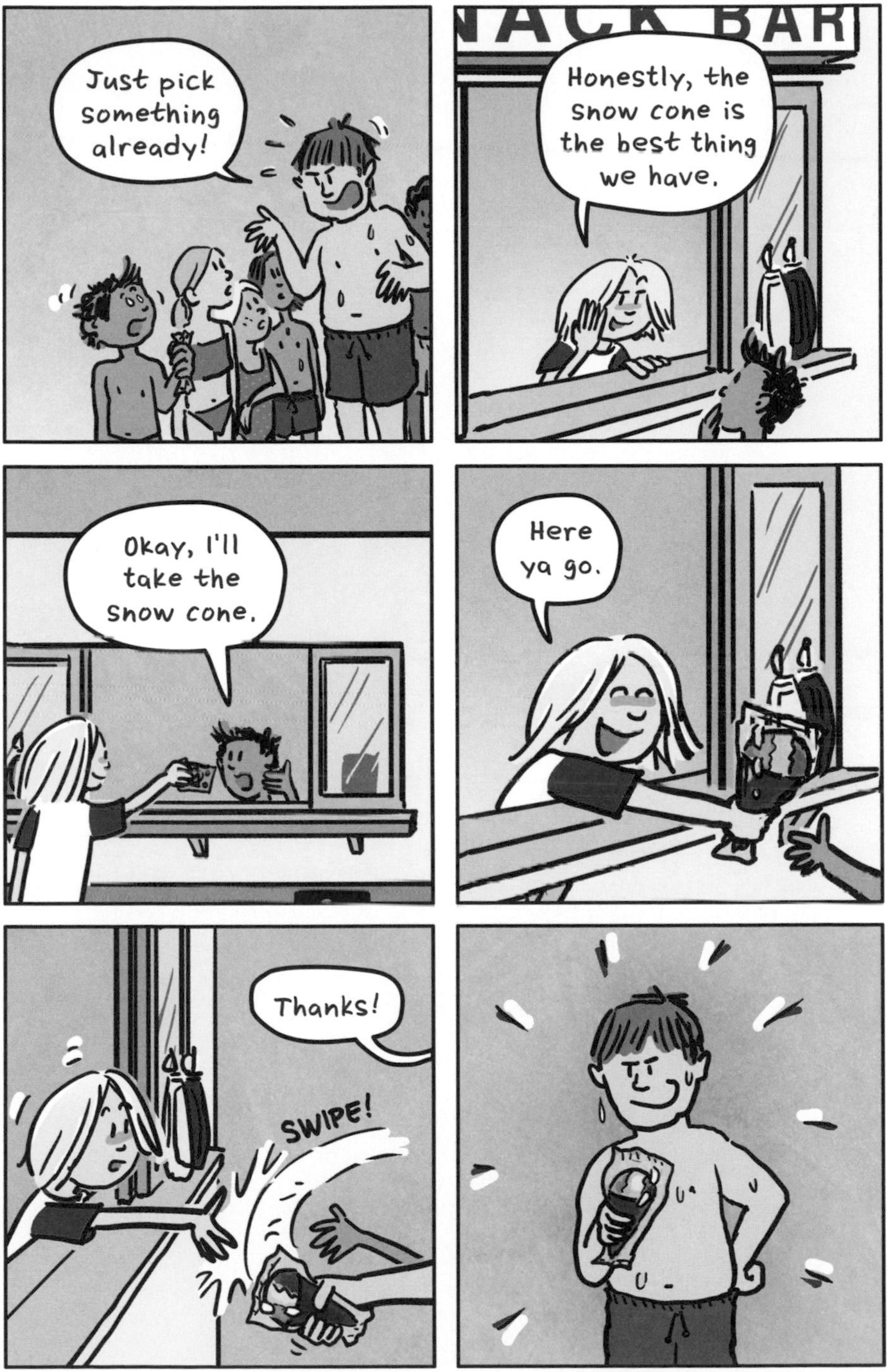
Just pick something already!
NACK BAR
Honestly, the snow cone is the best thing we have.
Okay, I'll take the snow cone.
Here ya go.
Thanks!
SWIPE!

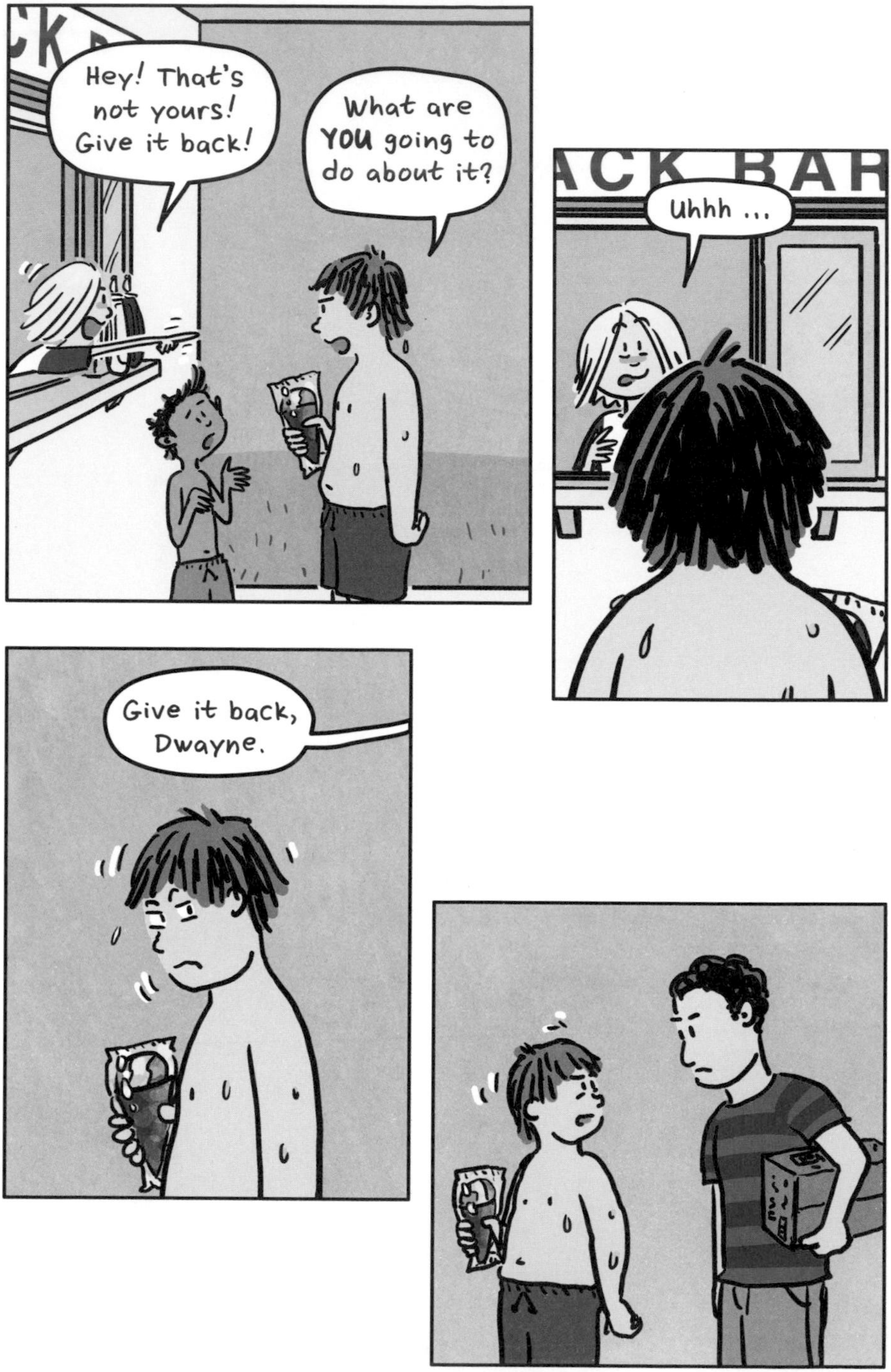
ACK BAR
Hey! That's not yours! Give it back!
What are **YOU** going to do about it?
Uhhh ...
Give it back, Dwayne.

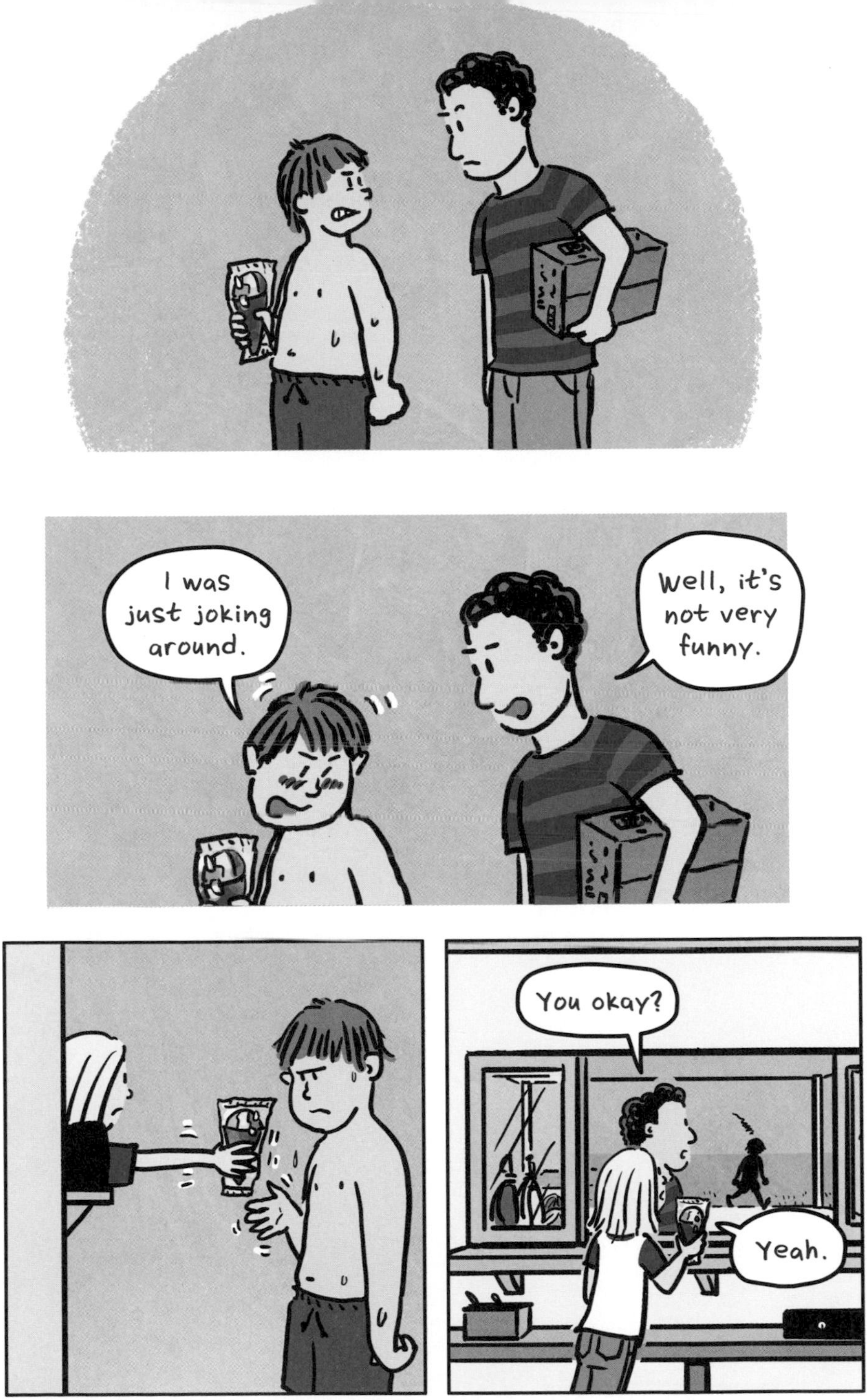
I was just joking around.
Well, it's not very funny.
You okay?
Yeah.

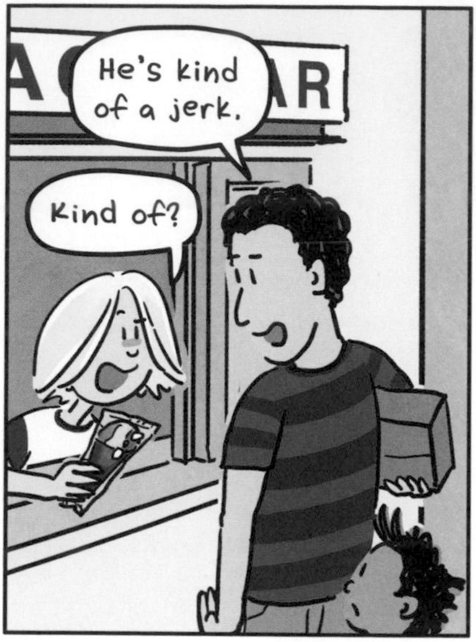
He's kind of a jerk.
Kind of?

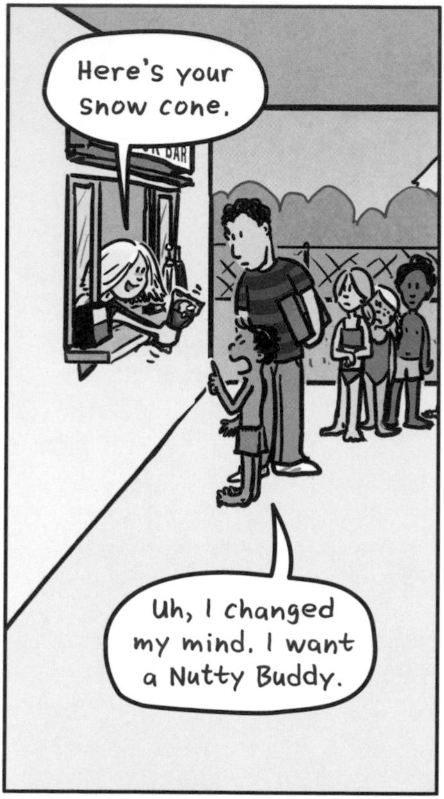
Here's your snow cone.
Uh, I changed my mind. I want a Nutty Buddy.

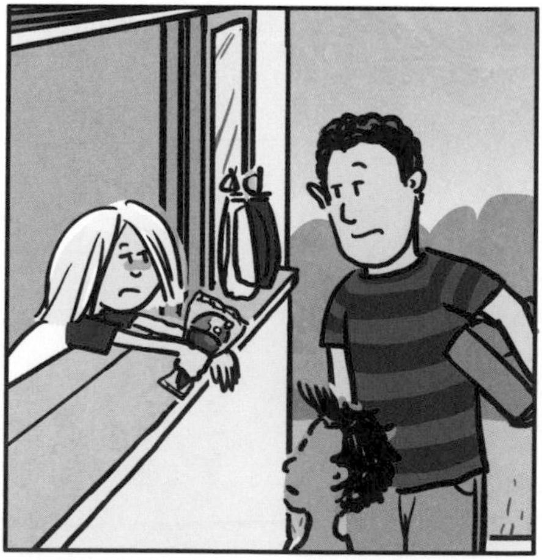

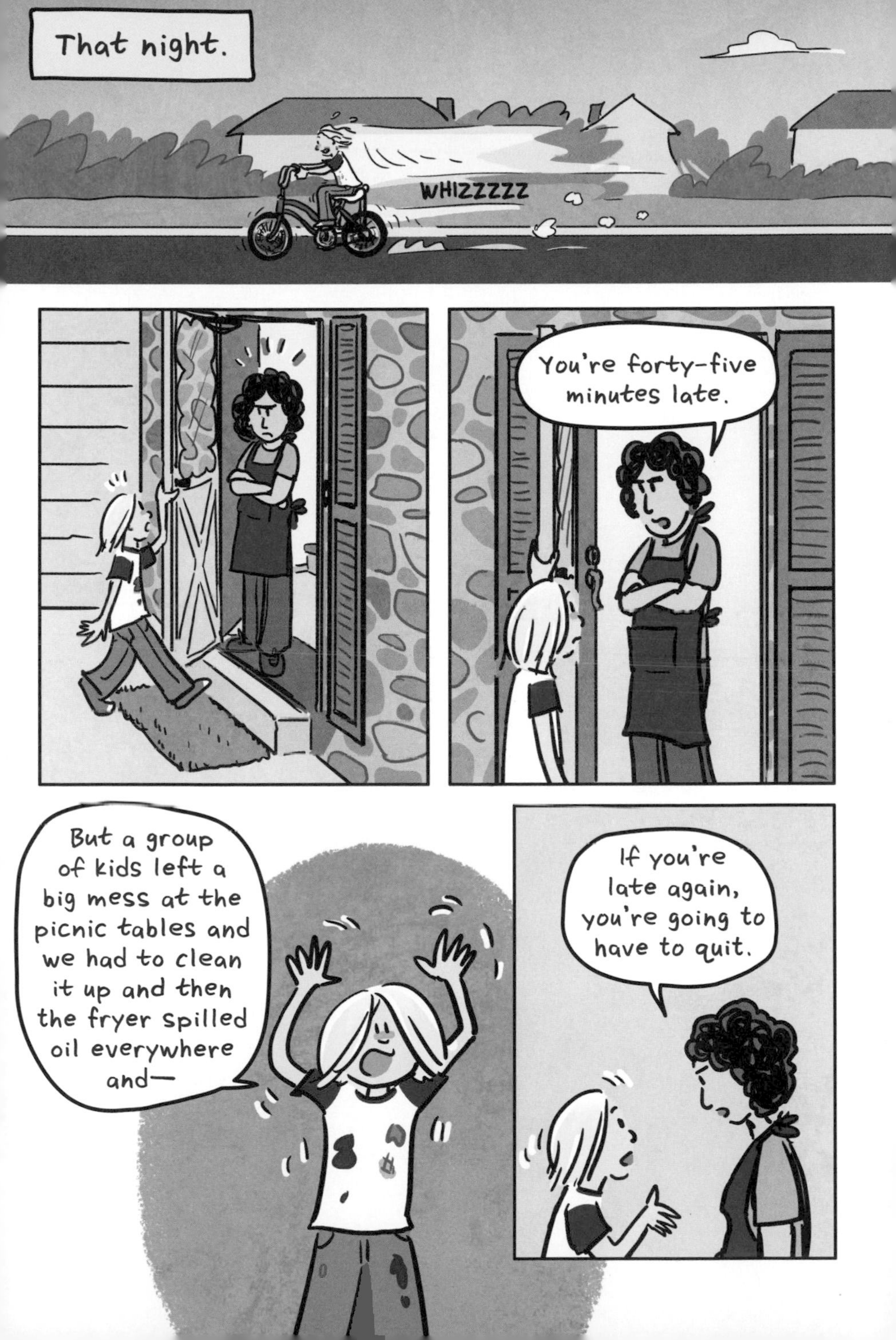
That night.
WHIZZZZZ
You're forty-five minutes late.
But a group of kids left a big mess at the picnic tables and we had to clean it up and then the fryer spilled oil everywhere and—
If you're late again, you're going to have to quit.

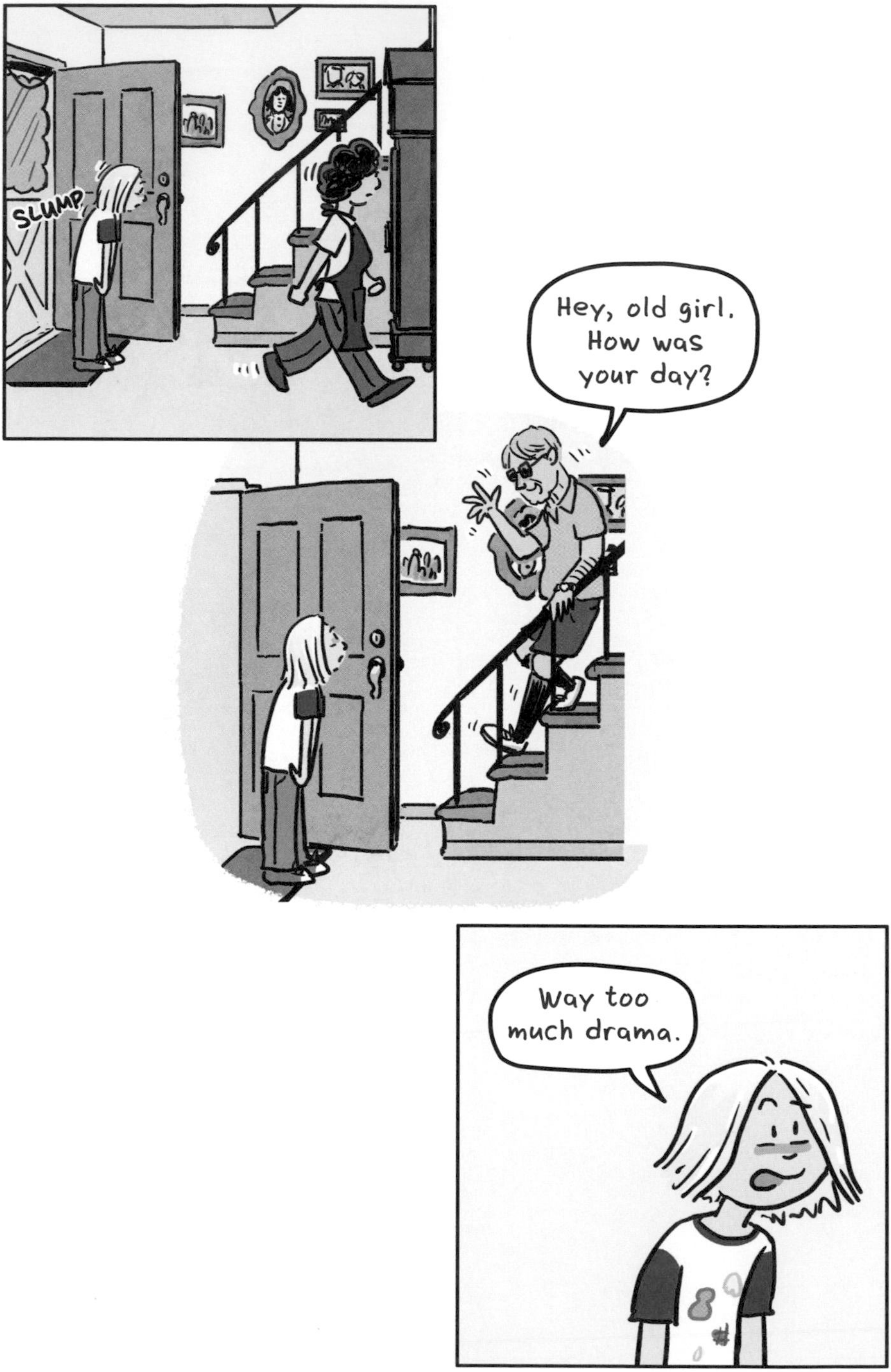
SLUMP
Hey, old girl. How was your day?
Way too much drama.

CHAPTER ELEVEN: Lightning Strikes

978 **Philadelphia Bulletin** 15-D

Weather Summary

TODAY'S FORECAST

Hot with chance of afternoon showers

Seattle
San Francisco
Phoenix
Chicago
Philadelphia
New York
Charleston
New Orleans
Miami
WARM
H
L
L
H

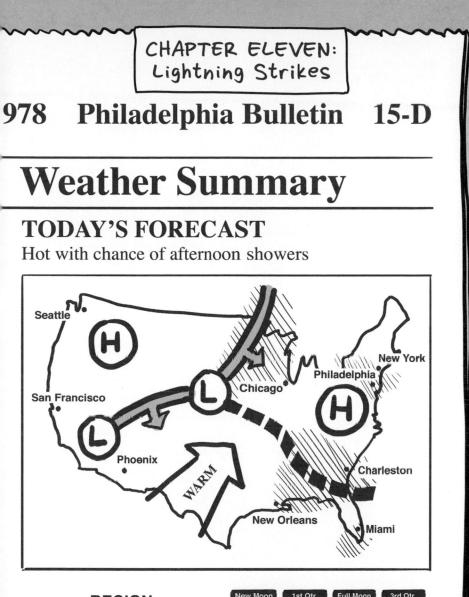

REGION

	High	Low
Allentown	72	53
Atlantic City	74	66
Harrisburg	75	63
Philadelphia	80	67
Pittsburgh	74	53
Scranton	72	53
Wilmington	78	65

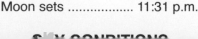

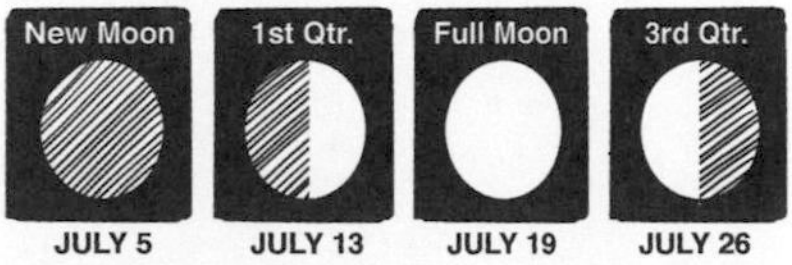

New Moon
1st Qtr.
Full Moon
3rd Qtr.
JULY 5
JULY 13
JULY 19
JULY 26

SUN AND MOON

Sun sets .... 8:31 p.m.
Sun rises .... 5:42 a.m.
Moon sets .... 11:31 p.m.

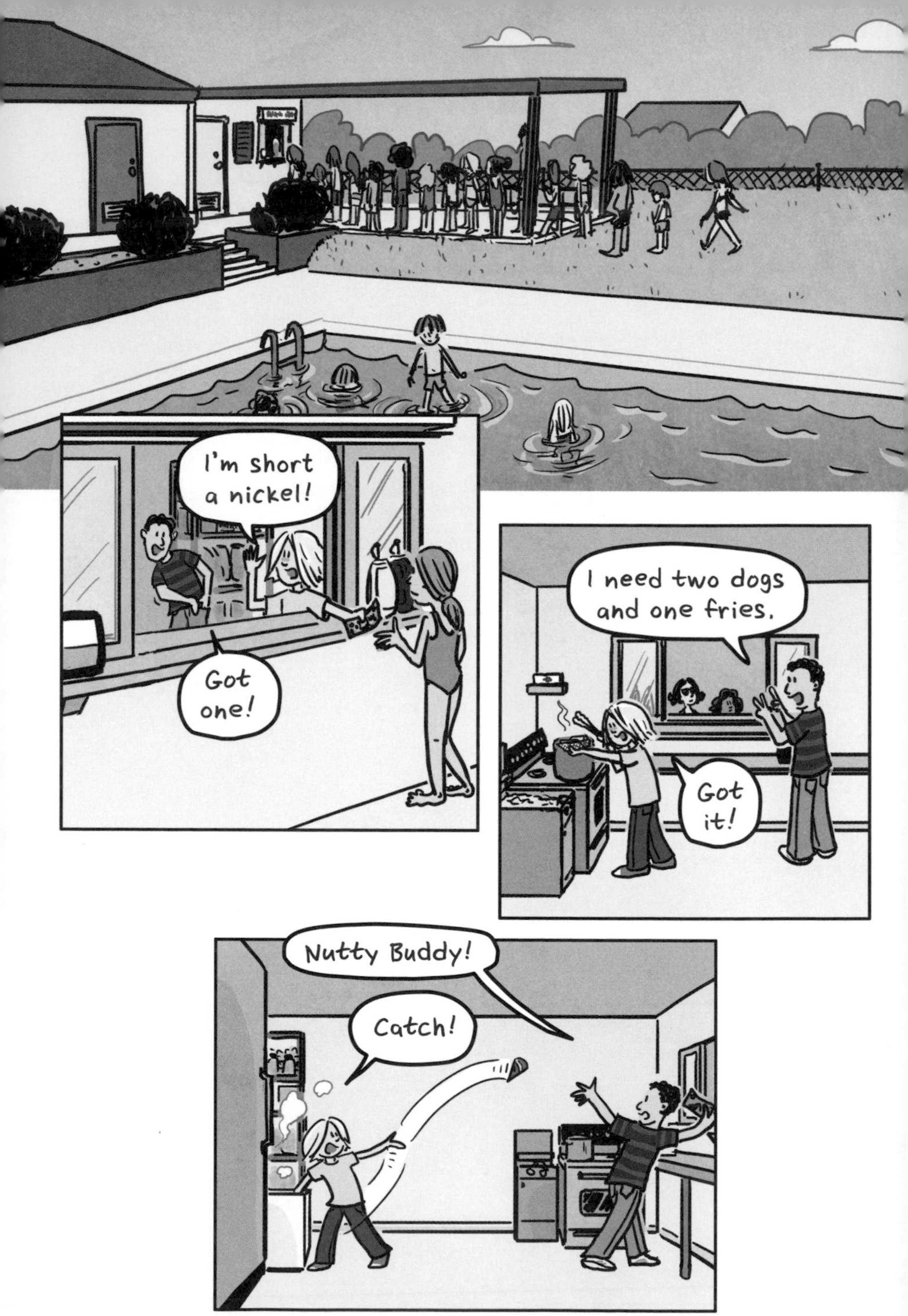
I'm short a nickel!
Got one!
I need two dogs and one fries.
Got it!
Nutty Buddy!
Catch!

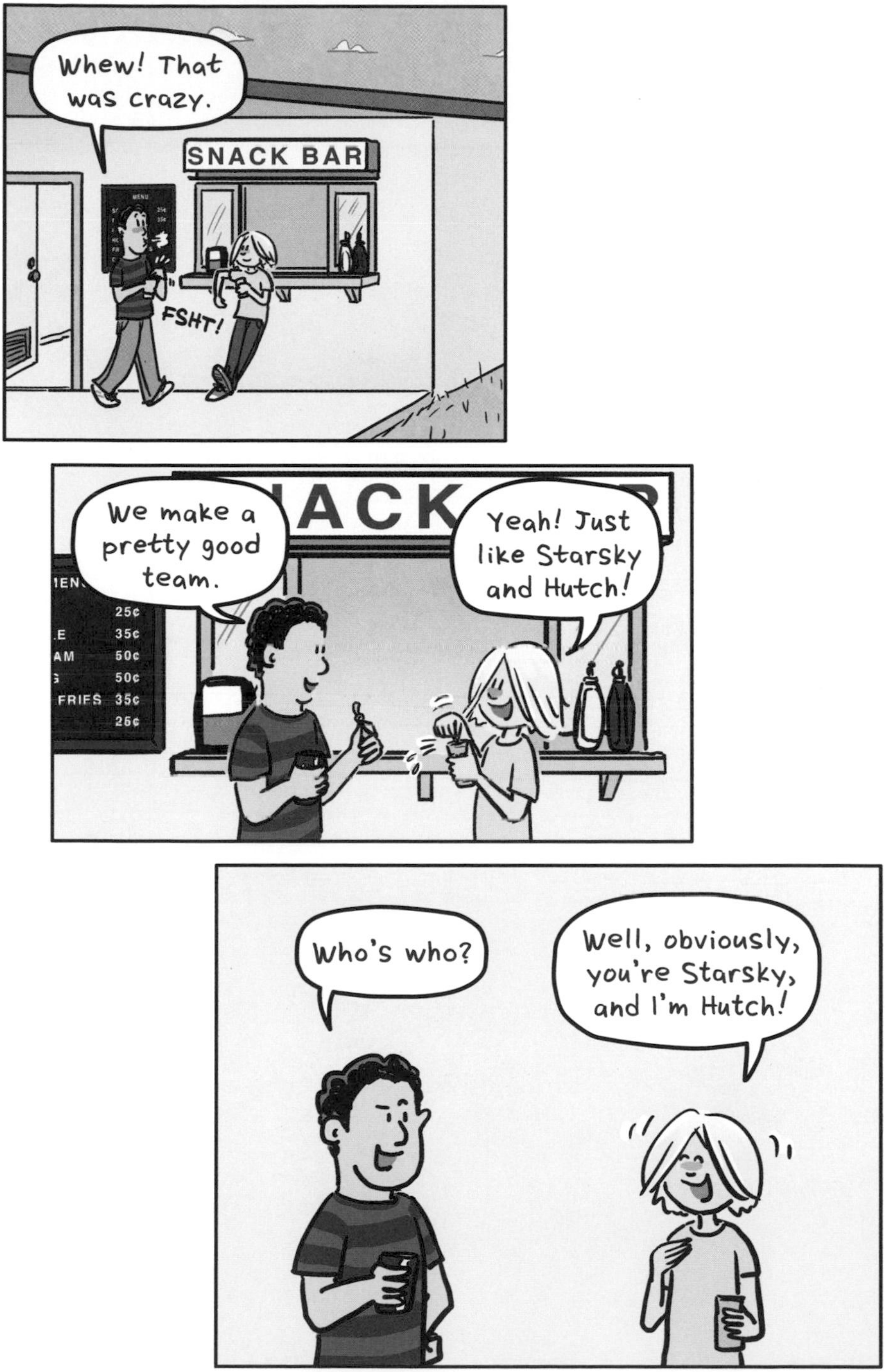

Whew! That was crazy.
SNACK BAR
FSHT!
We make a pretty good team.
Yeah! Just like Starsky and Hutch!
Who's who?
Well, obviously, you're Starsky, and I'm Hutch!

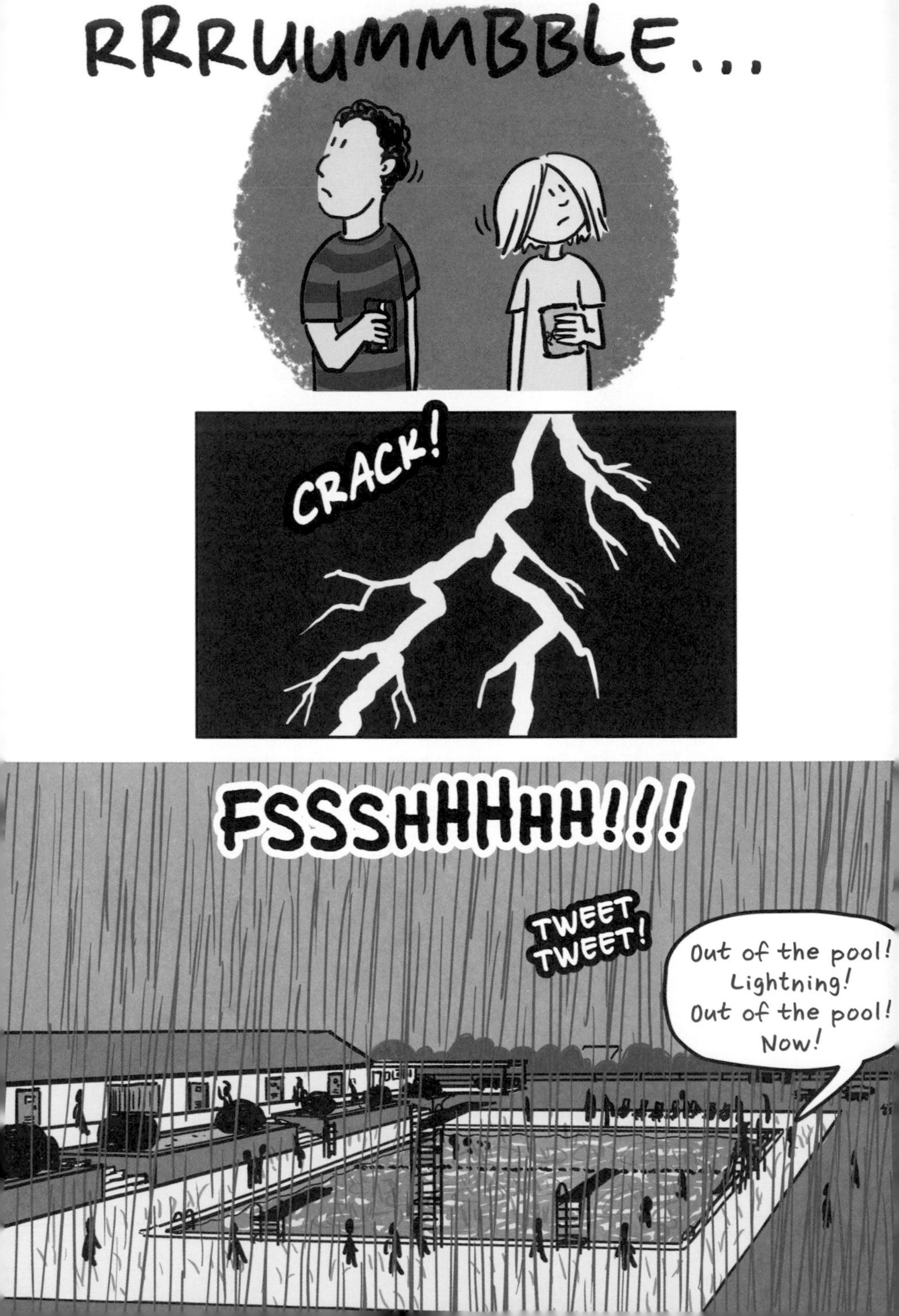
RRRUUMMBBLE...
CRACK!
FSSSHHHHH!!!
TWEET TWEET!
Out of the pool! Lightning! Out of the pool! Now!

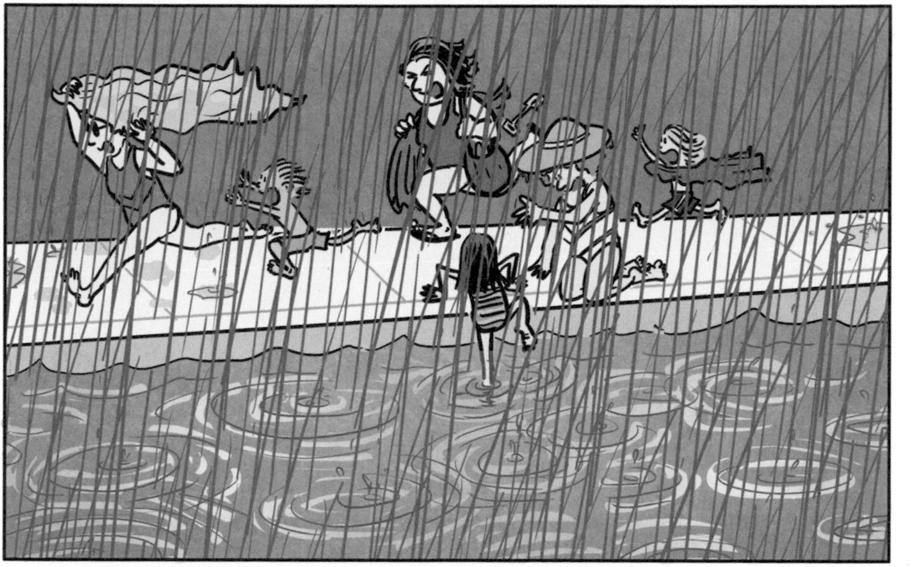

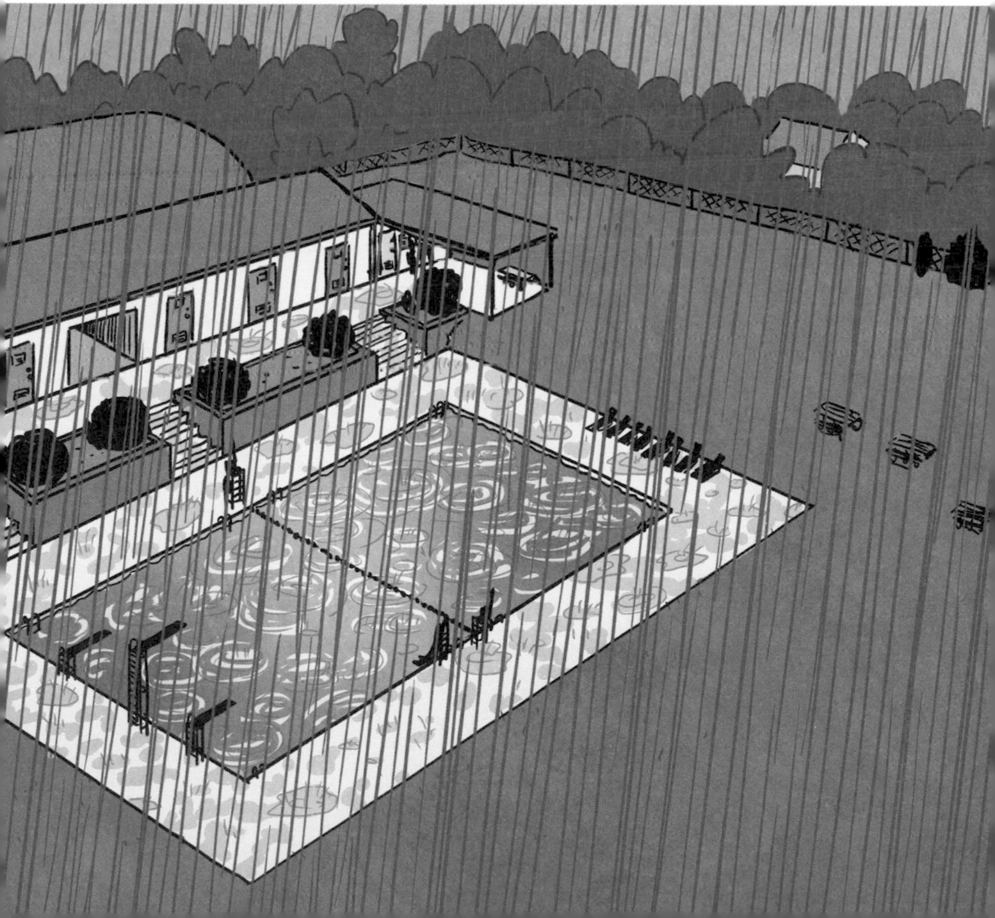

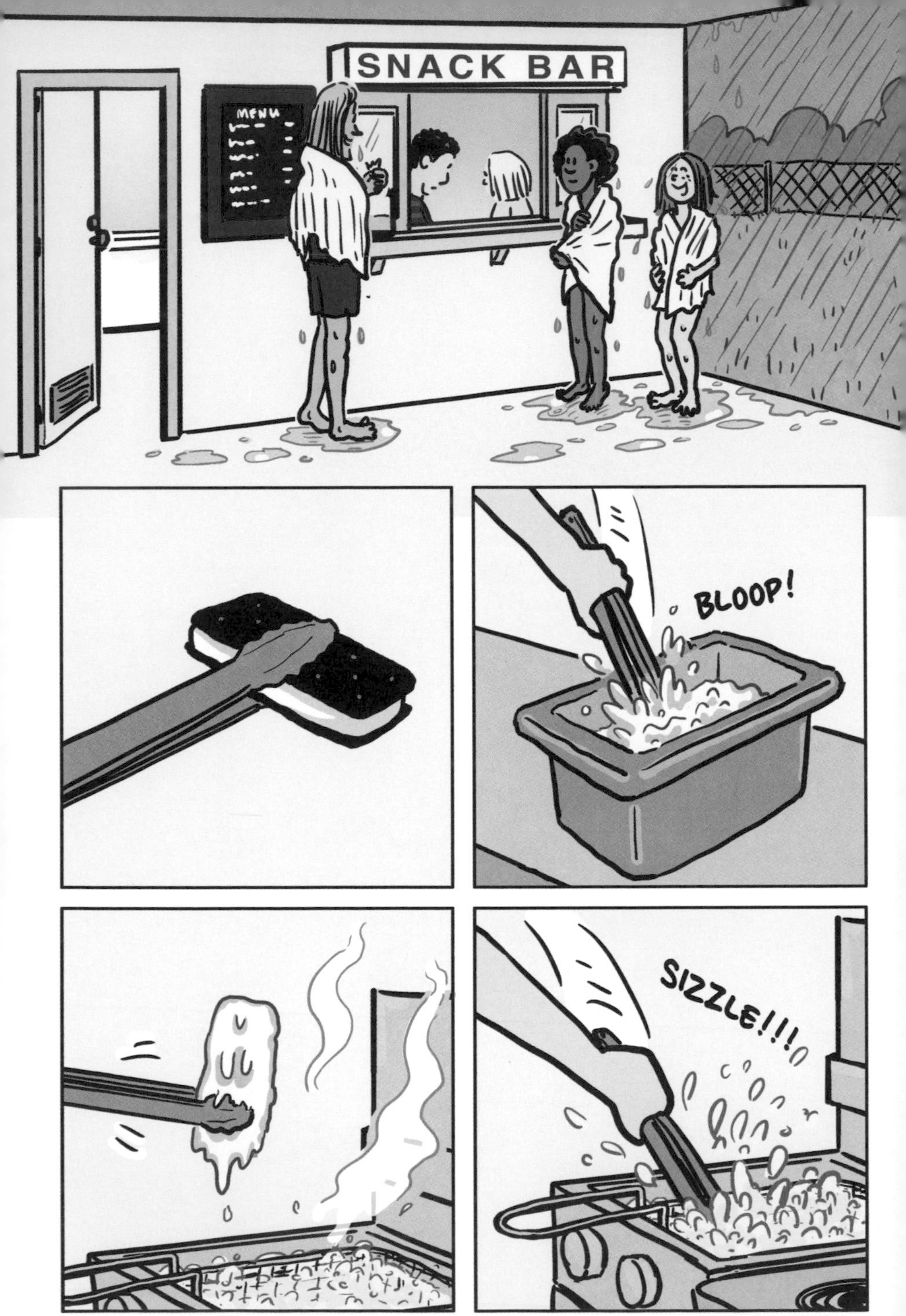
SNACK BAR
MENU
BLOOP!
SIZZLE!!!!

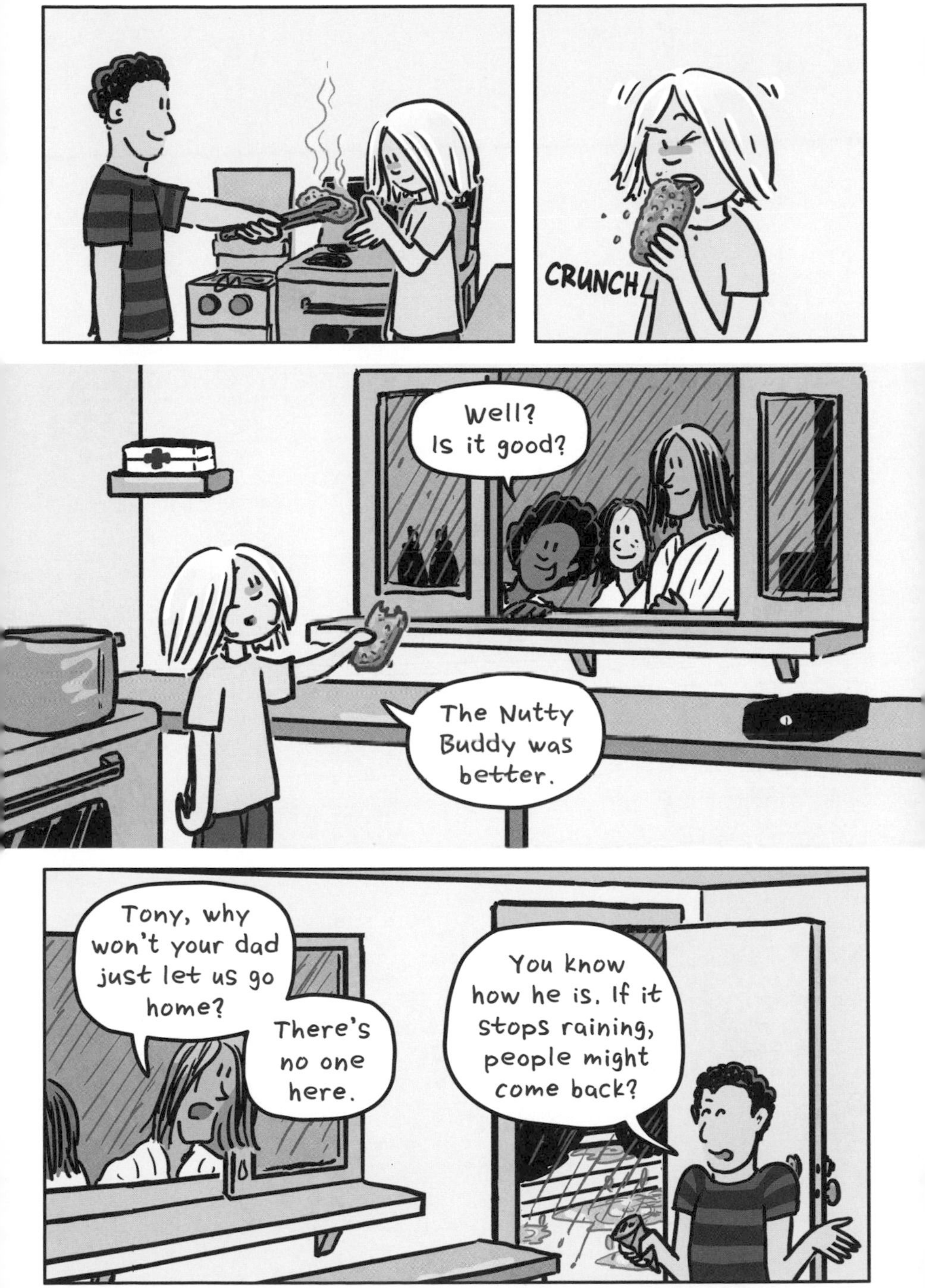
CRUNCH
Well? Is it good?
The Nutty Buddy was better.
Tony, why won't your dad just let us go home?
There's no one here.
You know how he is. If it stops raining, people might come back?

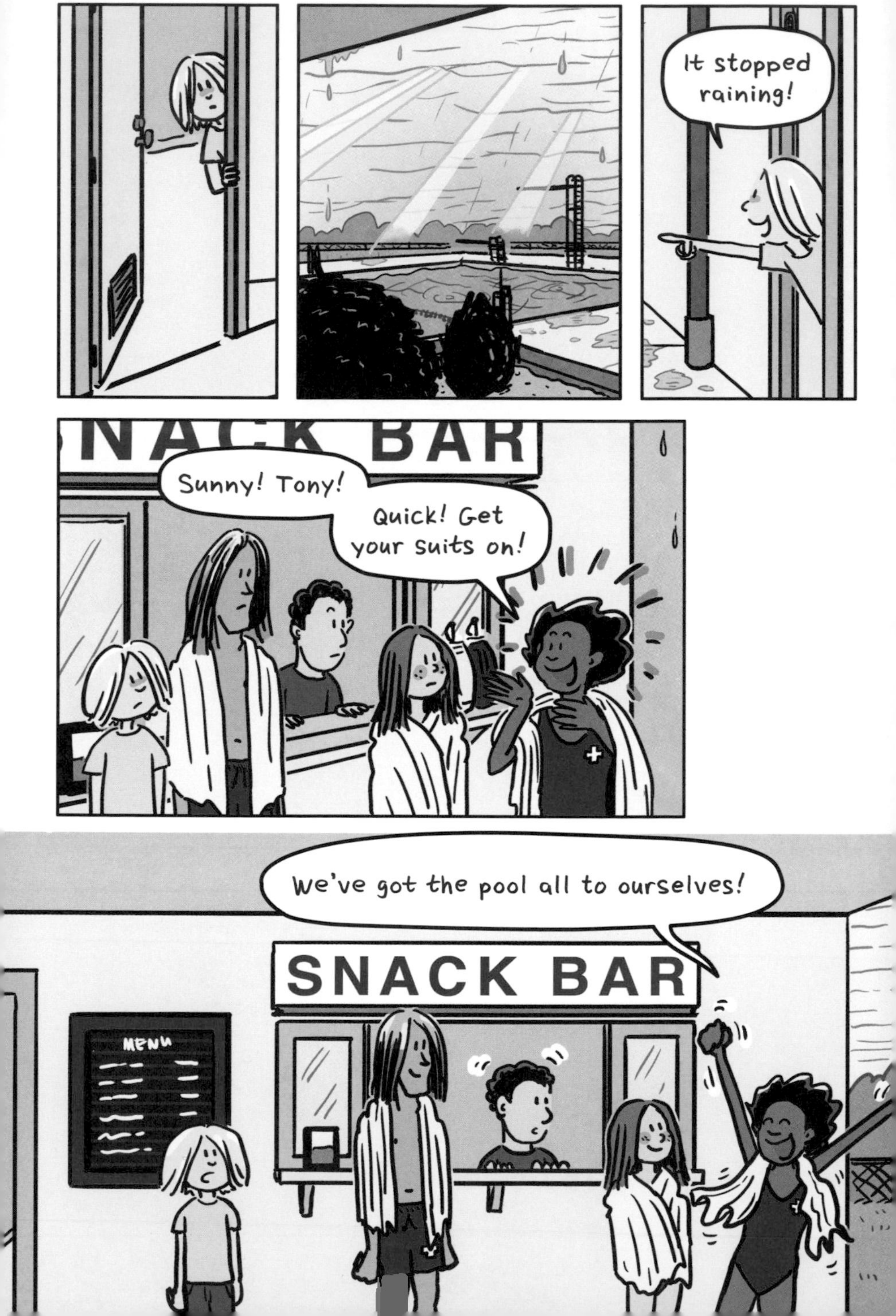

It stopped raining!
NACK BAR
Sunny! Tony!
Quick! Get your suits on!
We've got the pool all to ourselves!
SNACK BAR
MENU

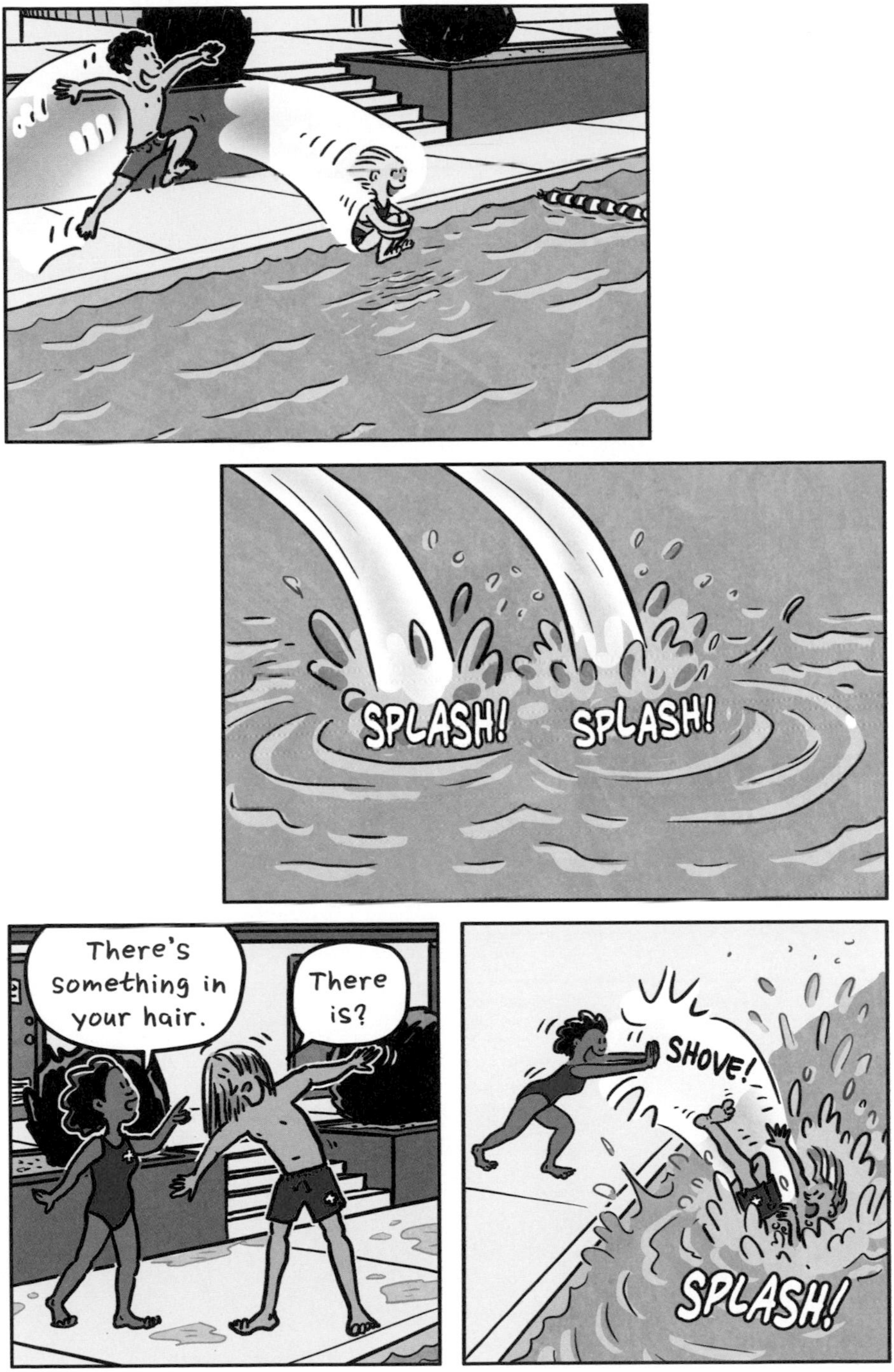
SPLASH!
SPLASH!
There's something in your hair.
There is?
SHOVE!
SPLASH!

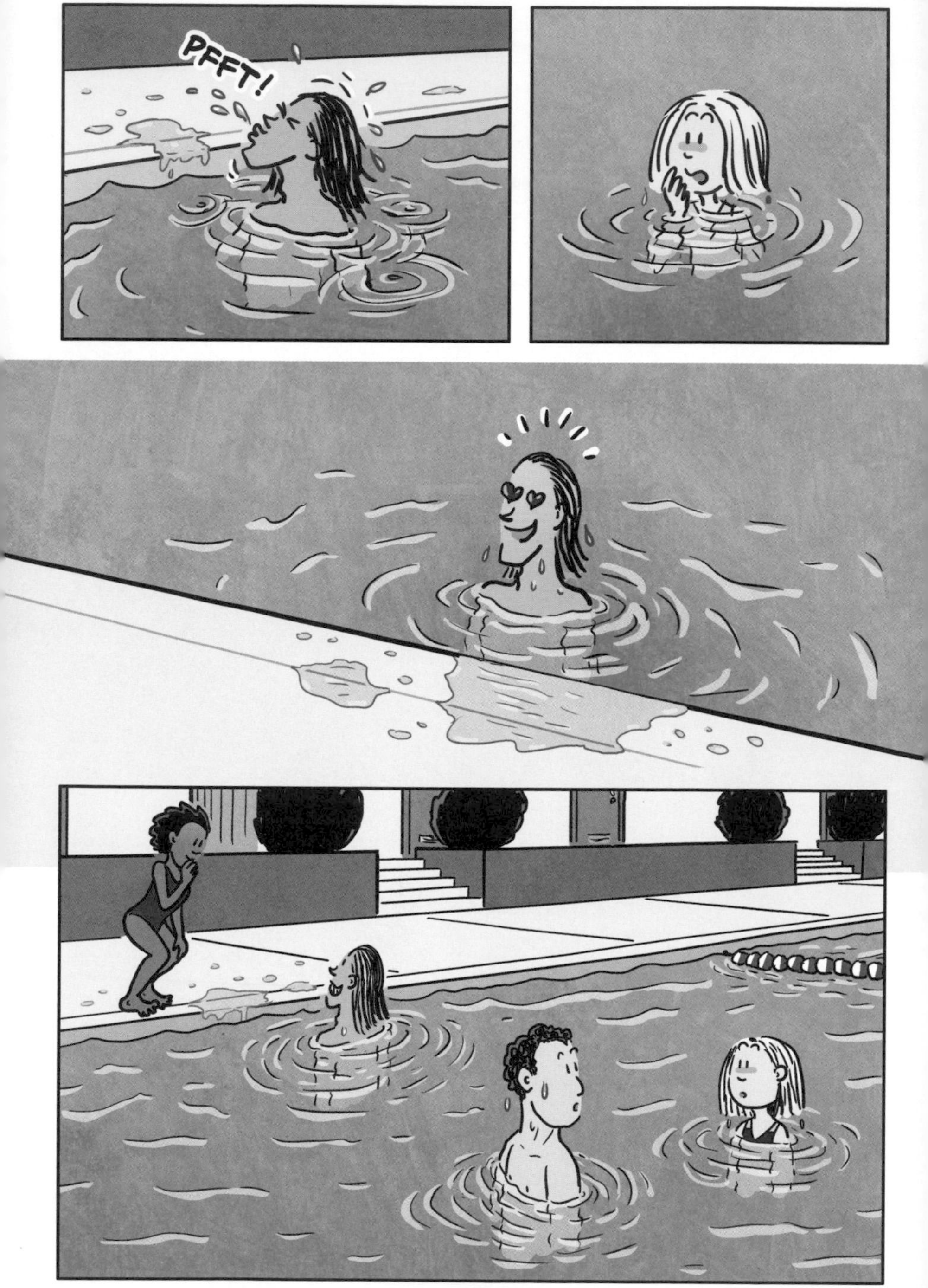
PFFT!

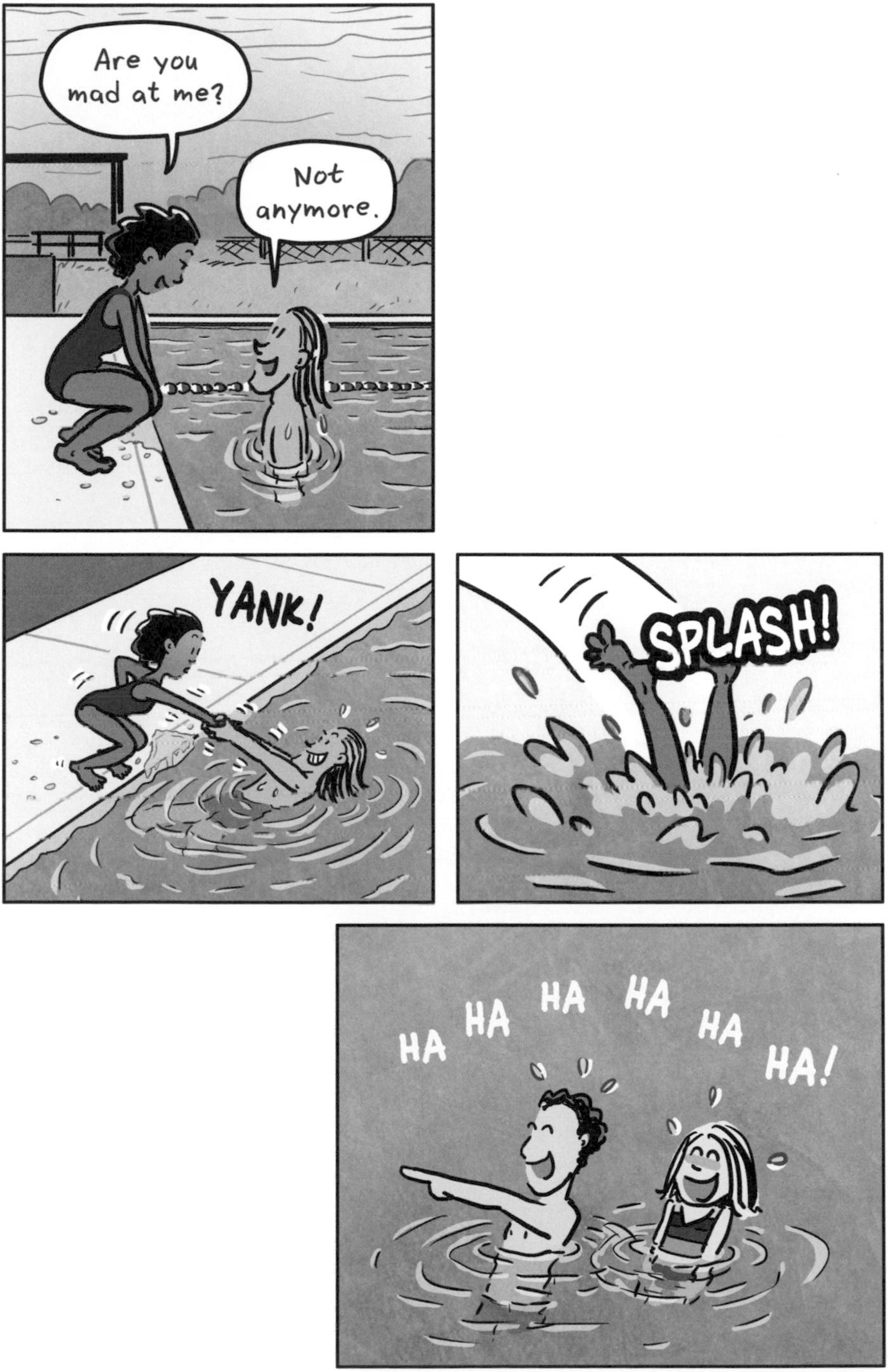
Are you mad at me?
Not anymore.
YANK!
SPLASH!
HA HA HA HA HA HA!

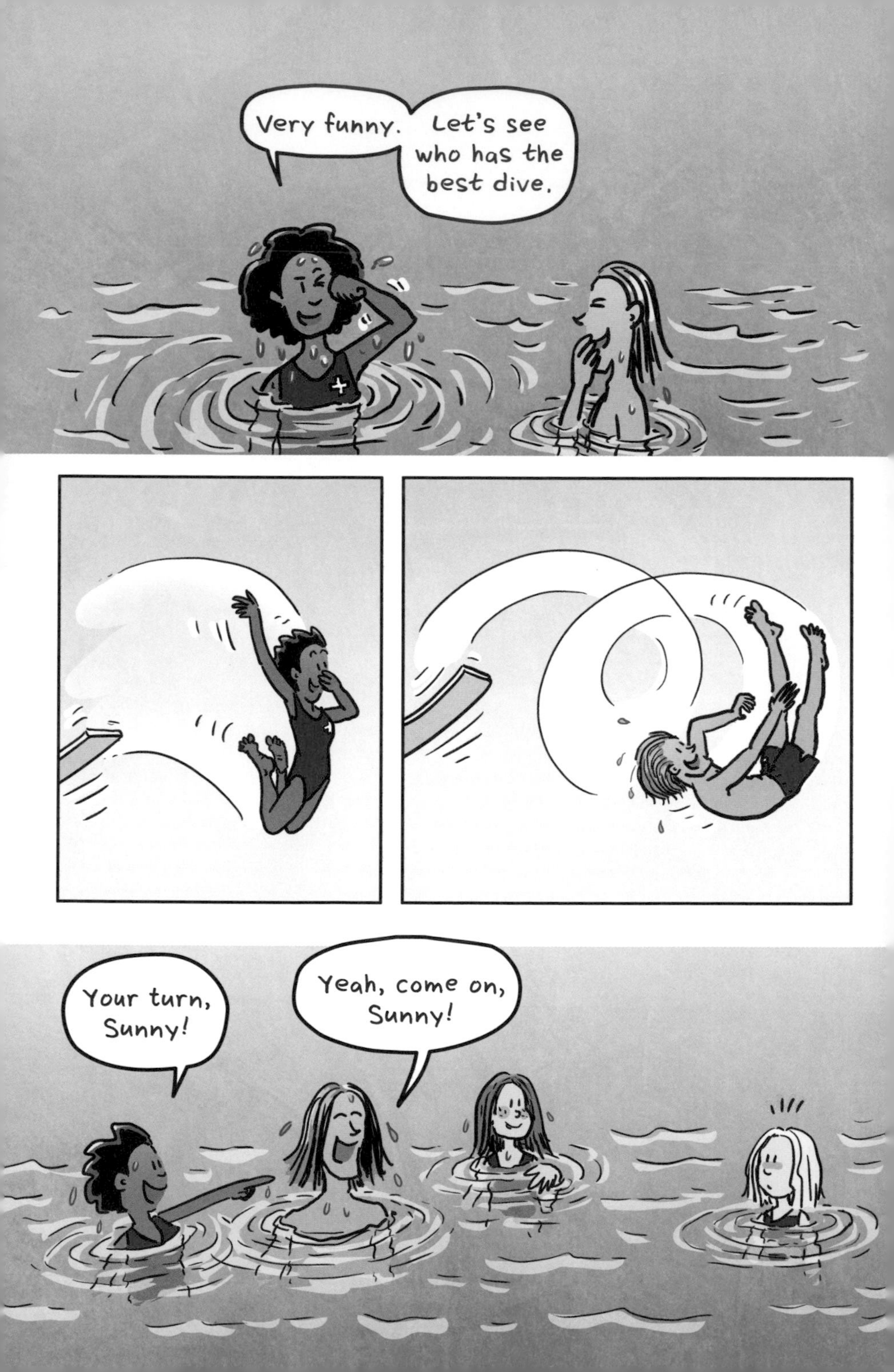
Very funny.
Let's see who has the best dive.
Your turn, Sunny!
Yeah, come on, Sunny!

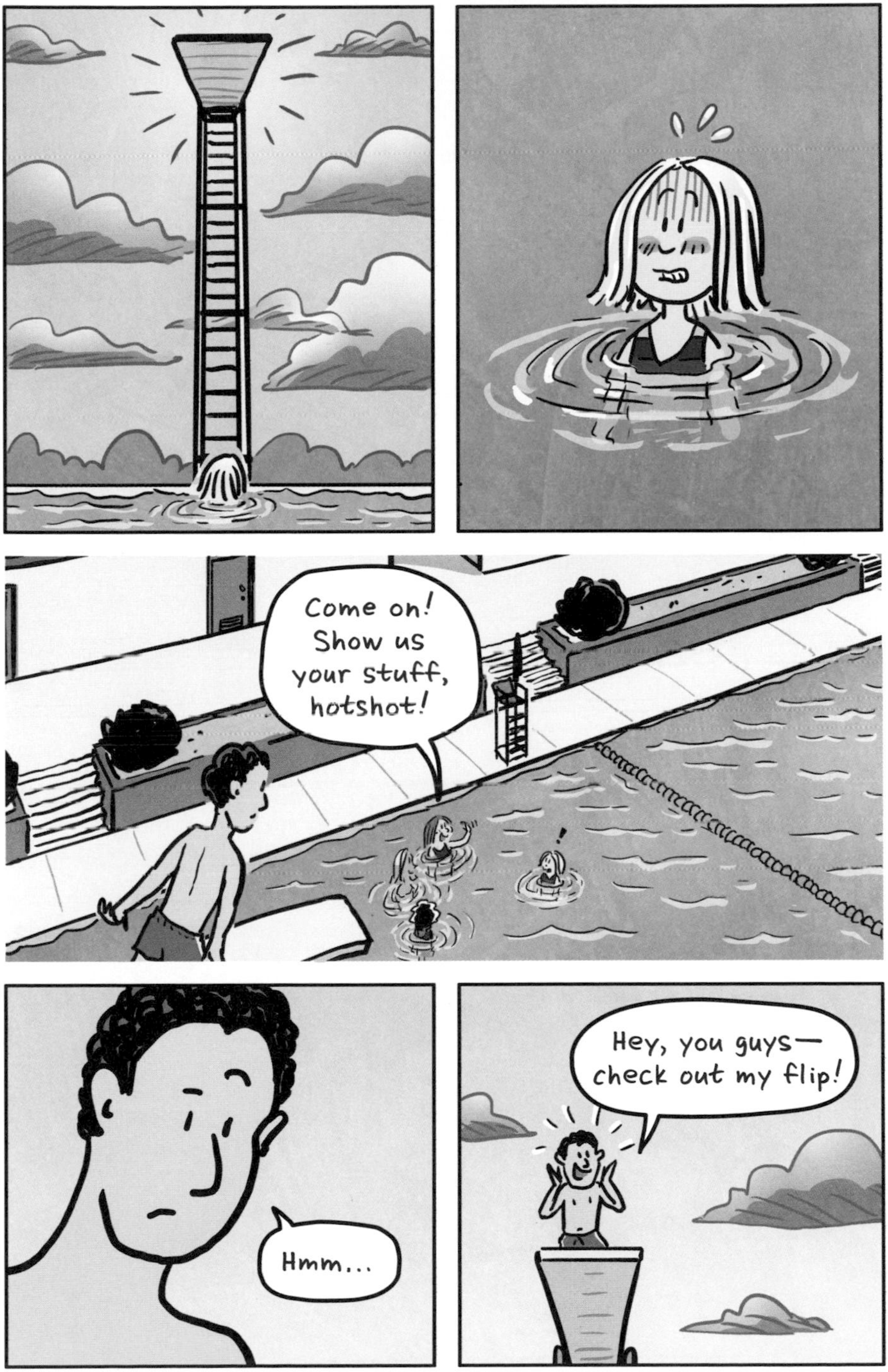
Come on! Show us your stuff, hotshot!
Hmm...
Hey, you guys— check out my flip!

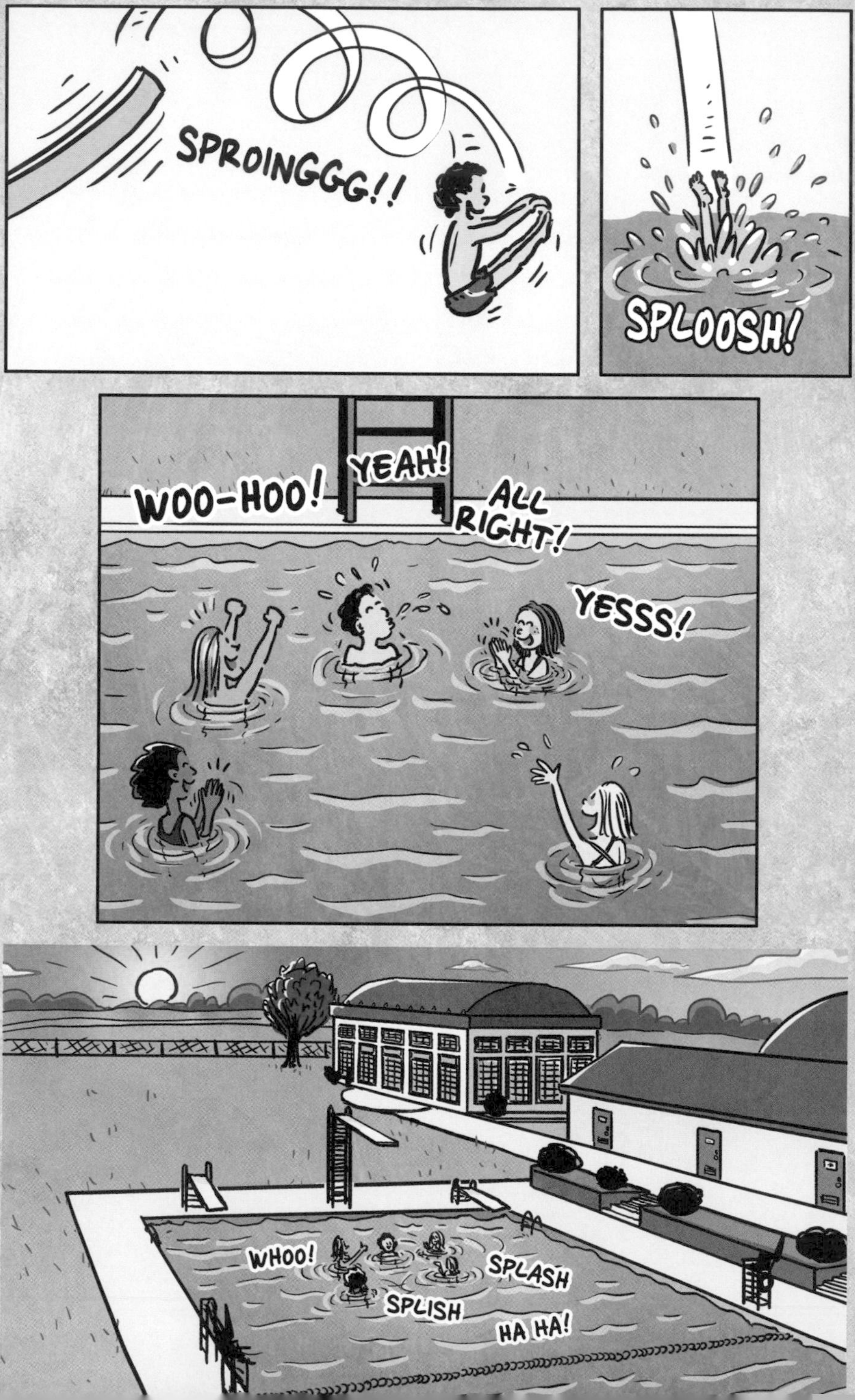
SPROINGGG!!
SPLOOSH!
WOO-HOO!
YEAH!
ALL RIGHT!
YESSS!
WHOO!
SPLASH
SPLISH
HA HA!

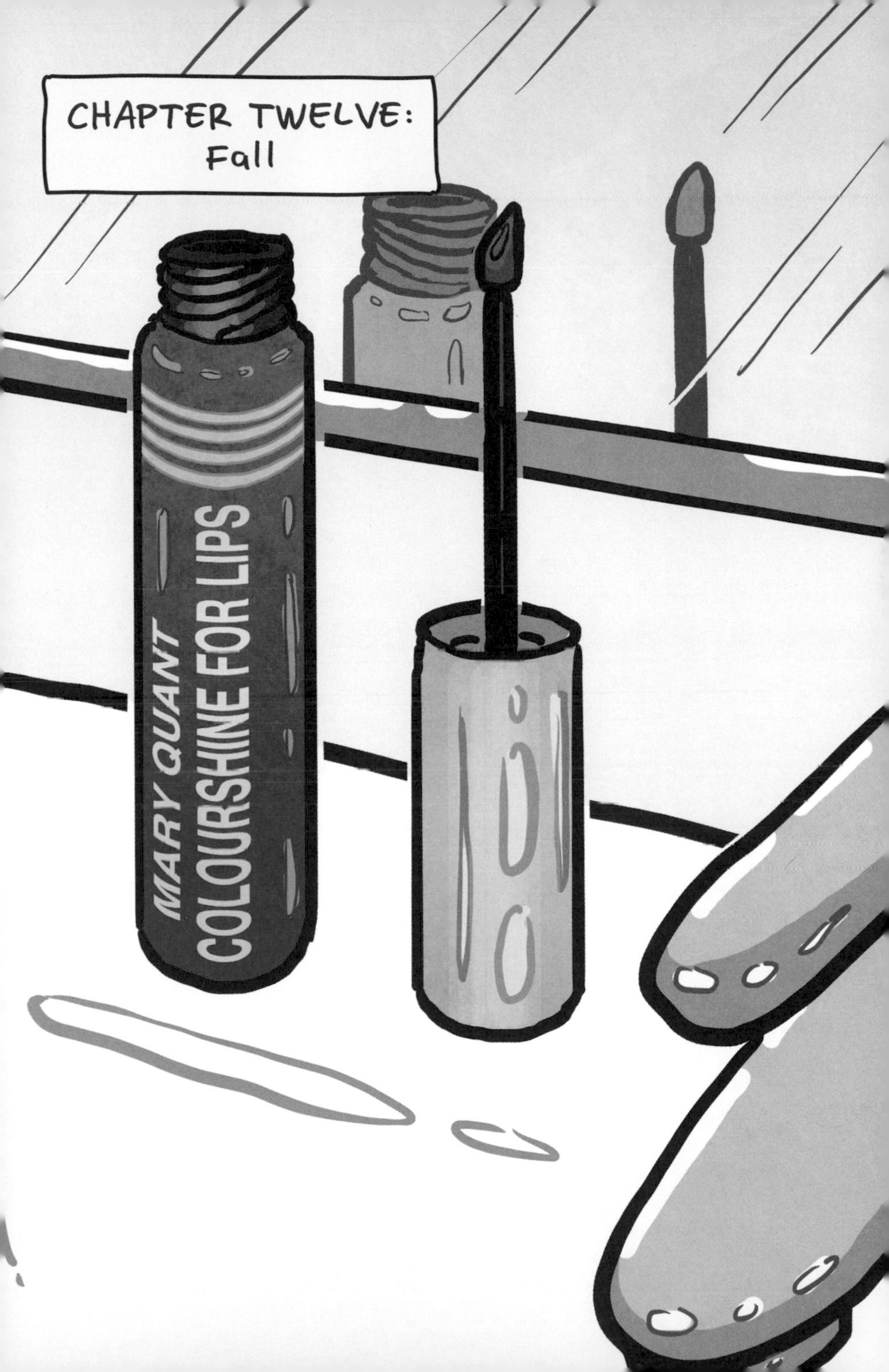
CHAPTER TWELVE:
Fall
MARY QUANT
COLOURSHINE FOR LIPS

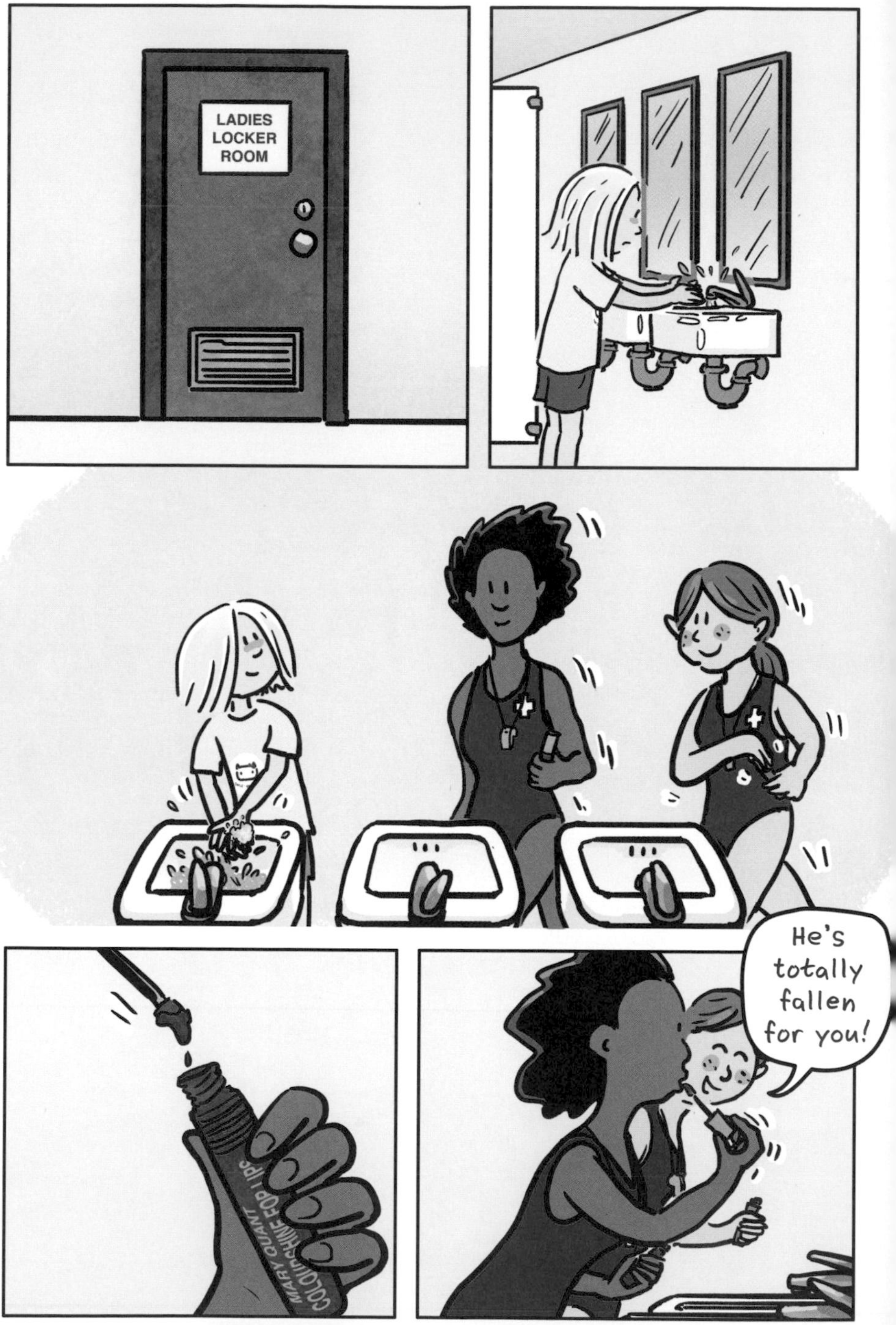
LADIES
LOCKER
ROOM
MARY QUANT
He's totally fallen for you!

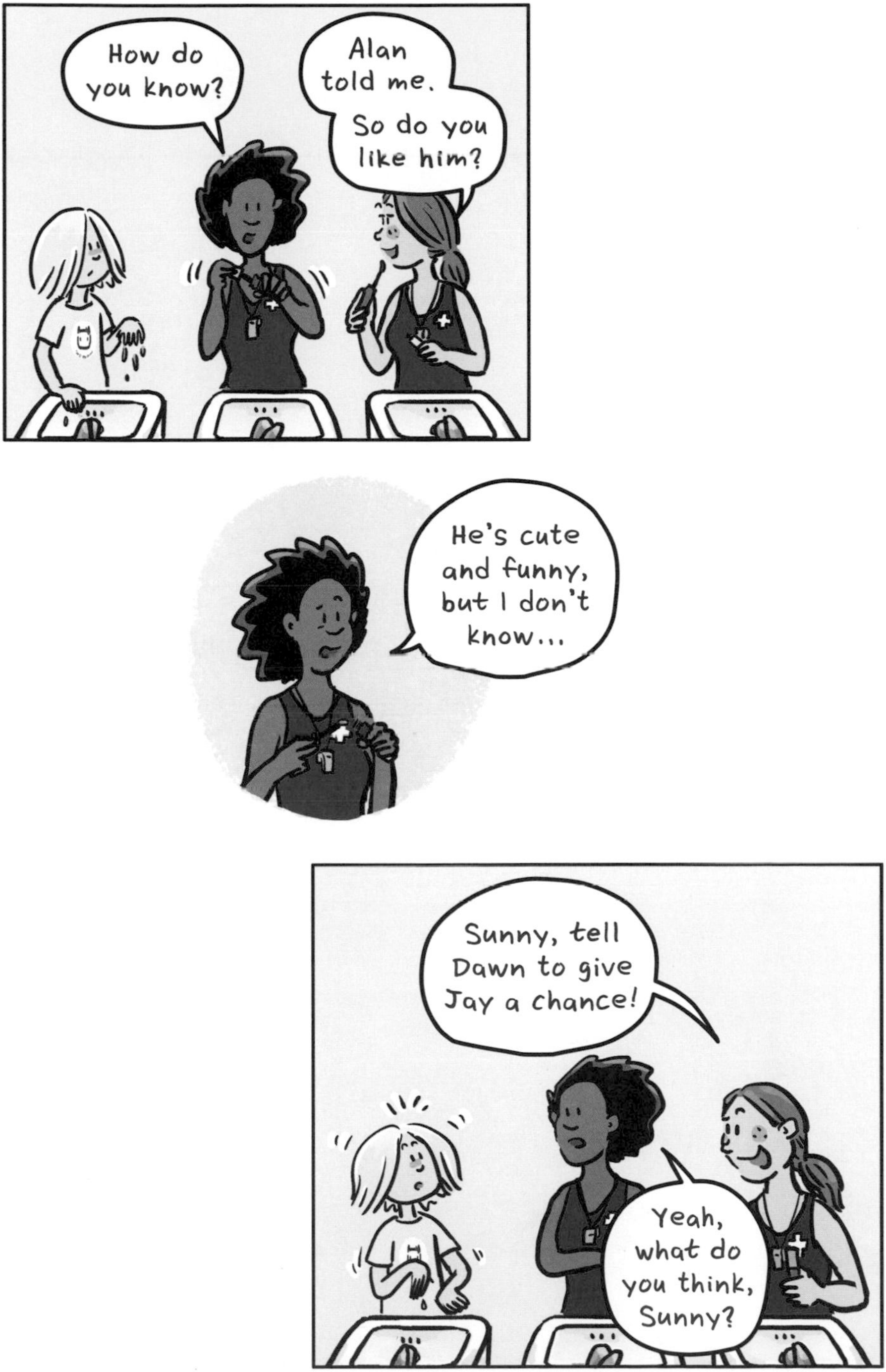
How do you know?
Alan told me.
So do you like him?
He's cute and funny, but I don't know...
Sunny, tell Dawn to give Jay a chance!
Yeah, what do you think, Sunny?

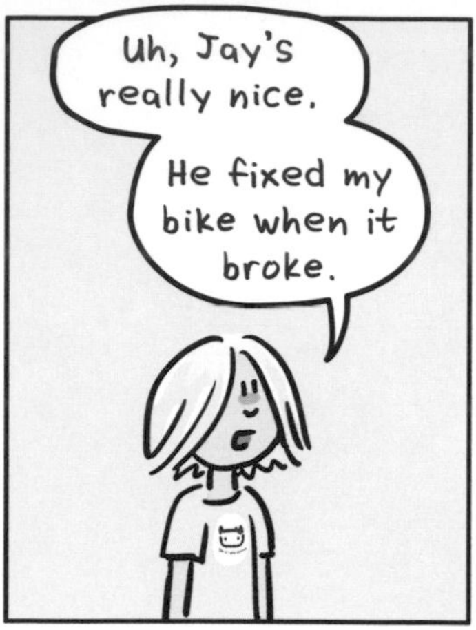
Uh, Jay's really nice.
He fixed my bike when it broke.

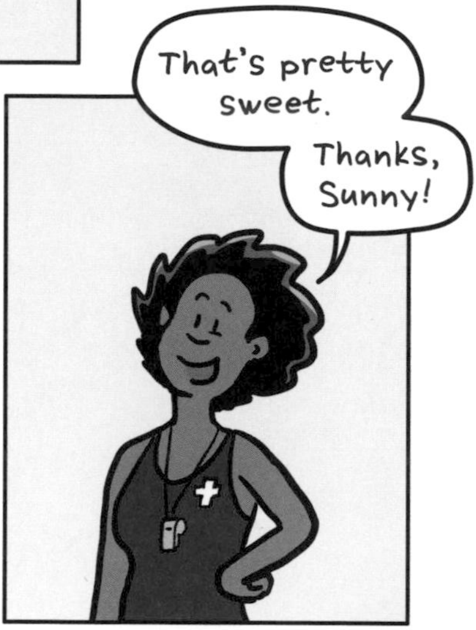
That's pretty sweet.
Thanks, Sunny!

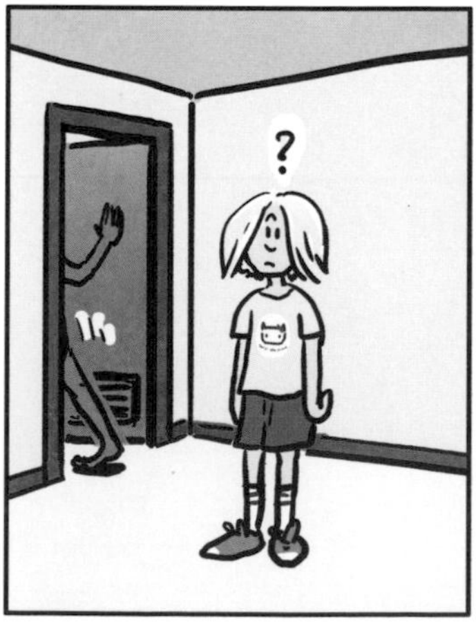
?

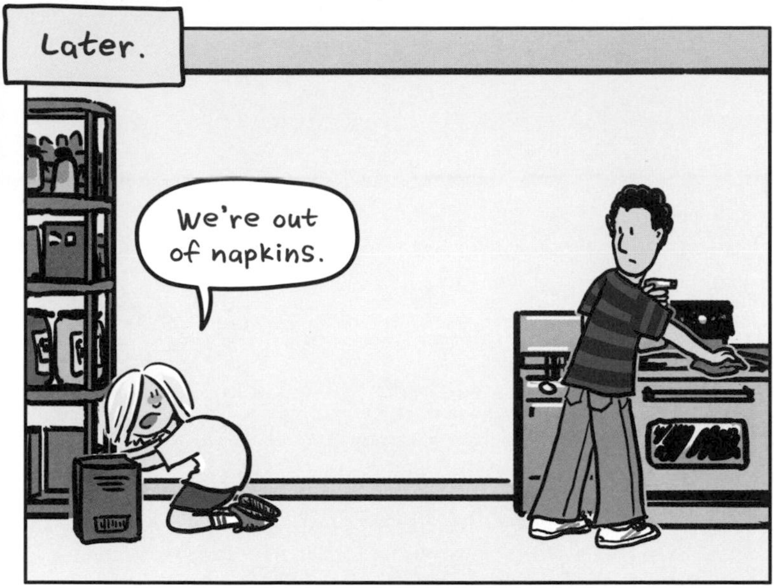
Later.
We're out of napkins.

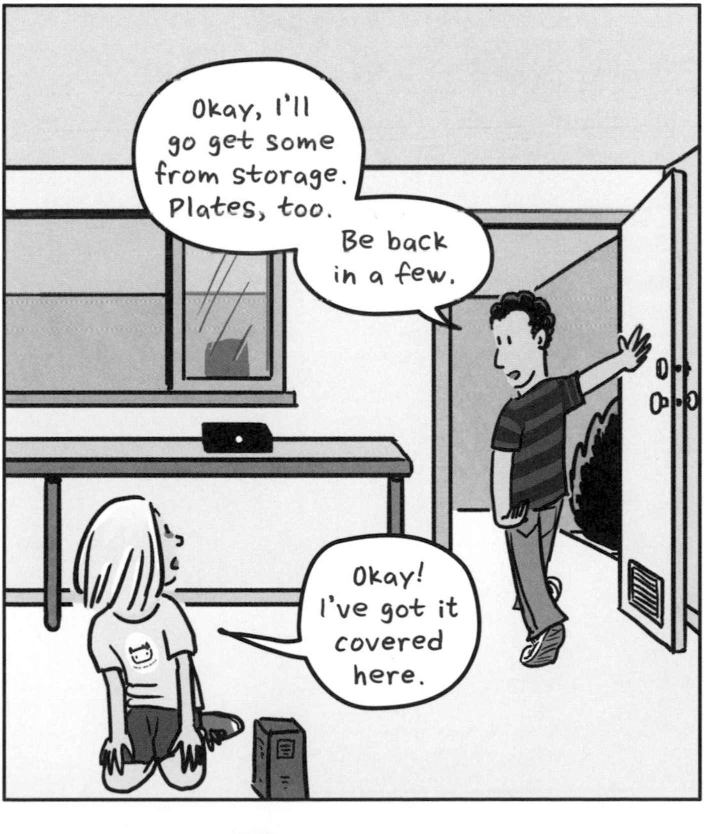
Okay, I'll go get some from storage. Plates, too.
Be back in a few.
Okay! I've got it covered here.

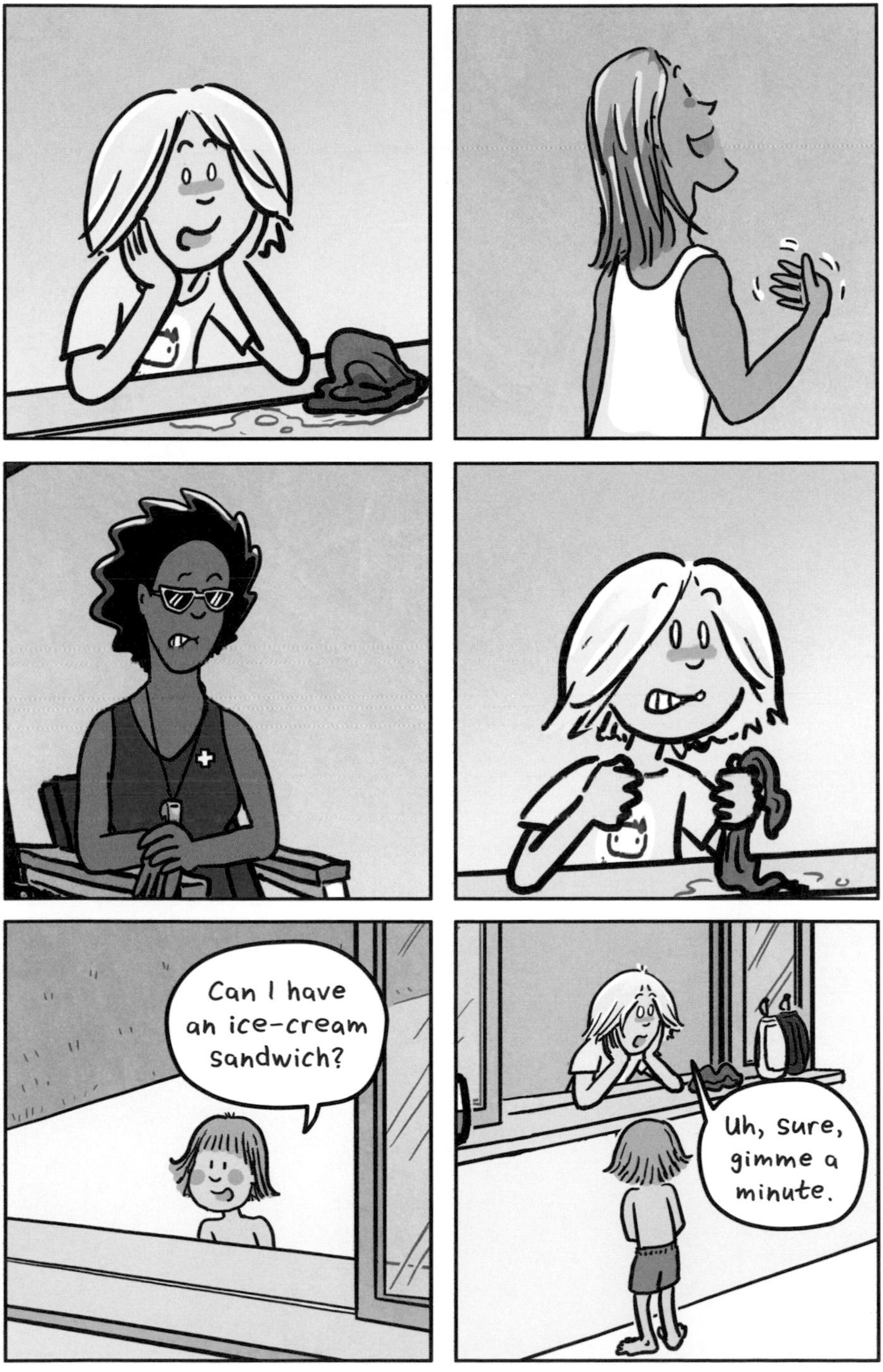

Can I have an ice-cream sandwich?
Uh, sure, gimme a minute.

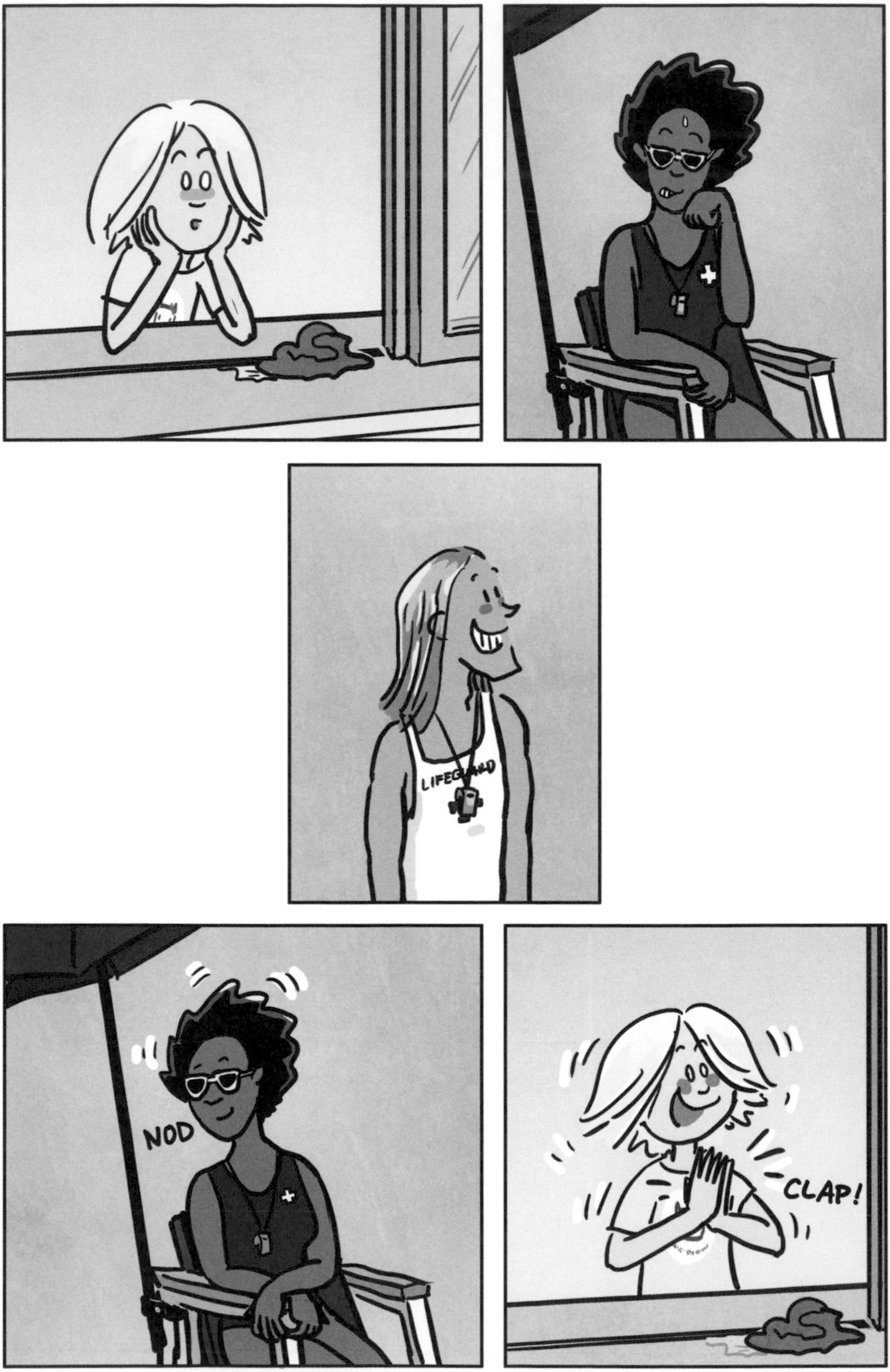
LIFEGUARD
NOD
CLAP!

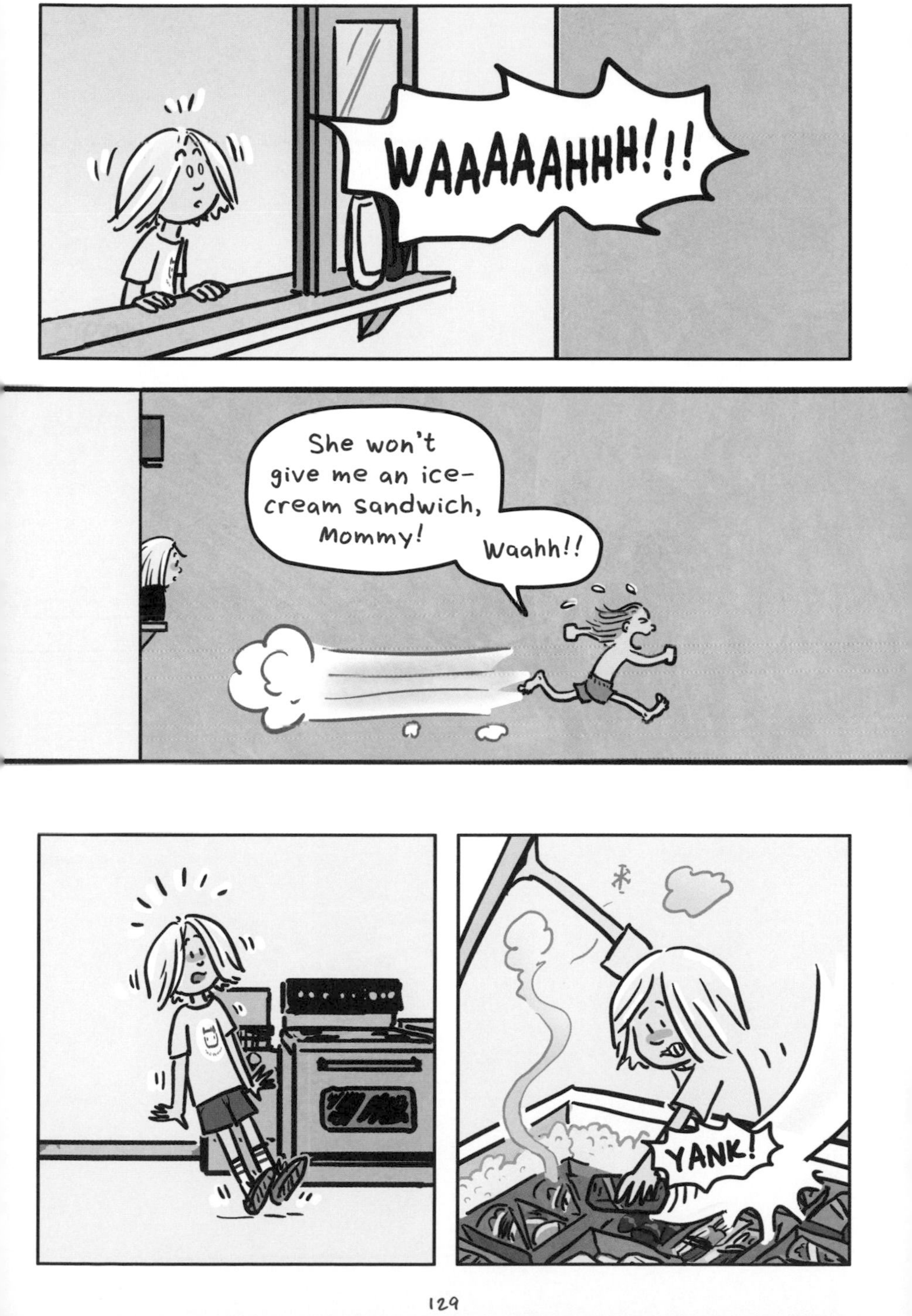
WAAAAAHHH!!!
She won't give me an ice-cream sandwich, Mommy!
Waahh!!
YANK!

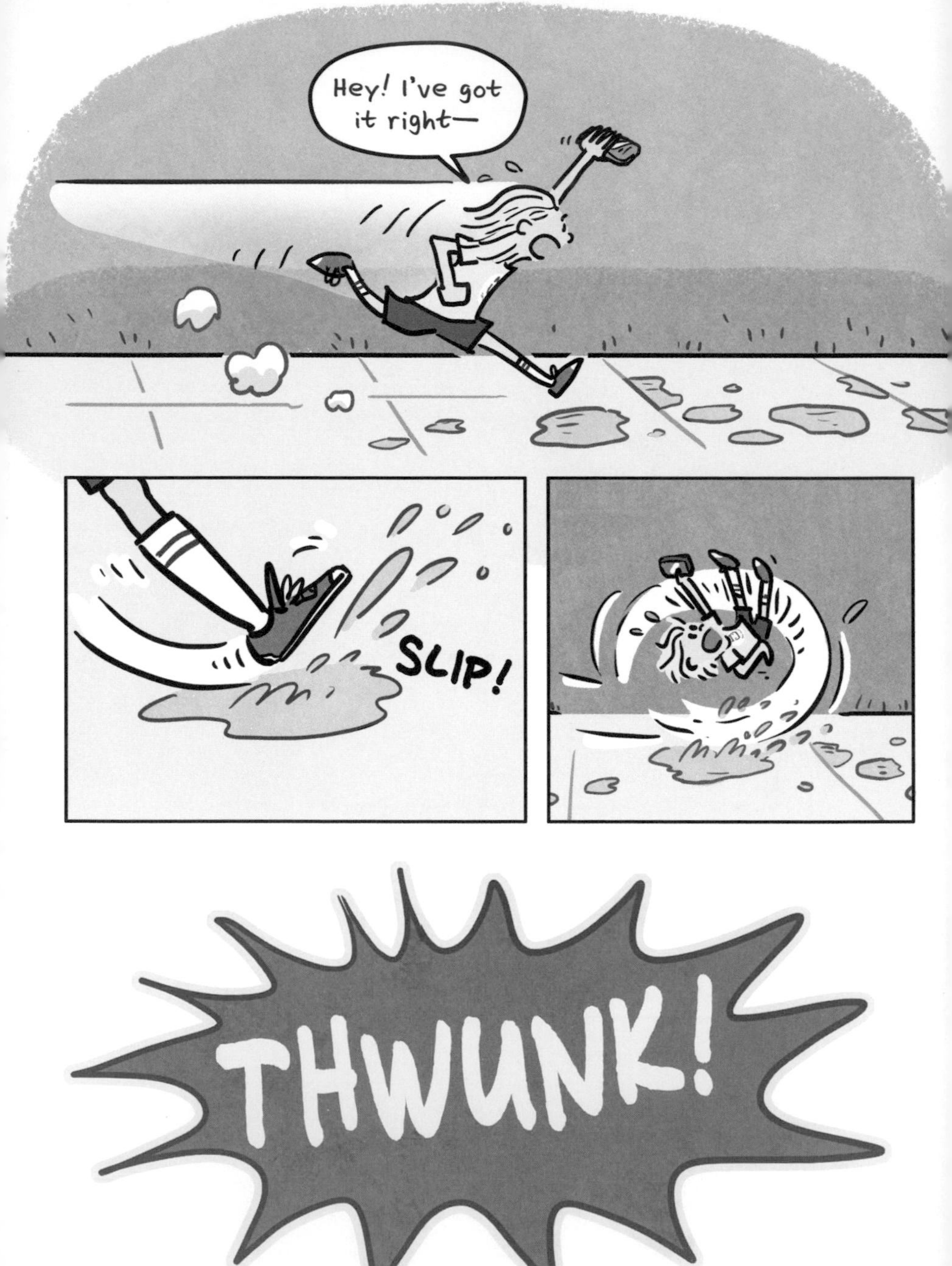
Hey! I've got it right—
SLIP!
THWUNK!

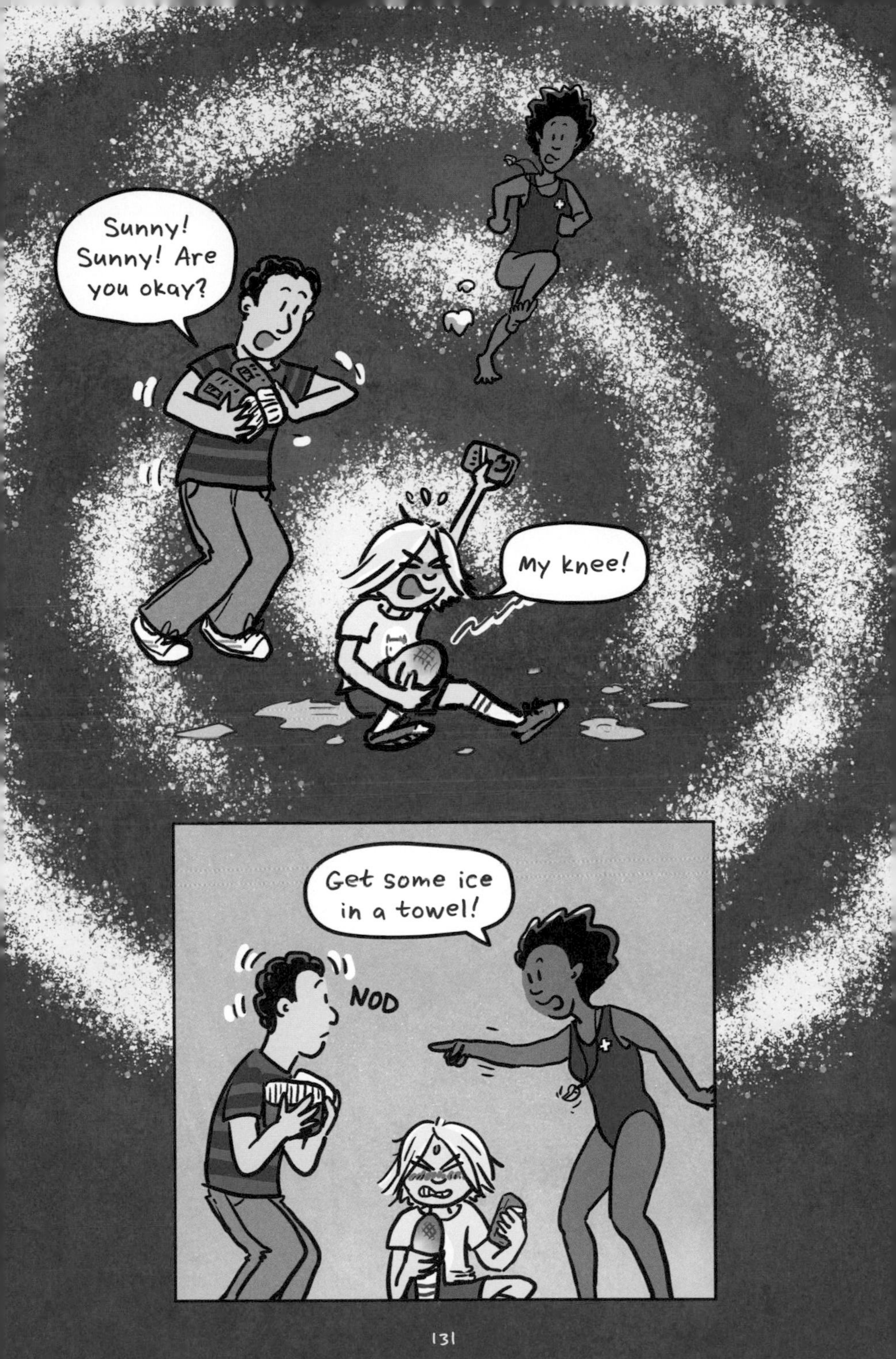
Sunny! Sunny! Are you okay?
My knee!
Get some ice in a towel!
NOD

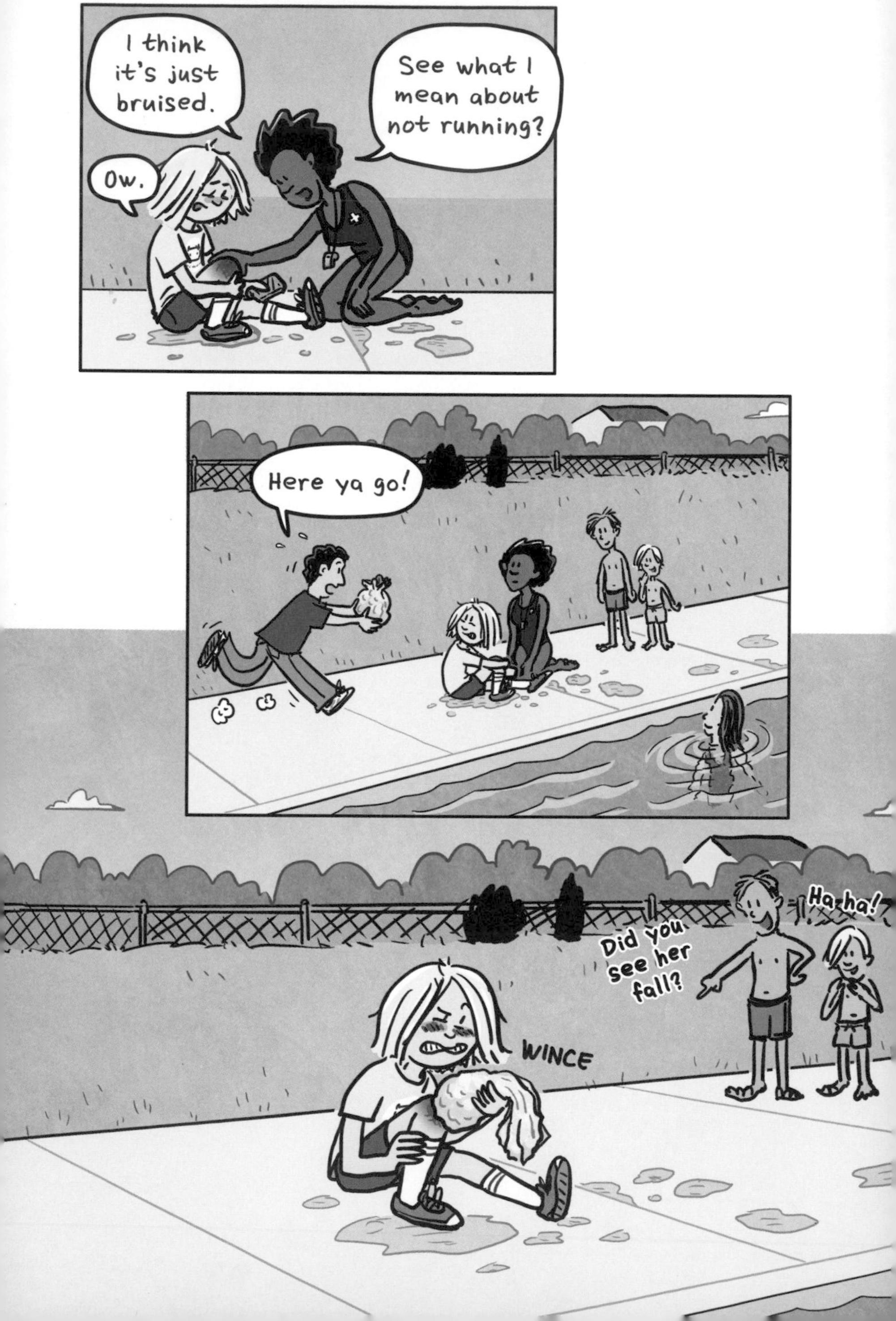
I think it's just bruised.
Ow.
See what I mean about not running?
Here ya go!
Did you see her fall?
Ha ha!
WINCE

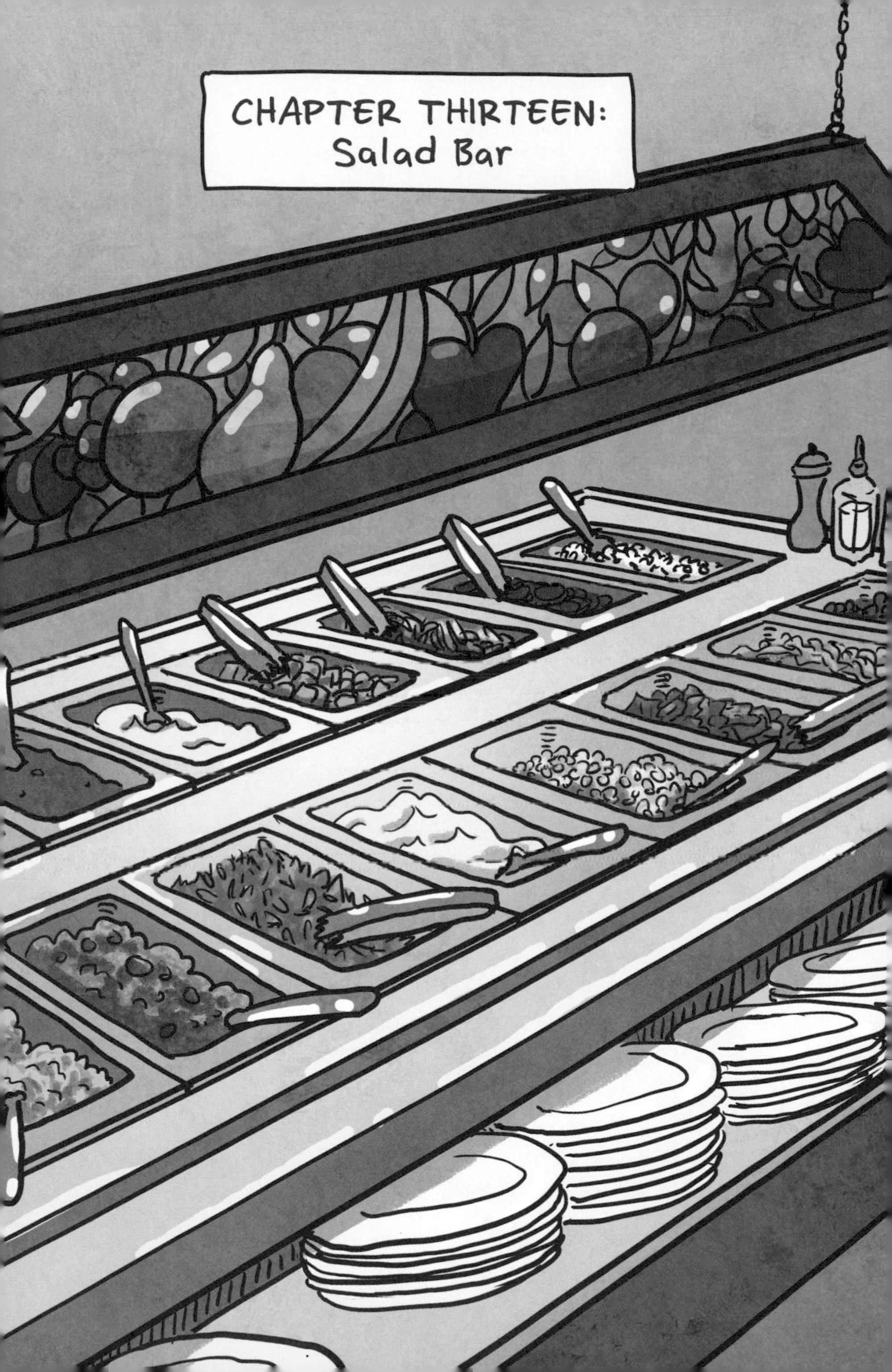
CHAPTER THIRTEEN:
Salad Bar

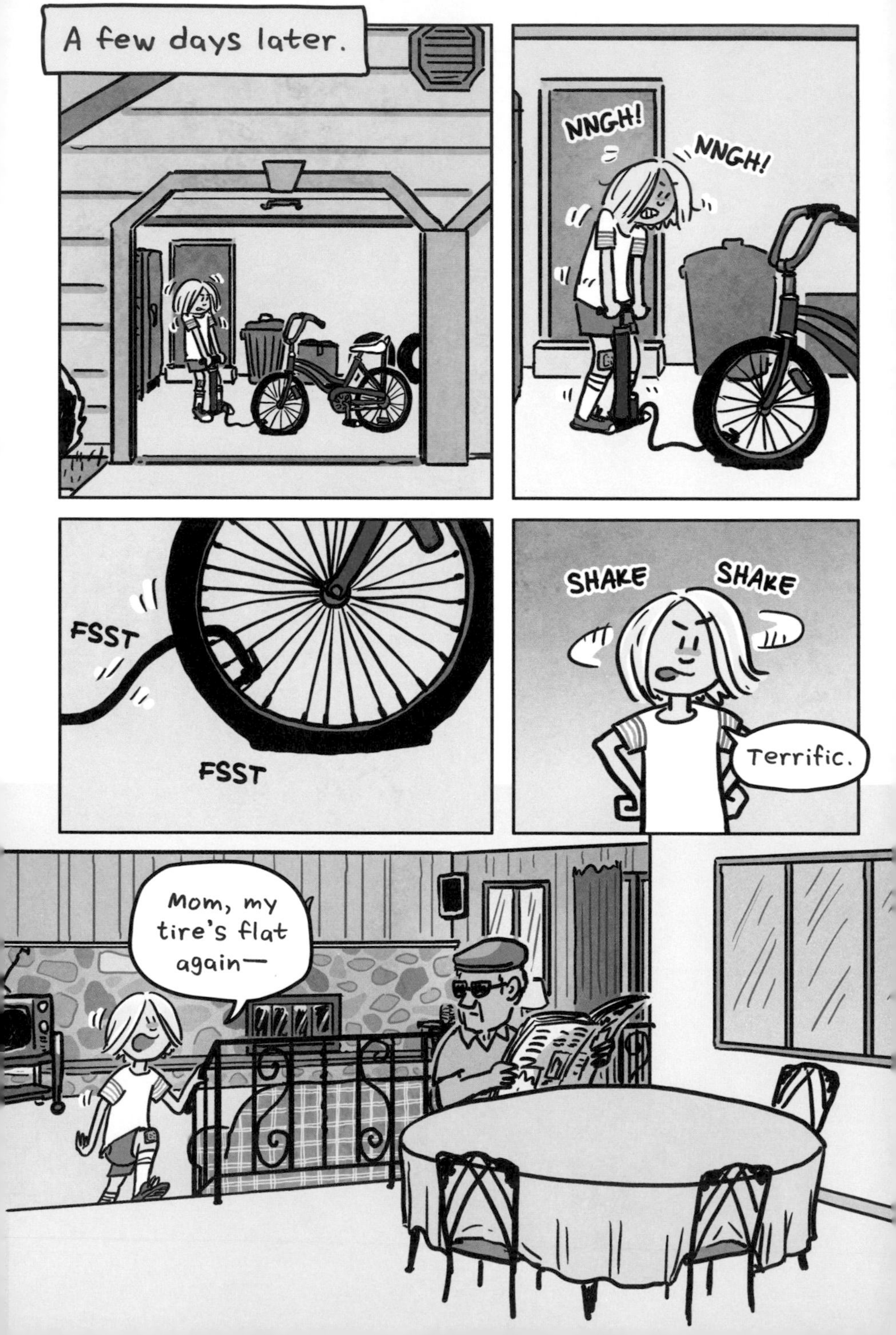
A few days later.
NNGH!
NNGH!
FSST
FSST
SHAKE
SHAKE
Terrific.
Mom, my tire's flat again—

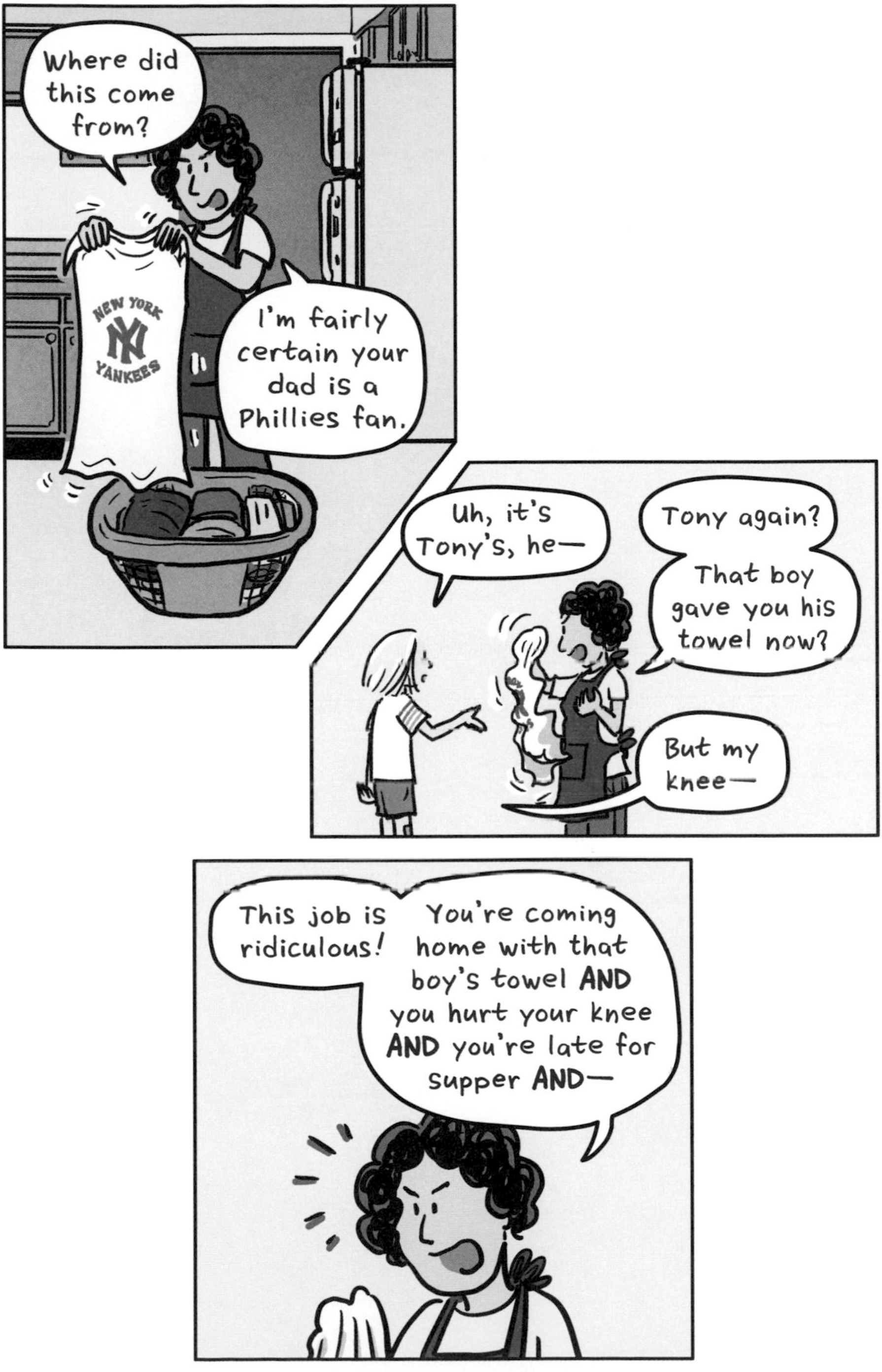
Where did this come from?
NEW YORK NY YANKEES
I'm fairly certain your dad is a Phillies fan.
Uh, it's Tony's, he—
Tony again?
That boy gave you his towel now?
But my knee—
This job is ridiculous!
You're coming home with that boy's towel **AND** you hurt your knee **AND** you're late for supper **AND**—

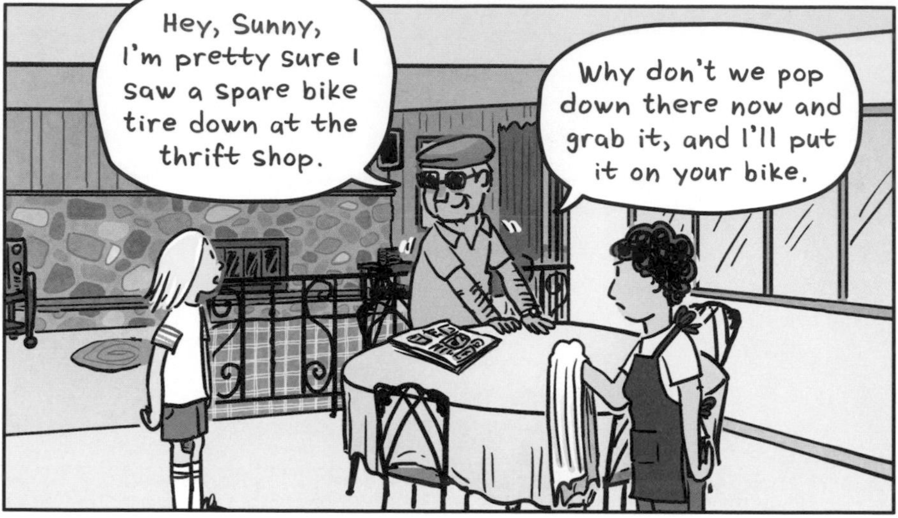
Hey, Sunny, I'm pretty sure I saw a spare bike tire down at the thrift shop.
Why don't we pop down there now and grab it, and I'll put it on your bike.

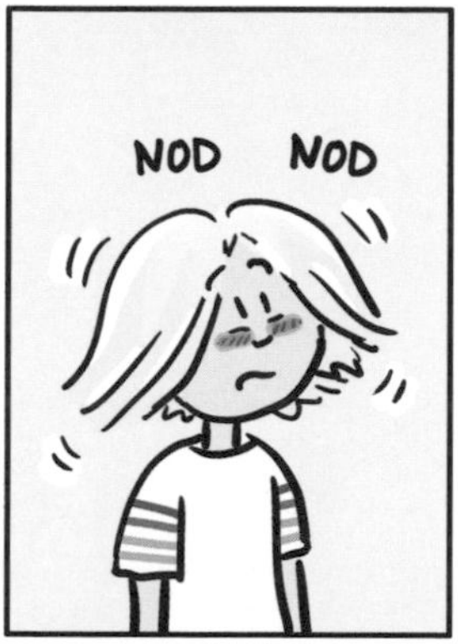
NOD NOD

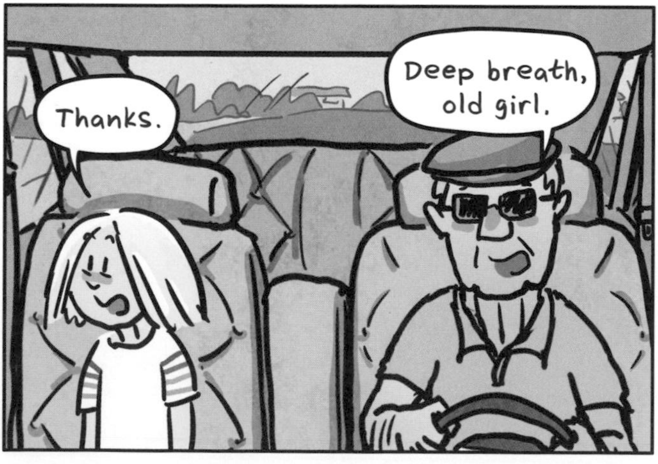
Deep breath, old girl.
Thanks.

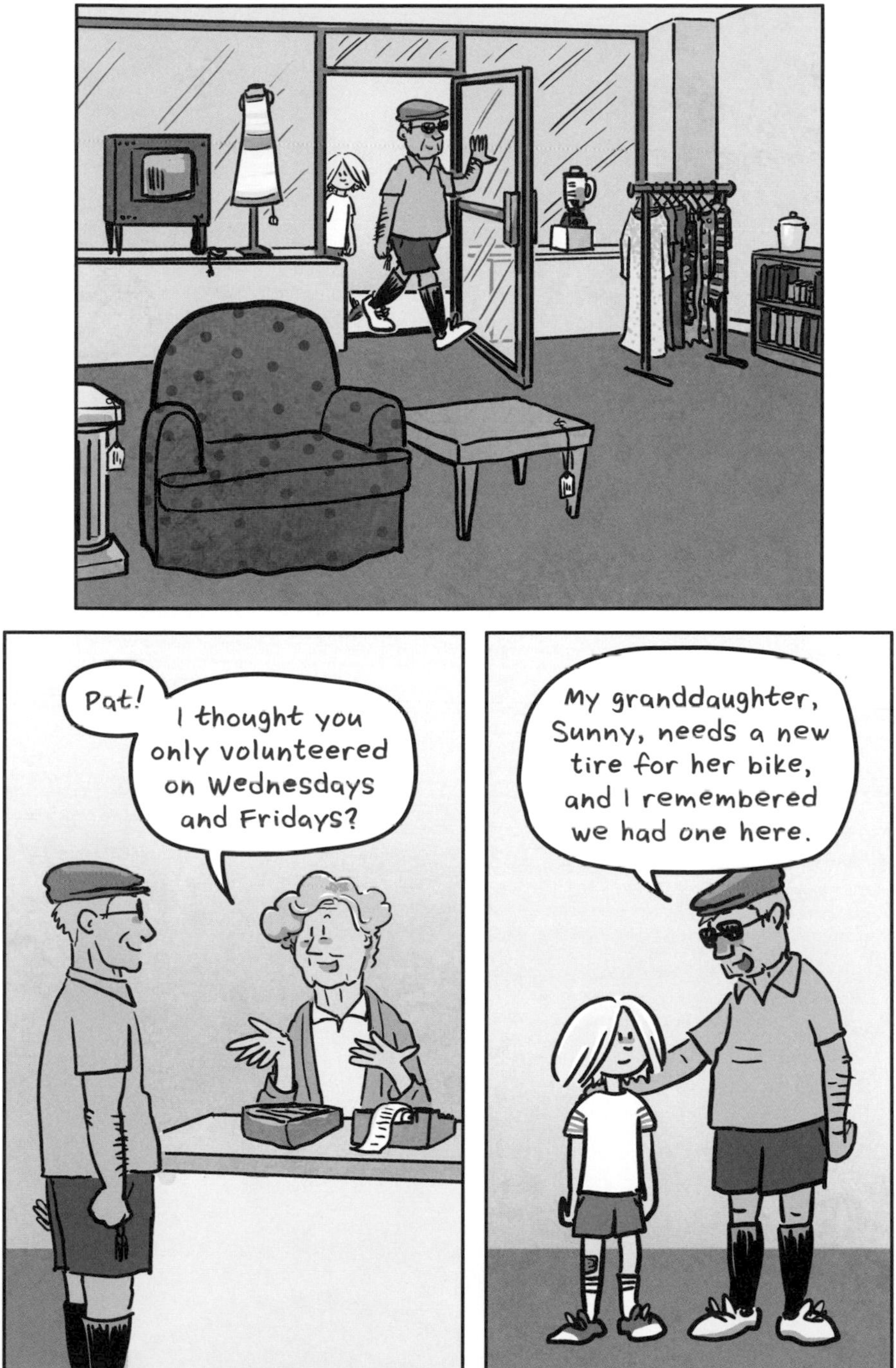
Pat!
I thought you only volunteered on Wednesdays and Fridays?
My granddaughter, Sunny, needs a new tire for her bike, and I remembered we had one here.

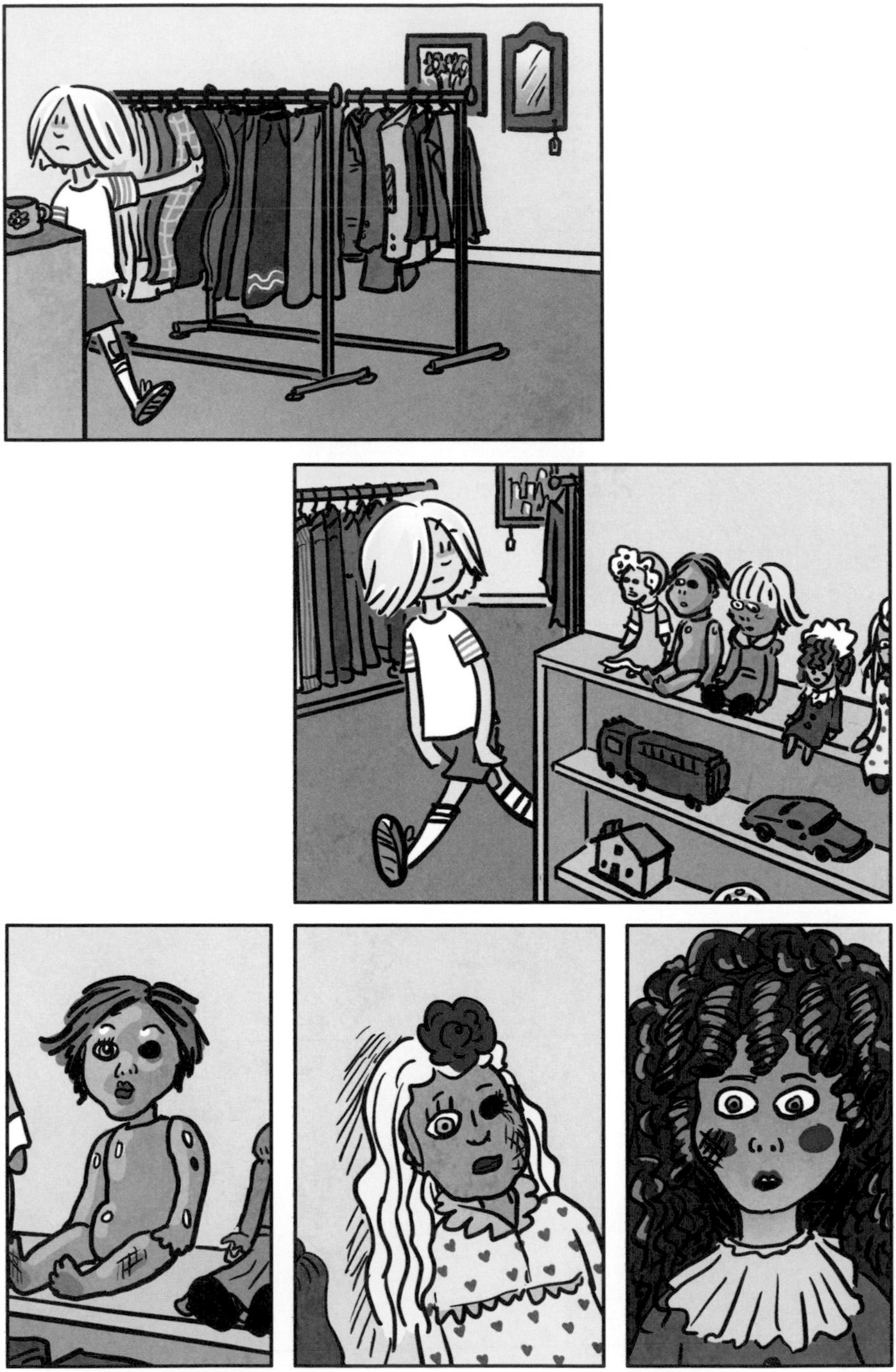

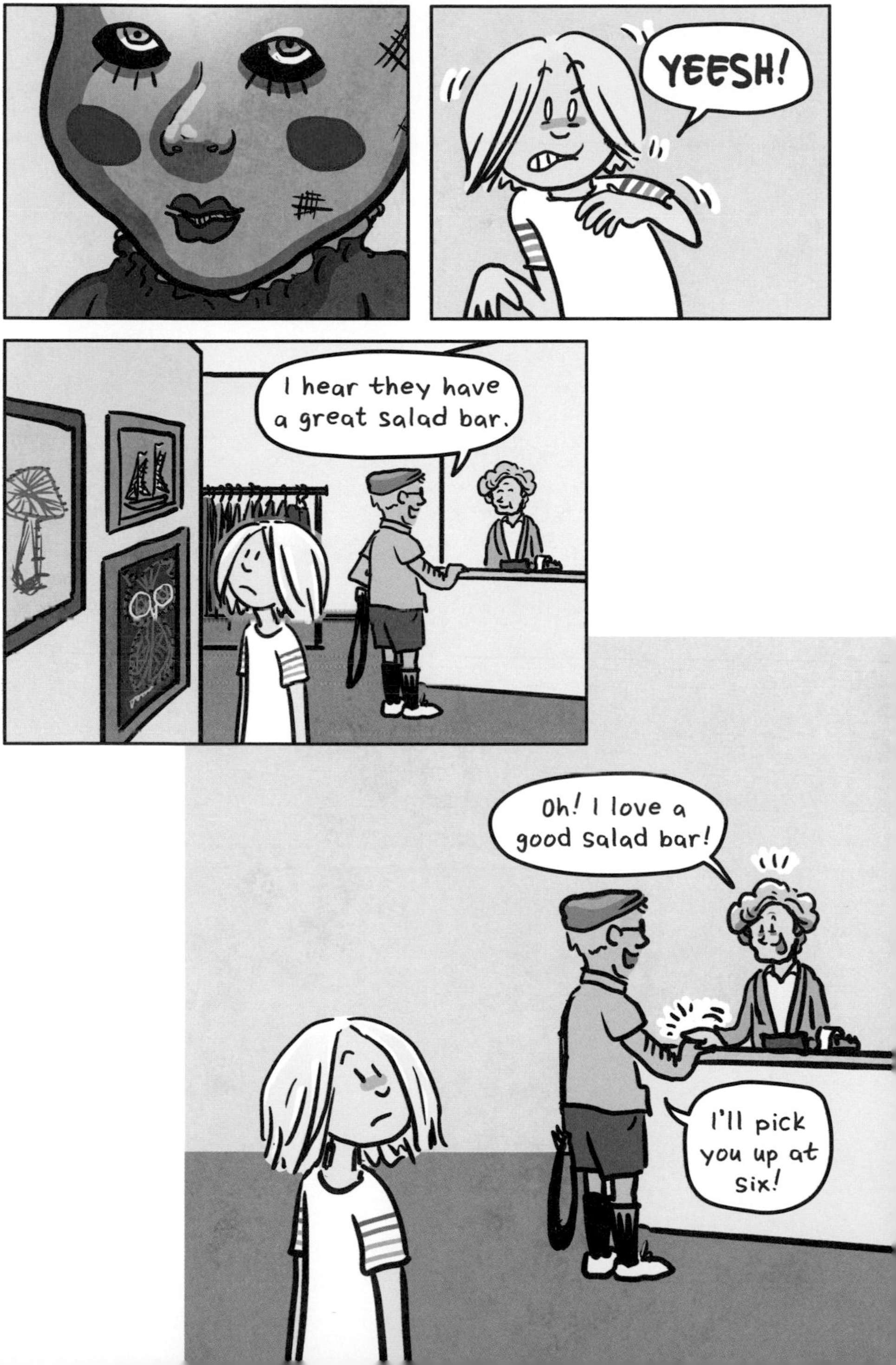
YEESH!
I hear they have a great salad bar.
Oh! I love a good salad bar!
I'll pick you up at six!

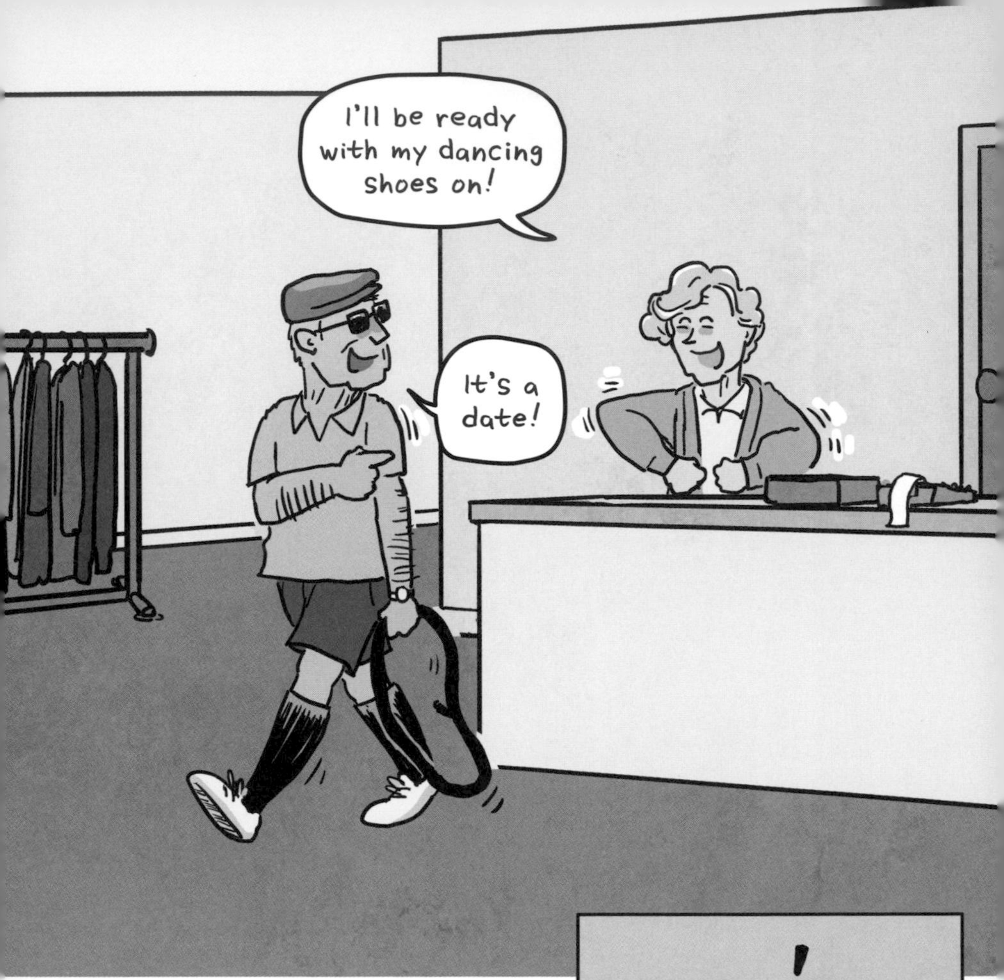
I'll be ready with my dancing shoes on!
It's a date!

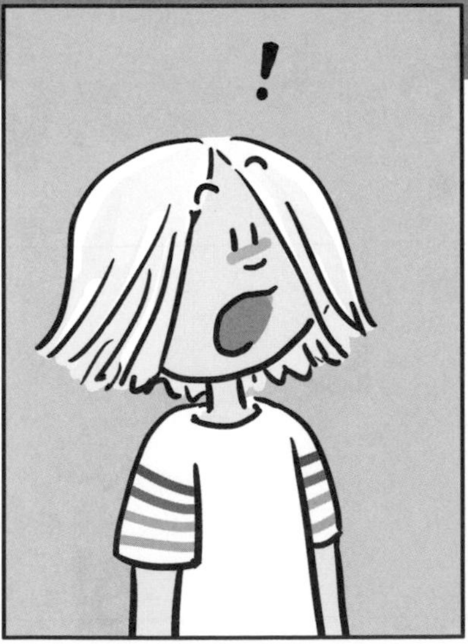
!

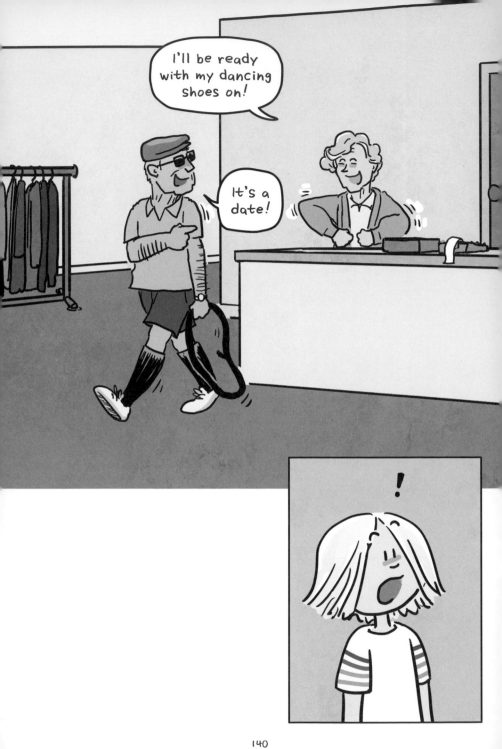

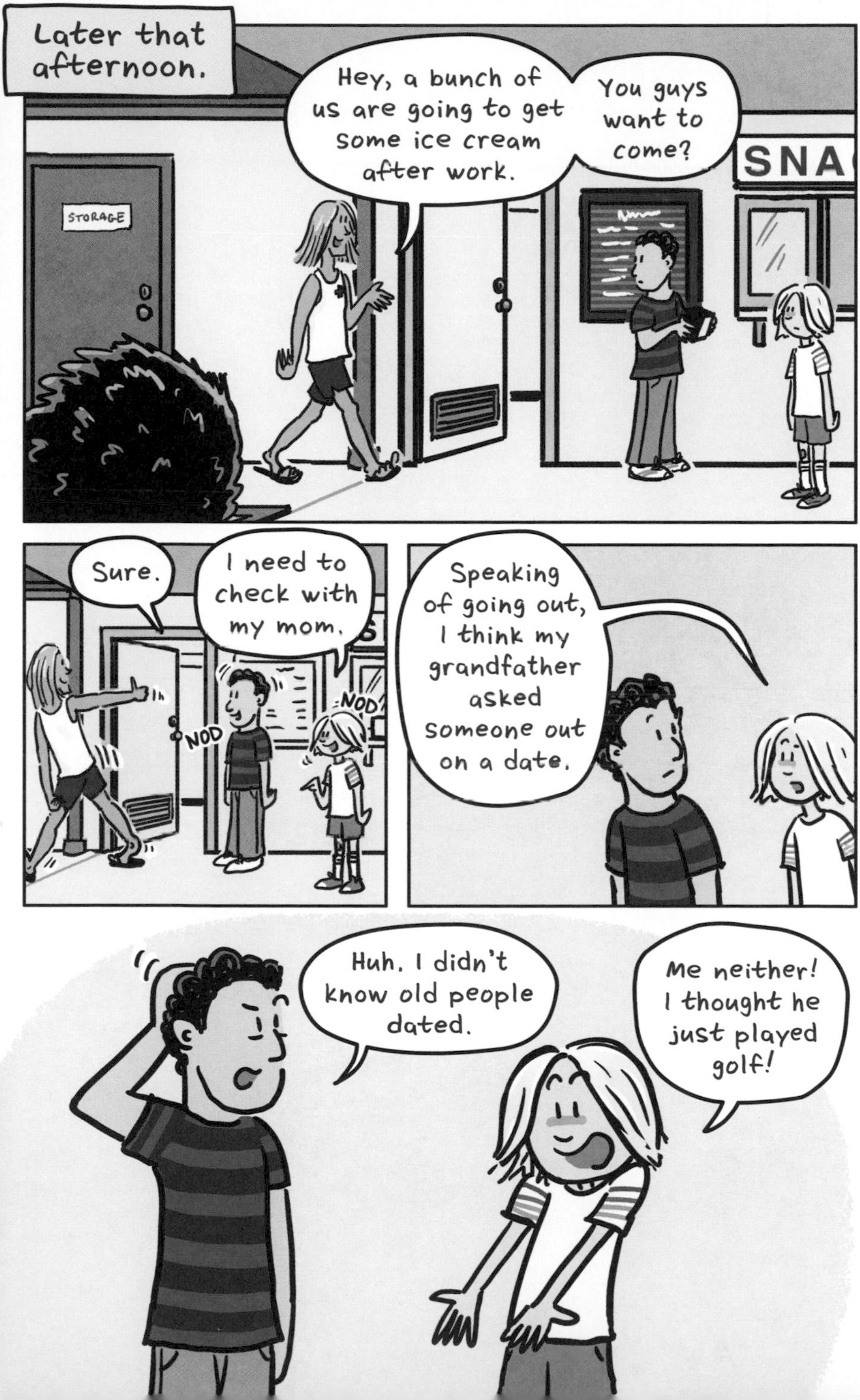
Later that afternoon.
Hey, a bunch of us are going to get some ice cream after work.
You guys want to come?
STORAGE
SNA
Sure.
I need to check with my mom.
NOD
NOD
Speaking of going out, I think my grandfather asked someone out on a date.
Huh. I didn't know old people dated.
Me neither! I thought he just played golf!

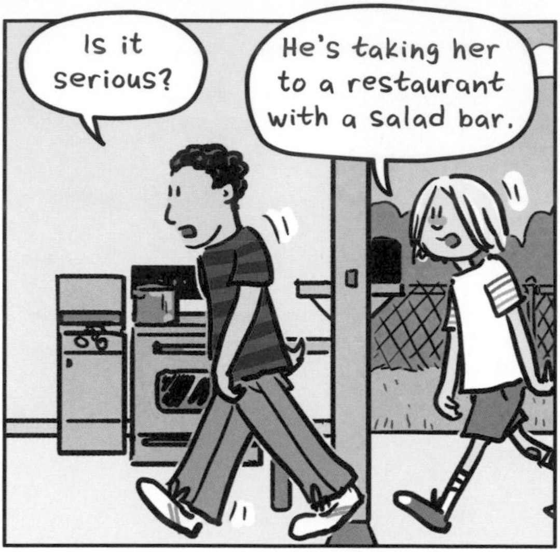
Is it serious?
He's taking her to a restaurant with a salad bar.

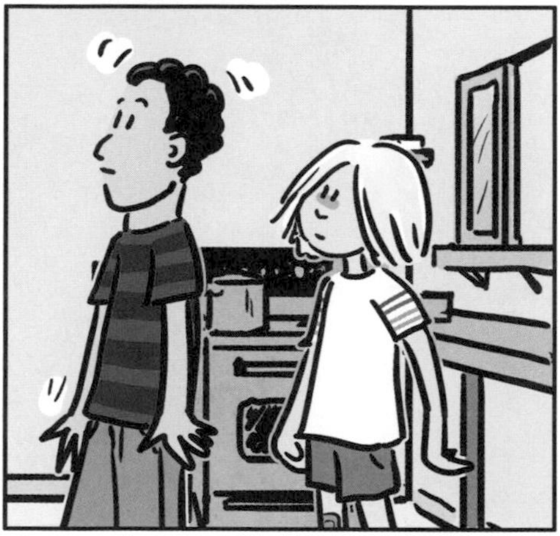

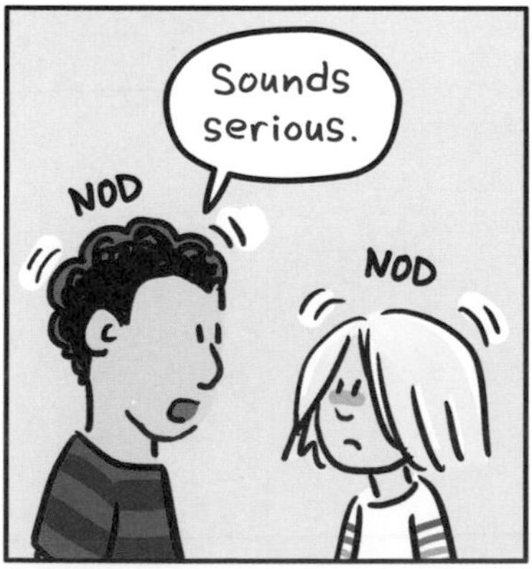
Sounds serious.
NOD
NOD

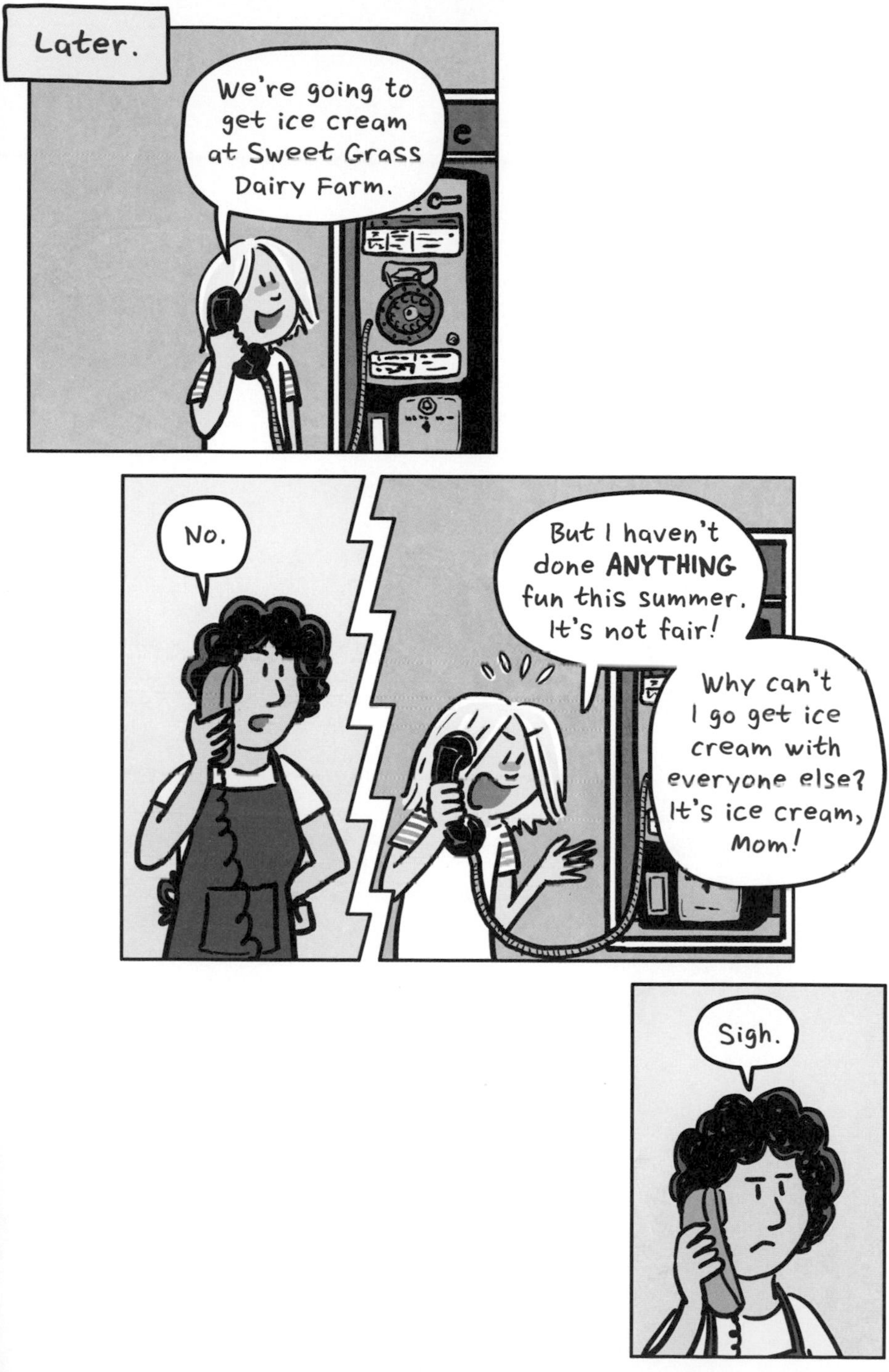
Later.
We're going to get ice cream at Sweet Grass Dairy Farm.
No.
But I haven't done **ANYTHING** fun this summer. It's not fair!
Why can't I go get ice cream with everyone else? It's ice cream, Mom!
Sigh.

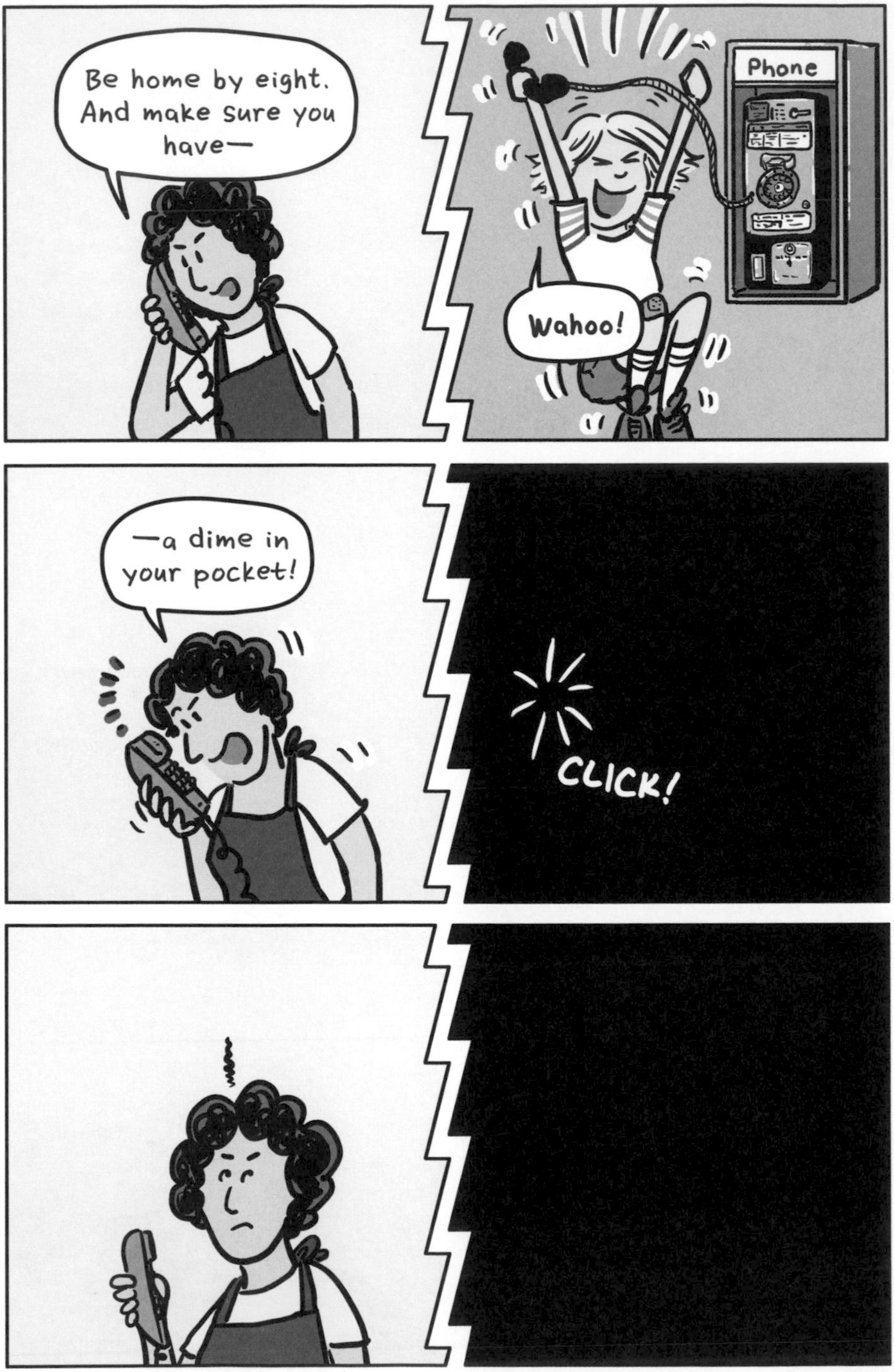
Be home by eight. And make sure you have—
Phone
Wahoo!
—a dime in your pocket!
CLICK!

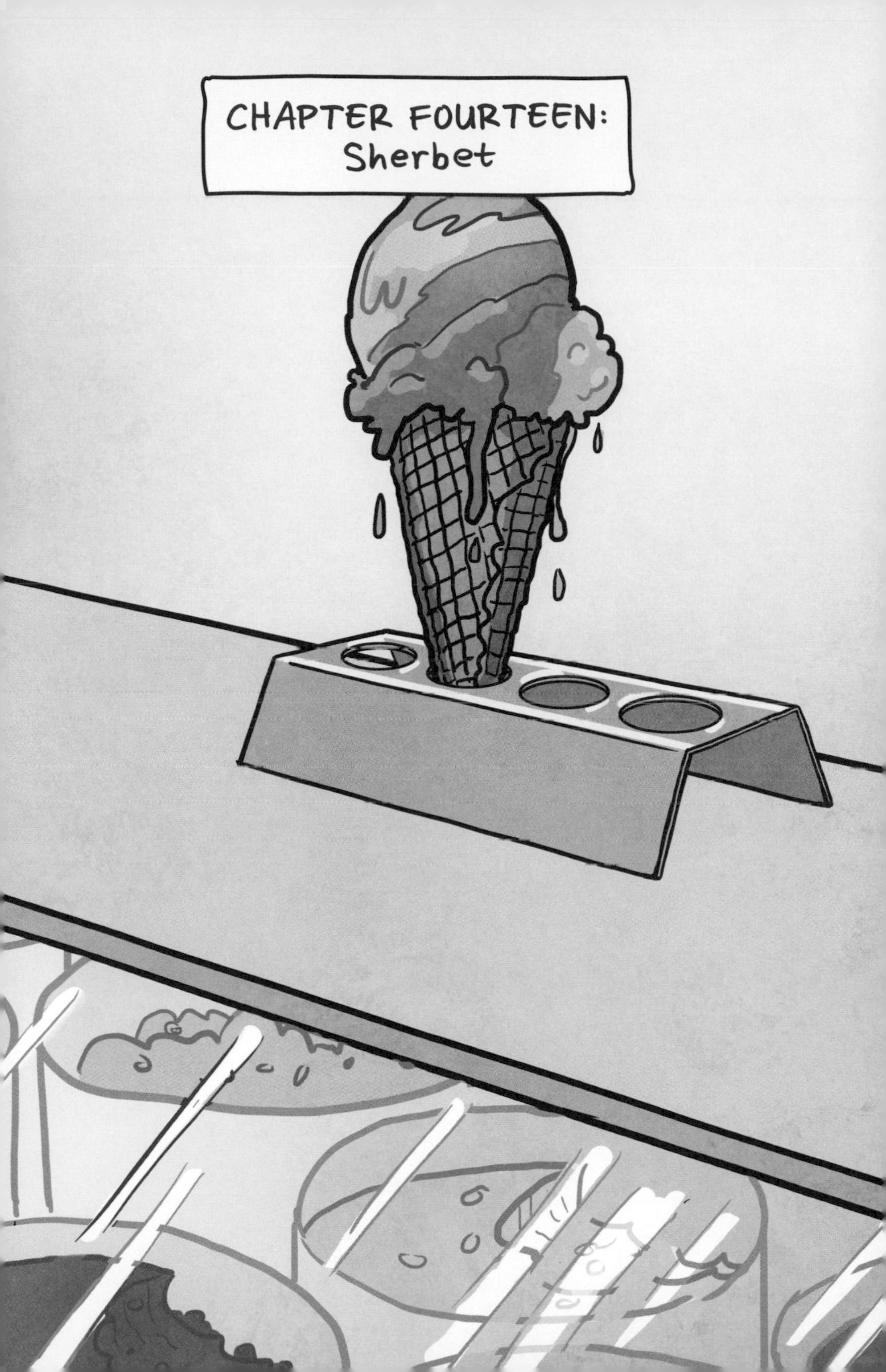
CHAPTER FOURTEEN:
Sherbet

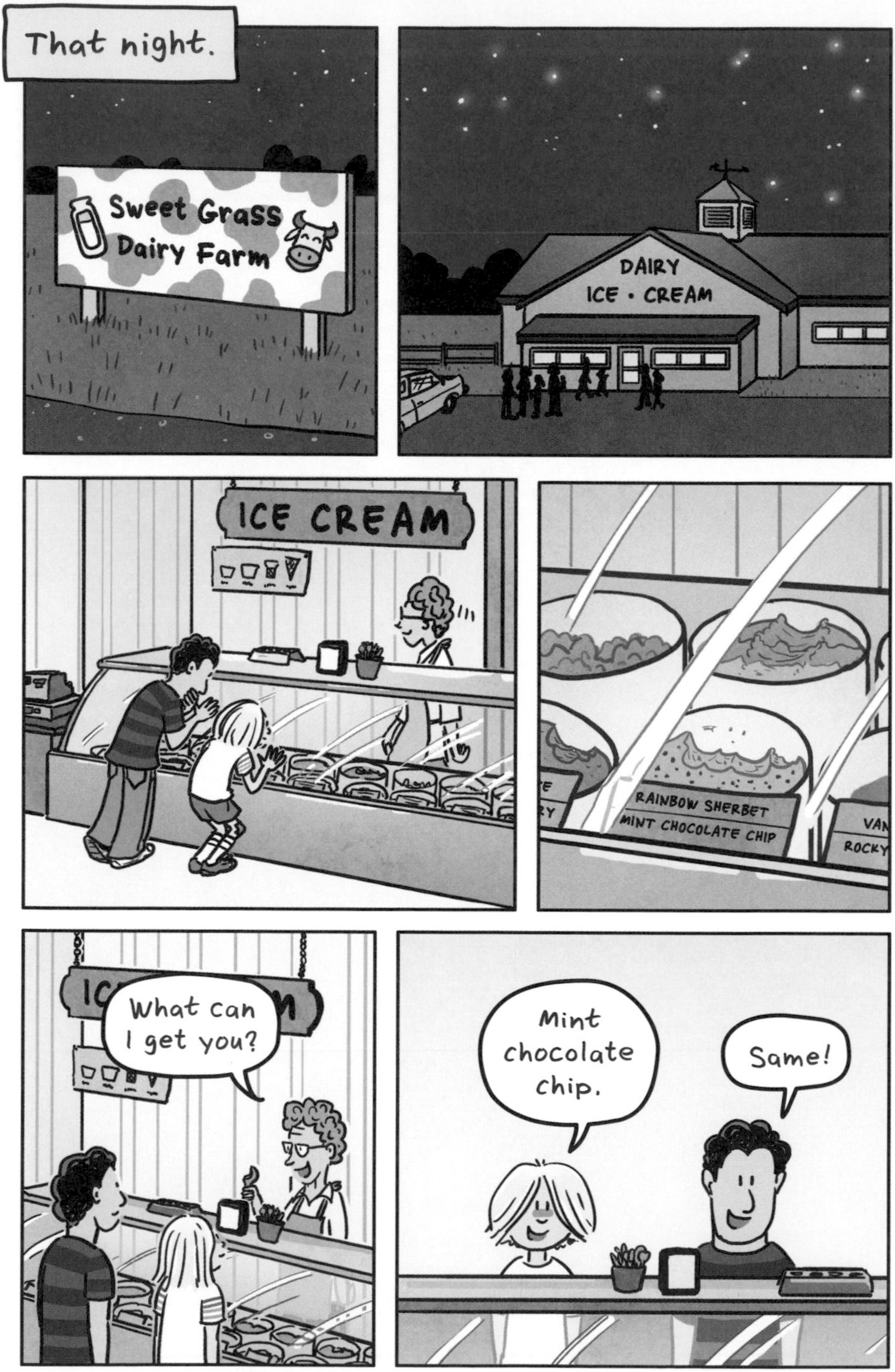
That night.
Sweet Grass Dairy Farm
DAIRY
ICE • CREAM
ICE CREAM
RAINBOW SHERBET
MINT CHOCOLATE CHIP
What can I get you?
Mint chocolate chip.
Same!

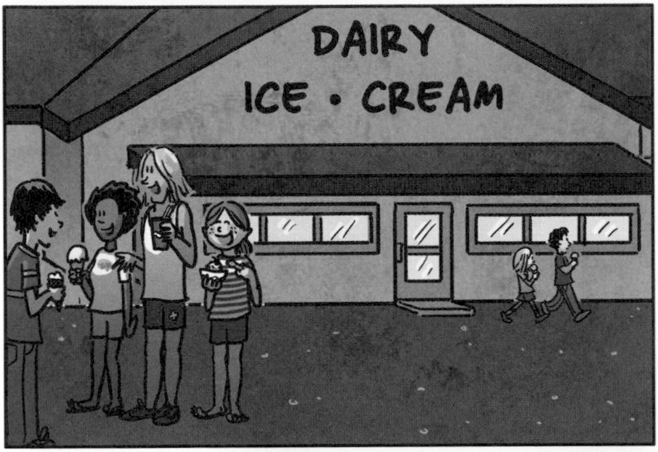
DAIRY
ICE • CREAM

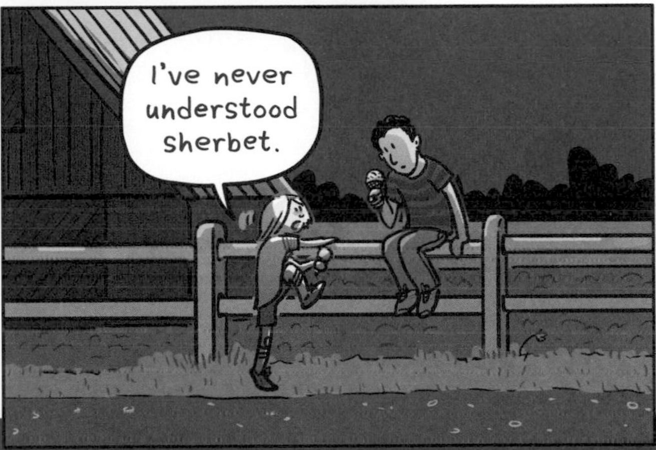
I've never understood sherbet.

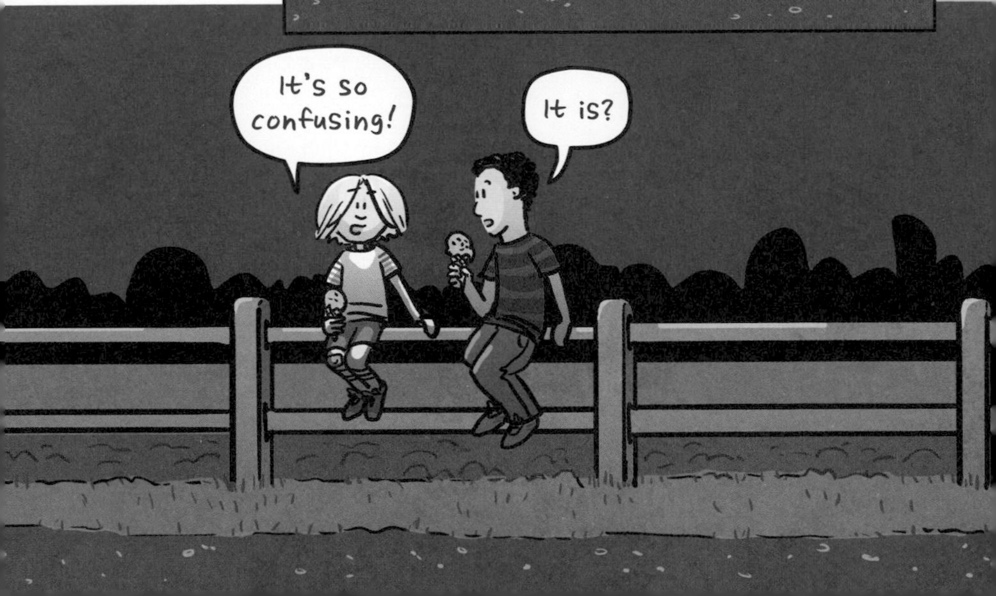
It's so confusing!
It is?

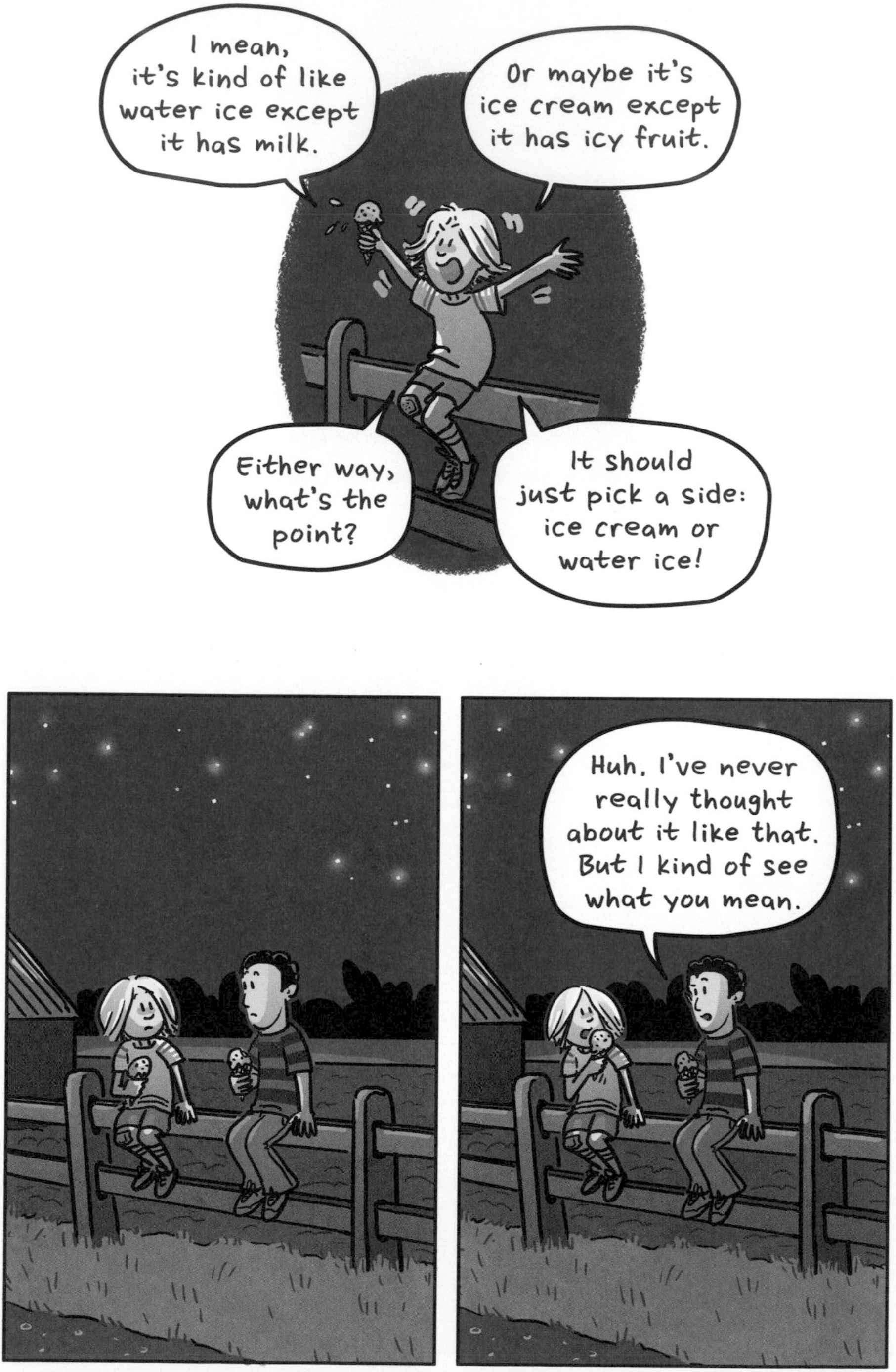
I mean, it's kind of like water ice except it has milk.
Or maybe it's ice cream except it has icy fruit.
Either way, what's the point?
It should just pick a side: ice cream or water ice!
Huh. I've never really thought about it like that. But I kind of see what you mean.

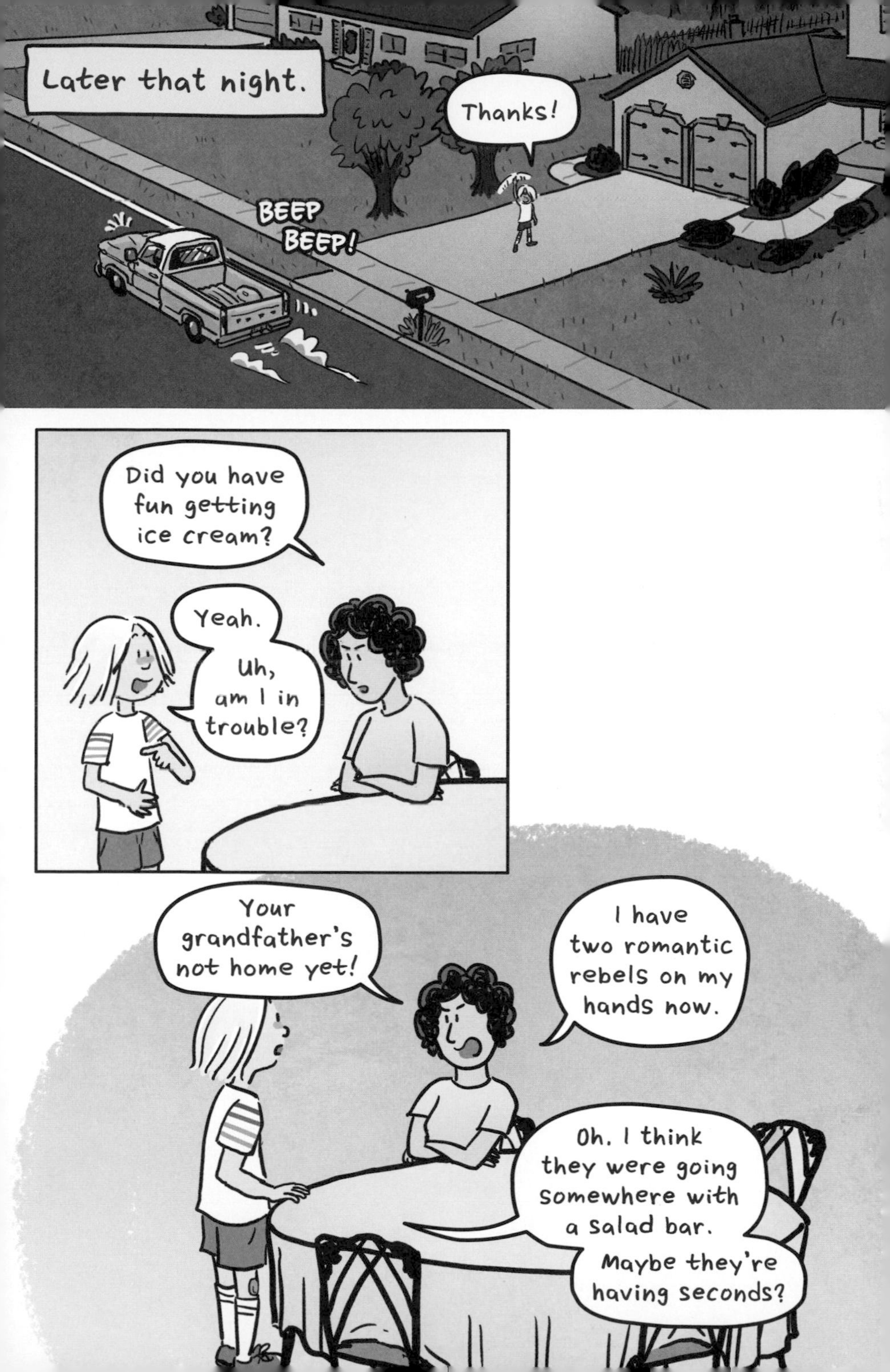
Later that night.
Thanks!
BEEP BEEP!
Did you have fun getting ice cream?
Yeah.
Uh, am I in trouble?
Your grandfather's not home yet!
I have two romantic rebels on my hands now.
Oh. I think they were going somewhere with a salad bar.
Maybe they're having seconds?

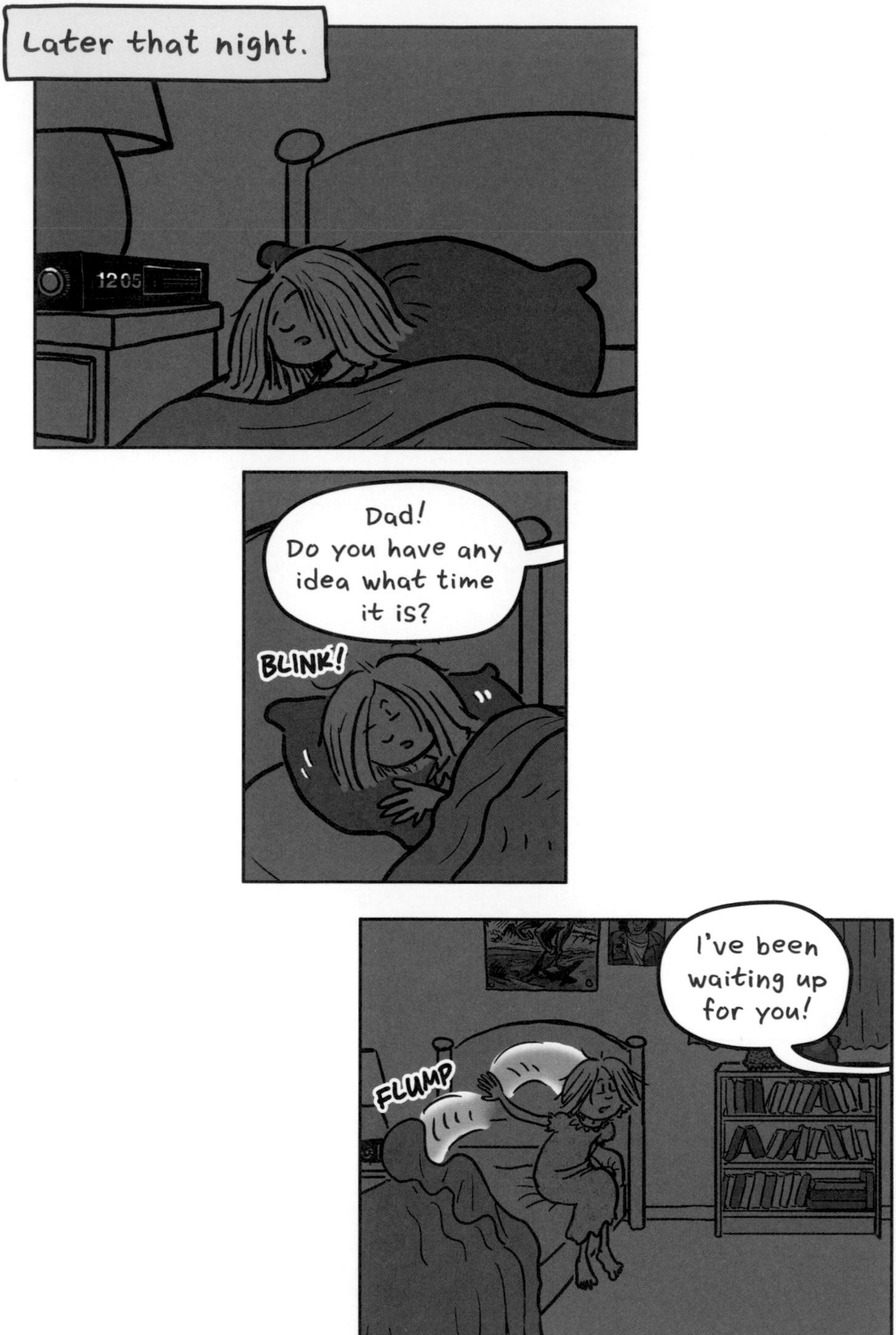
Later that night.
Dad!
Do you have any idea what time it is?
BLINK!
I've been waiting up for you!
FLUMP

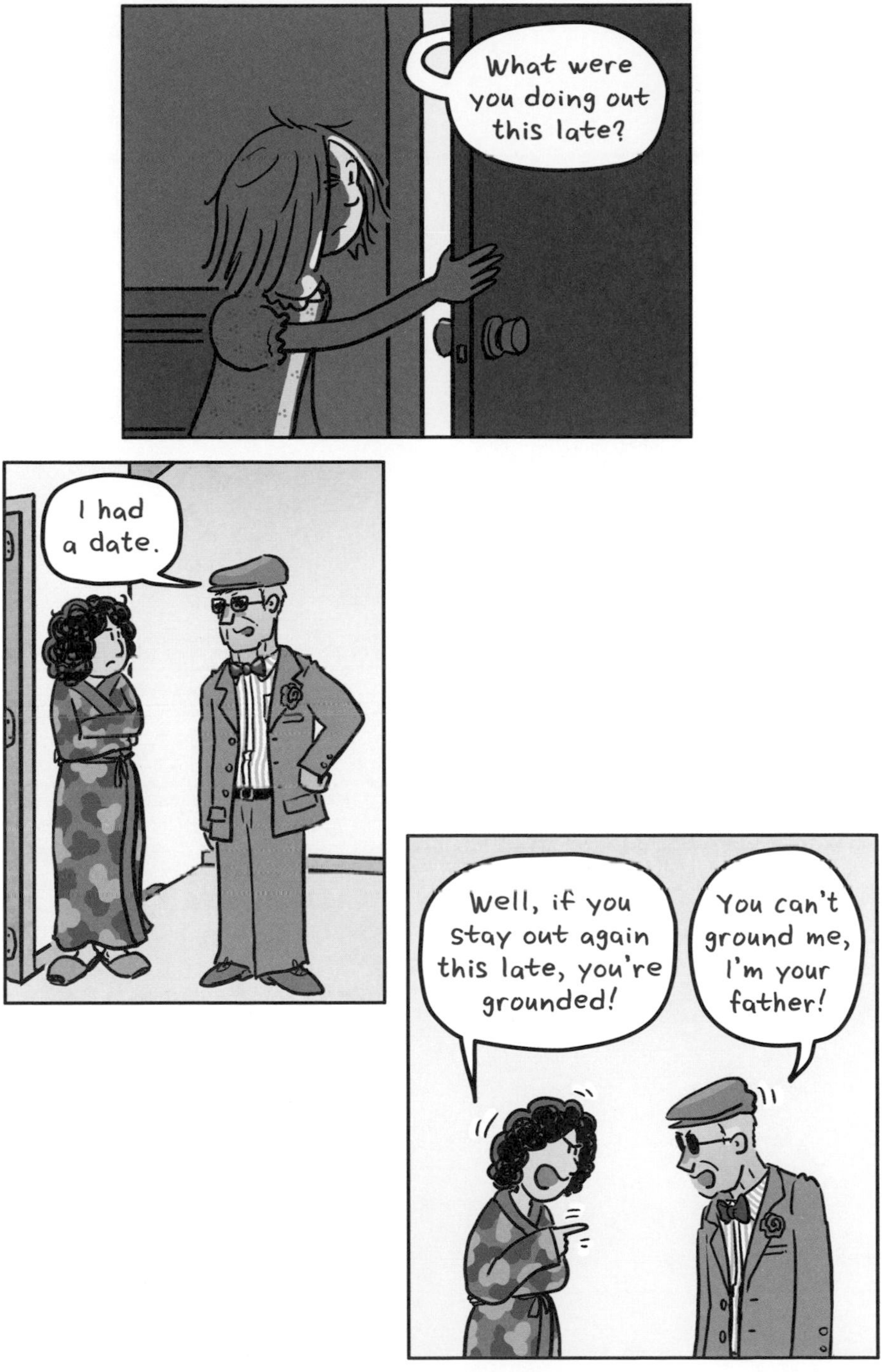
What were you doing out this late?
I had a date.
Well, if you stay out again this late, you're grounded!
You can't ground me, I'm your father!

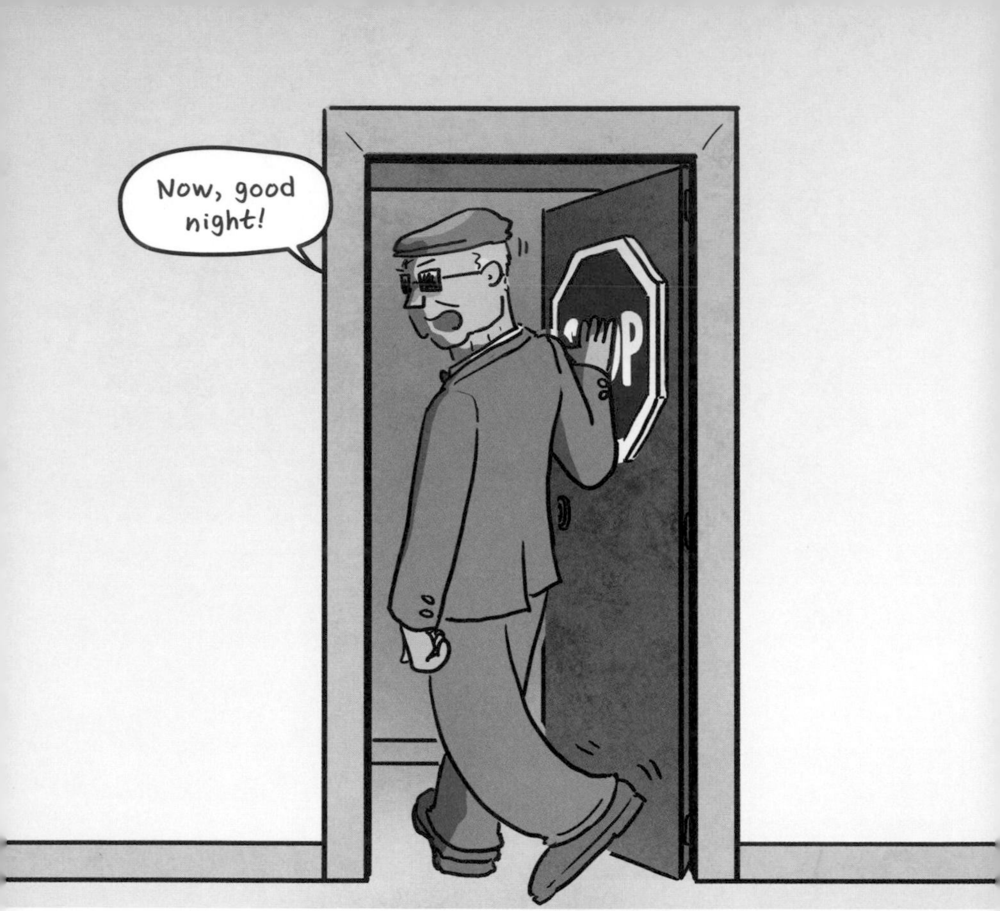
Now, good night!

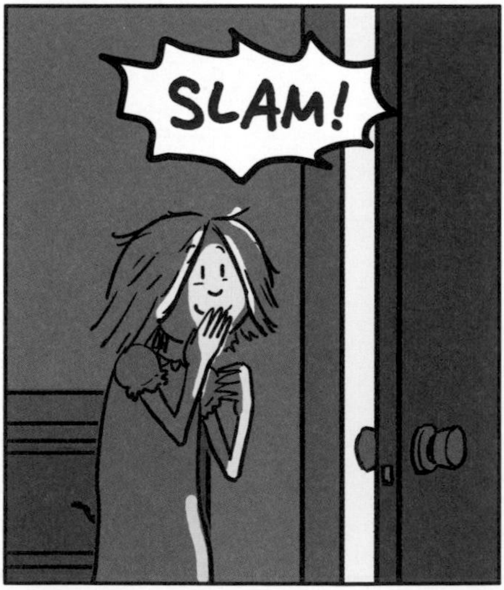
SLAM!

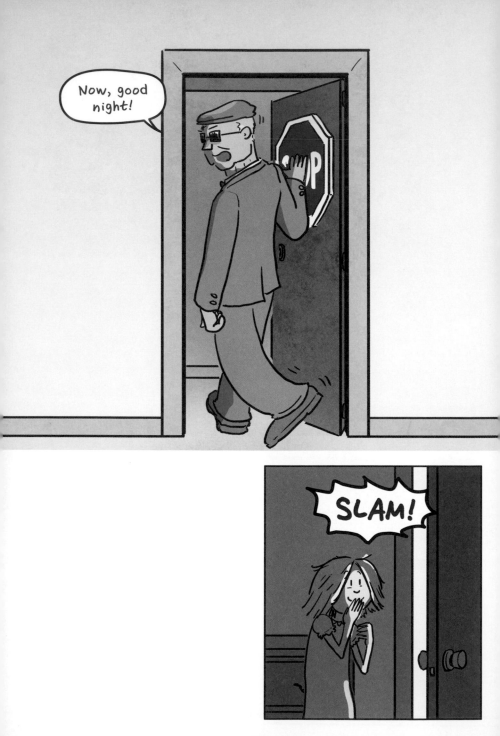

CHAPTER FIFTEEN: Surprise

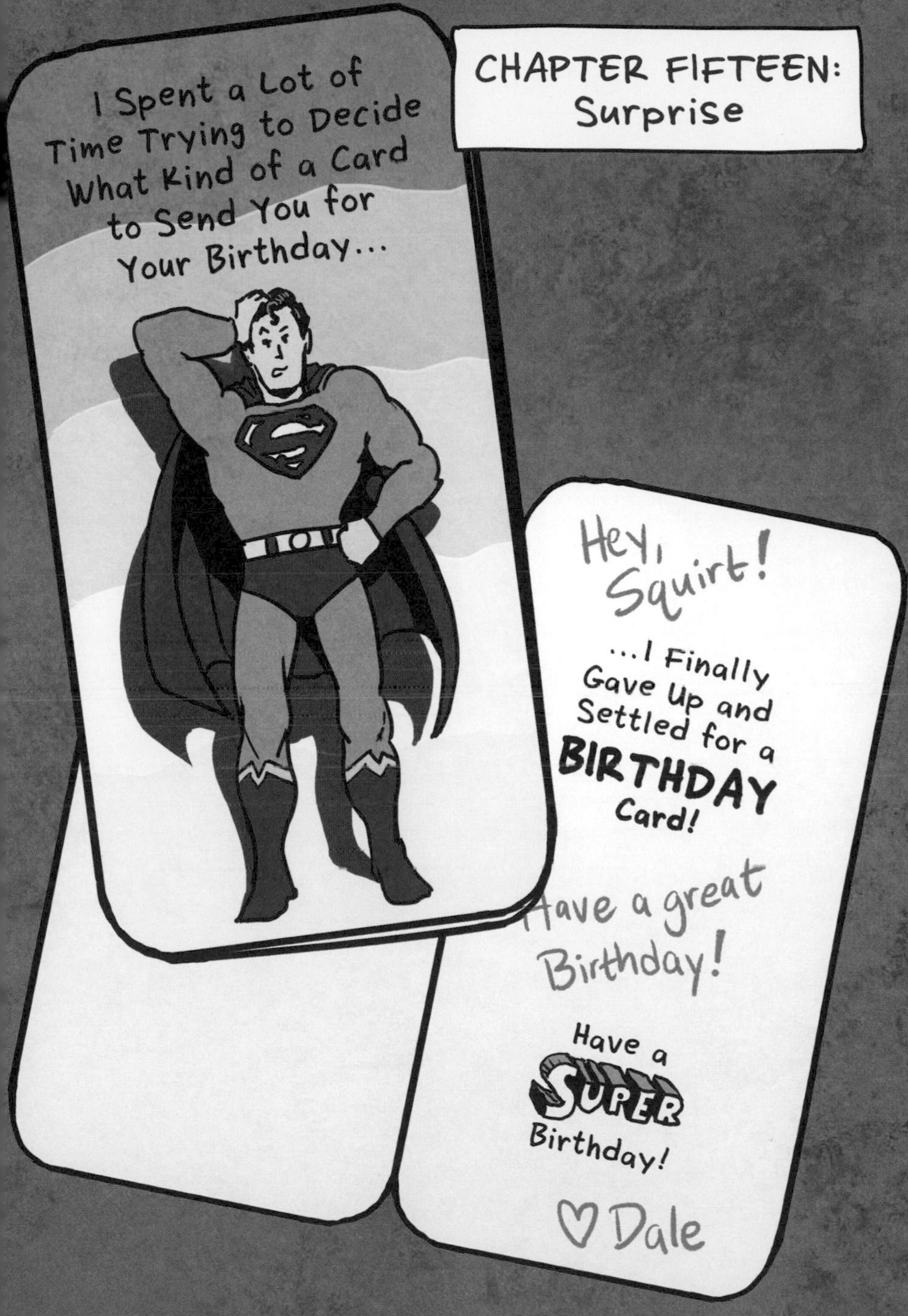
I Spent a Lot of Time Trying to Decide What Kind of a Card to Send You for Your Birthday...
Hey, Squirt!
...I Finally Gave Up and Settled for a BIRTHDAY Card!
Have a great Birthday!
Have a SUPER Birthday!
♡ Dale

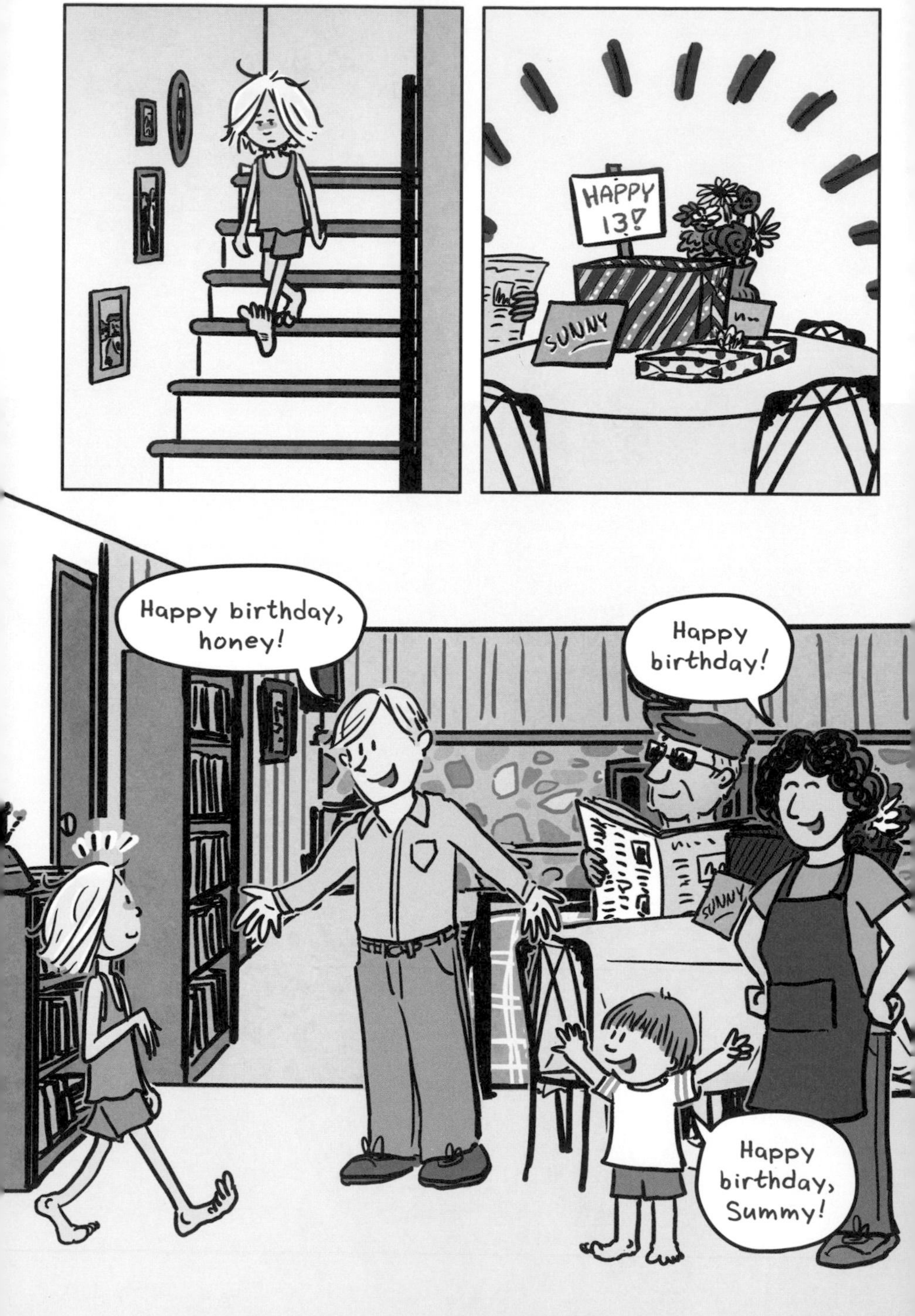
HAPPY 13!
SUNNY
Happy birthday, honey!
Happy birthday!
SUNNY
Happy birthday, Summy!

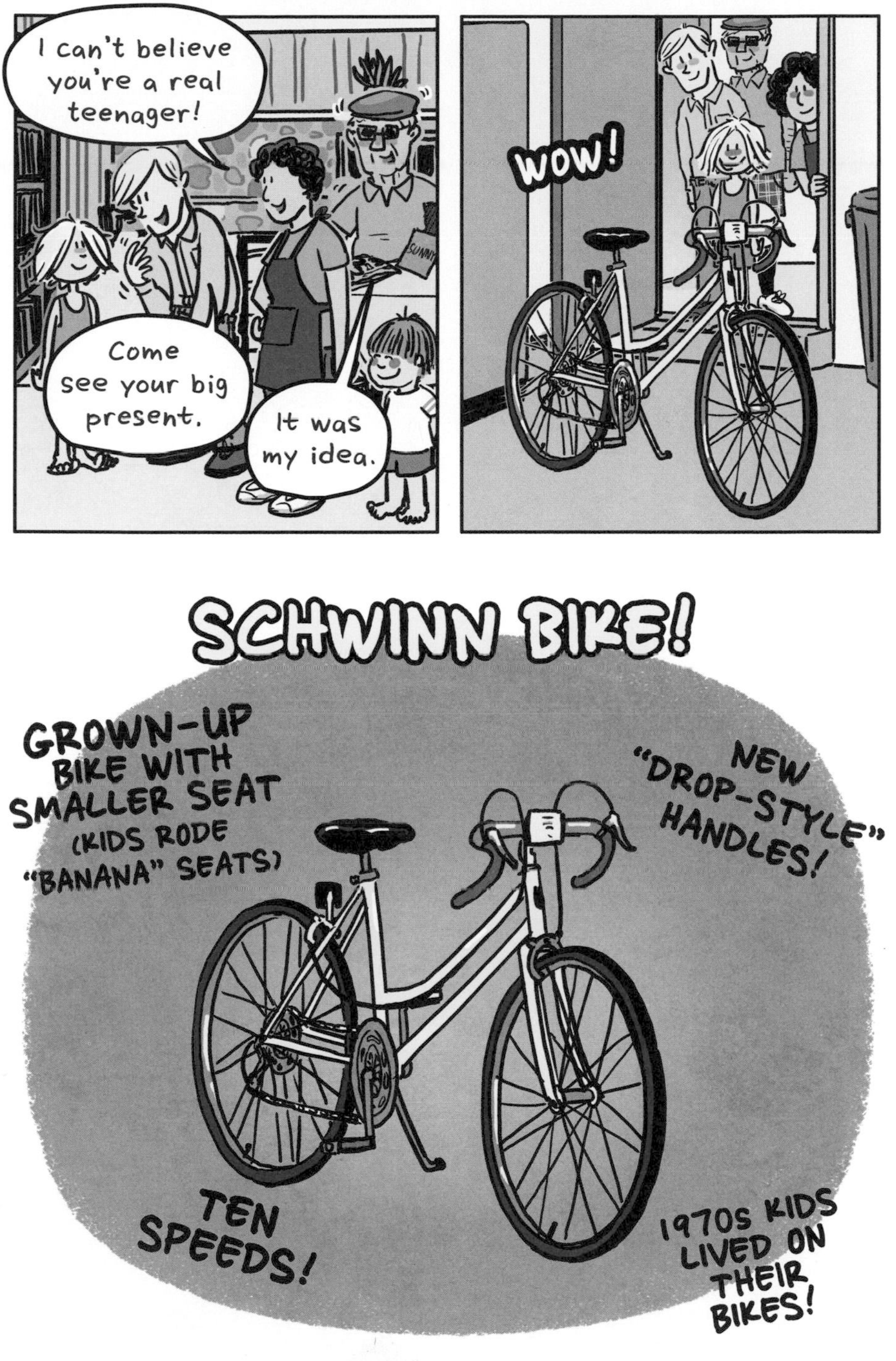
I can't believe you're a real teenager!
Come see your big present.
It was my idea.
WOW!
SCHWINN BIKE!
GROWN-UP BIKE WITH SMALLER SEAT (KIDS RODE "BANANA" SEATS)
NEW "DROP-STYLE" HANDLES!
TEN SPEEDS!
1970S KIDS LIVED ON THEIR BIKES!

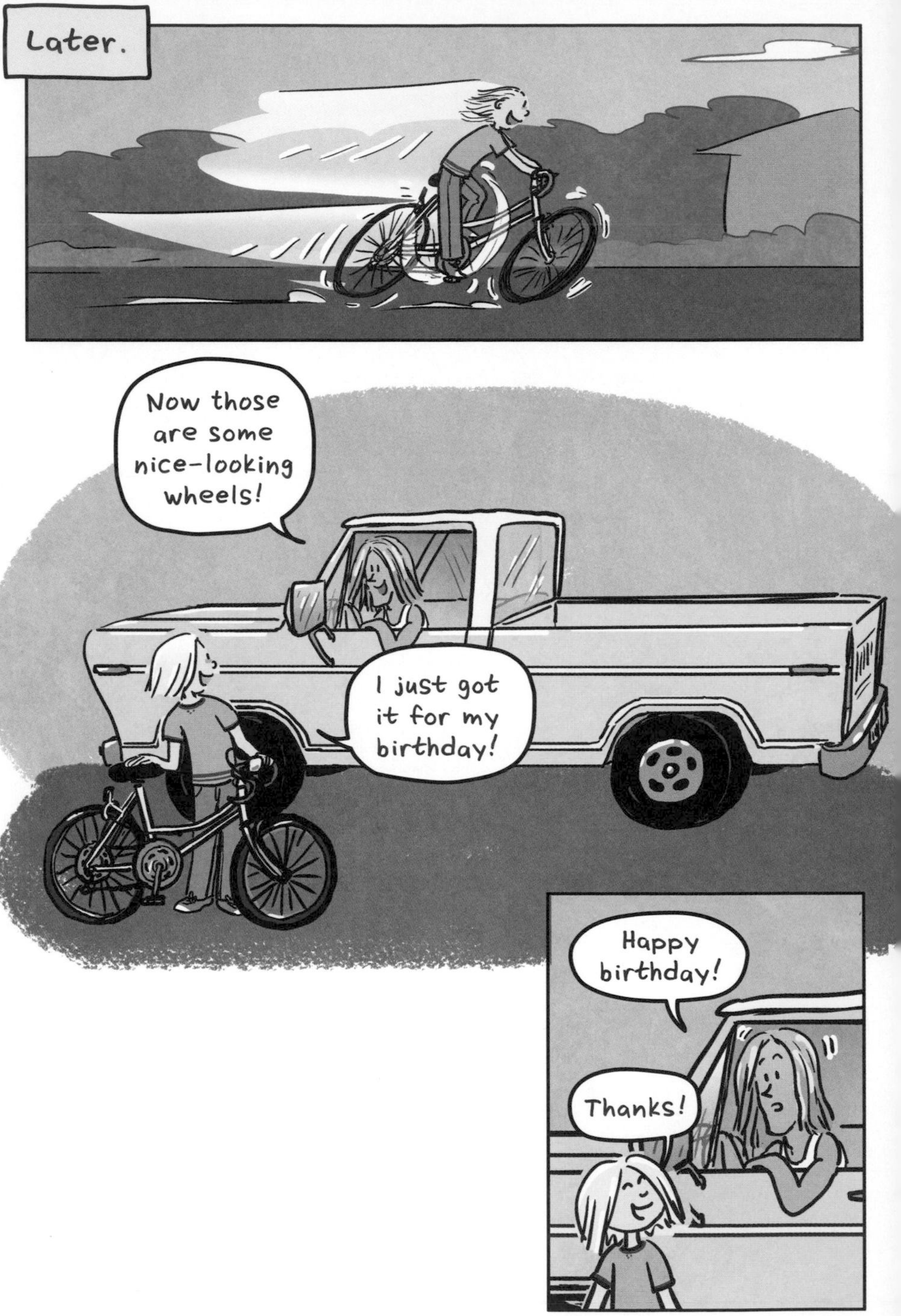
Later.
Now those are some nice-looking wheels!
I just got it for my birthday!
Happy birthday!
Thanks!

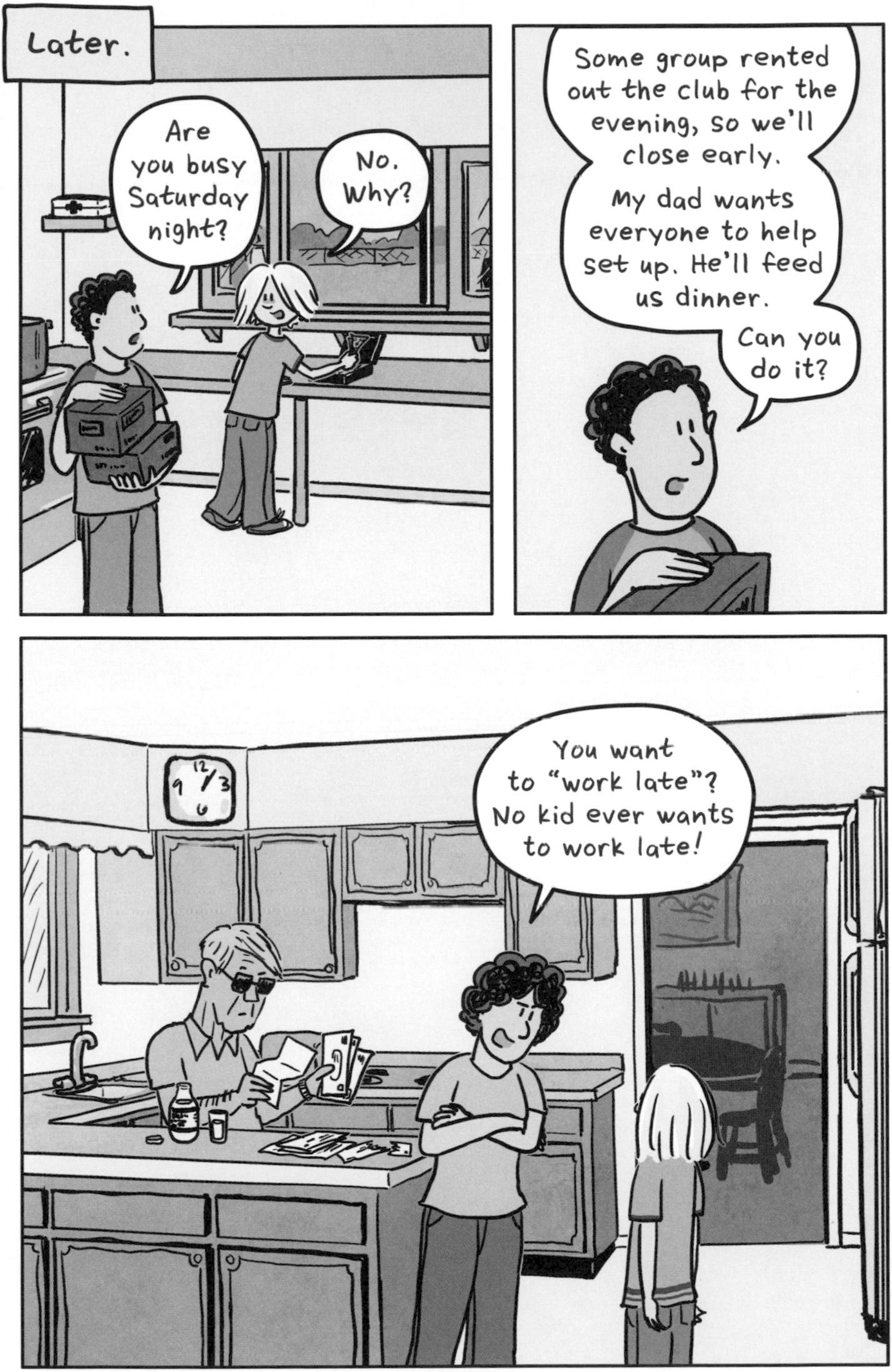
Later.
Are you busy Saturday night?
No. Why?
Some group rented out the club for the evening, so we'll close early.
My dad wants everyone to help set up. He'll feed us dinner.
Can you do it?
You want to "work late"? No kid ever wants to work late!

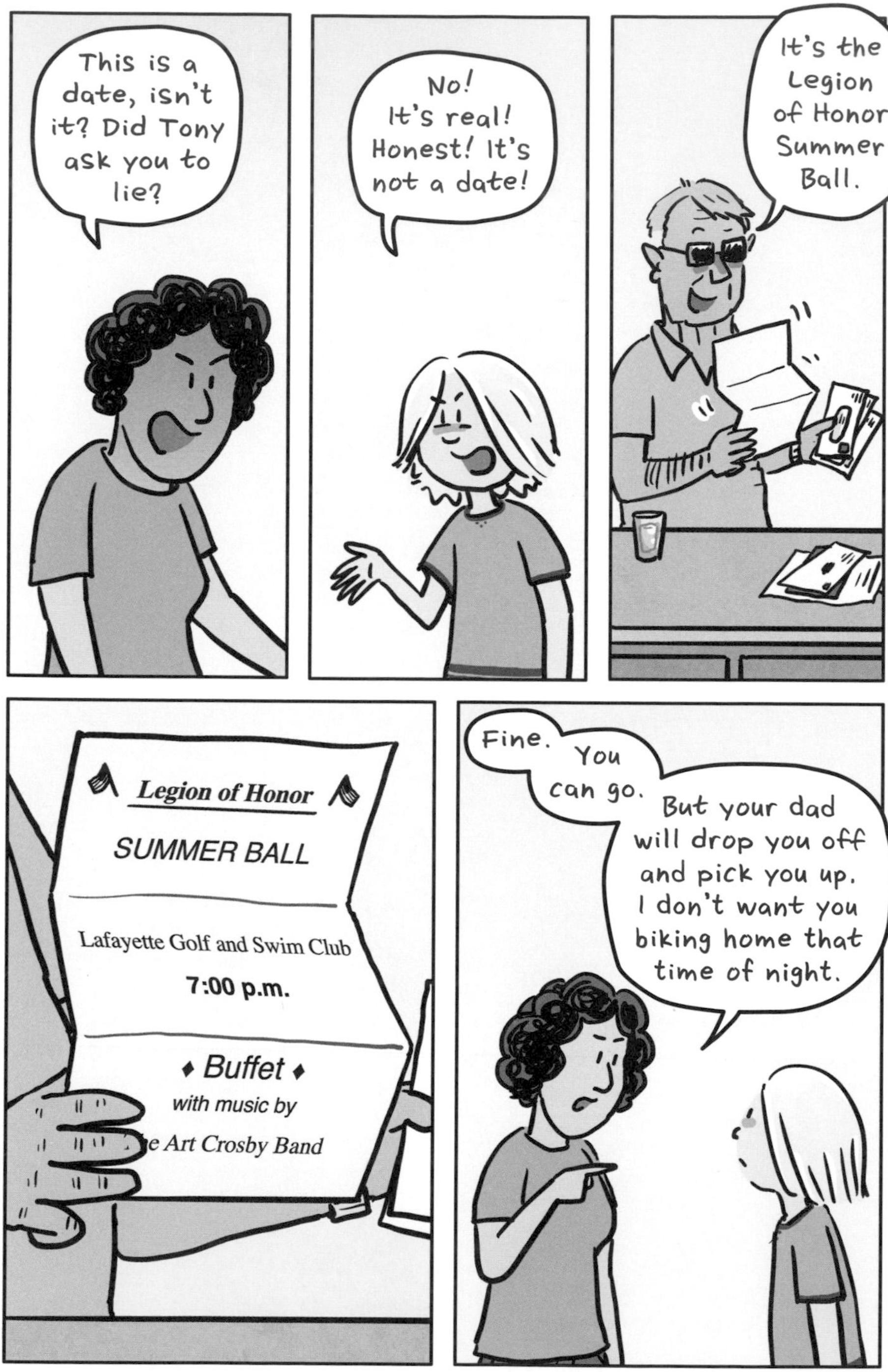
This is a date, isn't it? Did Tony ask you to lie?
No! It's real! Honest! It's not a date!
It's the Legion of Honor Summer Ball.
Legion of Honor
SUMMER BALL
Lafayette Golf and Swim Club
7:00 p.m.
Buffet
with music by
Art Crosby Band
Fine.
You can go.
But your dad will drop you off and pick you up. I don't want you biking home that time of night.

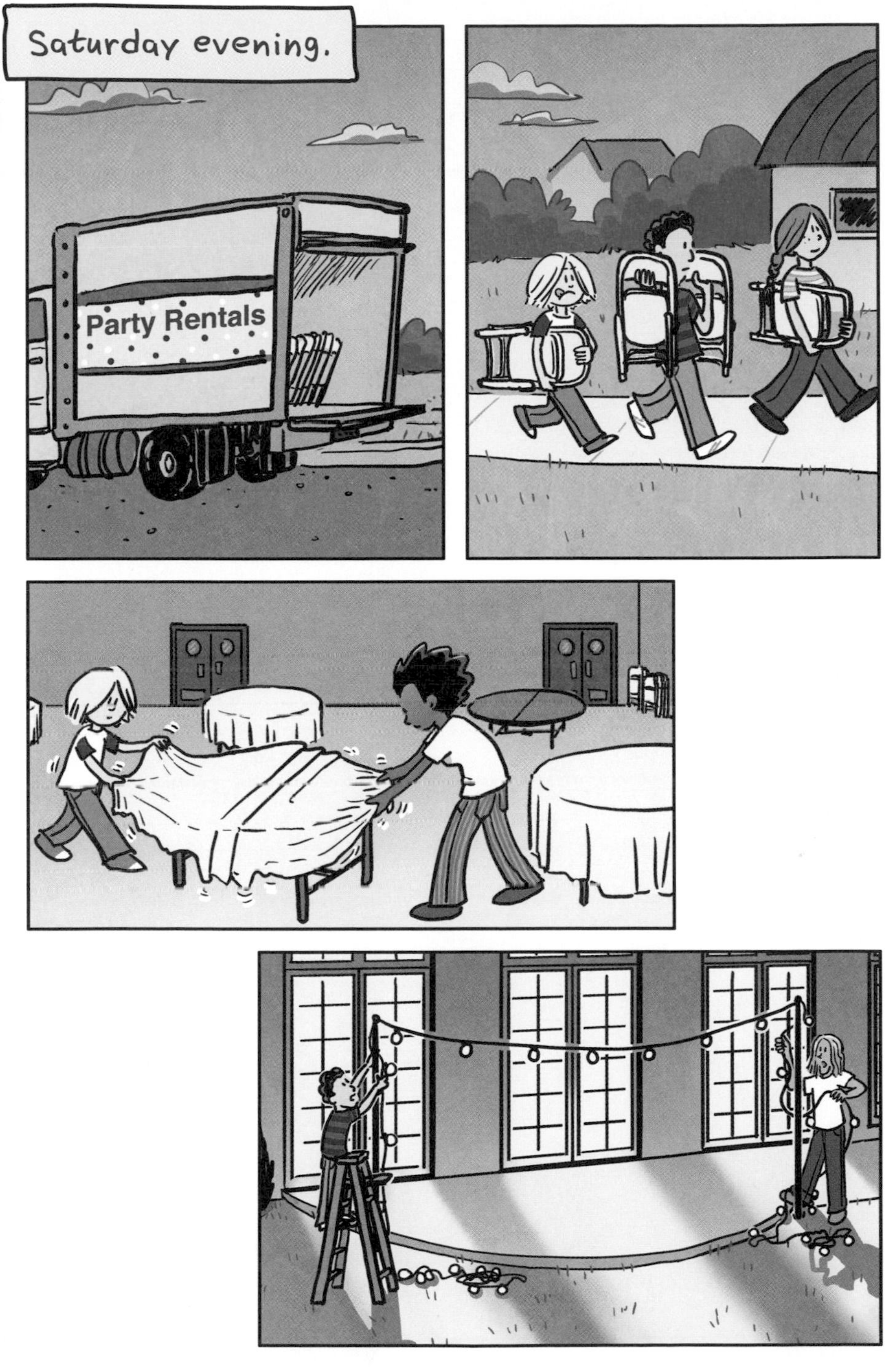
Saturday evening.
Party Rentals

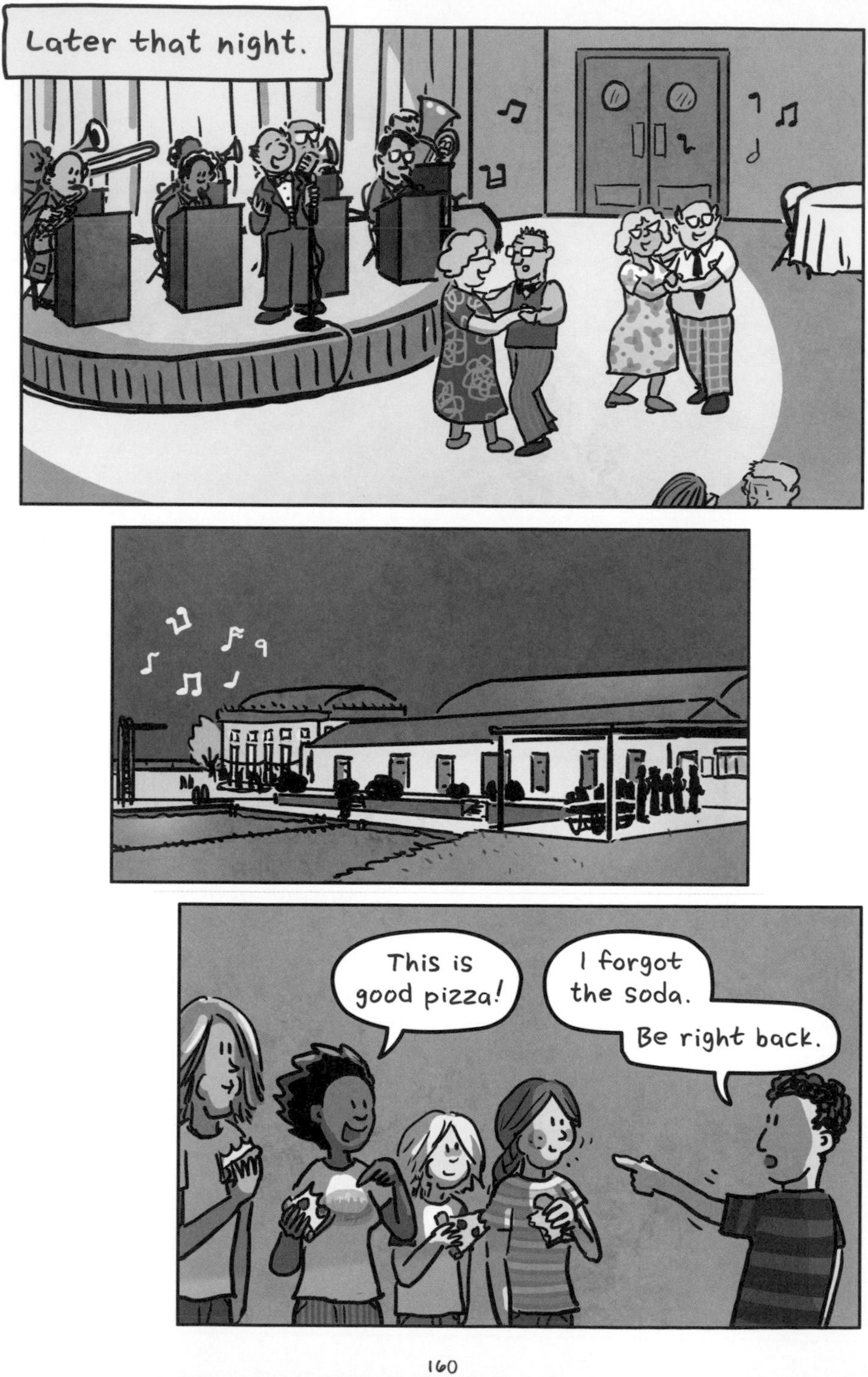

Later that night.
This is good pizza!
I forgot the soda.
Be right back.

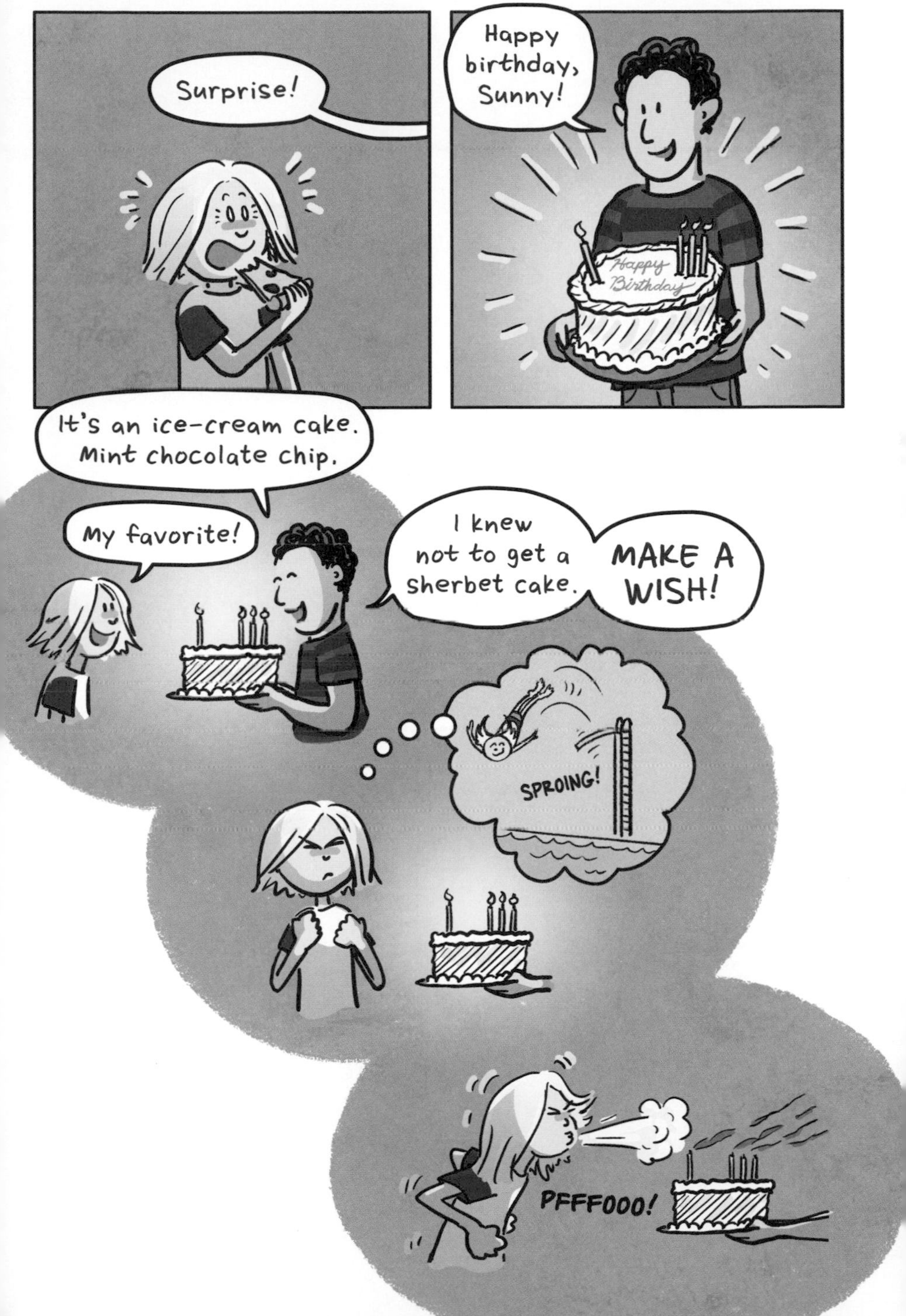
Surprise!
Happy birthday, Sunny!
Happy Birthday
It's an ice-cream cake. Mint chocolate chip.
My favorite!
I knew not to get a sherbet cake.
MAKE A WISH!
SPROING!
PFFFOOO!

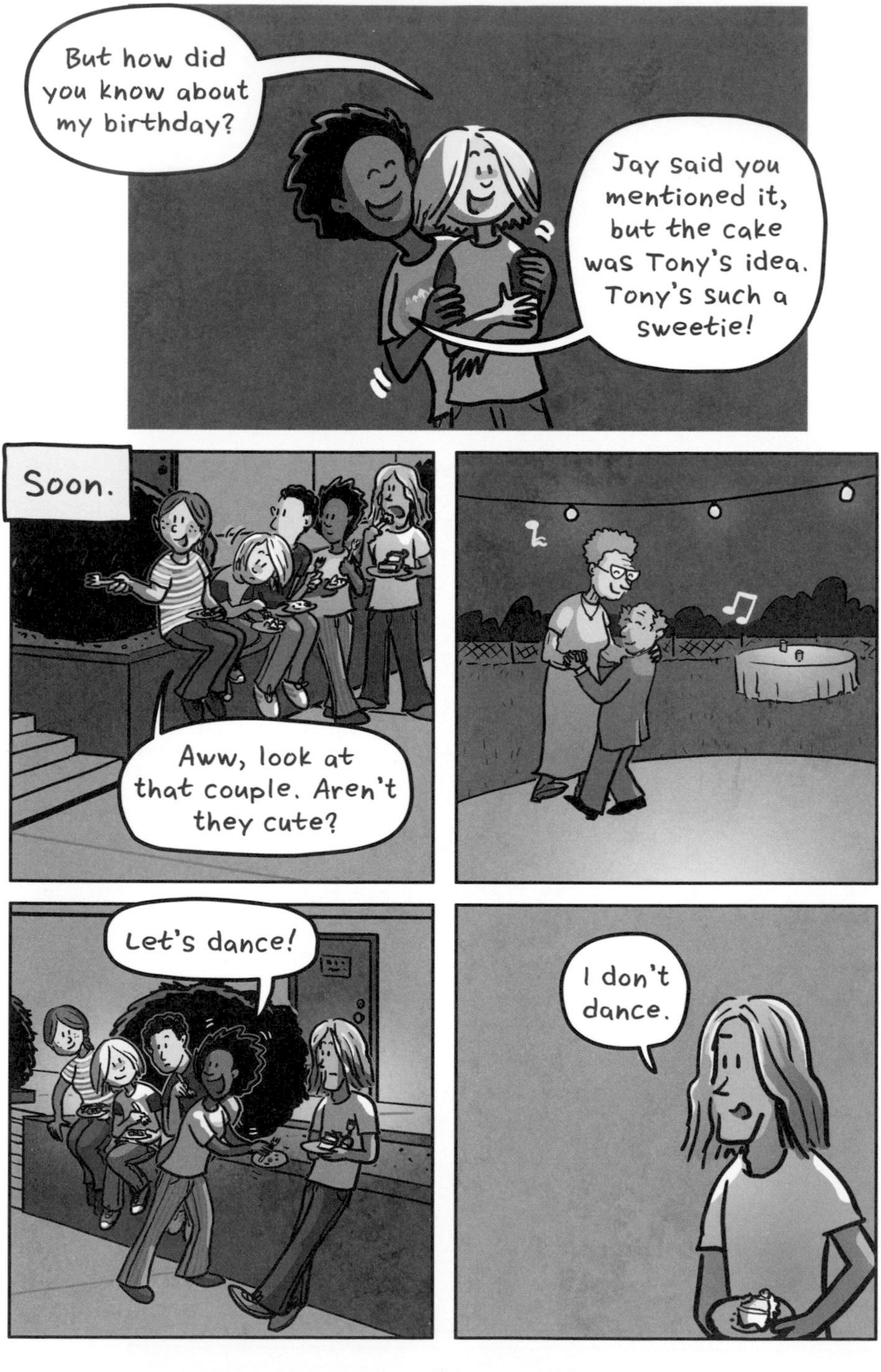
But how did you know about my birthday?
Jay said you mentioned it, but the cake was Tony's idea. Tony's such a sweetie!
Soon.
Aww, look at that couple. Aren't they cute?
Let's dance!
I don't dance.

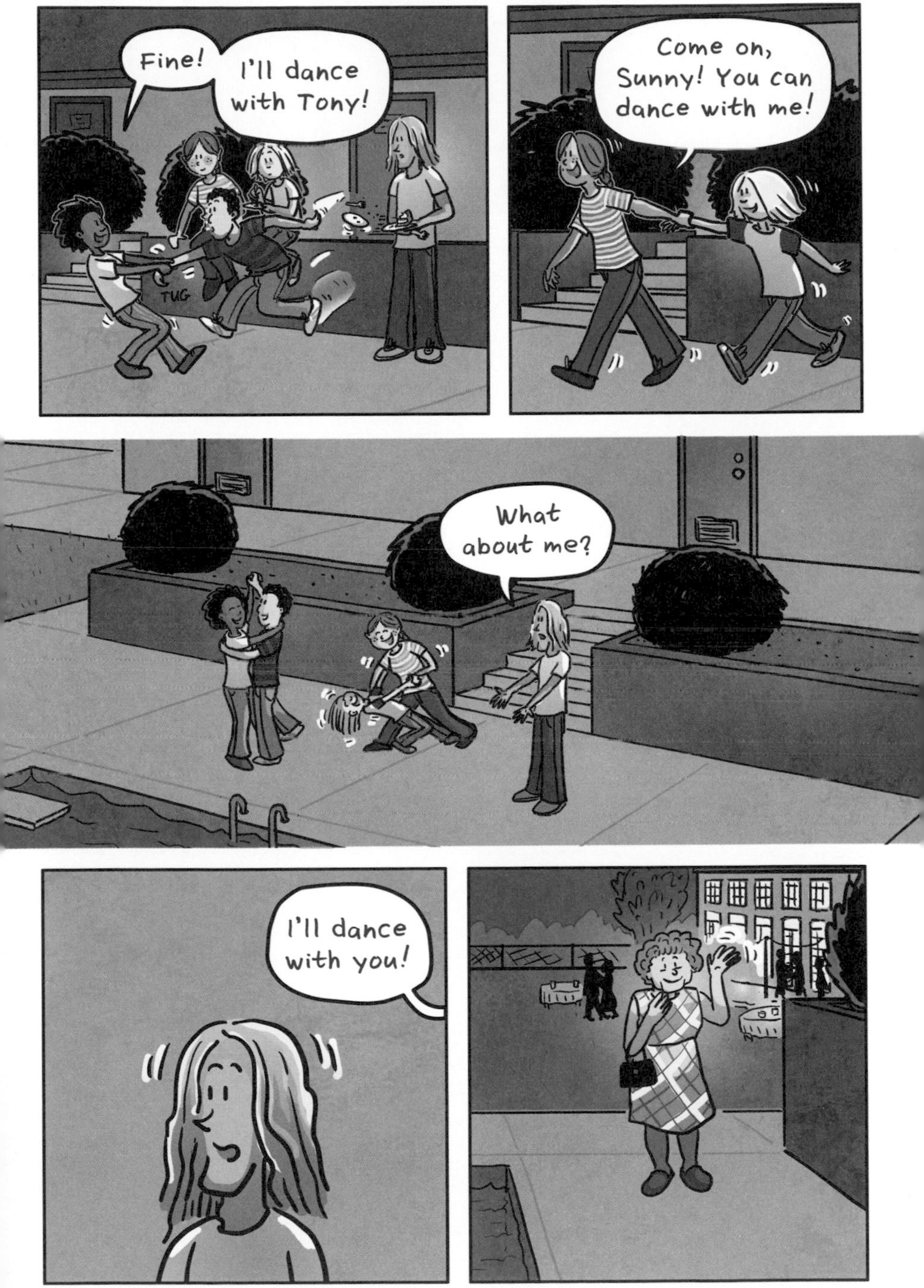
Fine!
I'll dance with Tony!
TUG
Come on, Sunny! You can dance with me!
What about me?
I'll dance with you!

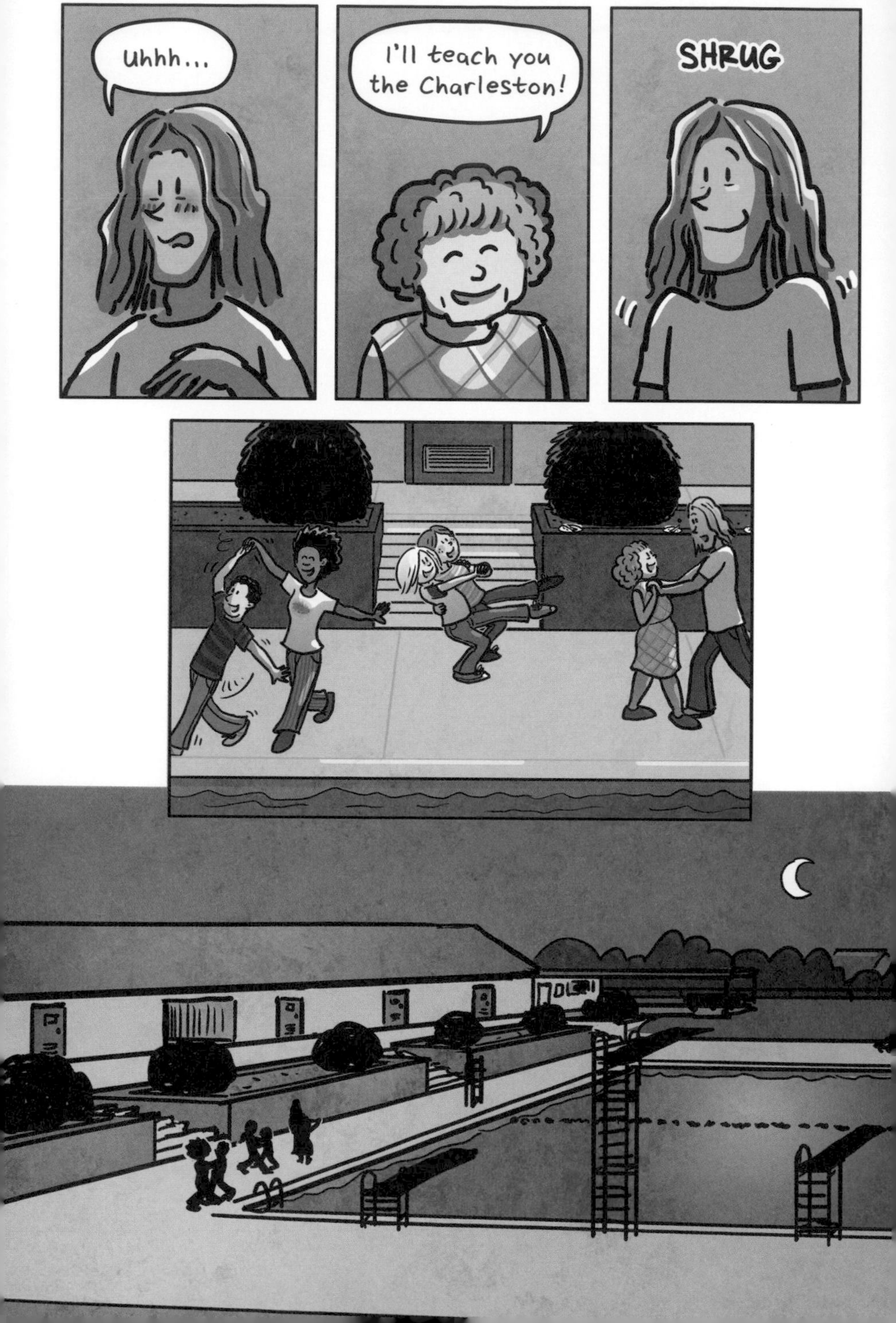
Uhhh...
I'll teach you the Charleston!
SHRUG

CHAPTER SIXTEEN:
Postcards

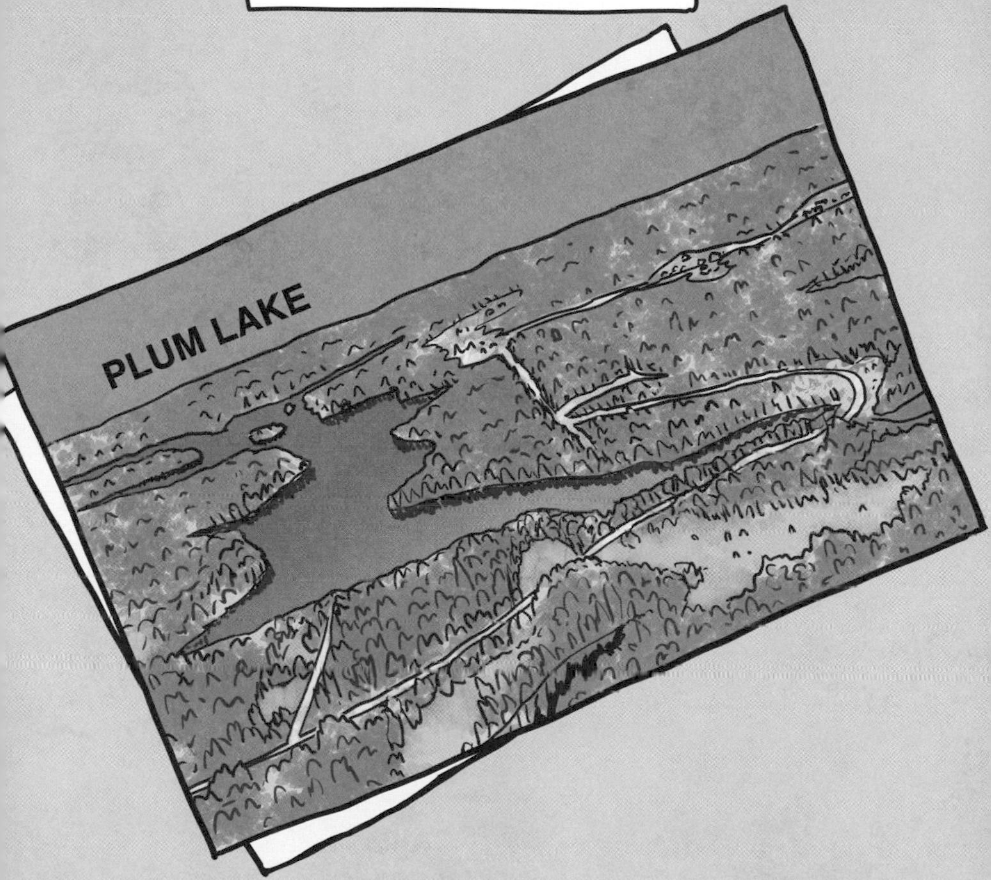
PLUM LAKE

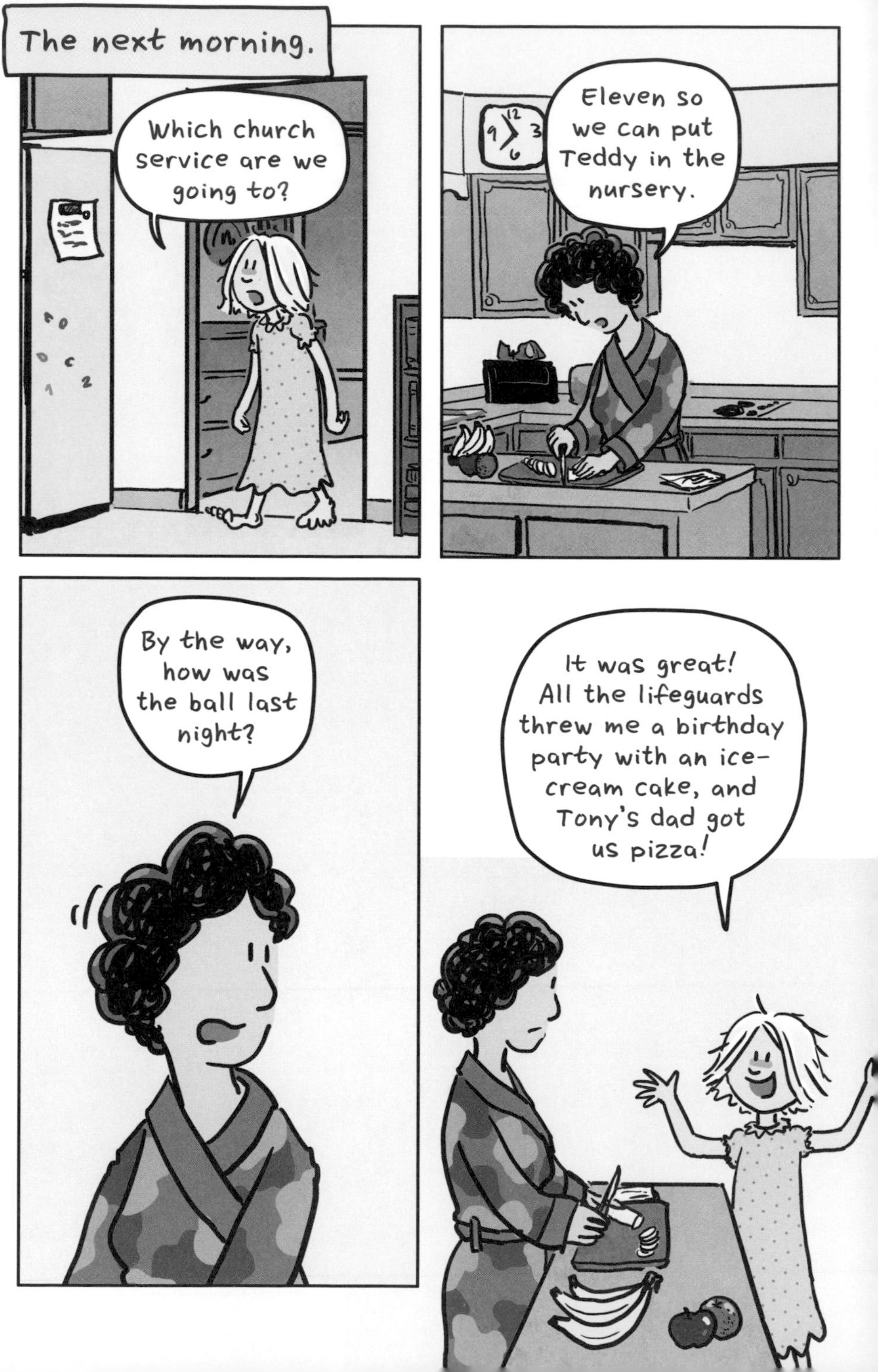
The next morning.
Which church service are we going to?
Eleven so we can put Teddy in the nursery.
By the way, how was the ball last night?
It was great! All the lifeguards threw me a birthday party with an ice-cream cake, and Tony's dad got us pizza!

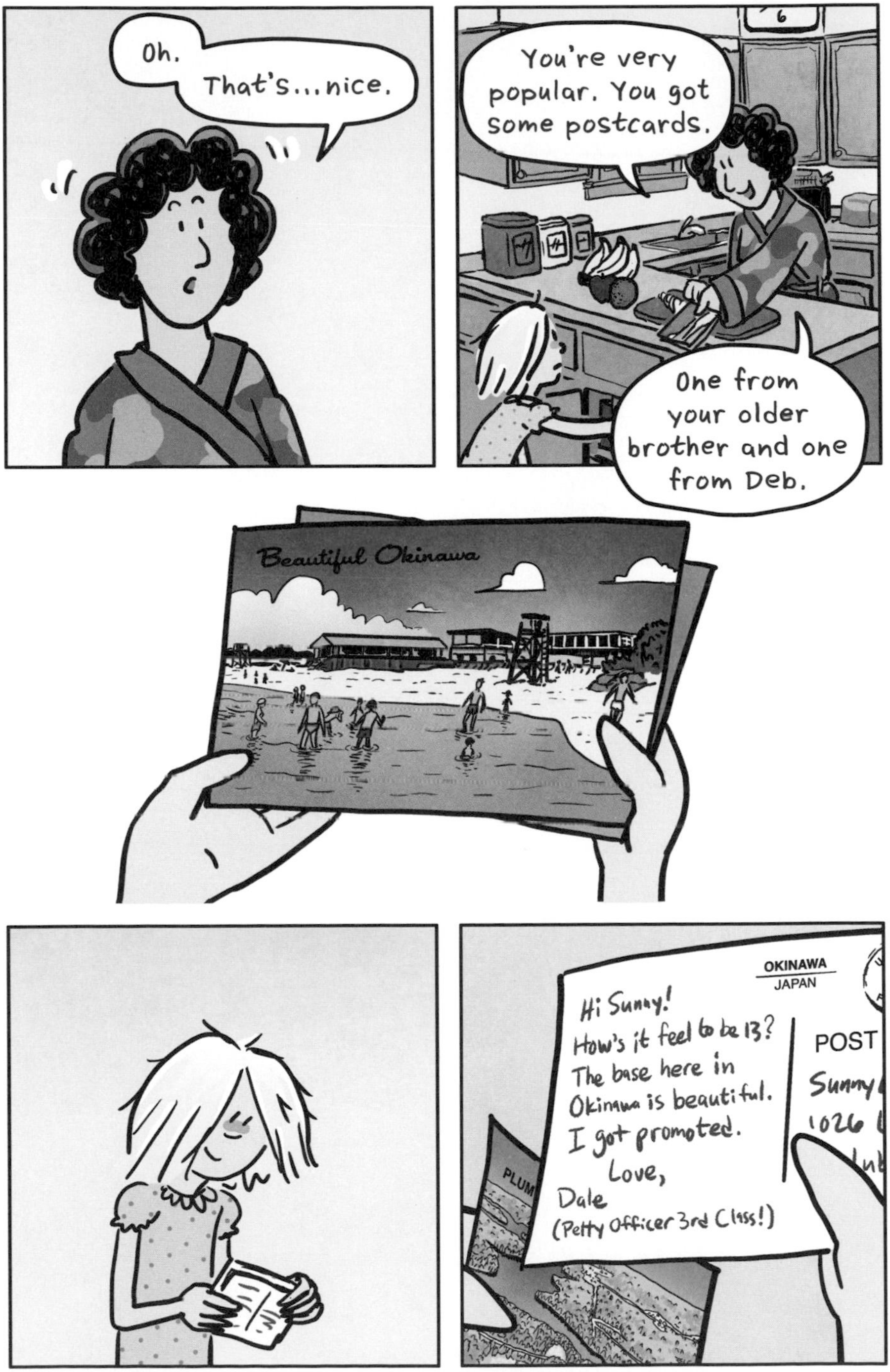
Oh. That's...nice.
You're very popular. You got some postcards.
One from your older brother and one from Deb.
Beautiful Okinawa
OKINAWA JAPAN
Hi Sunny!
How's it feel to be 13?
The base here in Okinawa is beautiful.
I got promoted.
Love,
Dale
(Petty Officer 3rd Class!)
POST
PLUM

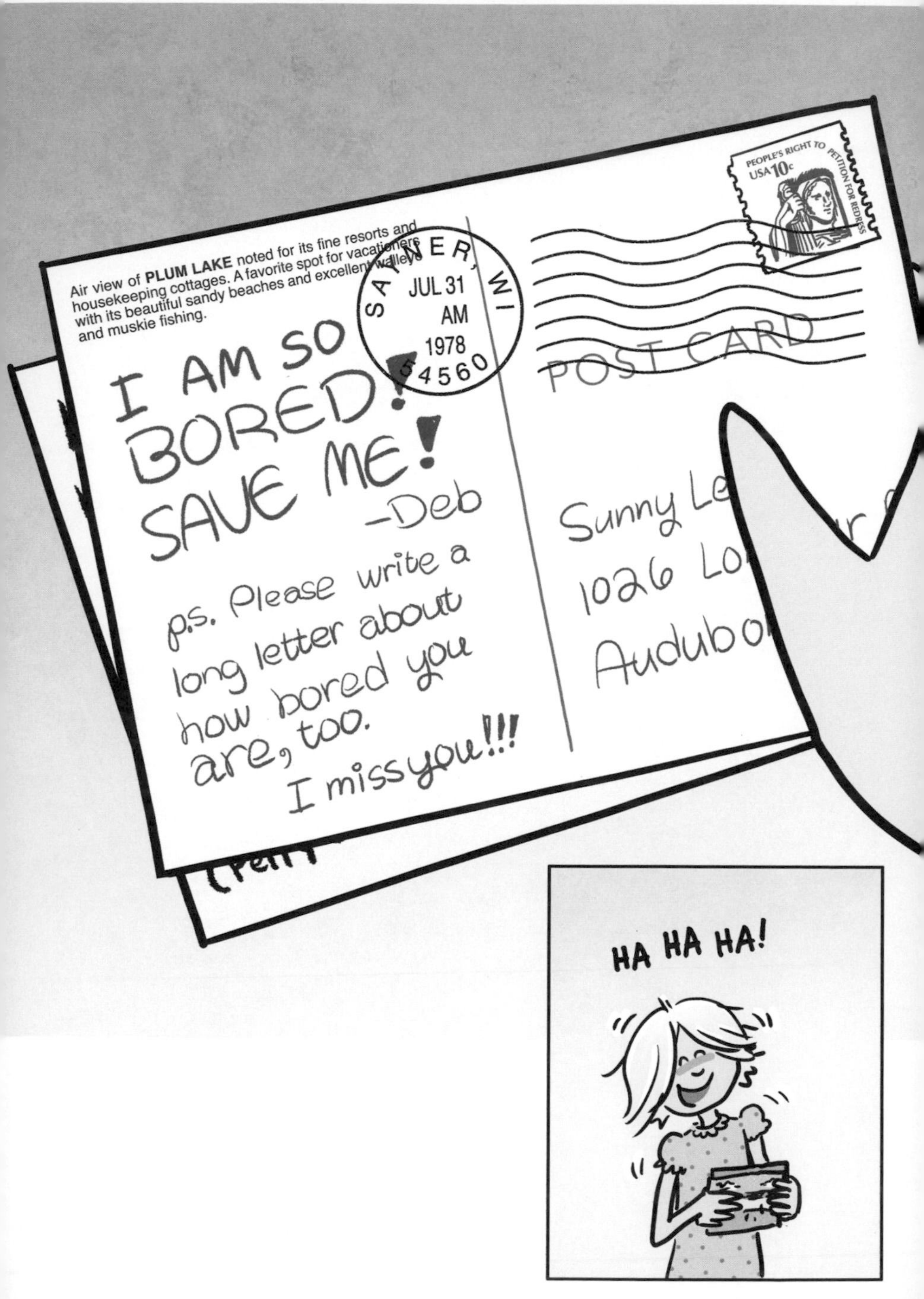

Air view of **PLUM LAKE** noted for its fine resorts and housekeeping cottages. A favorite spot for vacationers with its beautiful sandy beaches and excellent walleye and muskie fishing.
SAYNER, WI
JUL 31
AM
1978
54560
PEOPLE'S RIGHT TO PETITION FOR REDRESS
USA 10c
POST CARD
I AM SO BORED! SAVE ME!
-Deb
p.s. Please write a long letter about how bored you are, too.
I miss you!!!
Sunny Le
1026 Lo
Audubo
HA HA HA!

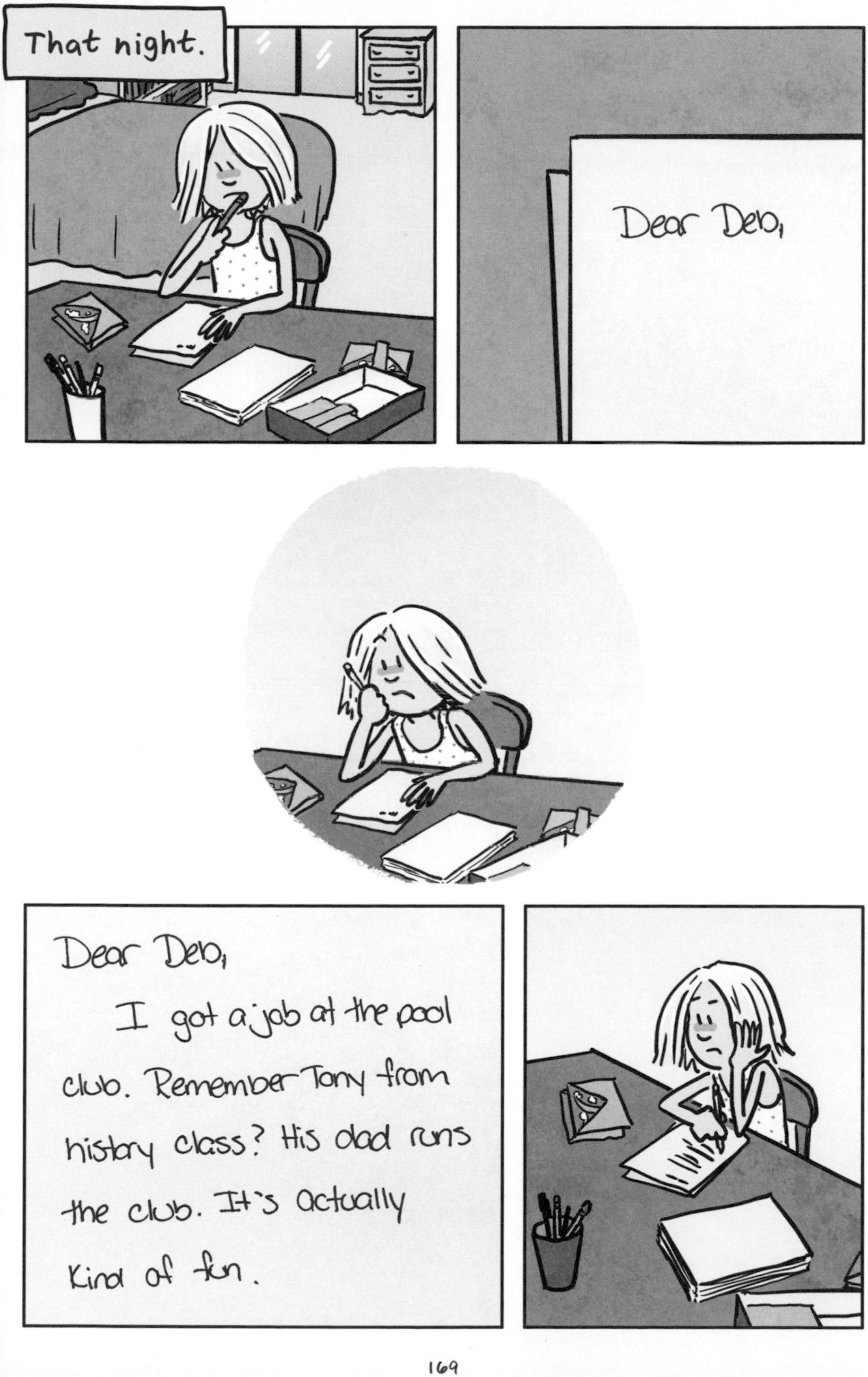
That night.
Dear Deb,
Dear Deb,
I got a job at the pool club. Remember Tony from history class? His dad runs the club. It's actually kind of fun.

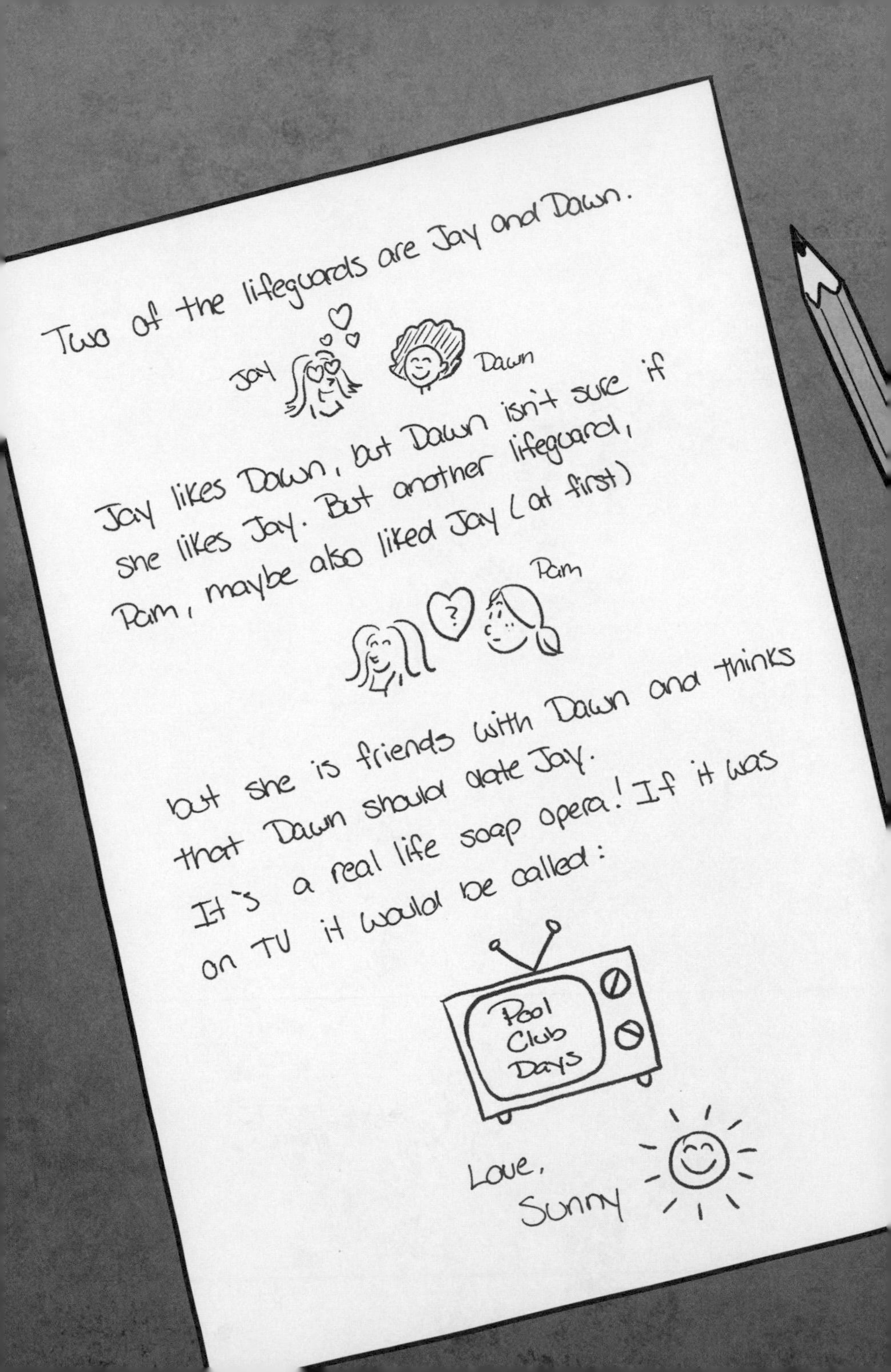
Two of the lifeguards are Jay and Dawn.
Jay
Dawn
Jay likes Dawn, but Dawn isn't sure if
she likes Jay. But another lifeguard,
Pam, maybe also liked Jay (at first)
Pam
but she is friends with Dawn and thinks
that Dawn should date Jay.
It's a real life soap opera! If it was
on TV it would be called:
Pool
Club
Days
Love,
Sunny

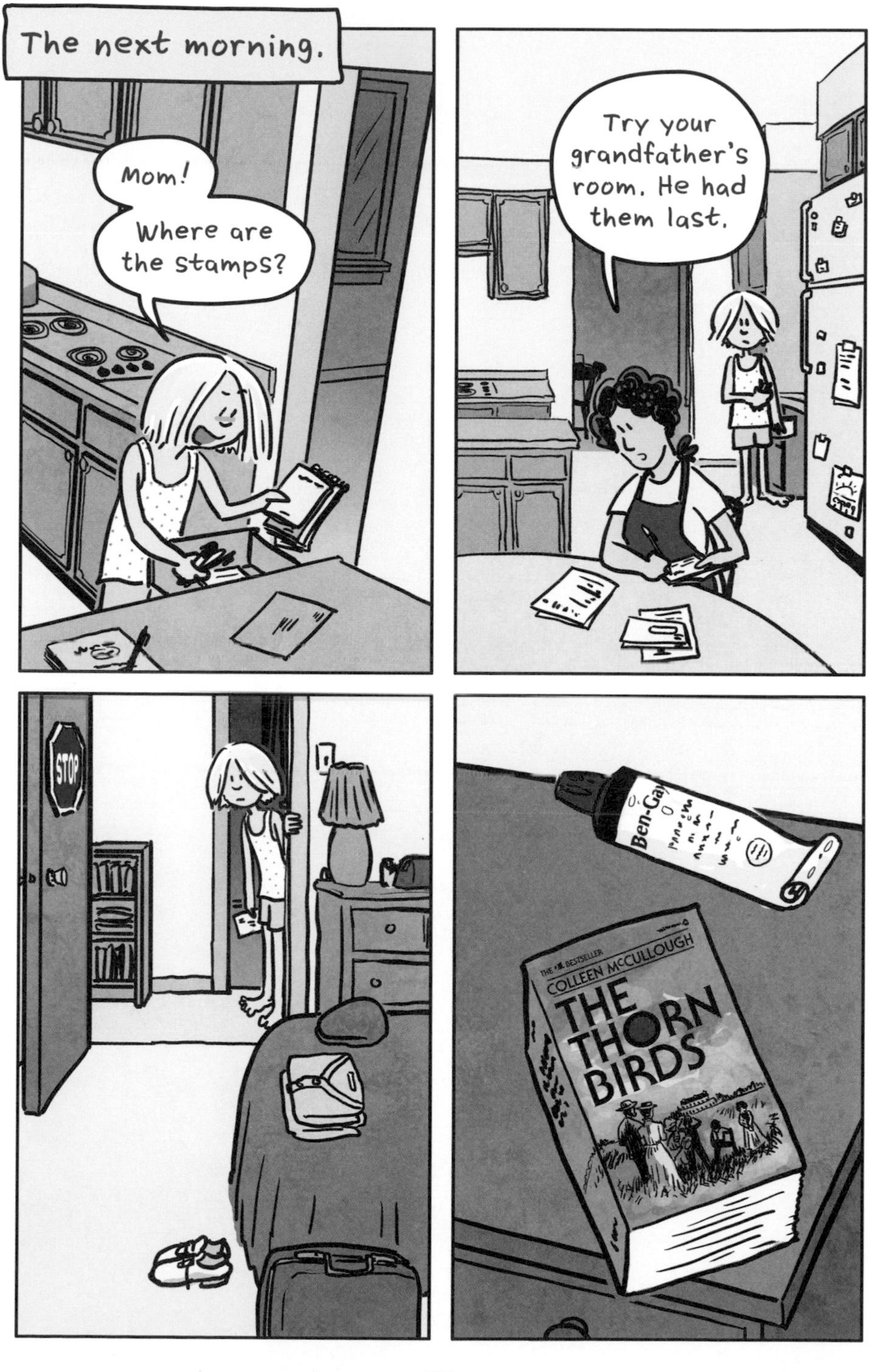
The next morning.
Mom!
Where are the stamps?
Try your grandfather's room. He had them last.
STOP
Ben-Gay
THE #1 BESTSELLER
COLLEEN McCULLOUGH
THE THORN BIRDS

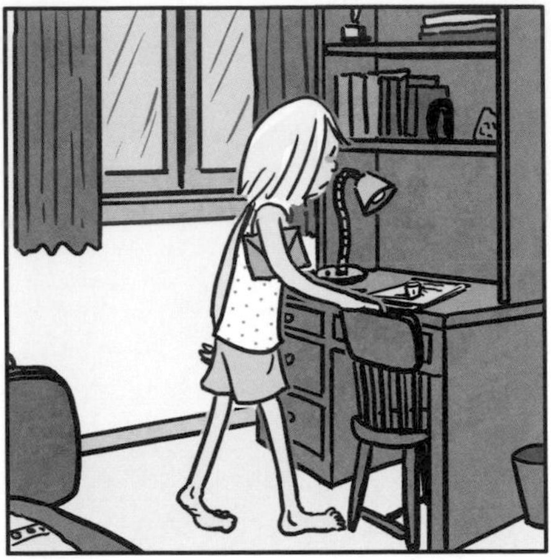

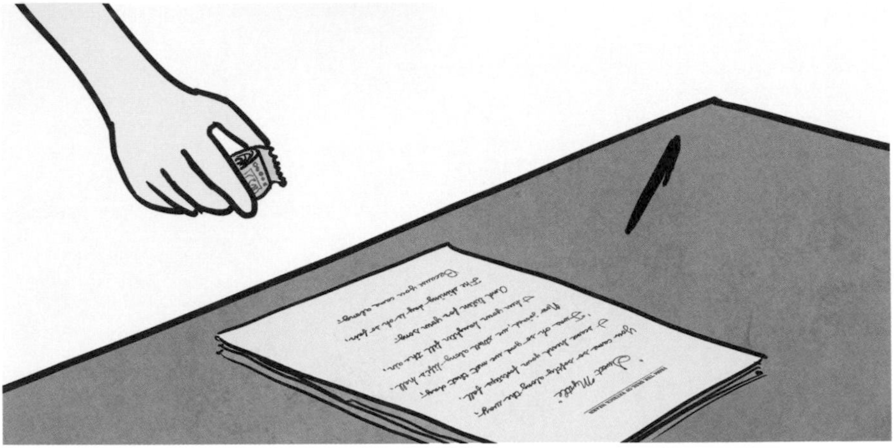

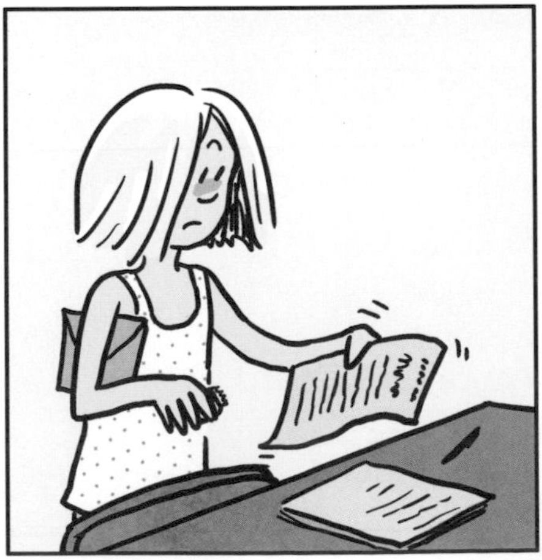

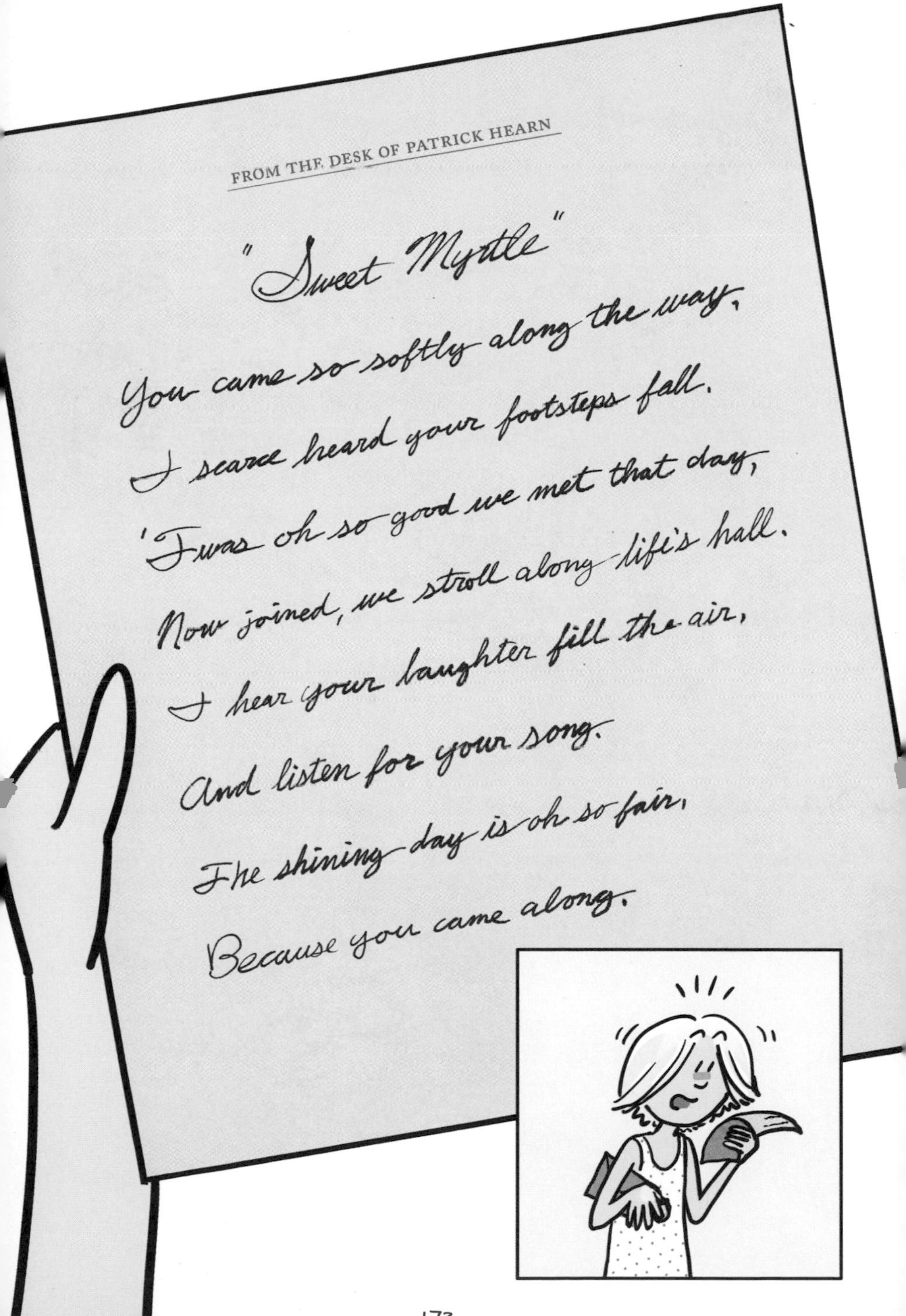
FROM THE DESK OF PATRICK HEARN
"Sweet Myrtle"
You came so softly along the way,
I scarce heard your footsteps fall.
'Twas oh so good we met that day,
Now joined, we stroll along life's hall.
I hear your laughter fill the air,
And listen for your song.
The shining day is oh so fair,
Because you came along.

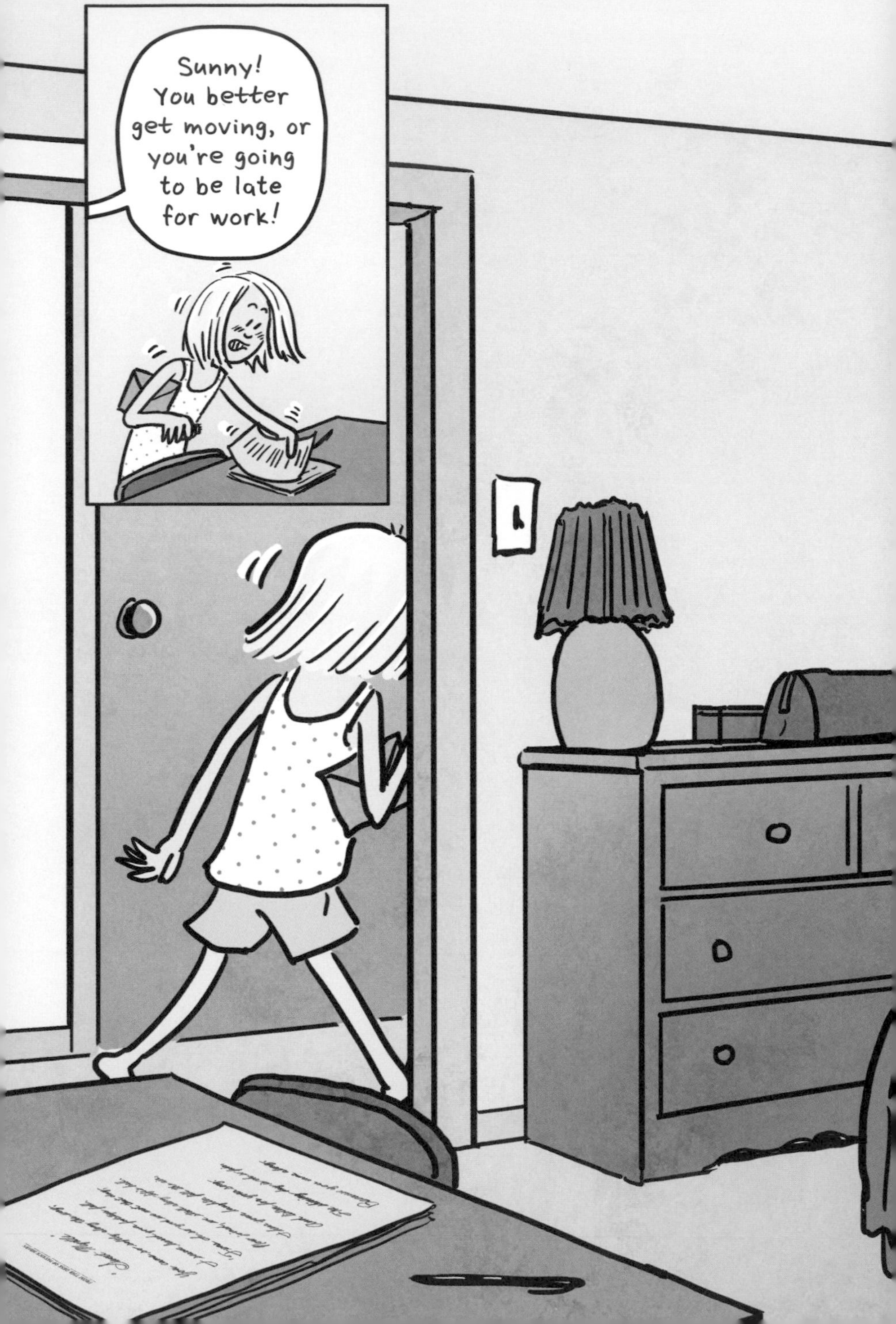
Sunny! You better get moving, or you're going to be late for work!

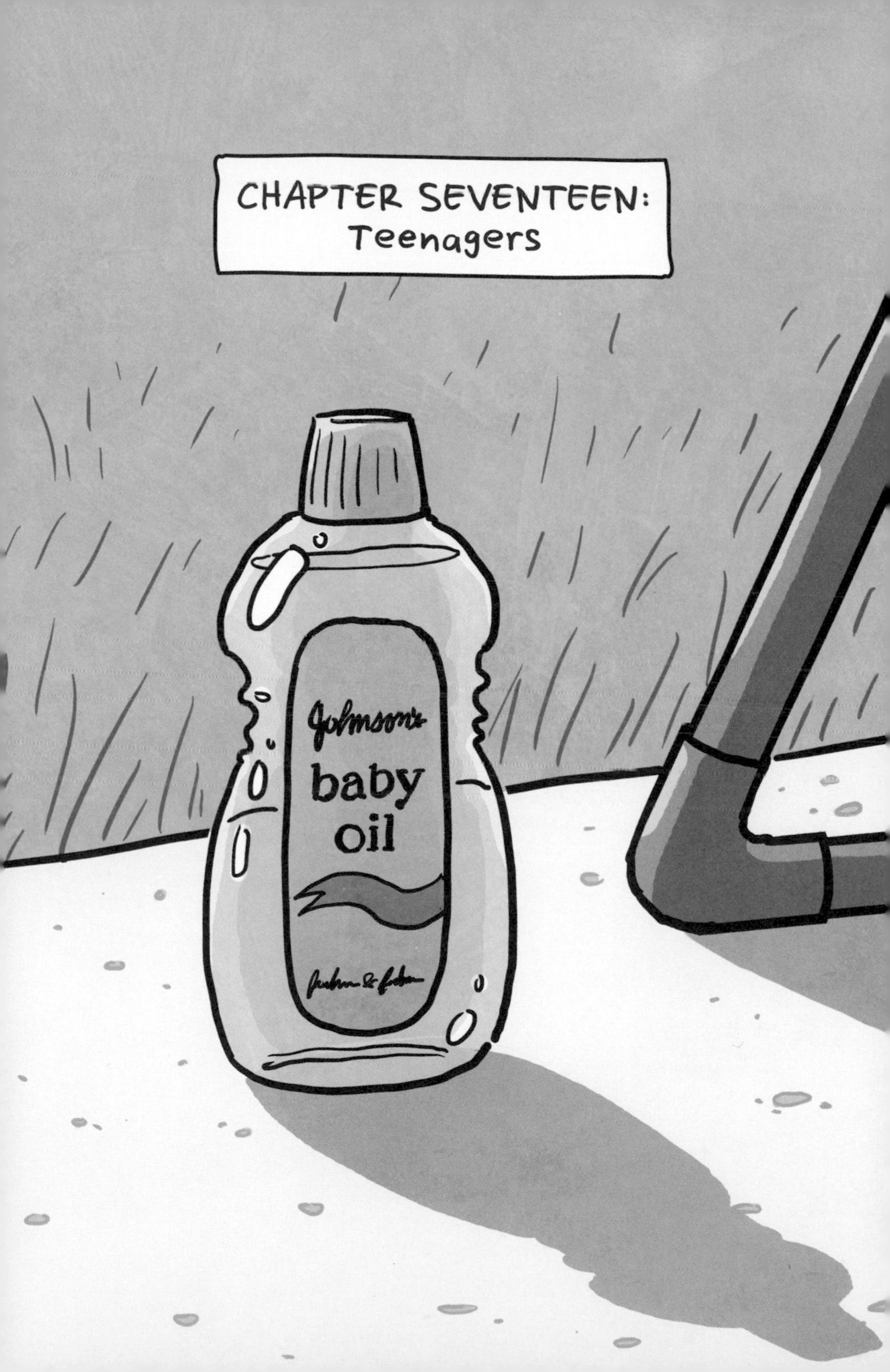
CHAPTER SEVENTEEN:
Teenagers
Johnson's
baby
oil

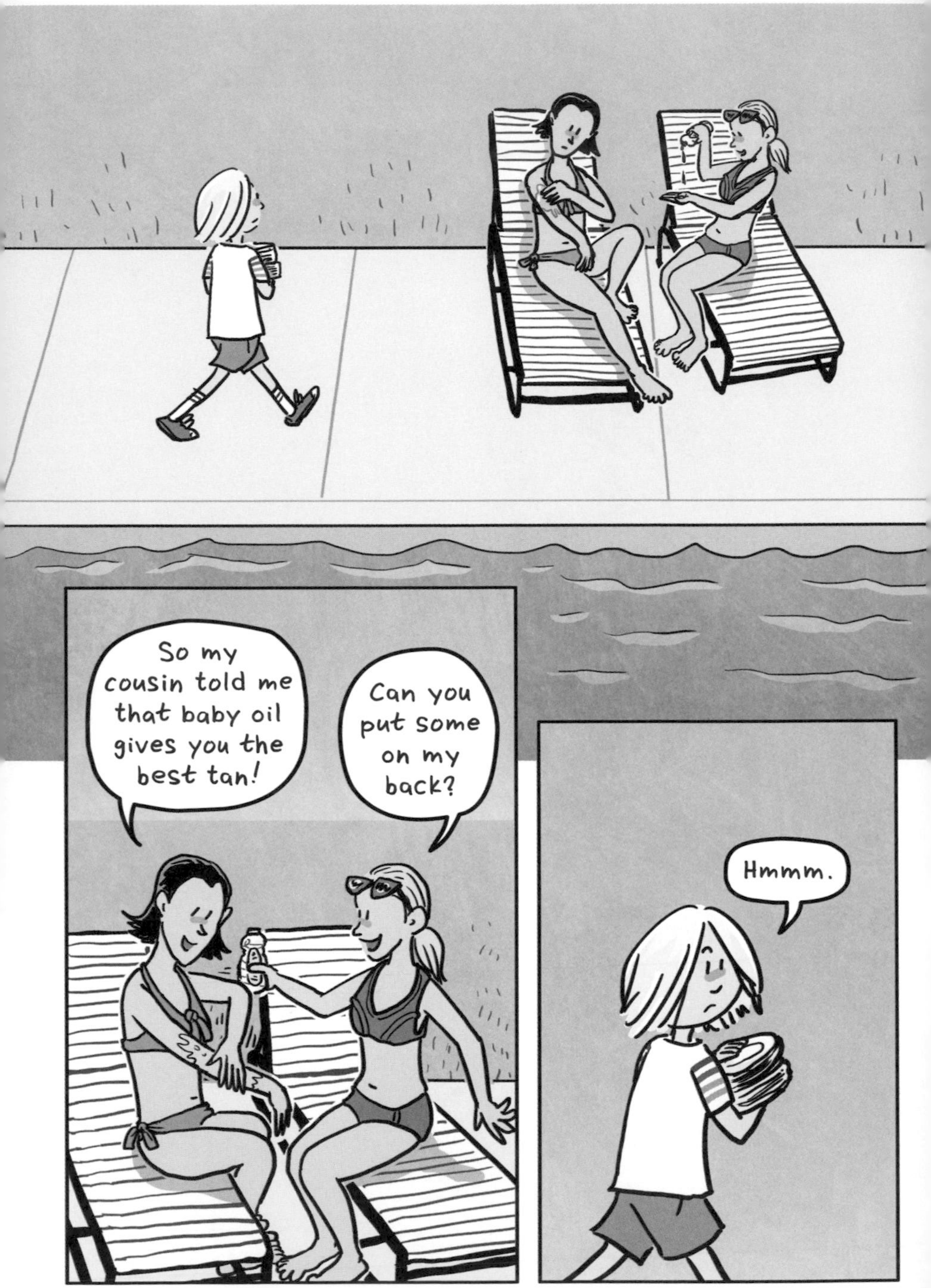
So my cousin told me that baby oil gives you the best tan!
Can you put some on my back?
Hmmm.

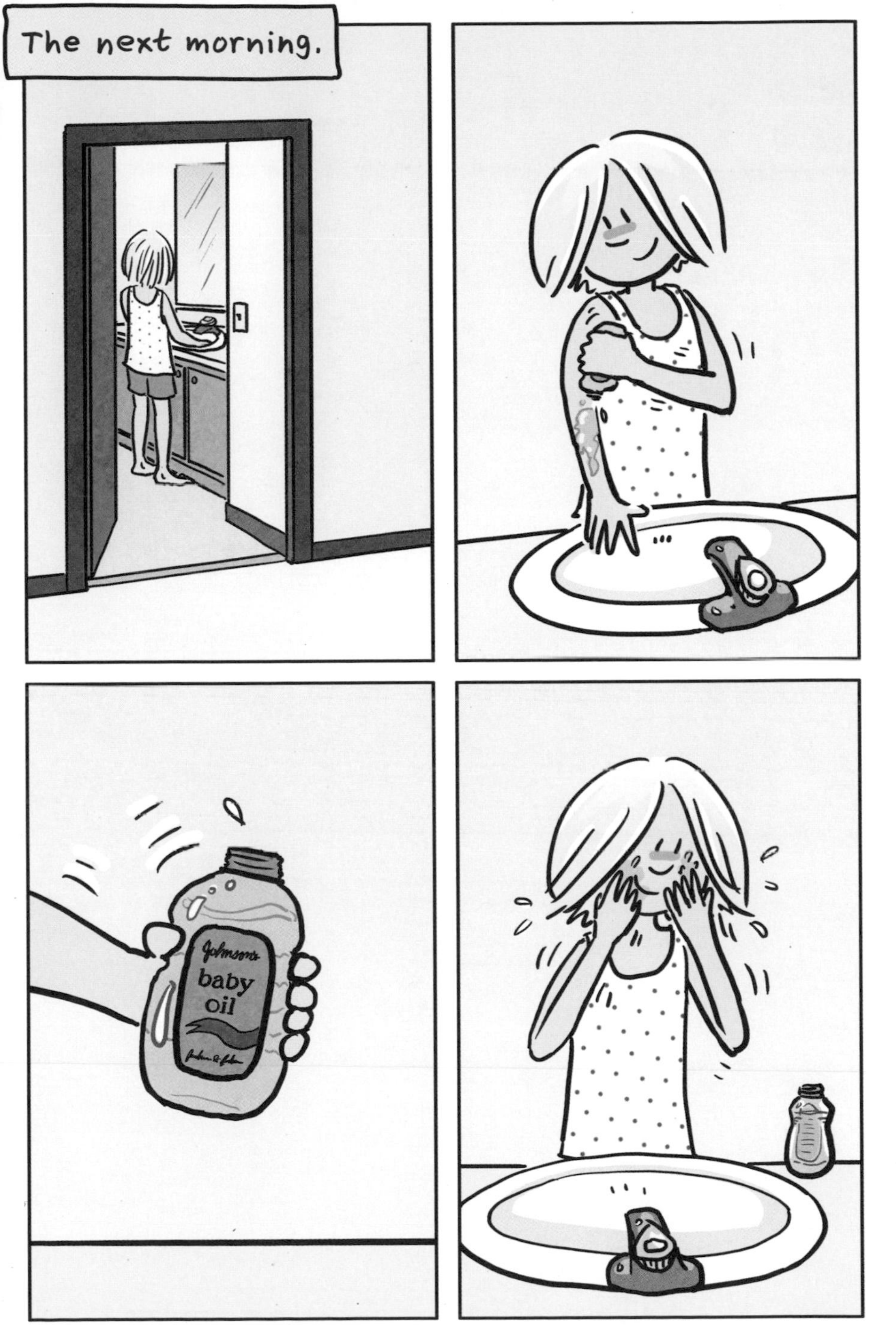
The next morning.
Johnson's
baby
oil

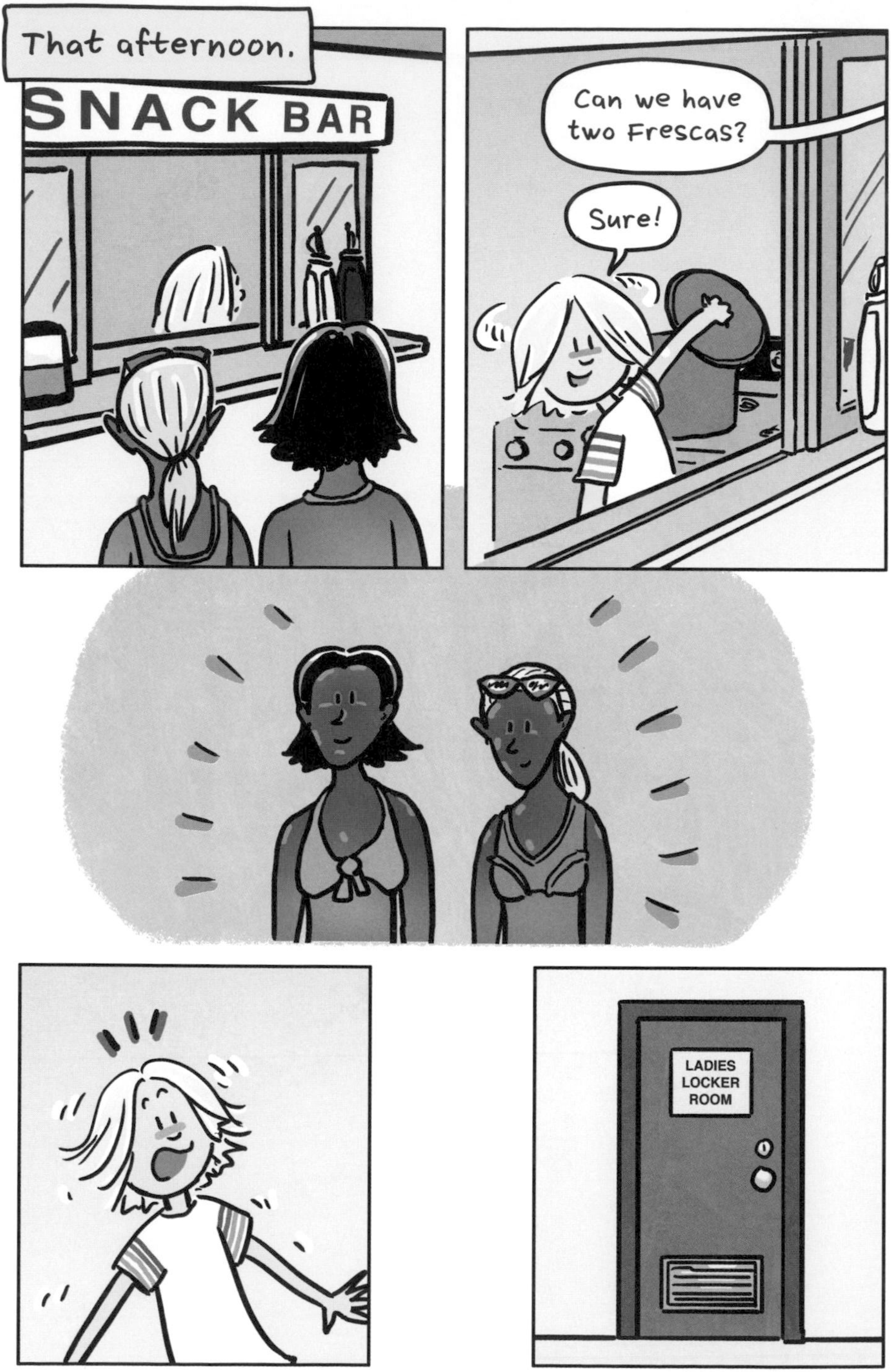
That afternoon.
SNACK BAR
Can we have two Frescas?
Sure!
LADIES LOCKER ROOM

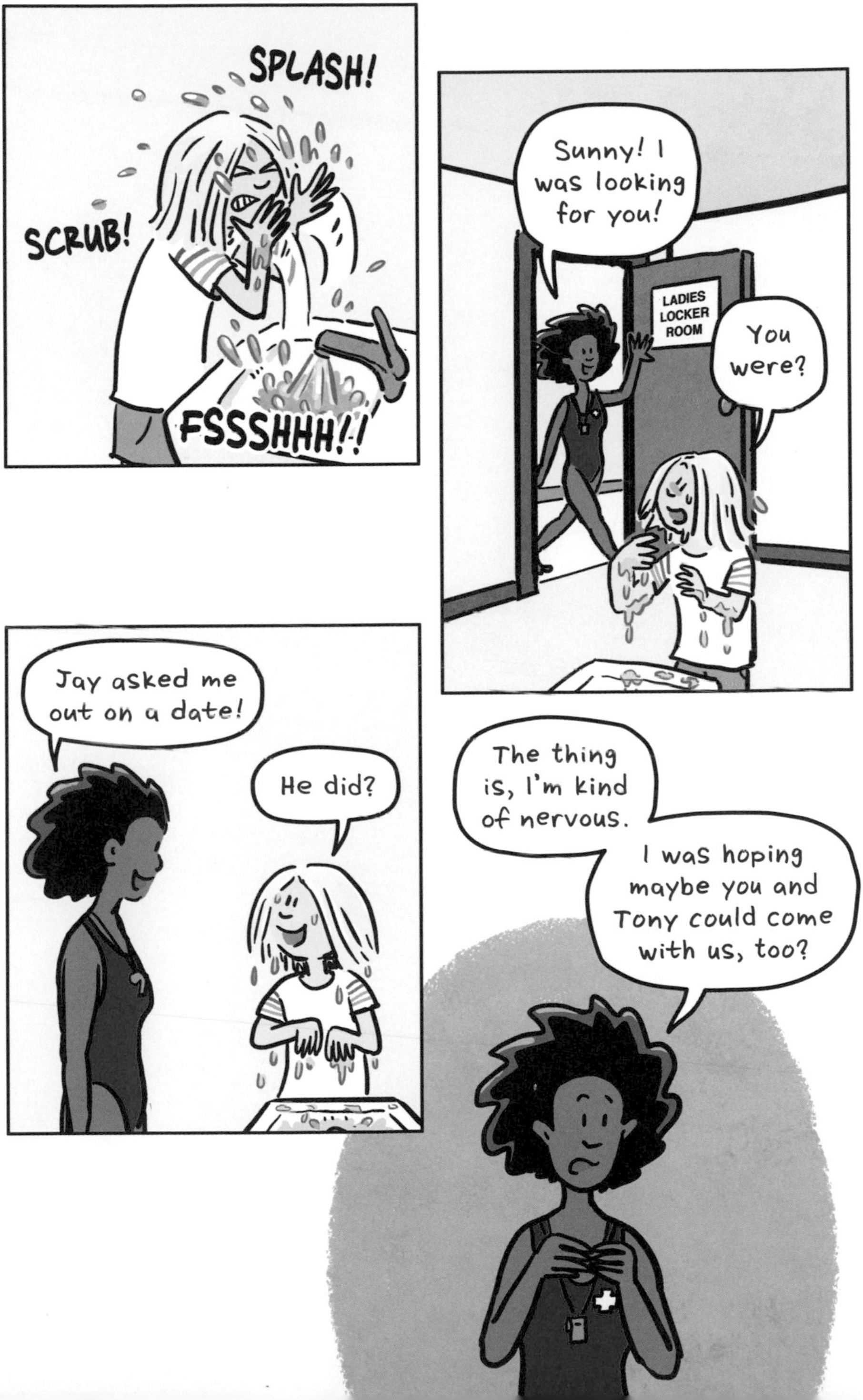
SPLASH!
SCRUB!
FSSSHHH!!
Sunny! I was looking for you!
LADIES LOCKER ROOM
You were?
Jay asked me out on a date!
He did?
The thing is, I'm kind of nervous.
I was hoping maybe you and Tony could come with us, too?

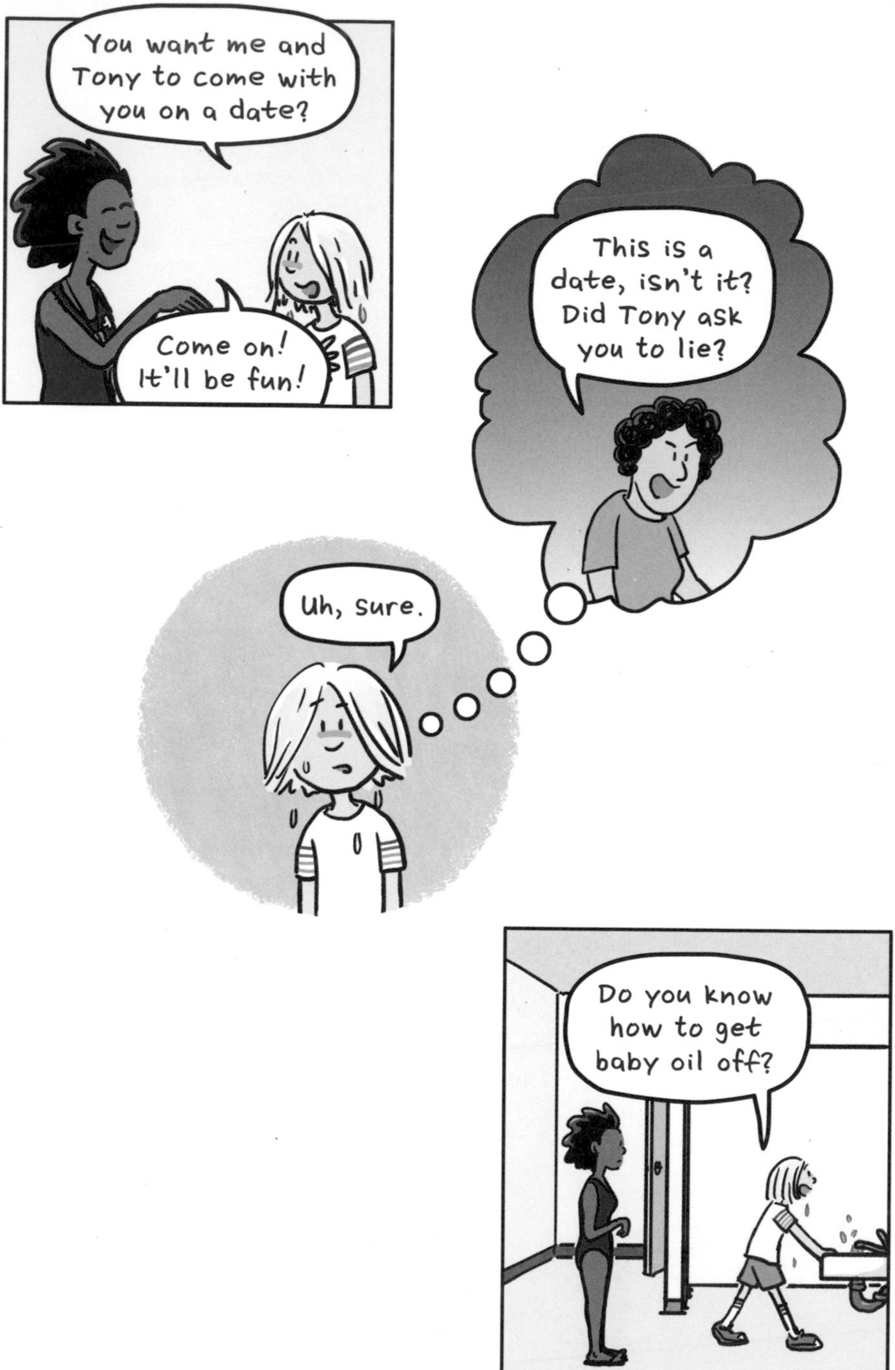
You want me and Tony to come with you on a date?
Come on! It'll be fun!
This is a date, isn't it? Did Tony ask you to lie?
Uh, sure.
Do you know how to get baby oil off?

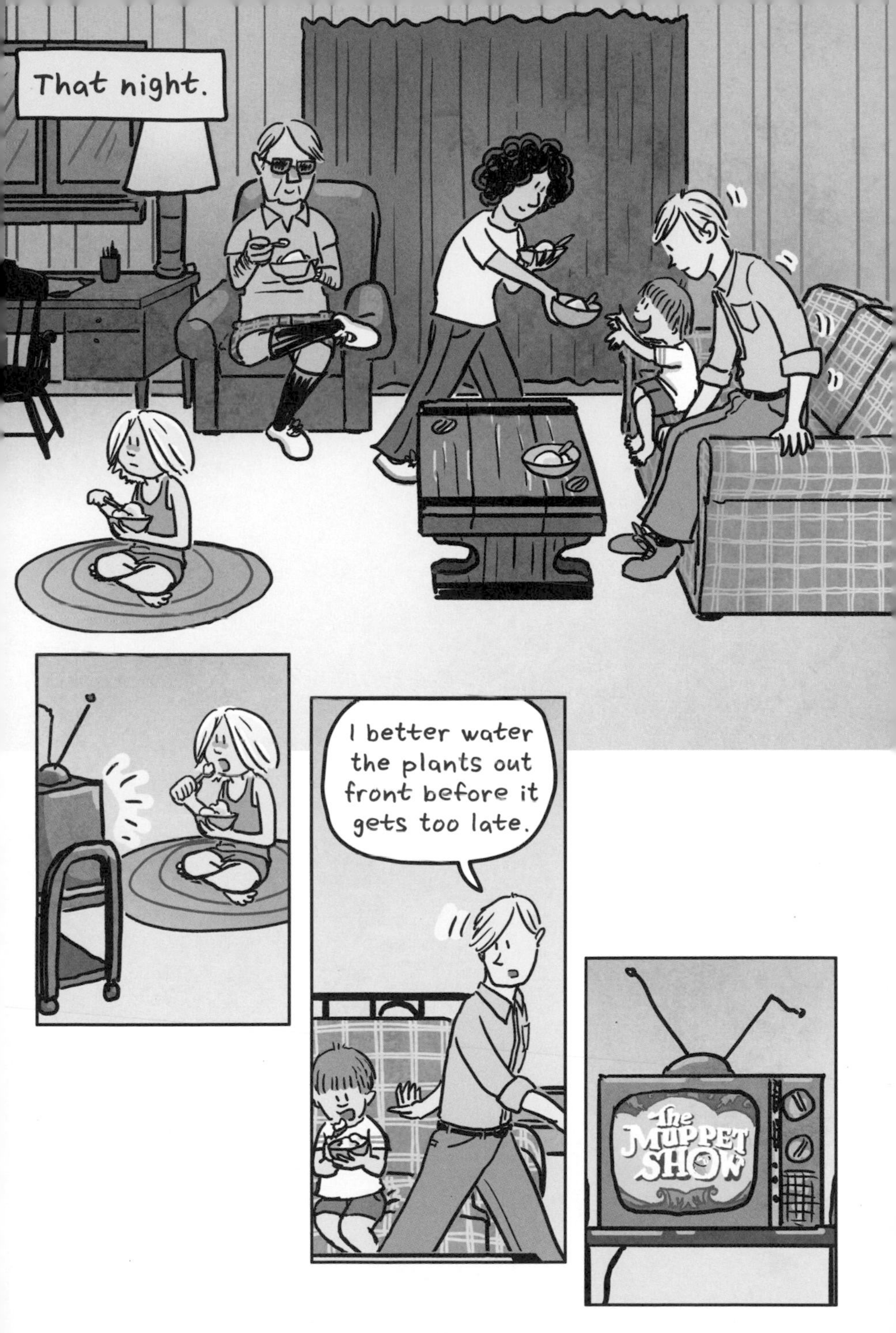
That night.
I better water the plants out front before it gets too late.
The Muppet Show

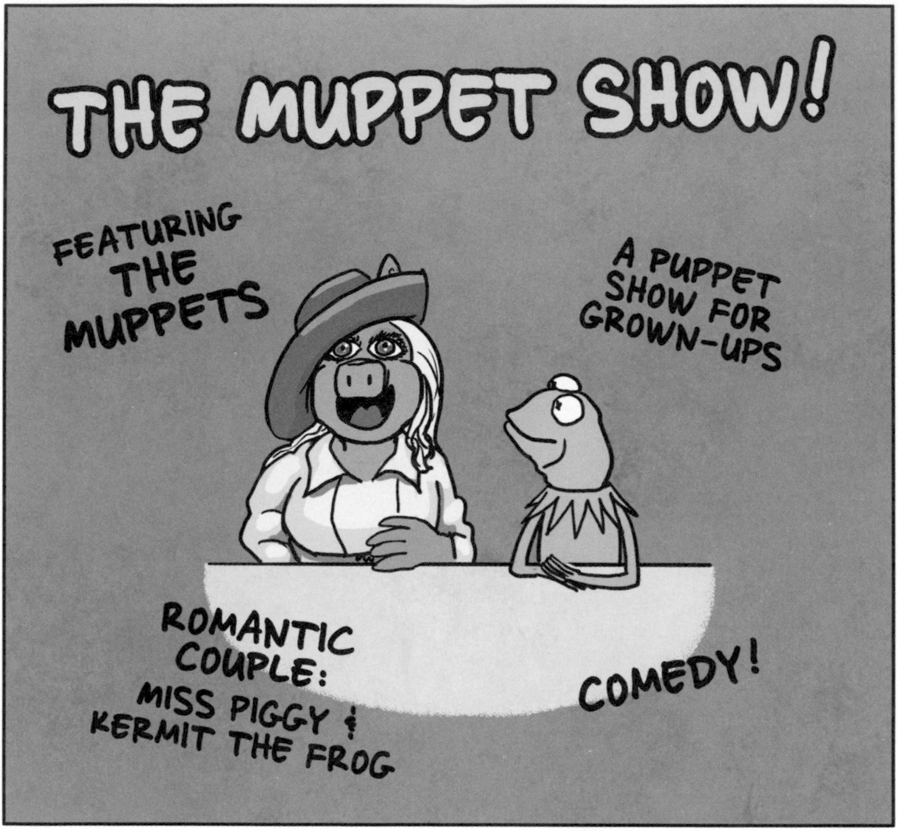
THE MUPPET SHOW!
FEATURING THE MUPPETS
A PUPPET SHOW FOR GROWN-UPS
ROMANTIC COUPLE: MISS PIGGY & KERMIT THE FROG
COMEDY!

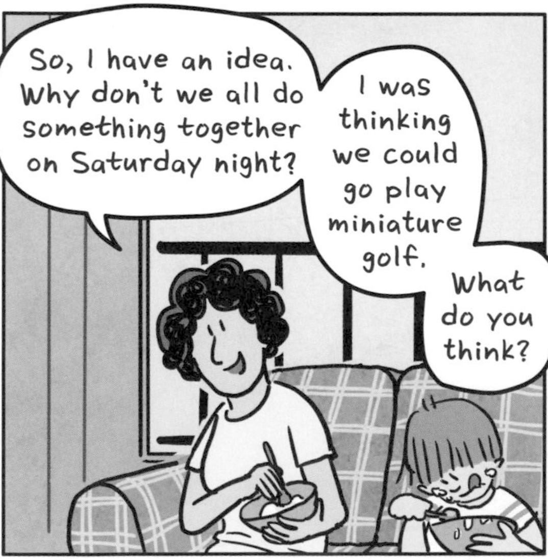
So, I have an idea. Why don't we all do something together on Saturday night?
I was thinking we could go play miniature golf.
What do you think?

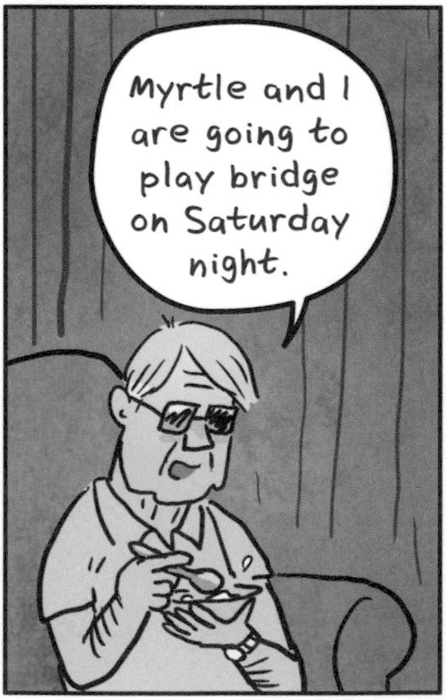
Myrtle and I are going to play bridge on Saturday night.

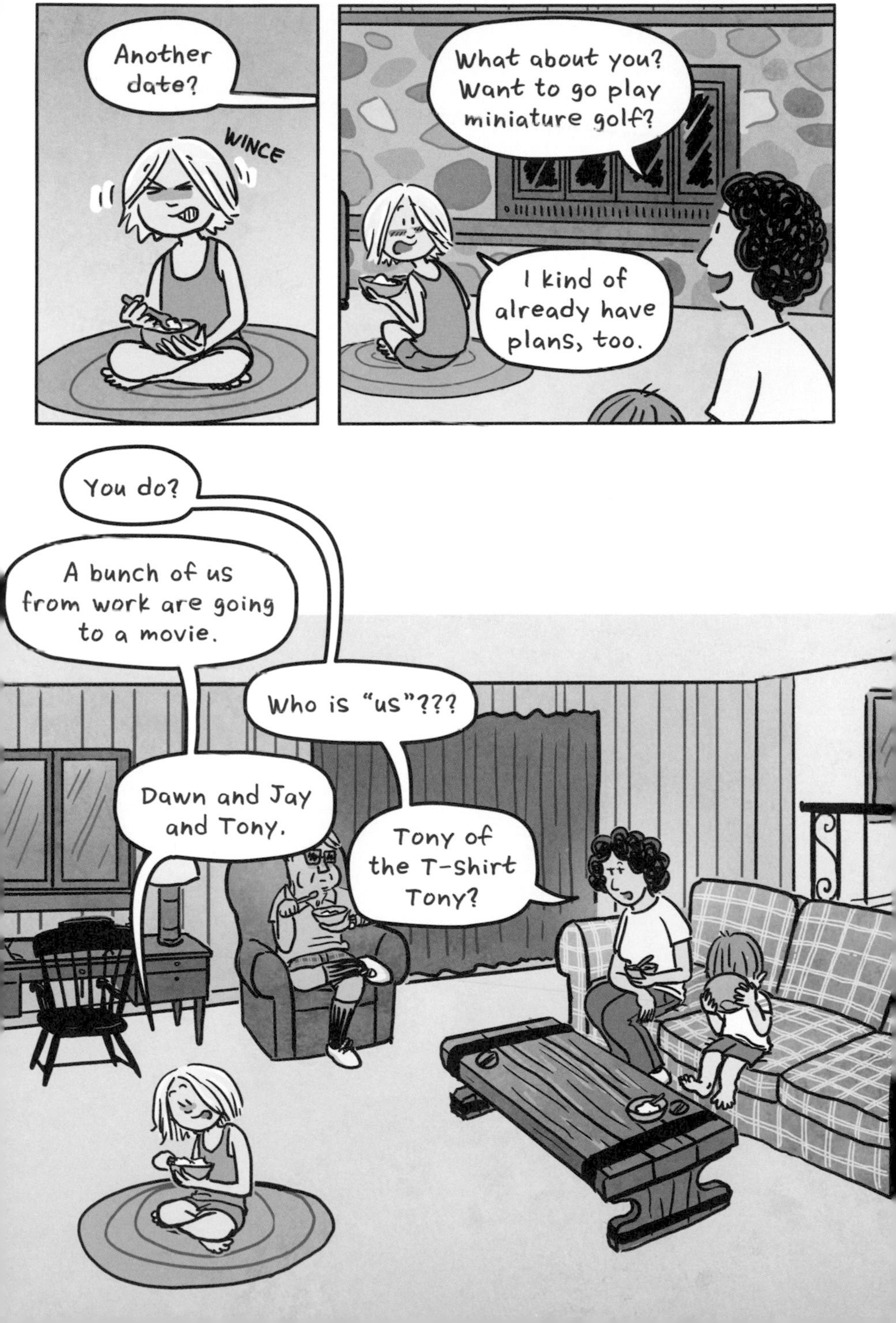
Another date?
WINCE
What about you? Want to go play miniature golf?
I kind of already have plans, too.
You do?
A bunch of us from work are going to a movie.
Who is "us"???
Dawn and Jay and Tony.
Tony of the T-shirt Tony?

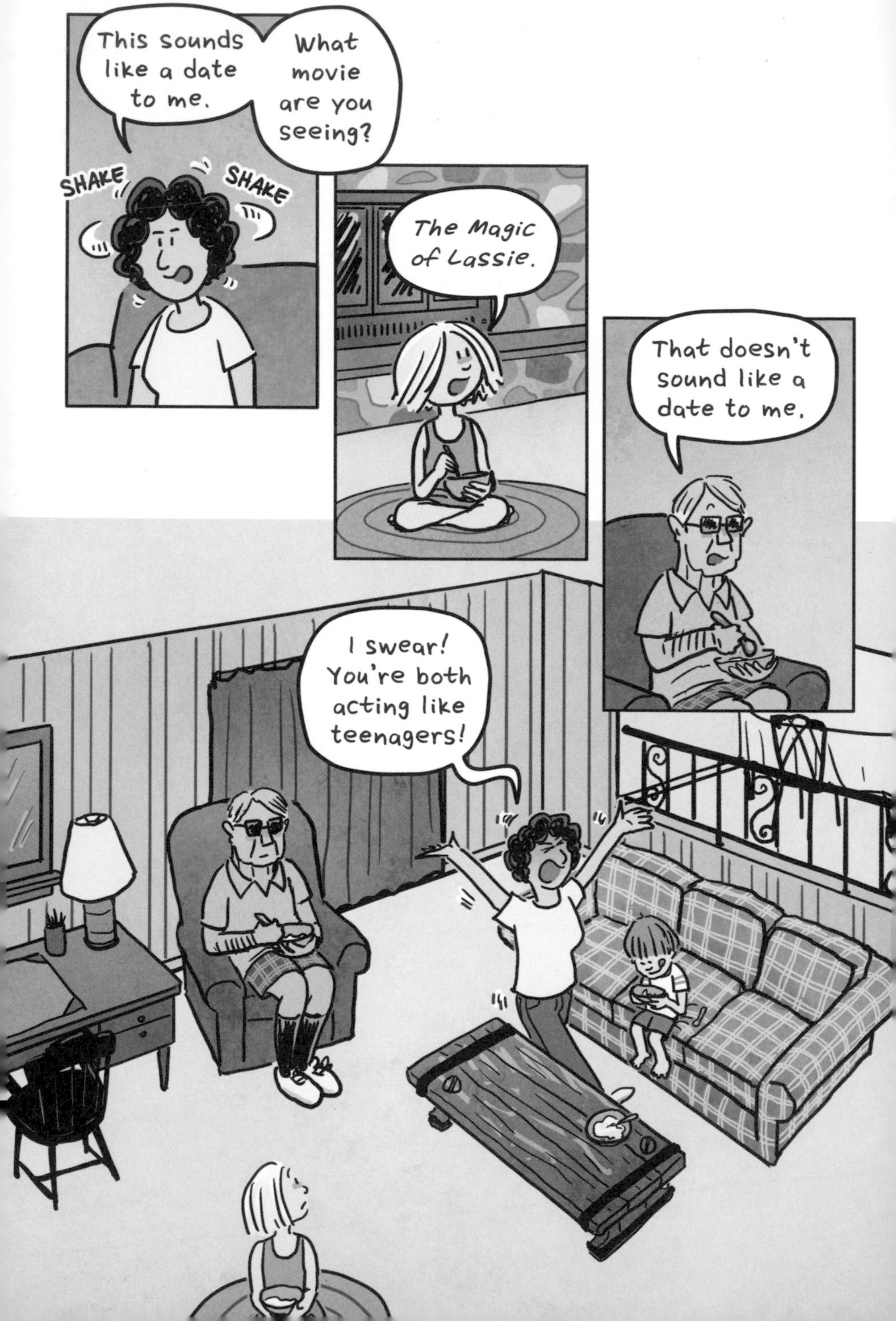
This sounds like a date to me.
What movie are you seeing?
SHAKE
SHAKE
The Magic of Lassie.
That doesn't sound like a date to me.
I swear! You're both acting like teenagers!

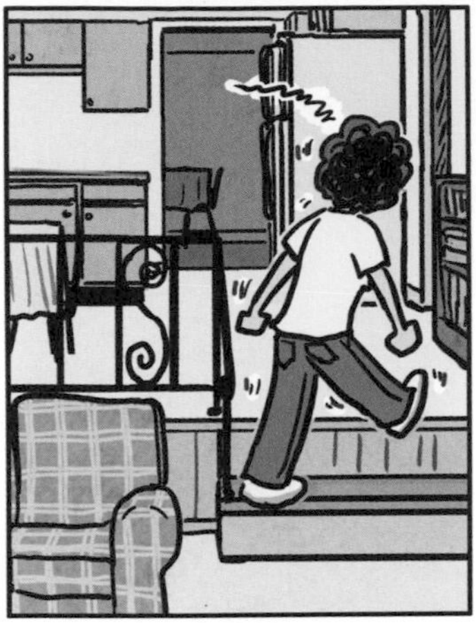

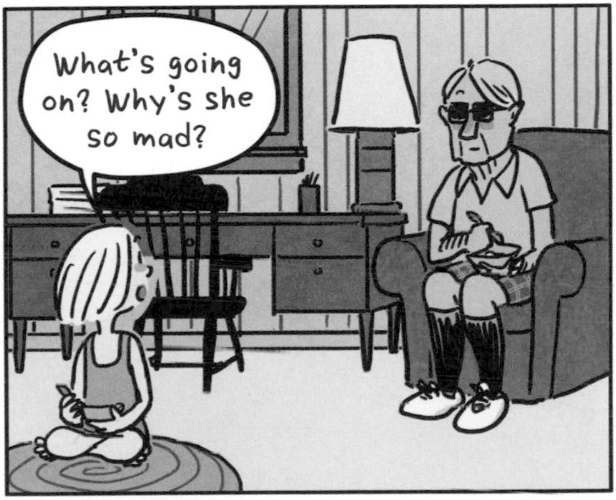
What's going on? Why's she so mad?

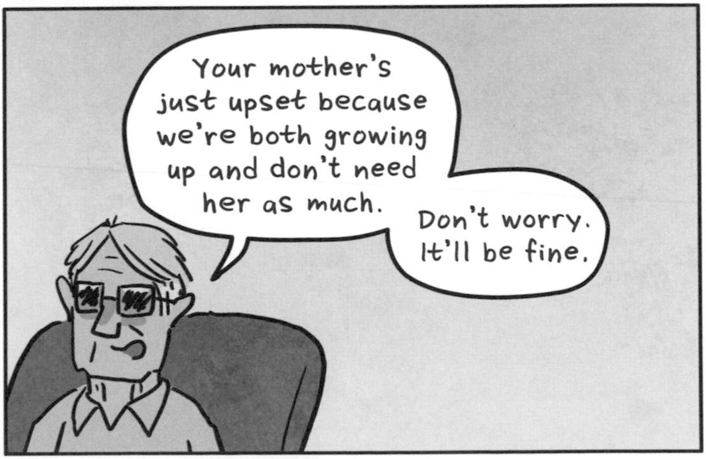
Your mother's just upset because we're both growing up and don't need her as much.
Don't worry. It'll be fine.

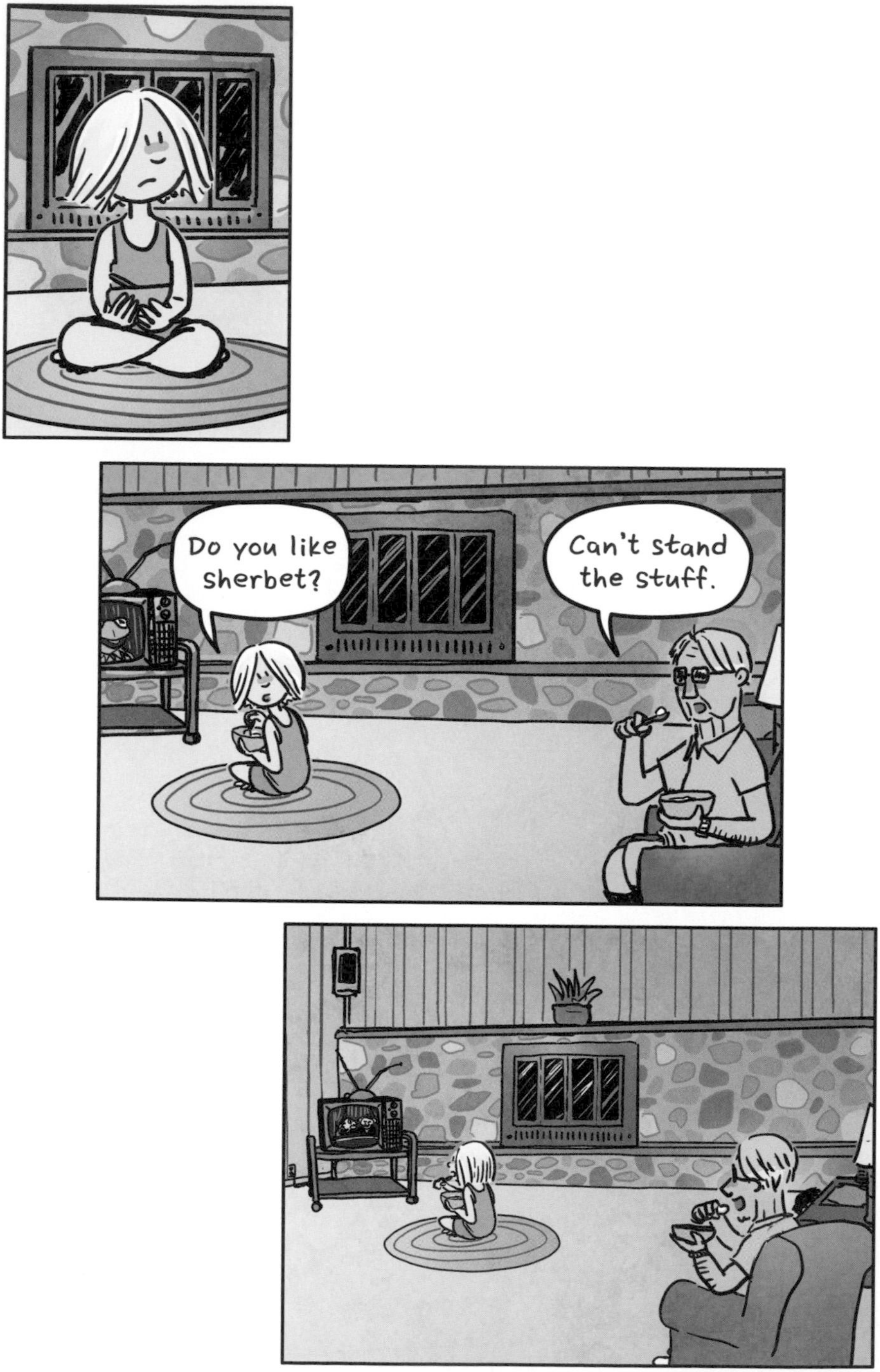
Do you like sherbet?
Can't stand the stuff.

CHAPTER EIGHTEEN: Fireworks

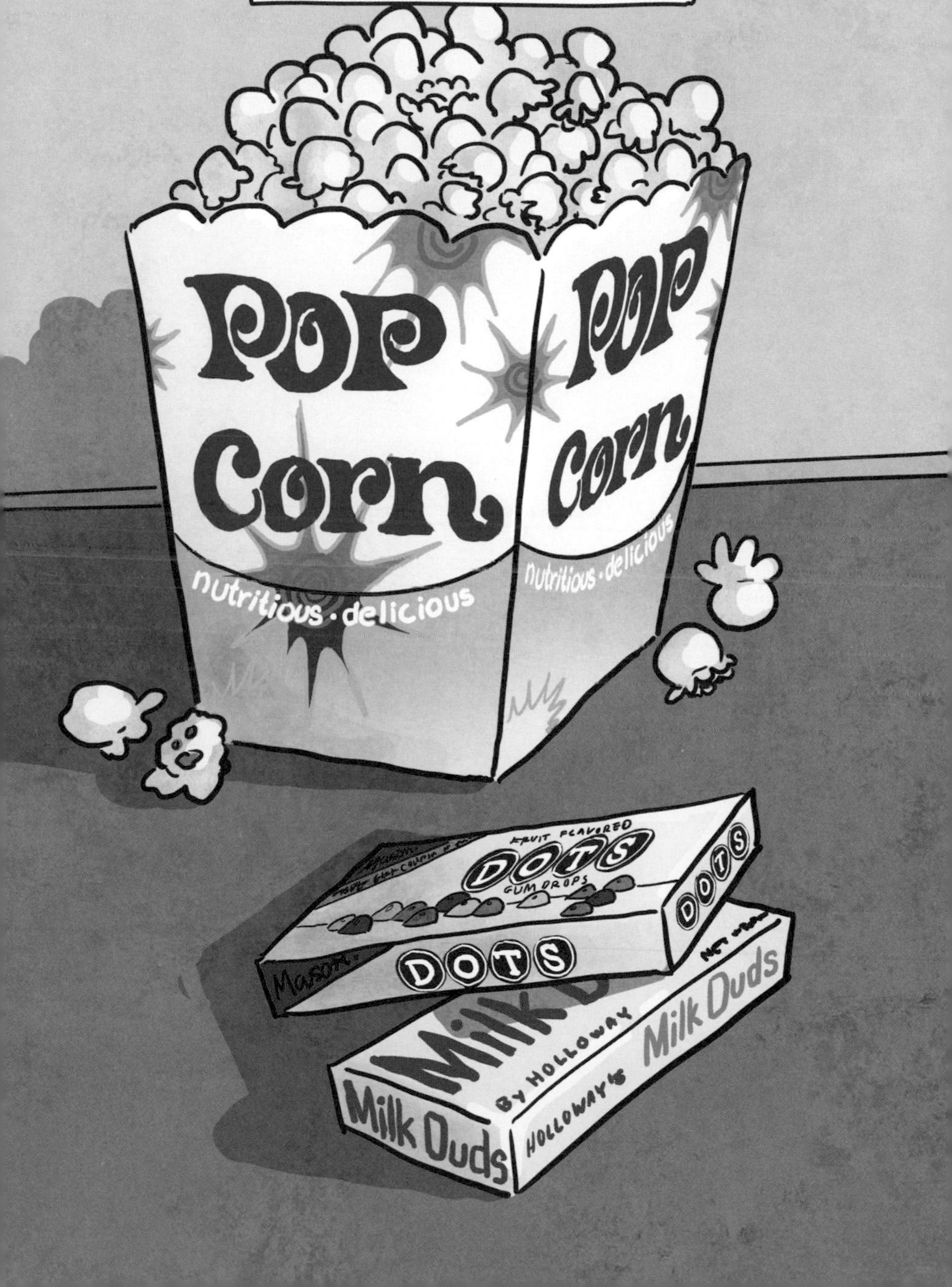
POP
CORN
nutritious · delicious
POP
CORN
nutritious · delicious
FRUIT FLAVORED
DOTS
GUM DROPS
DOTS
DOTS
Milk Duds
BY HOLLOWAY
Milk Duds
HOLLOWAY'S
Milk Duds

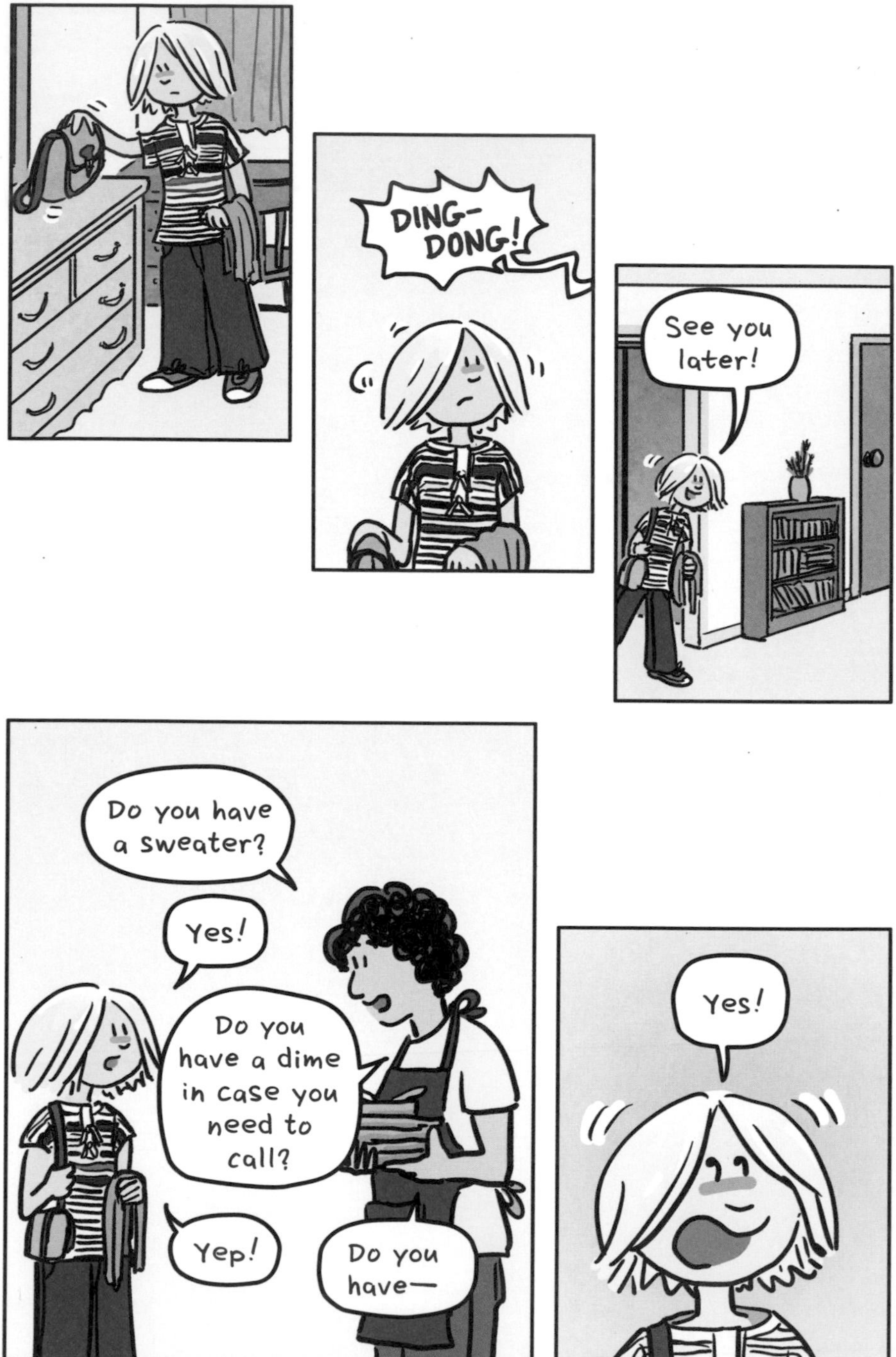
DING-DONG!
See you later!
Do you have a sweater?
Yes!
Do you have a dime in case you need to call?
Yep!
Do you have—
Yes!

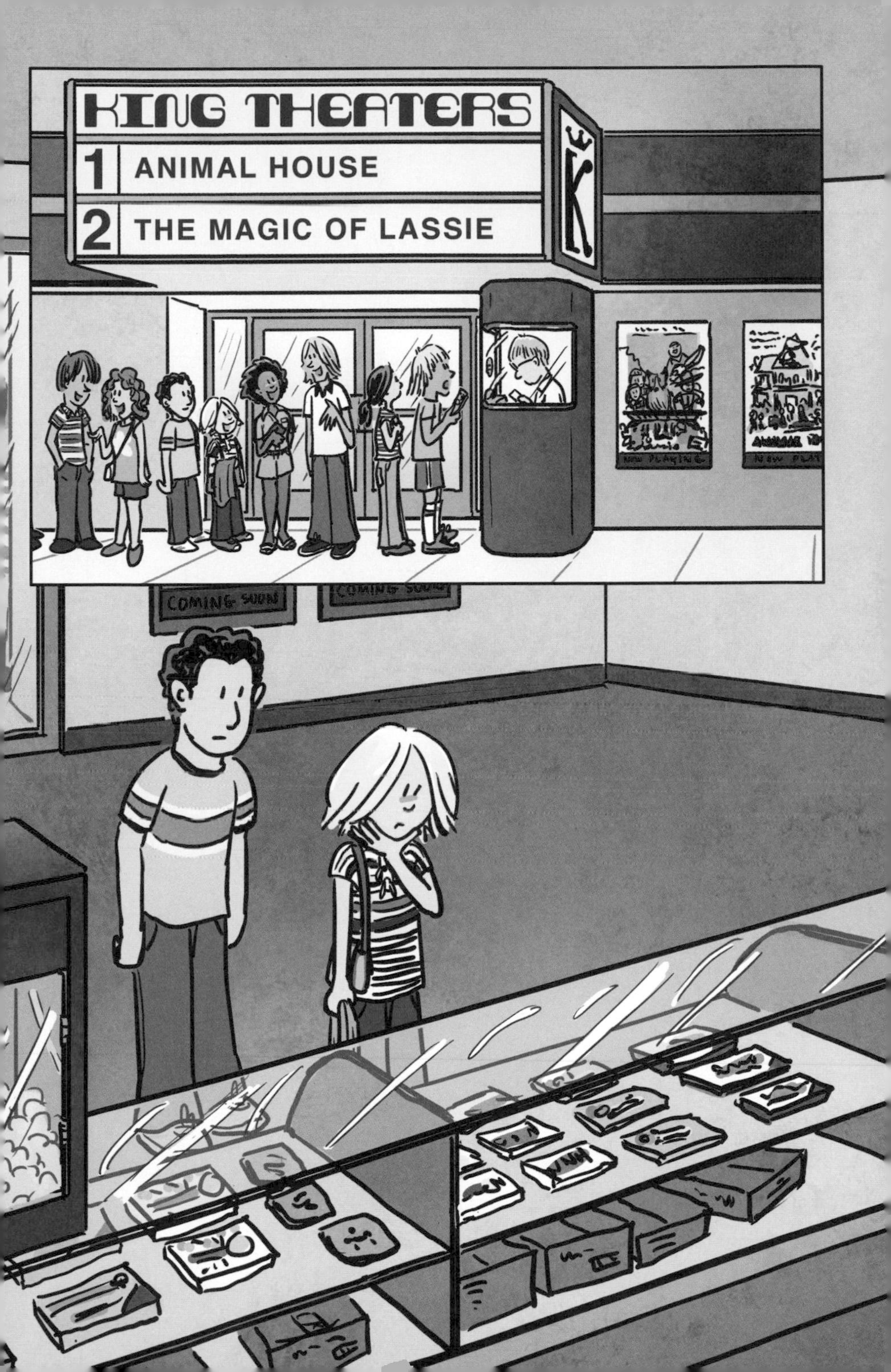
KING THEATERS
1 ANIMAL HOUSE
2 THE MAGIC OF LASSIE
K
COMING SOON
COMING SOON

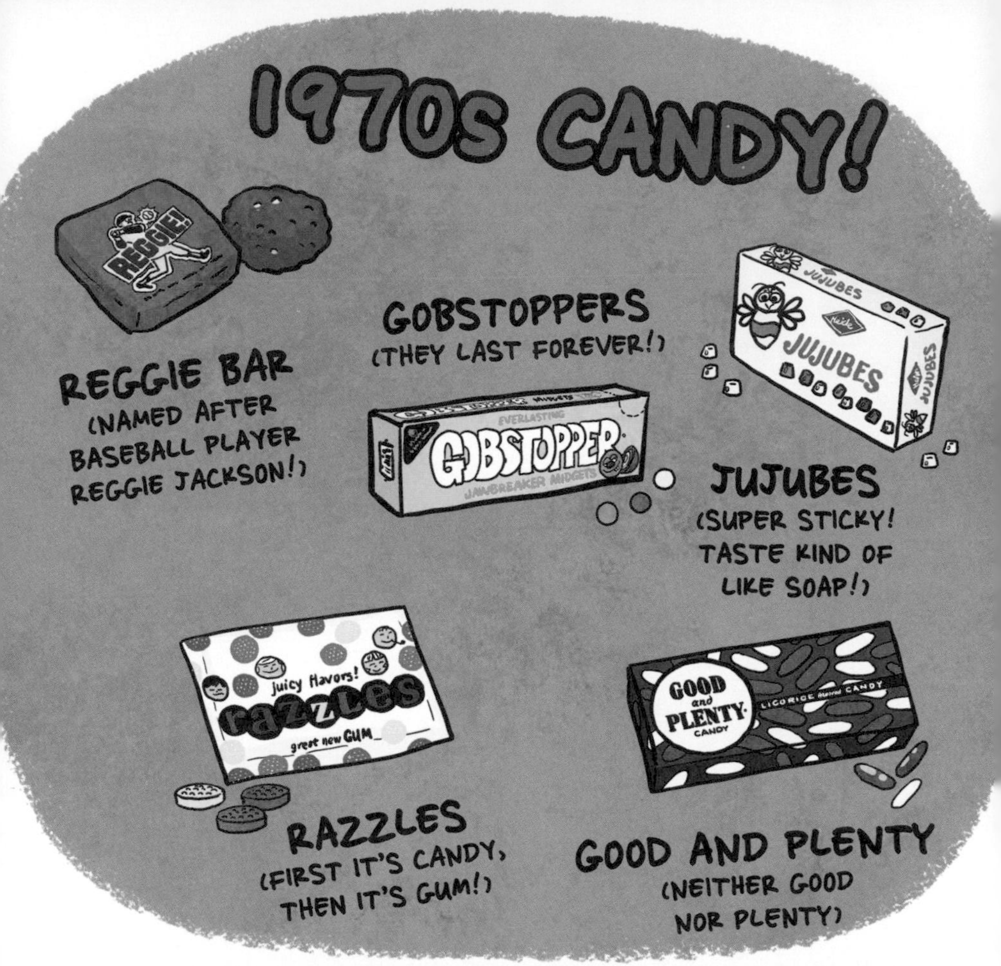
1970s CANDY!
REGGIE!
REGGIE BAR
(NAMED AFTER BASEBALL PLAYER REGGIE JACKSON!)
GOBSTOPPERS
(THEY LAST FOREVER!)
EVERLASTING
GOBSTOPPER
JAWBREAKER MIDGETS
JUJUBES
Heide
JUJUBES
(SUPER STICKY! TASTE KIND OF LIKE SOAP!)
juicy flavors!
razzles
great new GUM
RAZZLES
(FIRST IT'S CANDY, THEN IT'S GUM!)
GOOD and PLENTY
CANDY
LICORICE flavored CANDY
GOOD AND PLENTY
(NEITHER GOOD NOR PLENTY)

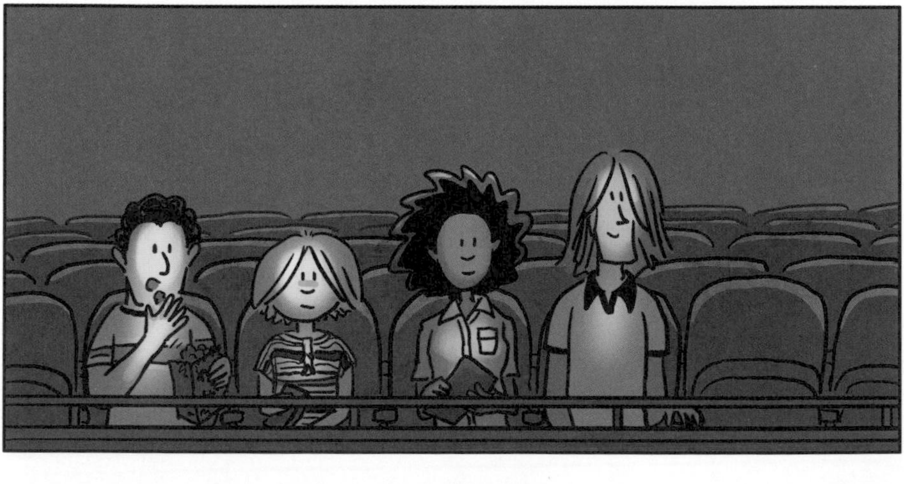

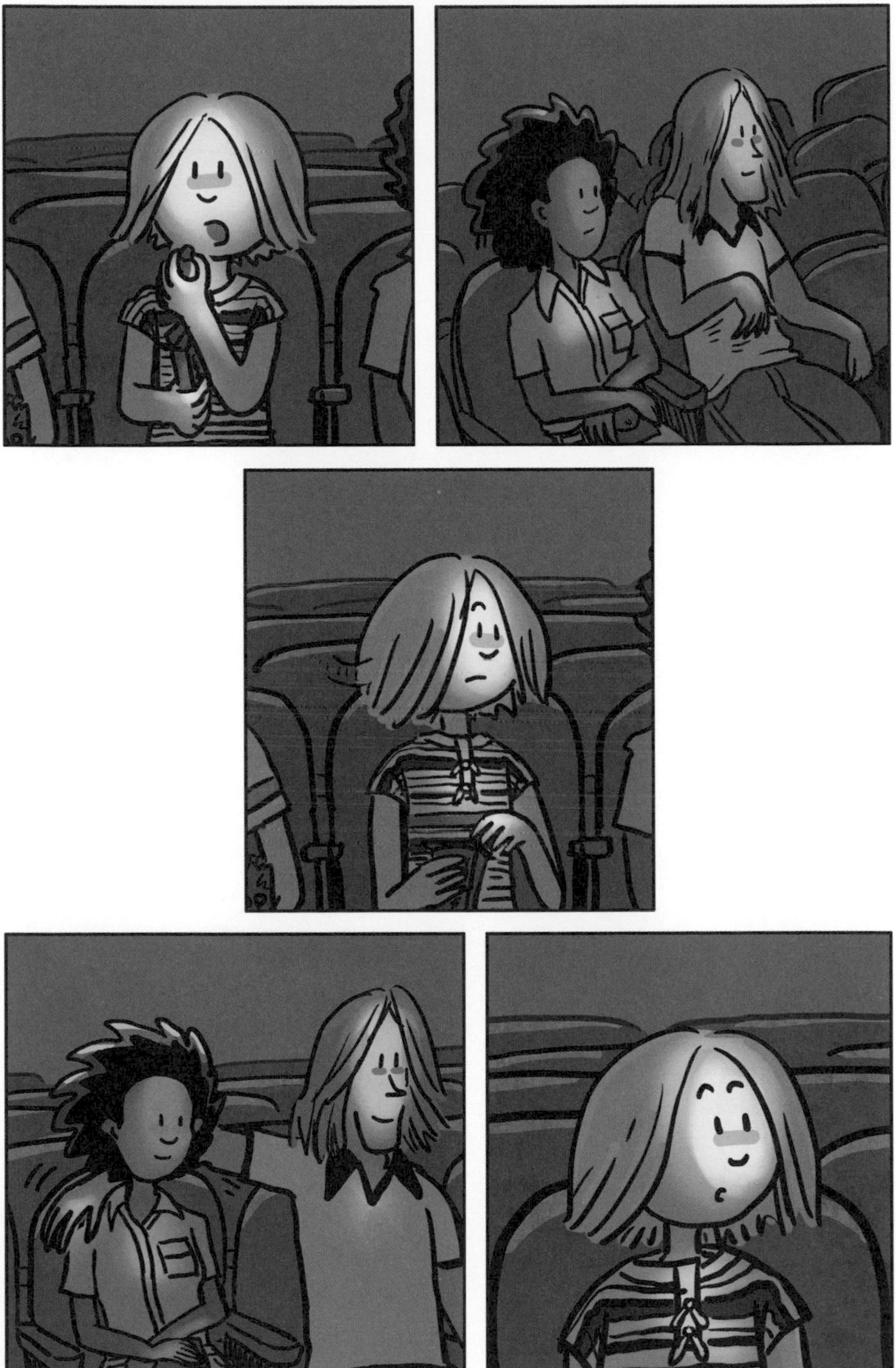

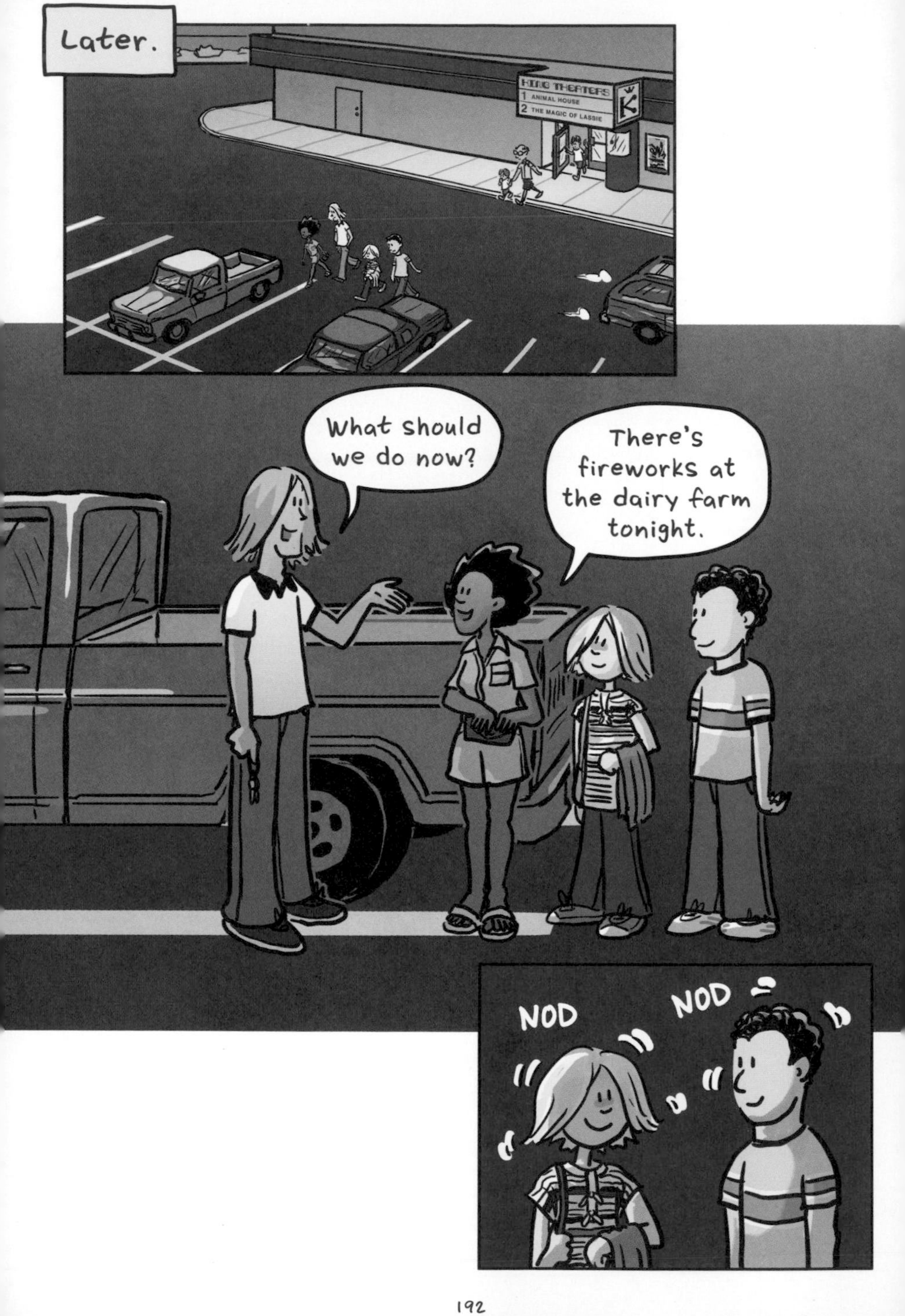
Later.
KING THEATERS
1 ANIMAL HOUSE
2 THE MAGIC OF LASSIE
What should we do now?
There's fireworks at the dairy farm tonight.
NOD
NOD

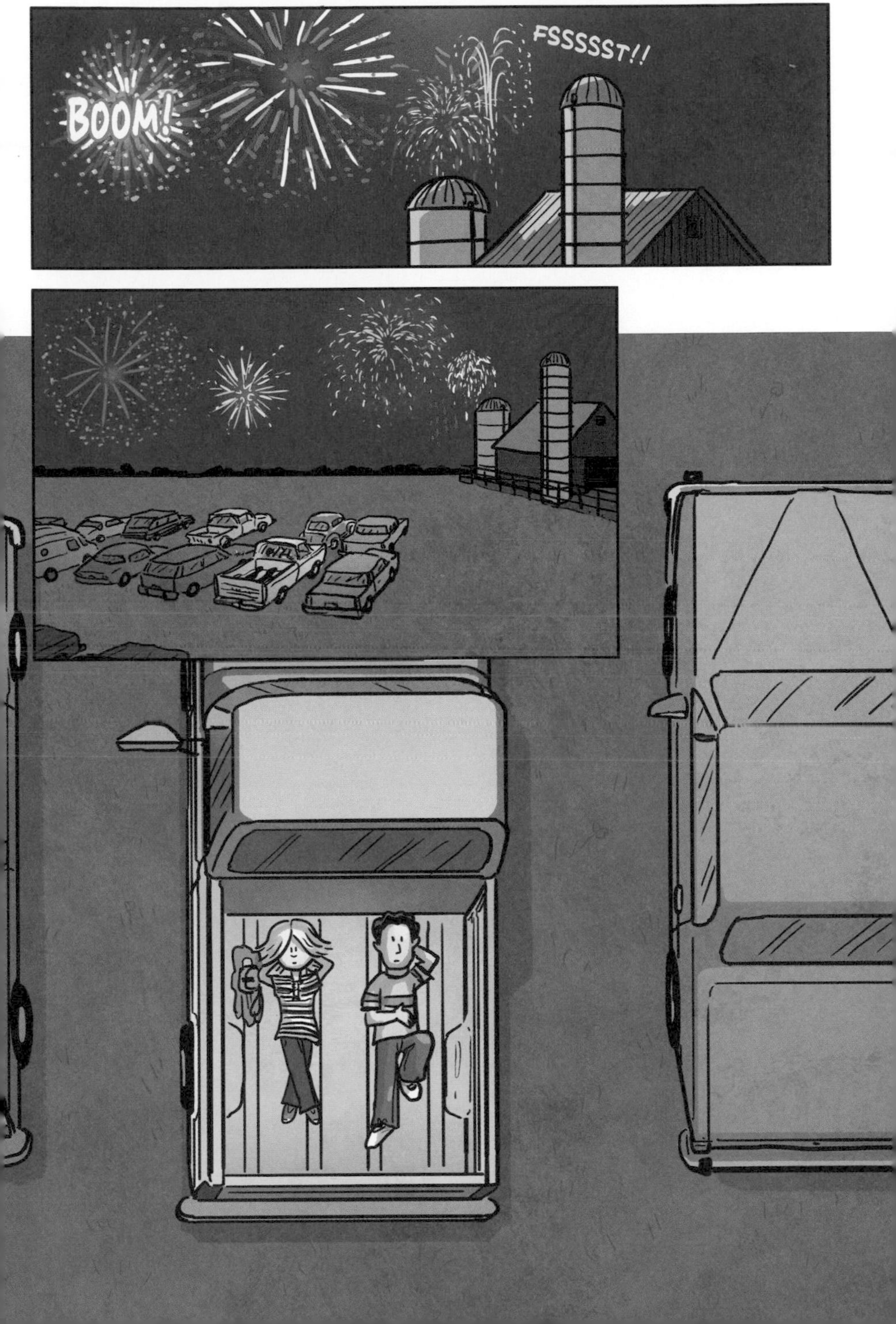
BOOM!
FSSSSST!!

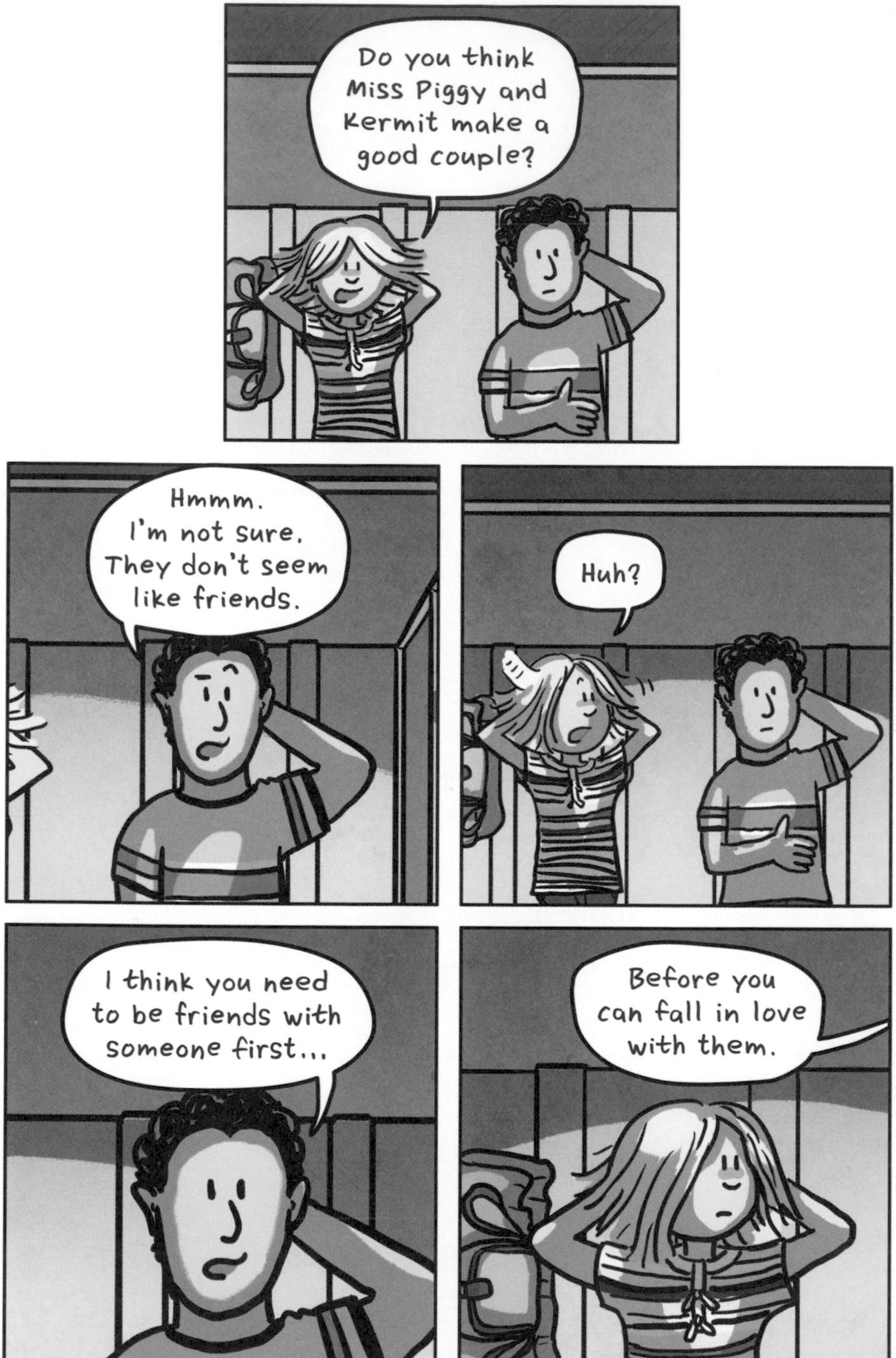
Do you think Miss Piggy and Kermit make a good couple?
Hmmm. I'm not sure. They don't seem like friends.
Huh?
I think you need to be friends with someone first...
Before you can fall in love with them.

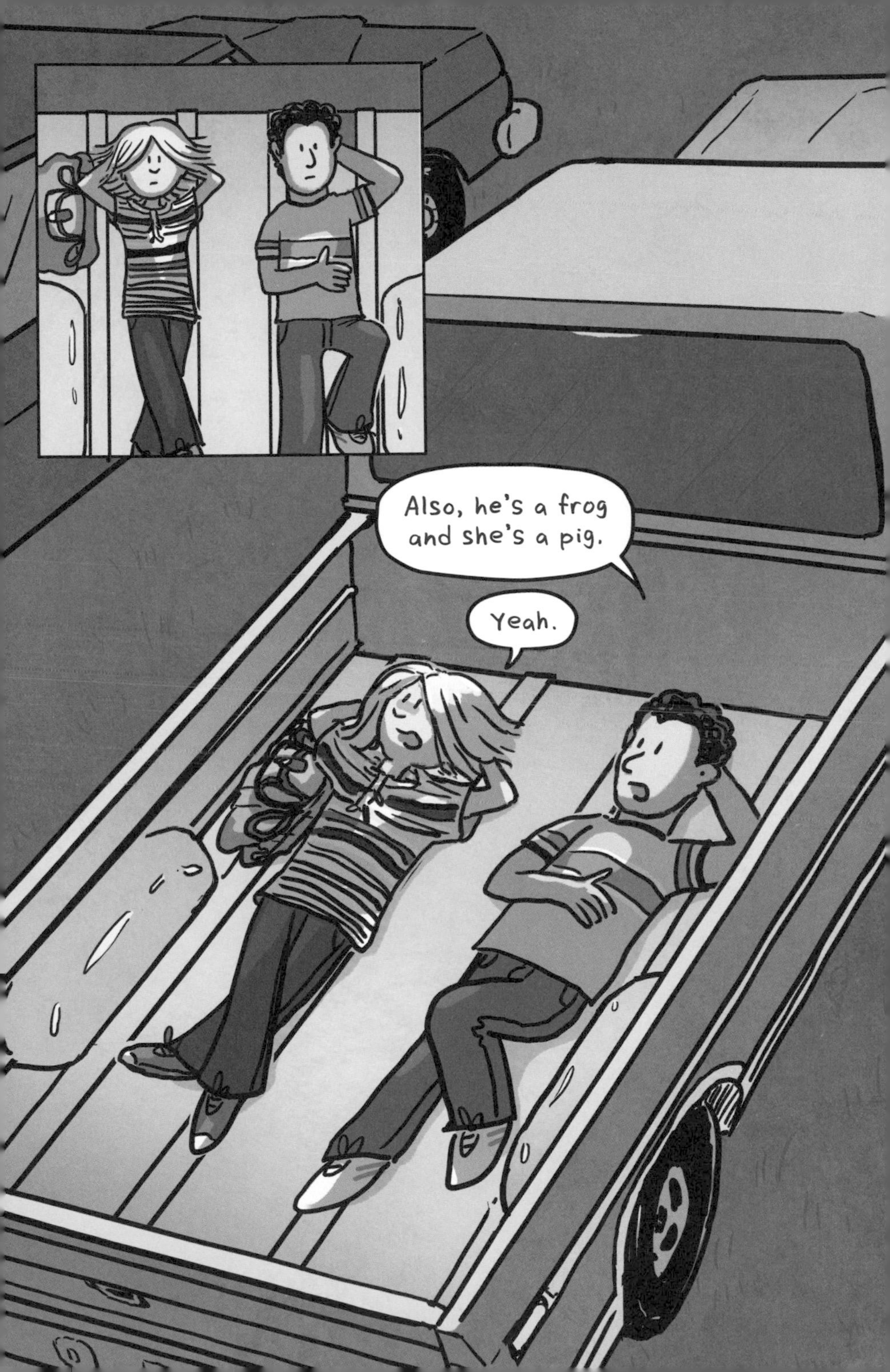
Also, he's a frog and she's a pig.
Yeah.

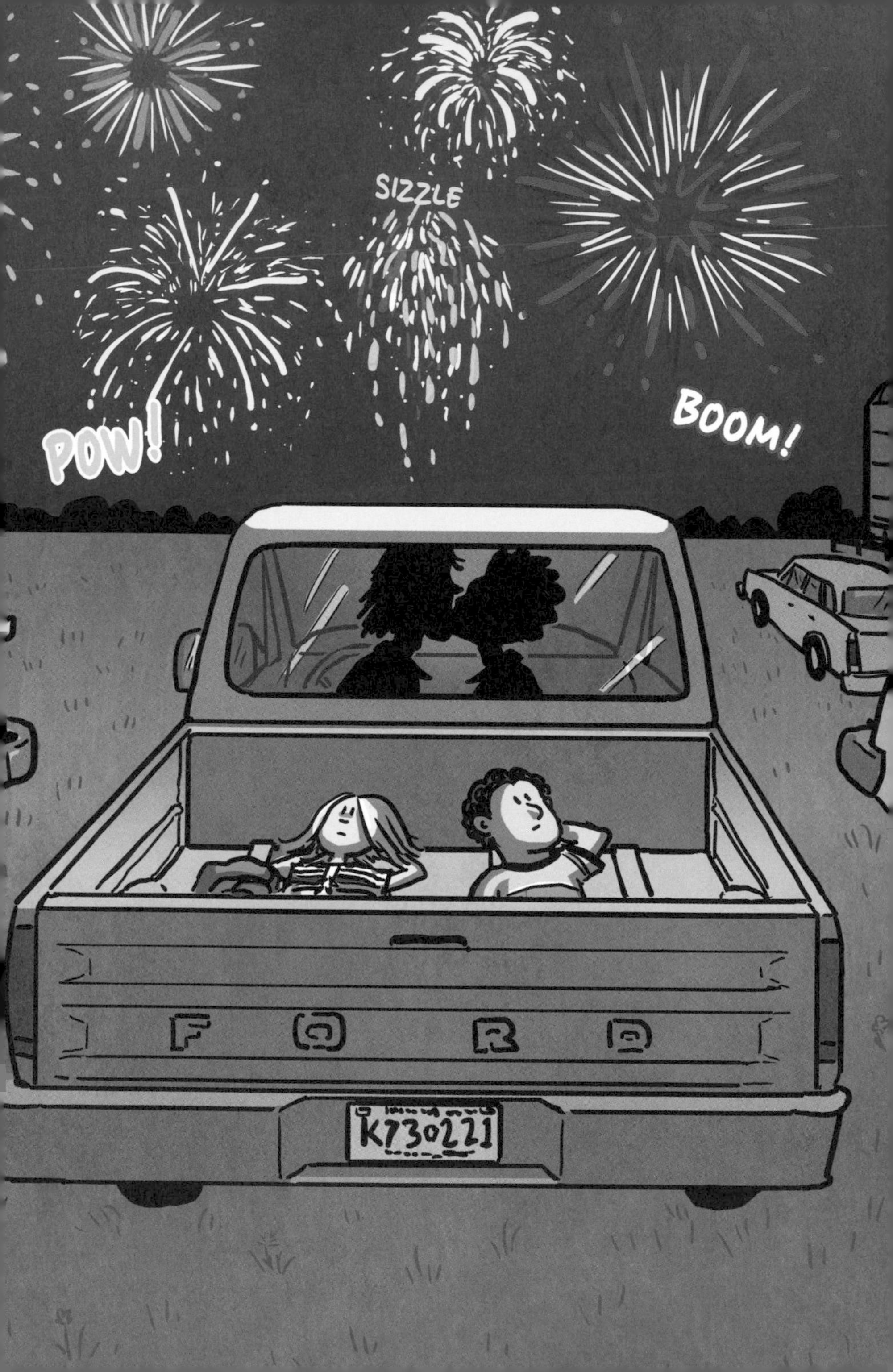
SIZZLE
POW!
BOOM!
FORD
K730221

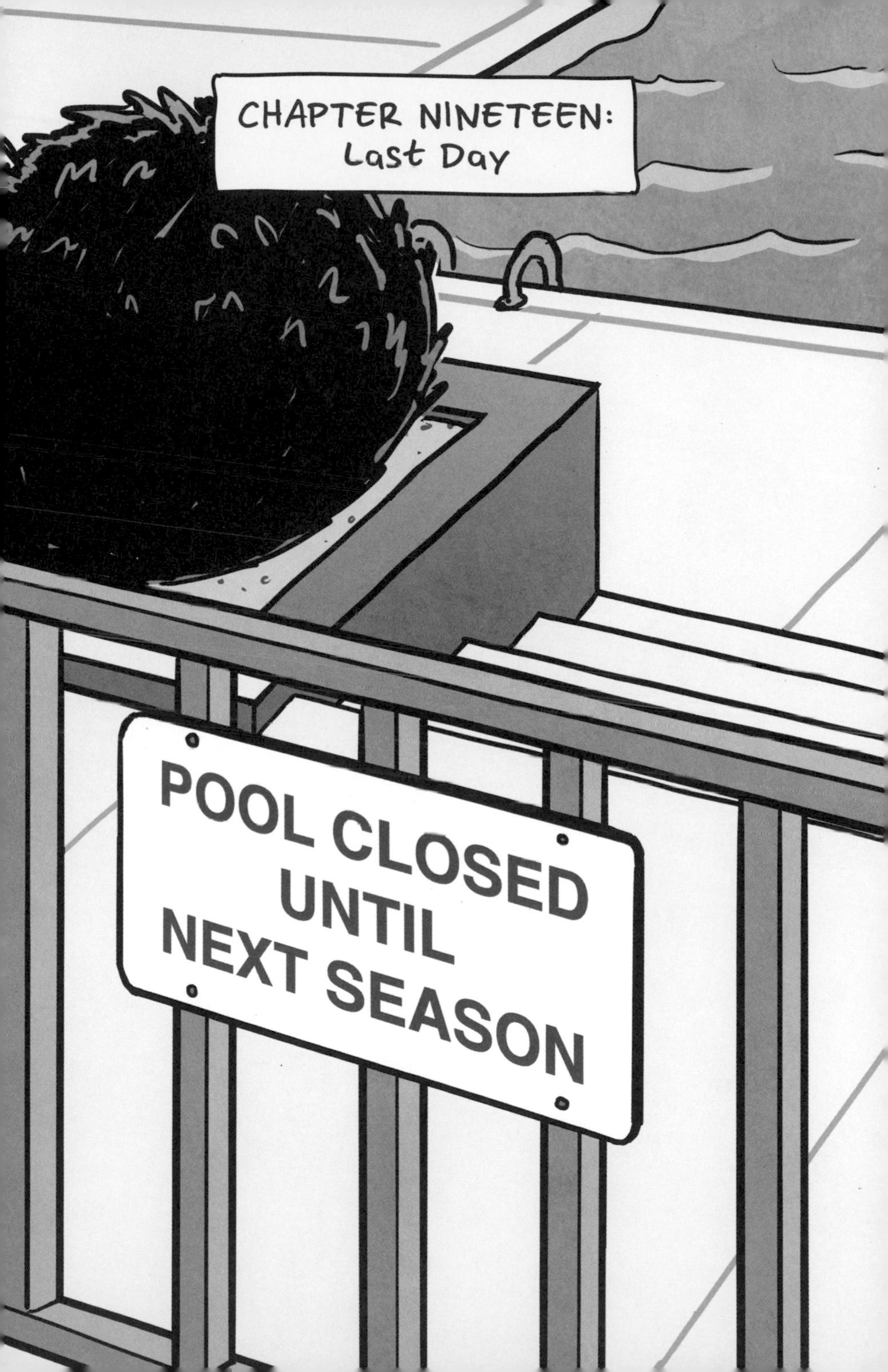
CHAPTER NINETEEN:
Last Day
POOL CLOSED
UNTIL
NEXT SEASON

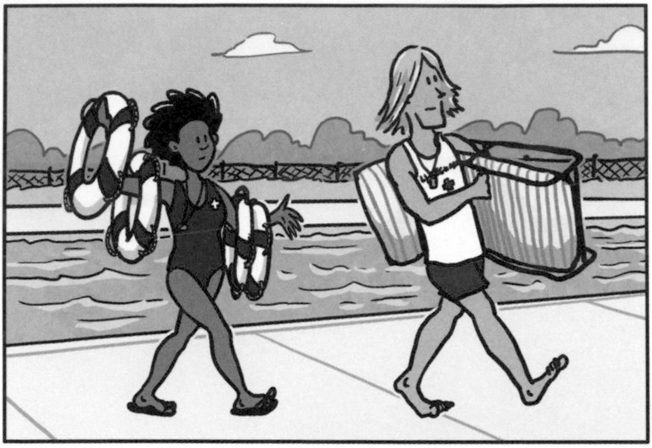

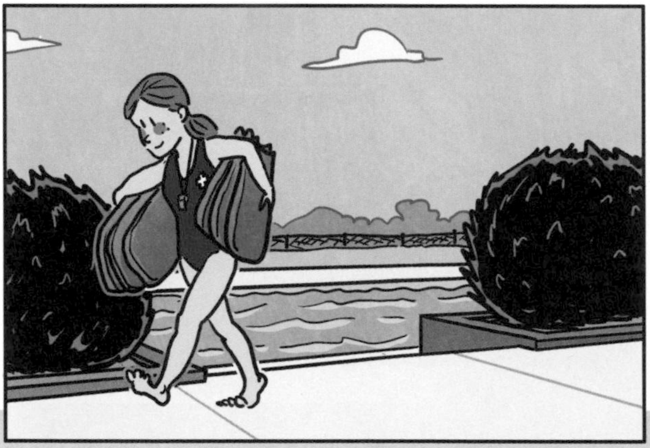

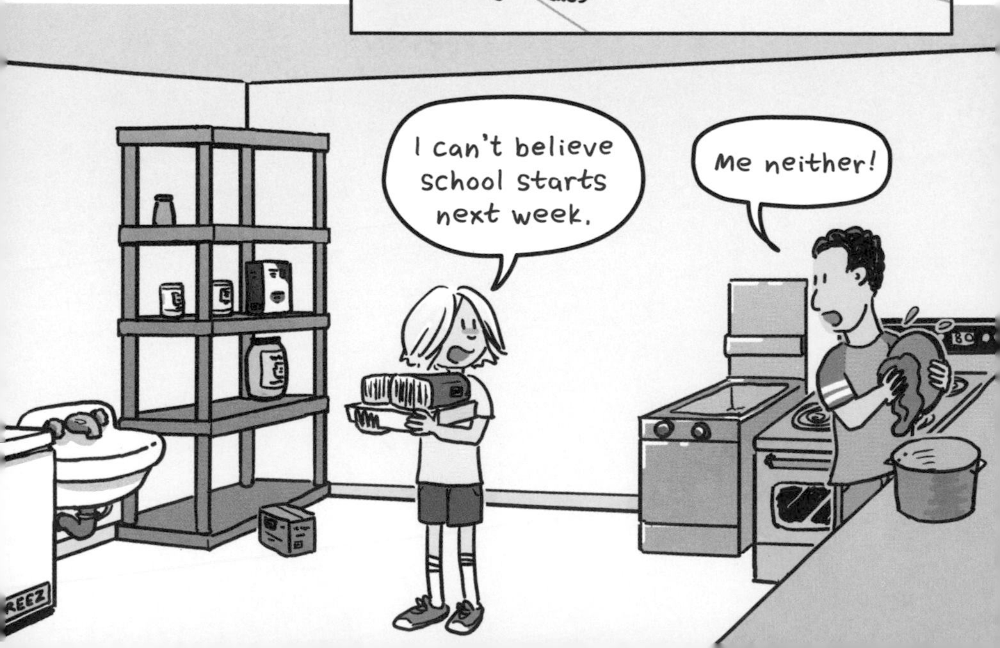
I can't believe school starts next week.
Me neither!

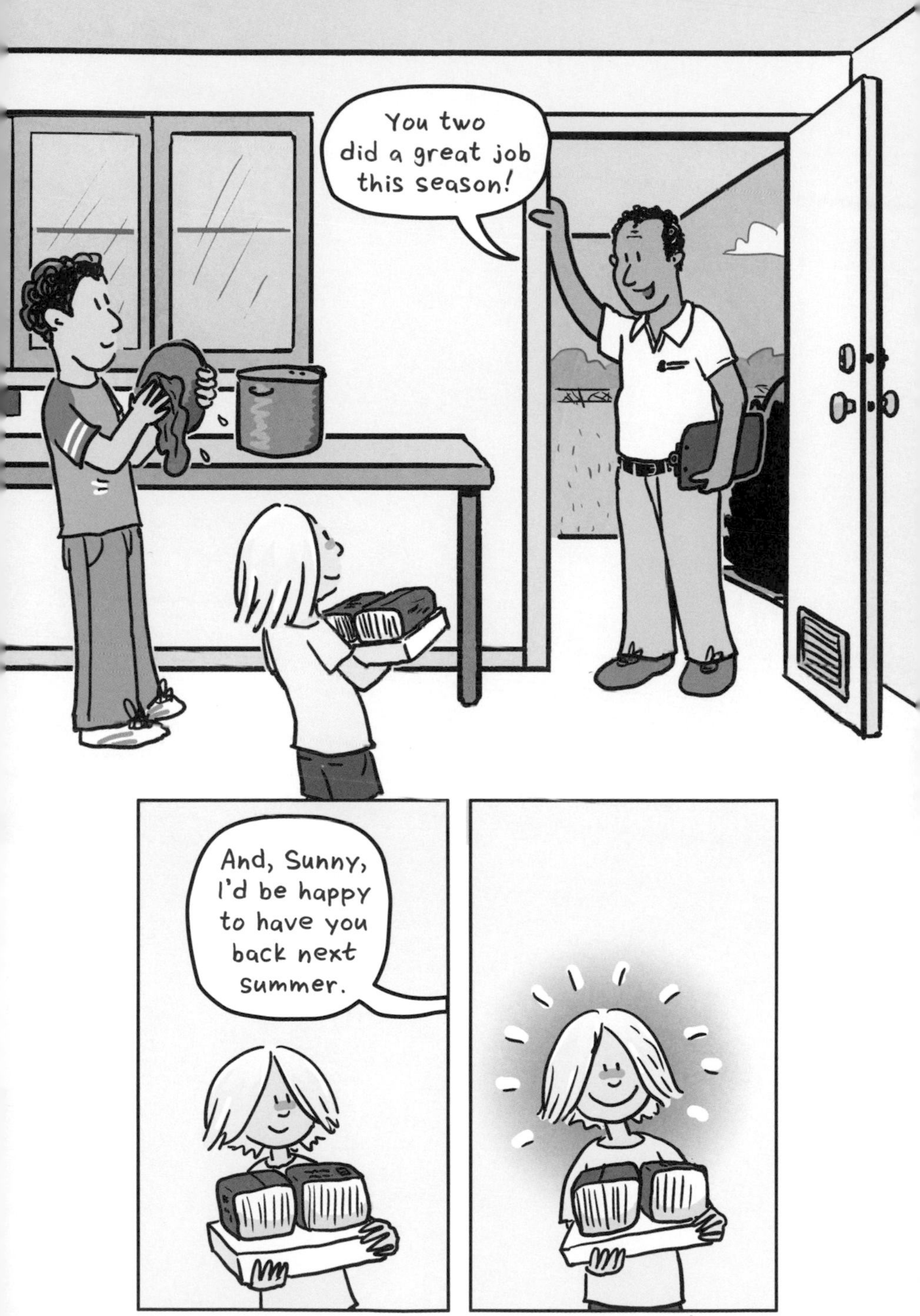
You two did a great job this season!
And, Sunny, I'd be happy to have you back next summer.

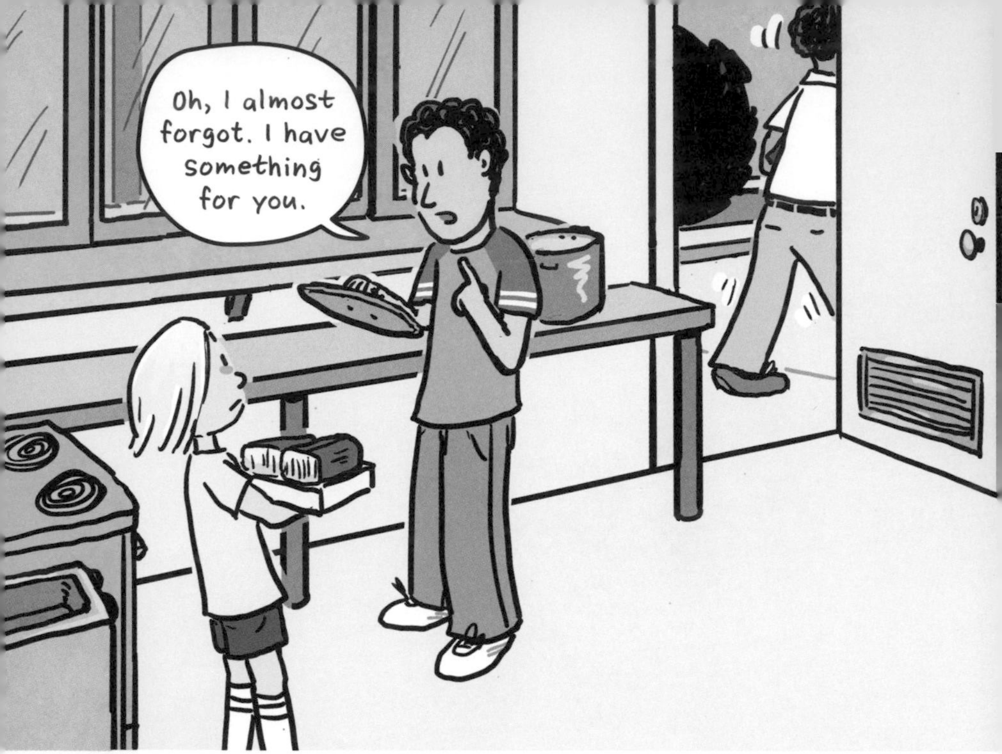
Oh, I almost forgot. I have something for you.

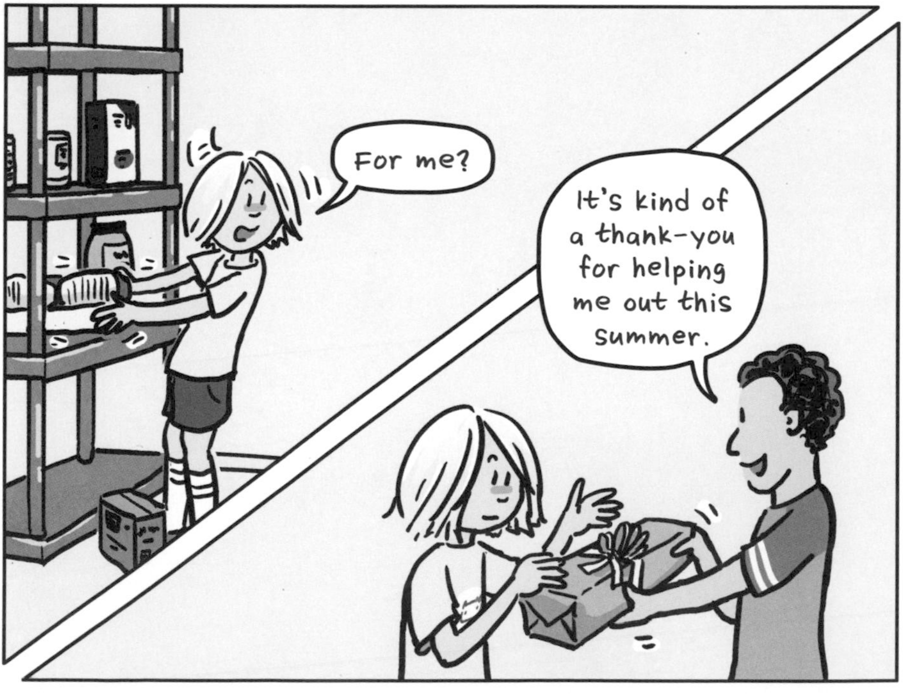
For me?
It's kind of a thank-you for helping me out this summer.

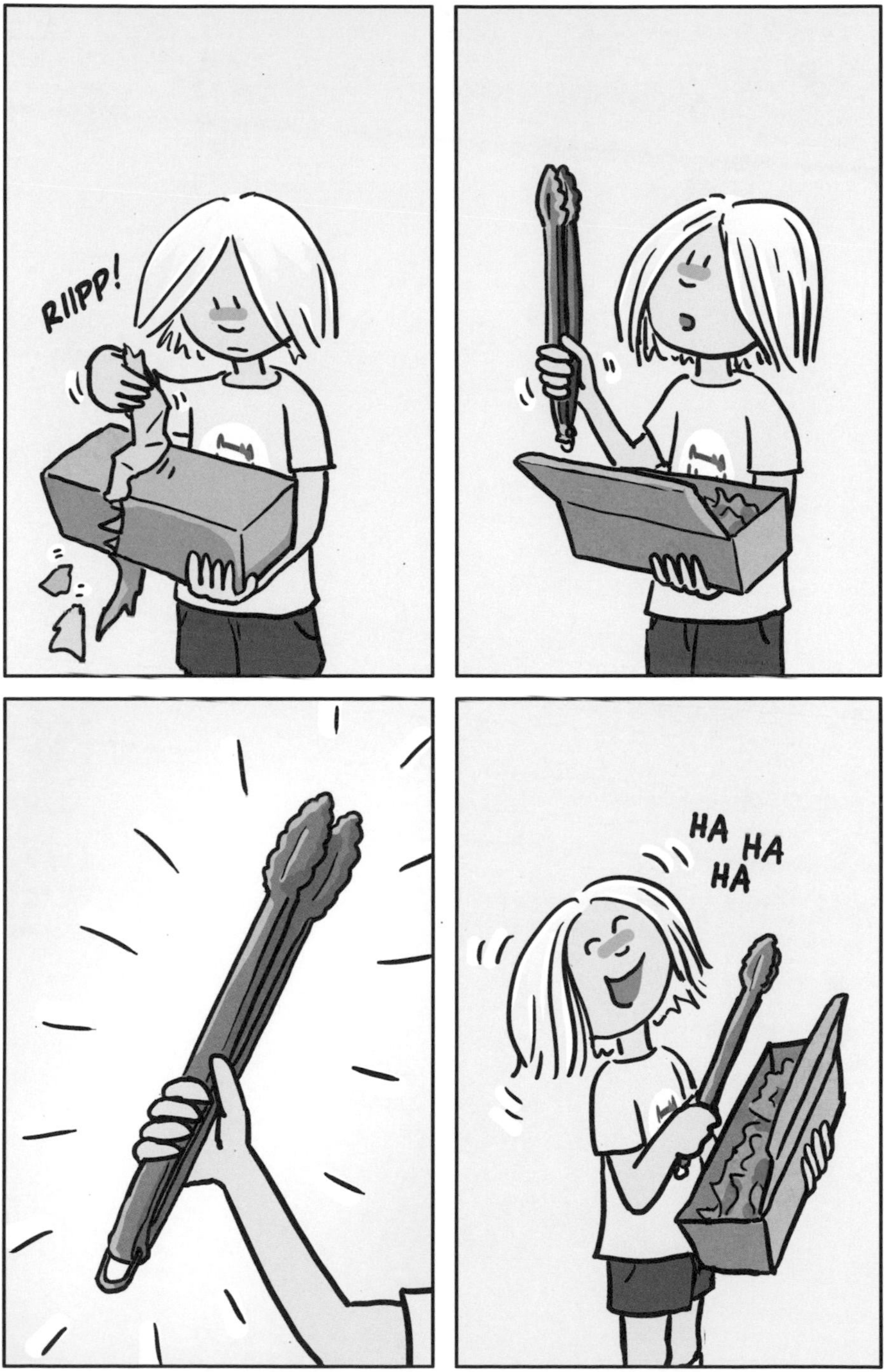
RIIPP!
HA HA
HA

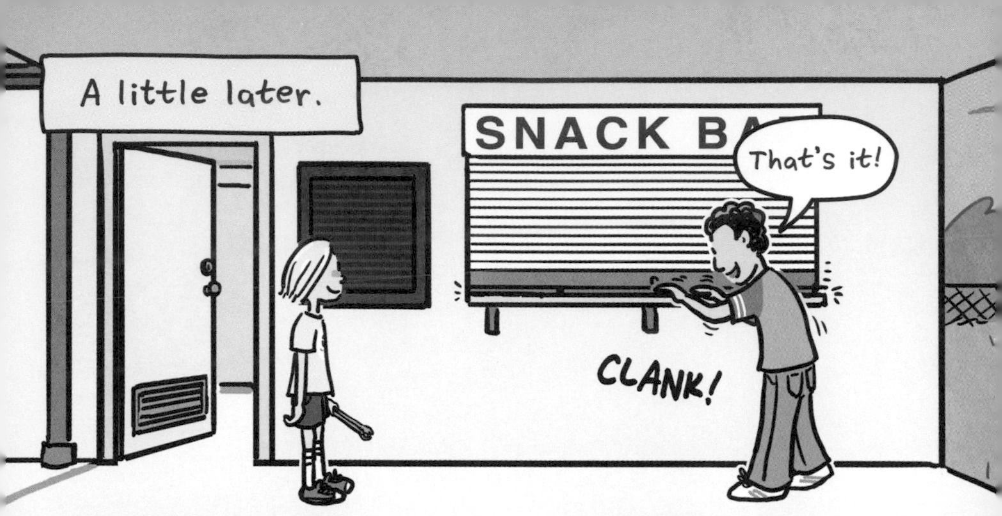
A little later.
SNACK BA
That's it!
CLANK!

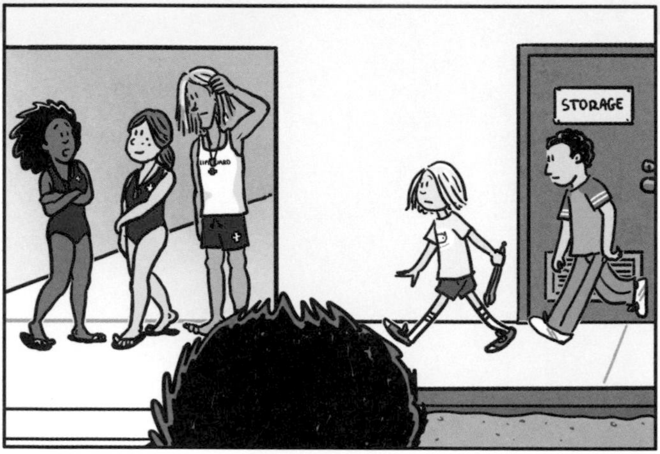
STORAGE

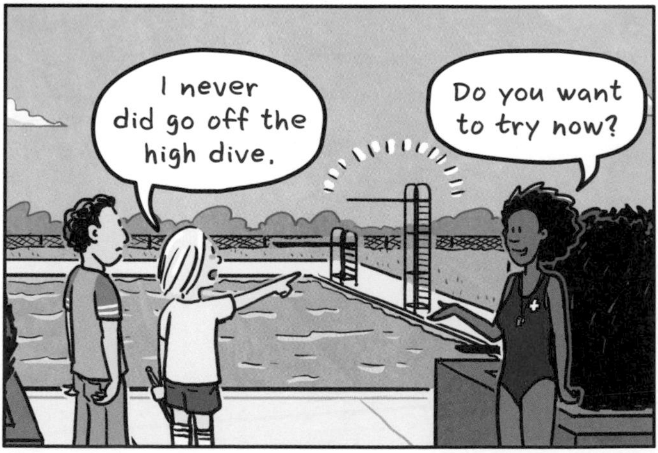
I never did go off the high dive.
Do you want to try now?

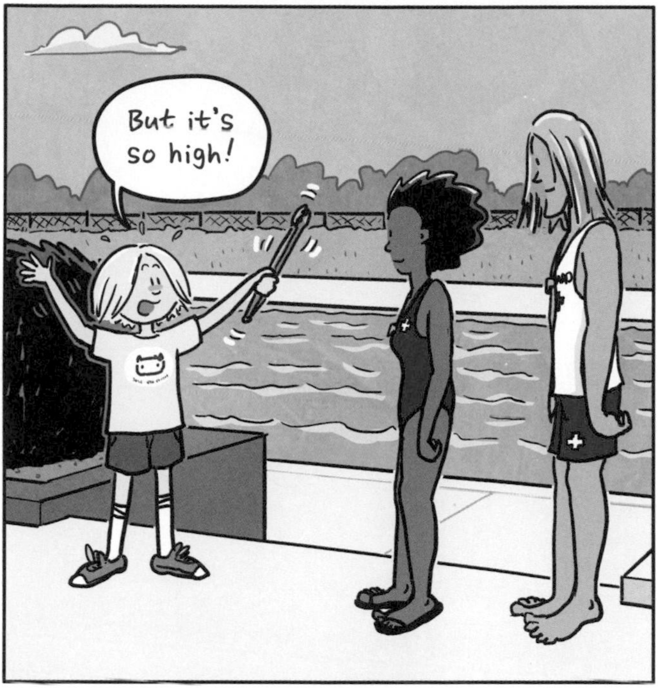
But it's so high!

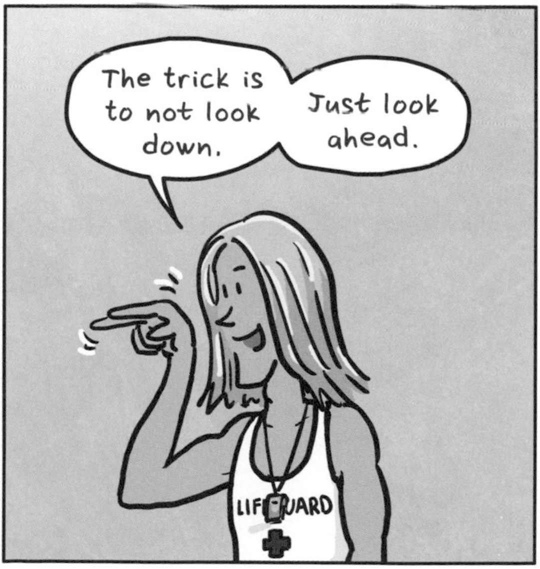
The trick is to not look down.
Just look ahead.
LIF UARD

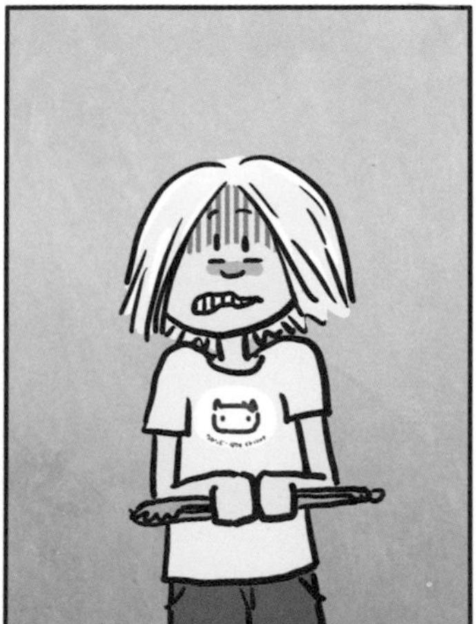

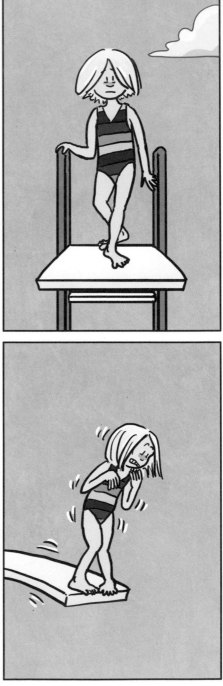

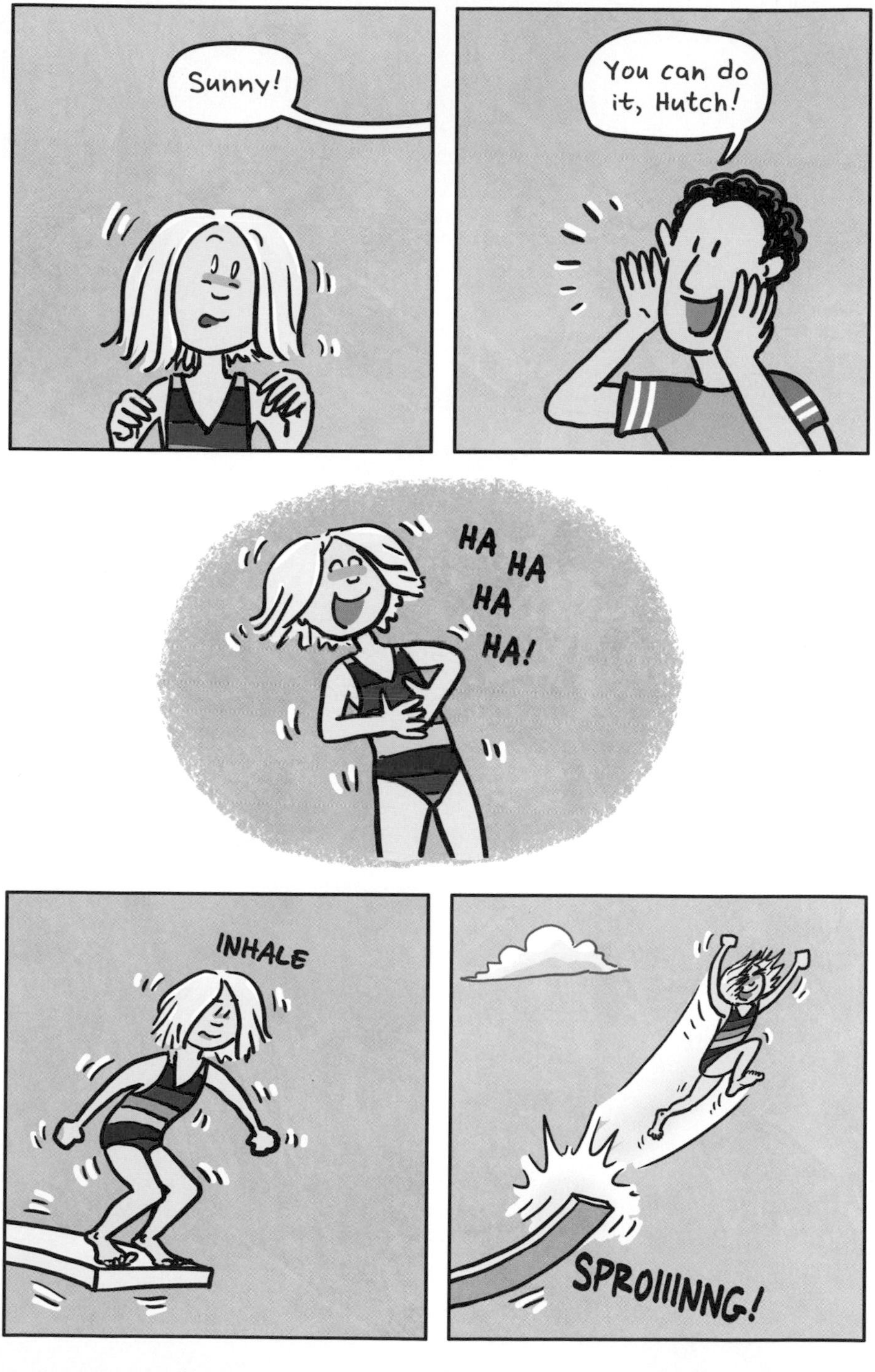
Sunny!
You can do it, Hutch!
HA HA HA HA!
INHALE
SPROIIINNG!

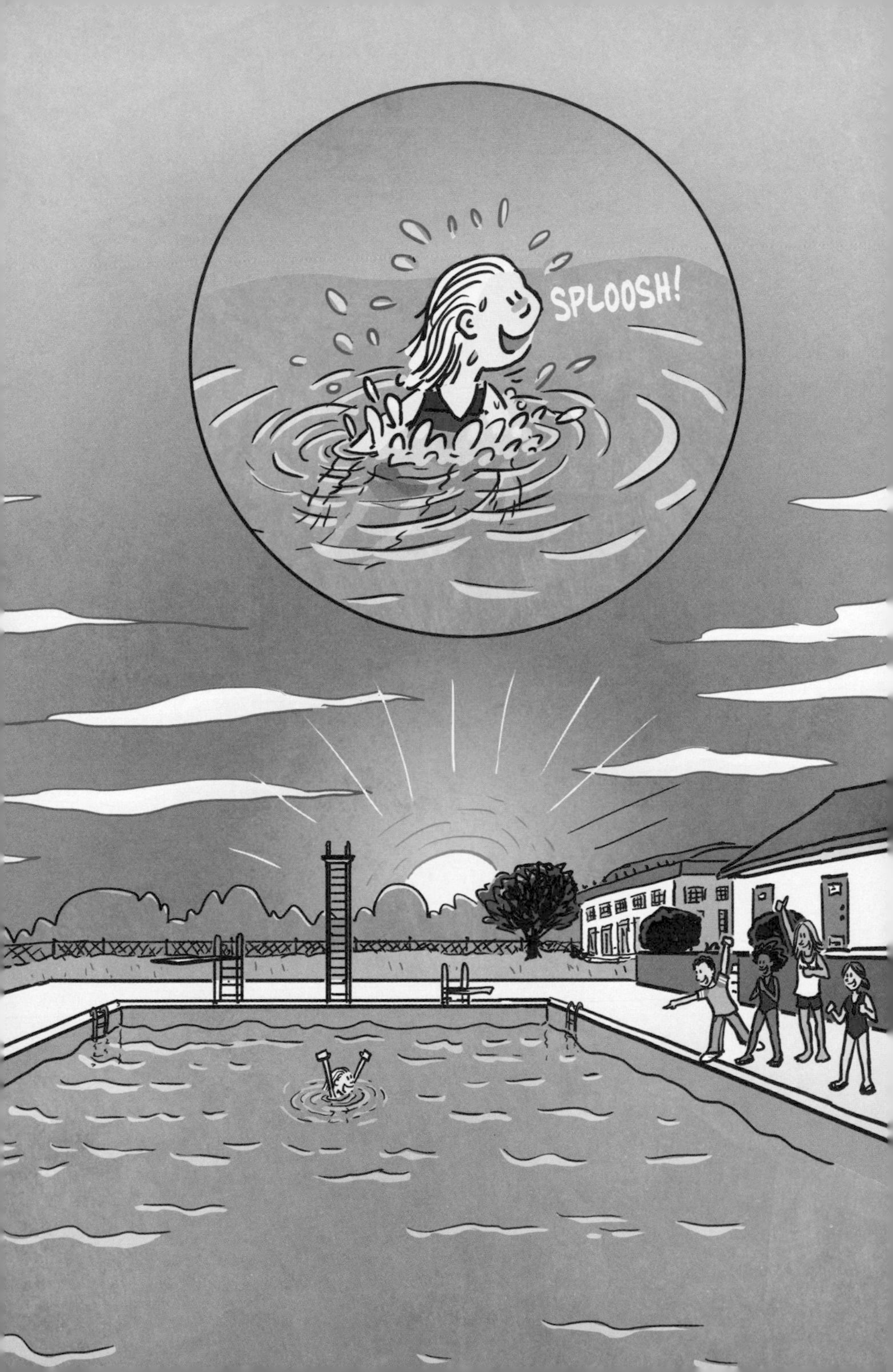
SPLOOSH!

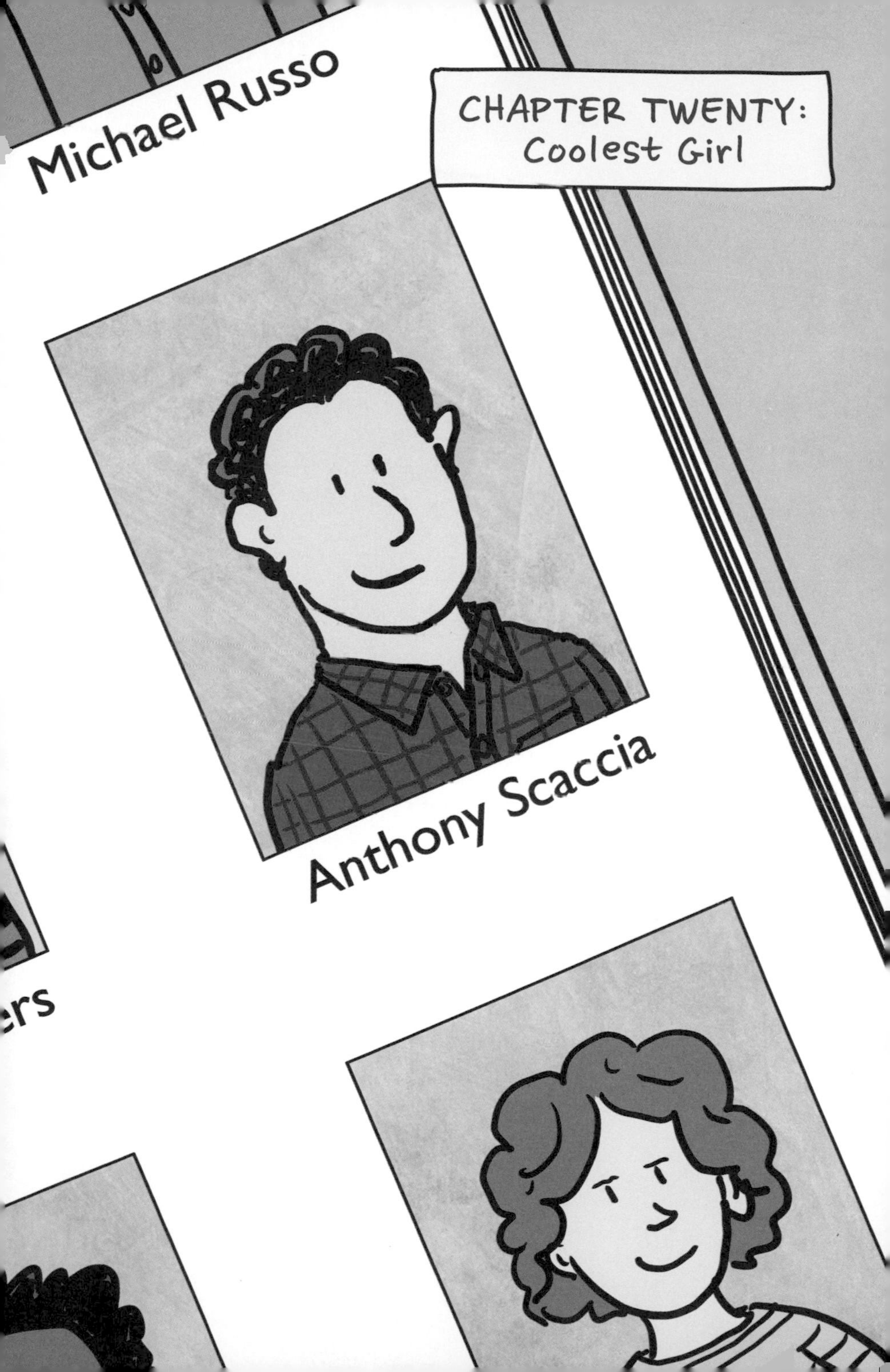
Michael Russo
CHAPTER TWENTY:
Coolest Girl
Anthony Scaccia

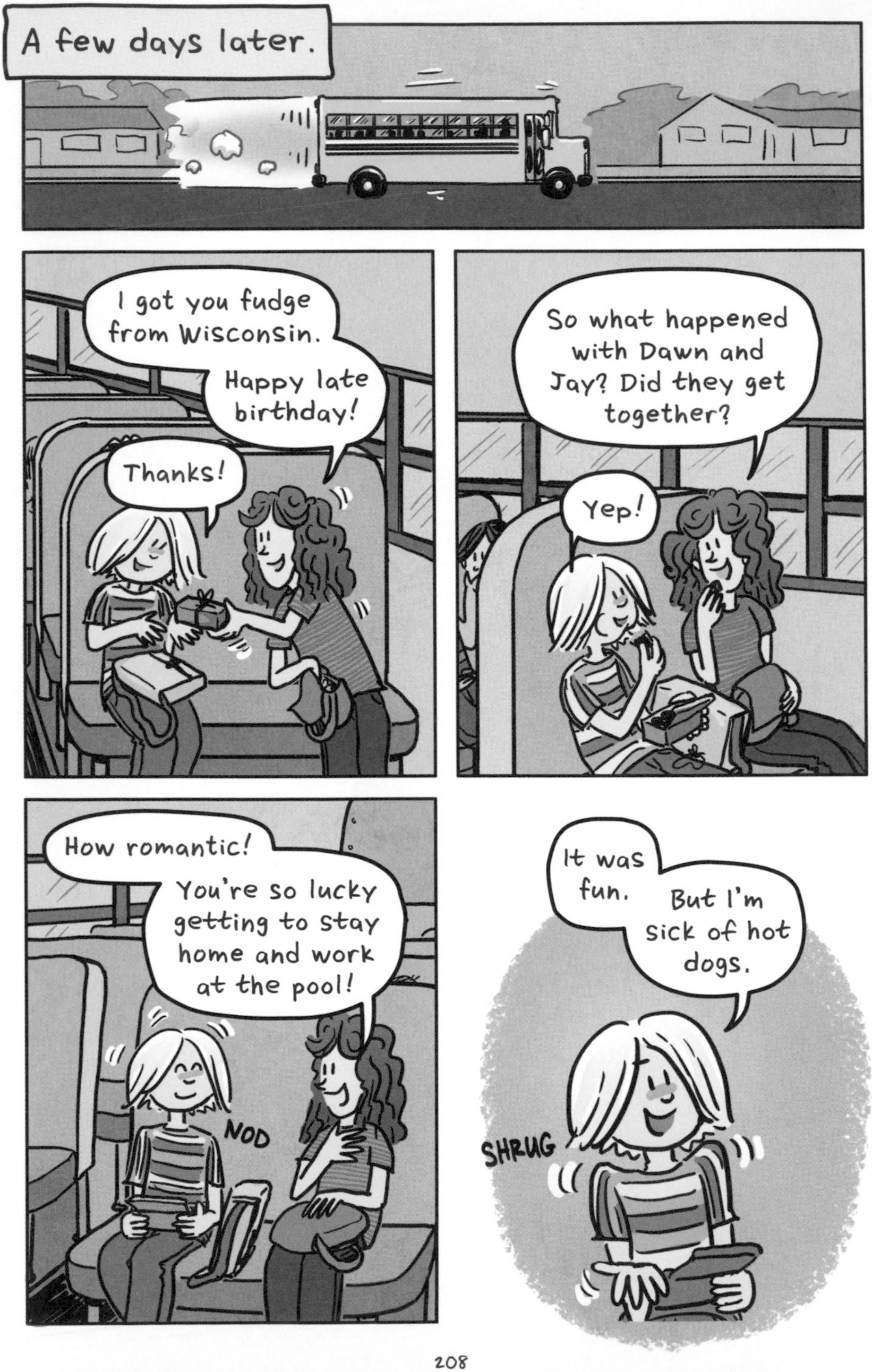
A few days later.
I got you fudge from Wisconsin.
Happy late birthday!
Thanks!
So what happened with Dawn and Jay? Did they get together?
Yep!
How romantic!
You're so lucky getting to stay home and work at the pool!
NOD
It was fun.
But I'm sick of hot dogs.
SHRUG

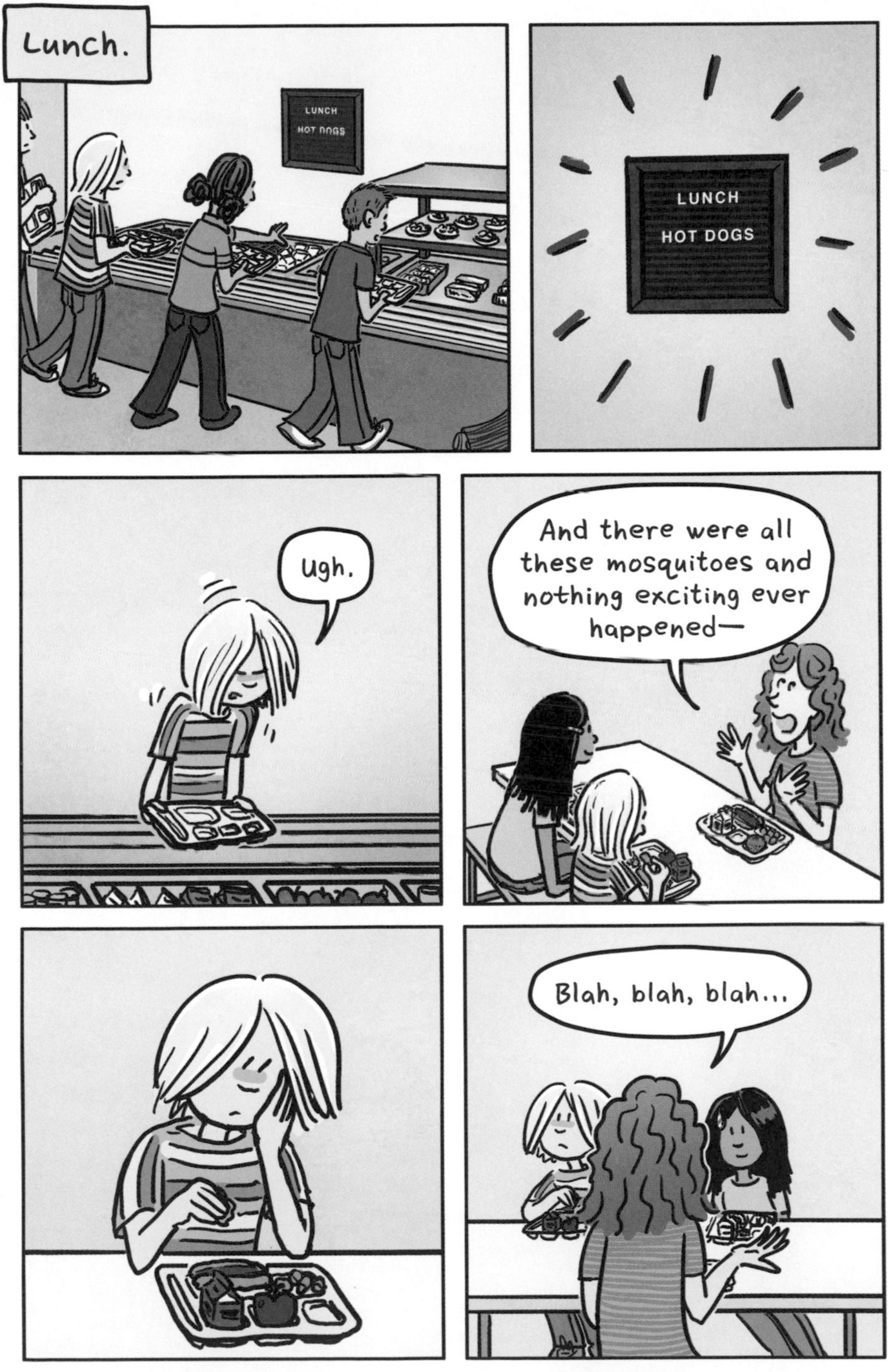
Lunch.
LUNCH
HOT DOGS
LUNCH
HOT DOGS
Ugh.
And there were all these mosquitoes and nothing exciting ever happened—
Blah, blah, blah...

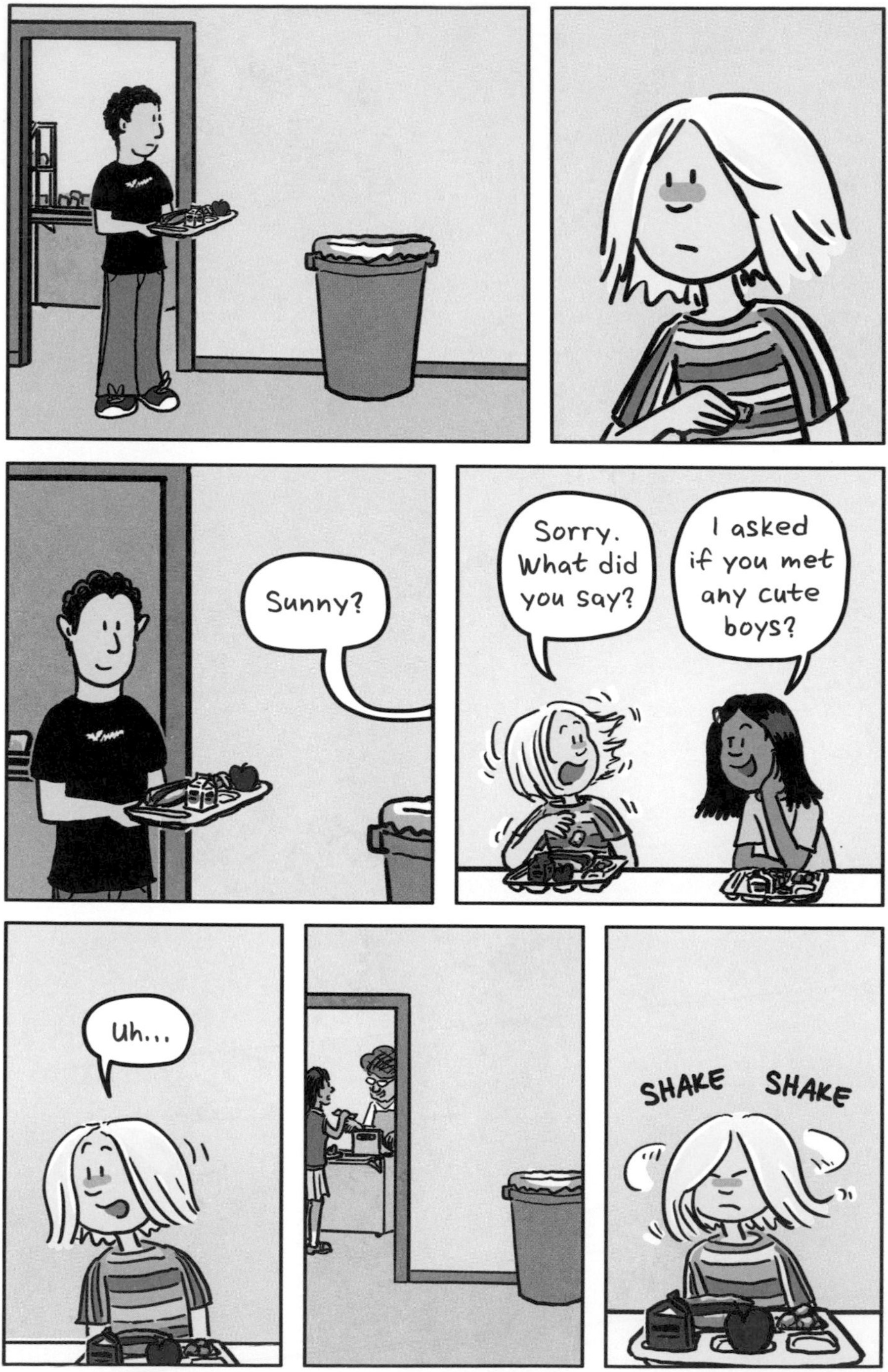
Sunny?
Sorry. What did you say?
I asked if you met any cute boys?
Uh...
SHAKE SHAKE

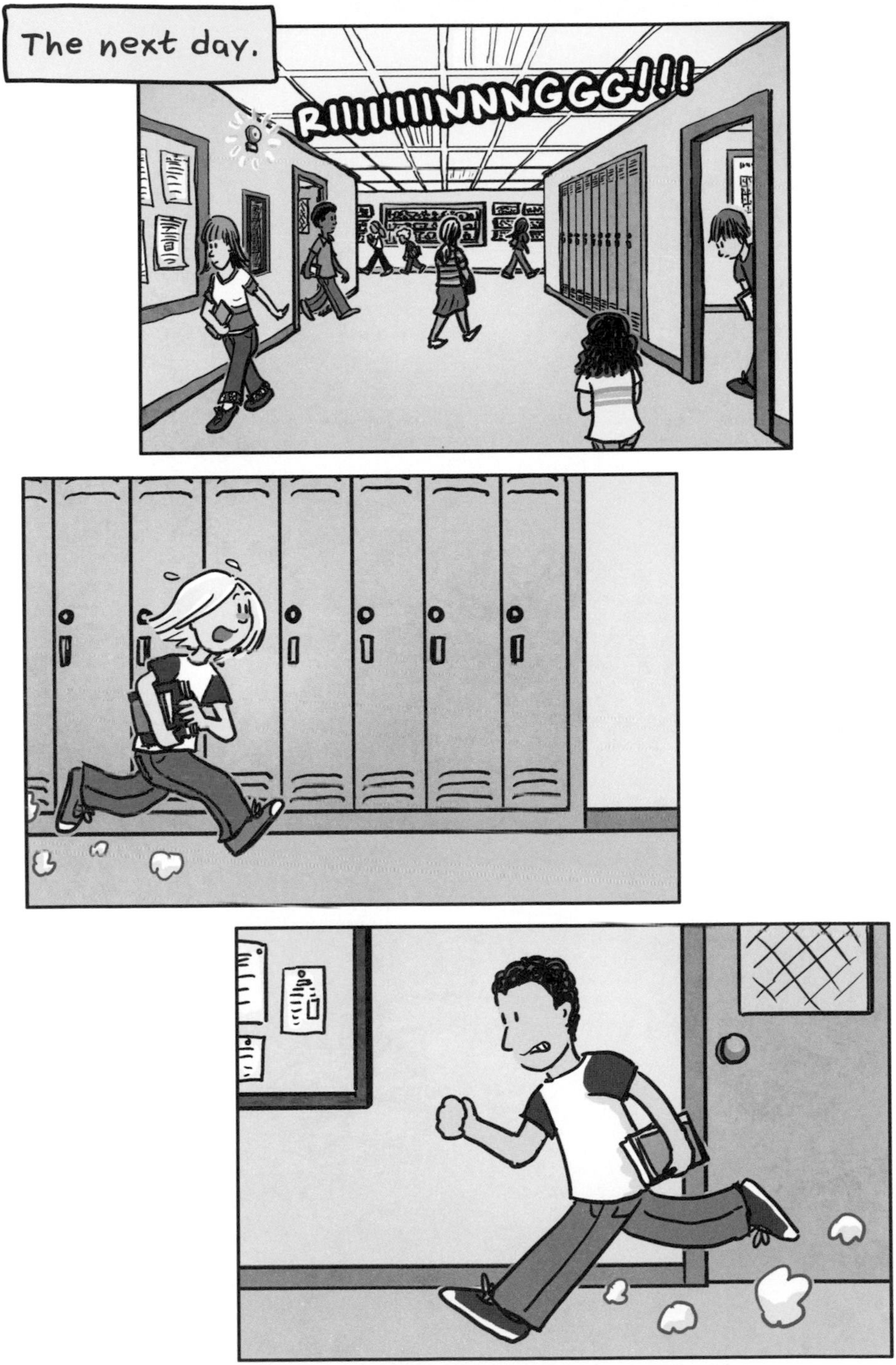
The next day.
RIIIIIIIINNNGGG!!!

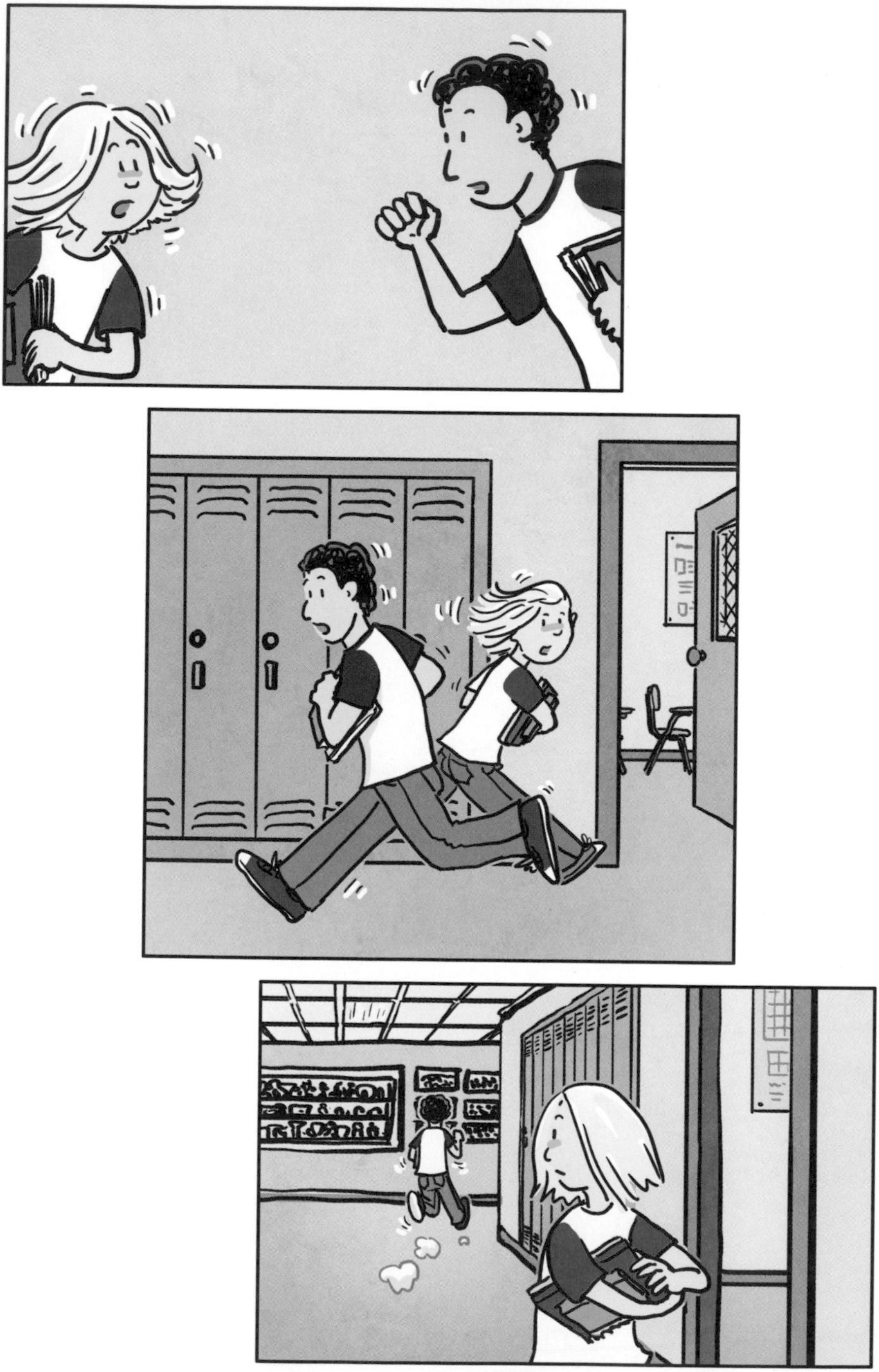

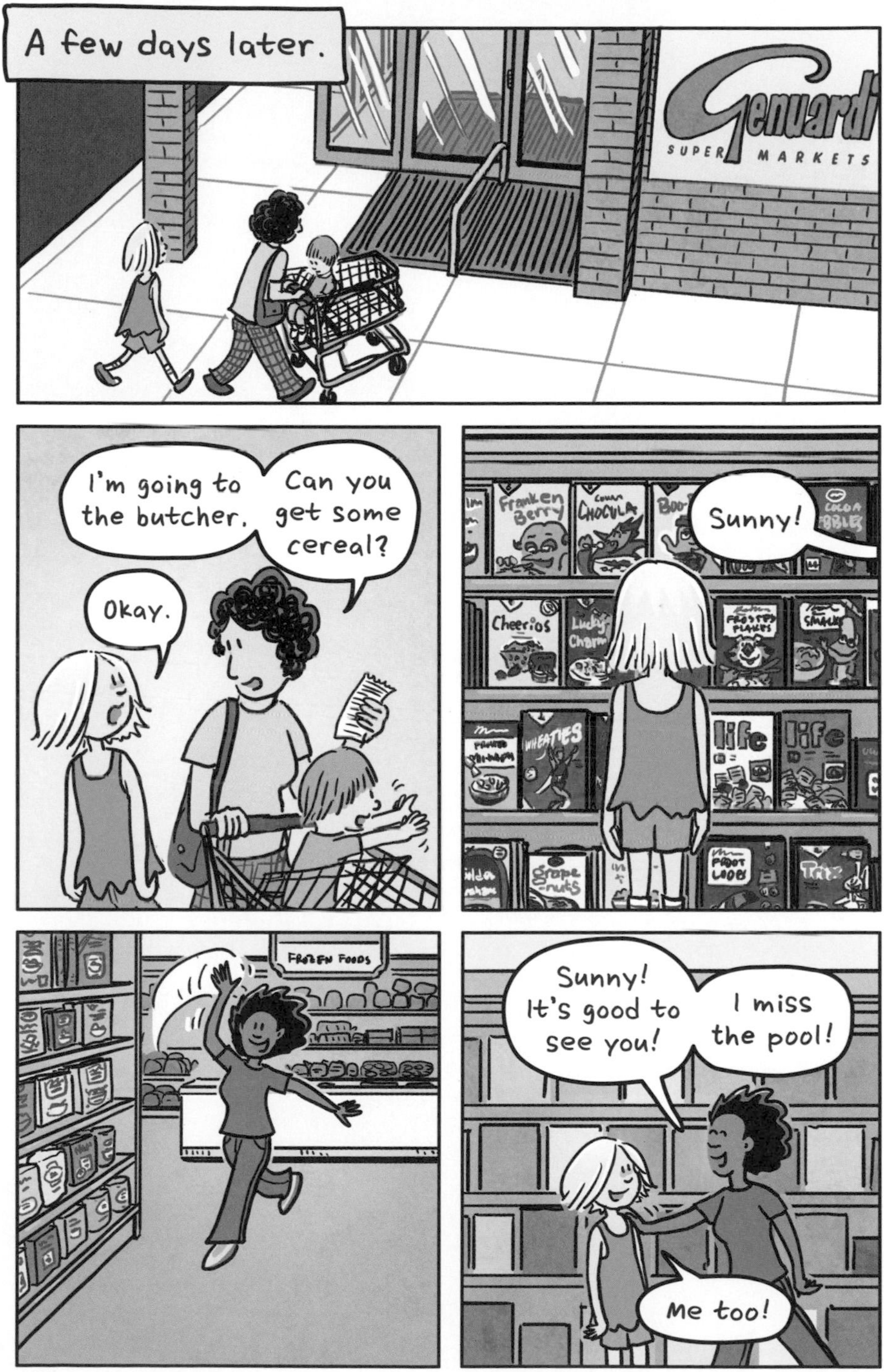
A few days later.
Genuardi SUPER MARKETS
I'm going to the butcher.
Can you get some cereal?
Okay.
Sunny!
FROZEN FOODS
Sunny! It's good to see you!
I miss the pool!
Me too!

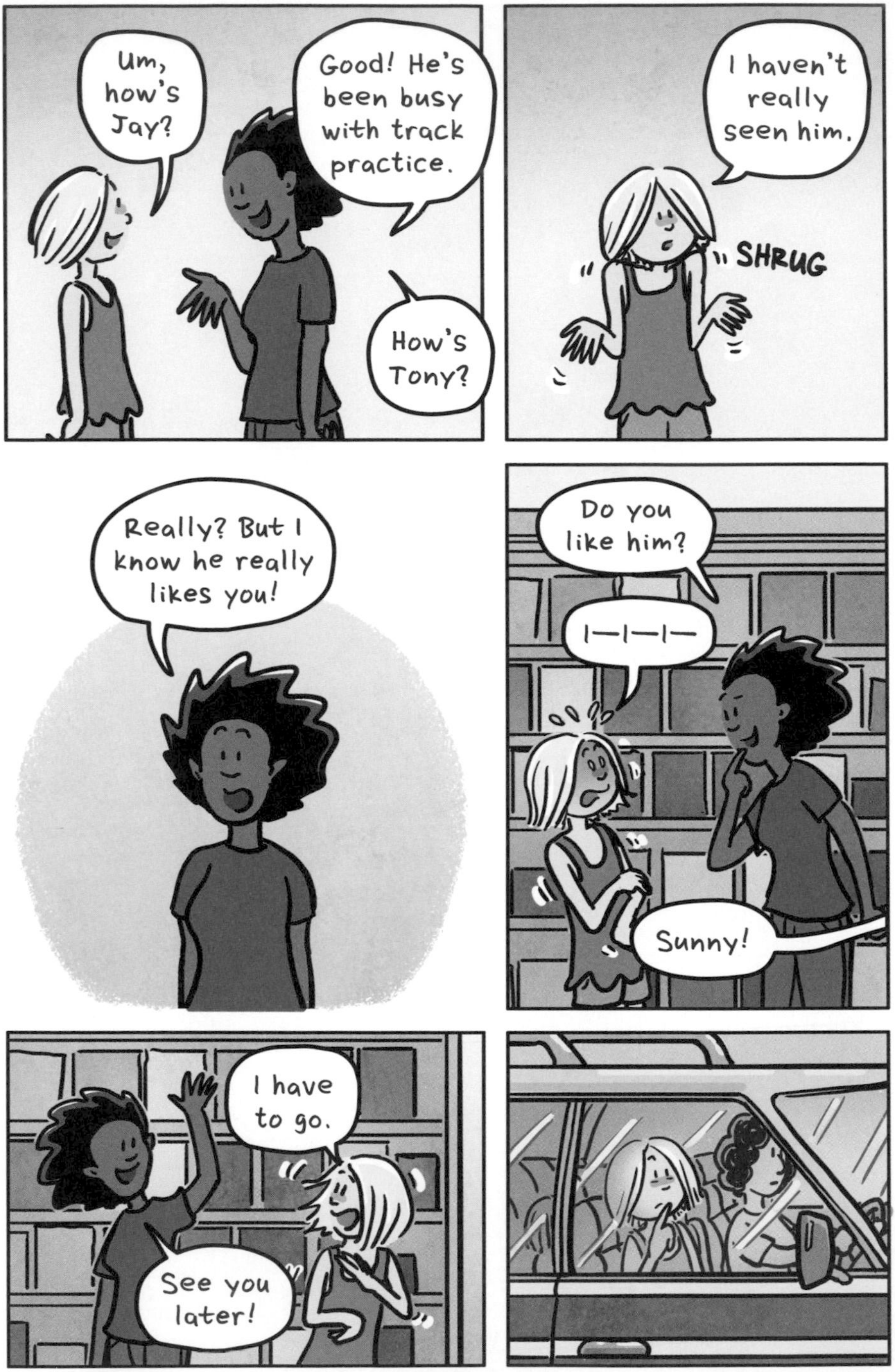
Um, how's Jay?
Good! He's been busy with track practice.
How's Tony?
I haven't really seen him.
SHRUG
Really? But I know he really likes you!
Do you like him?
I—I—I—
Sunny!
I have to go.
See you later!

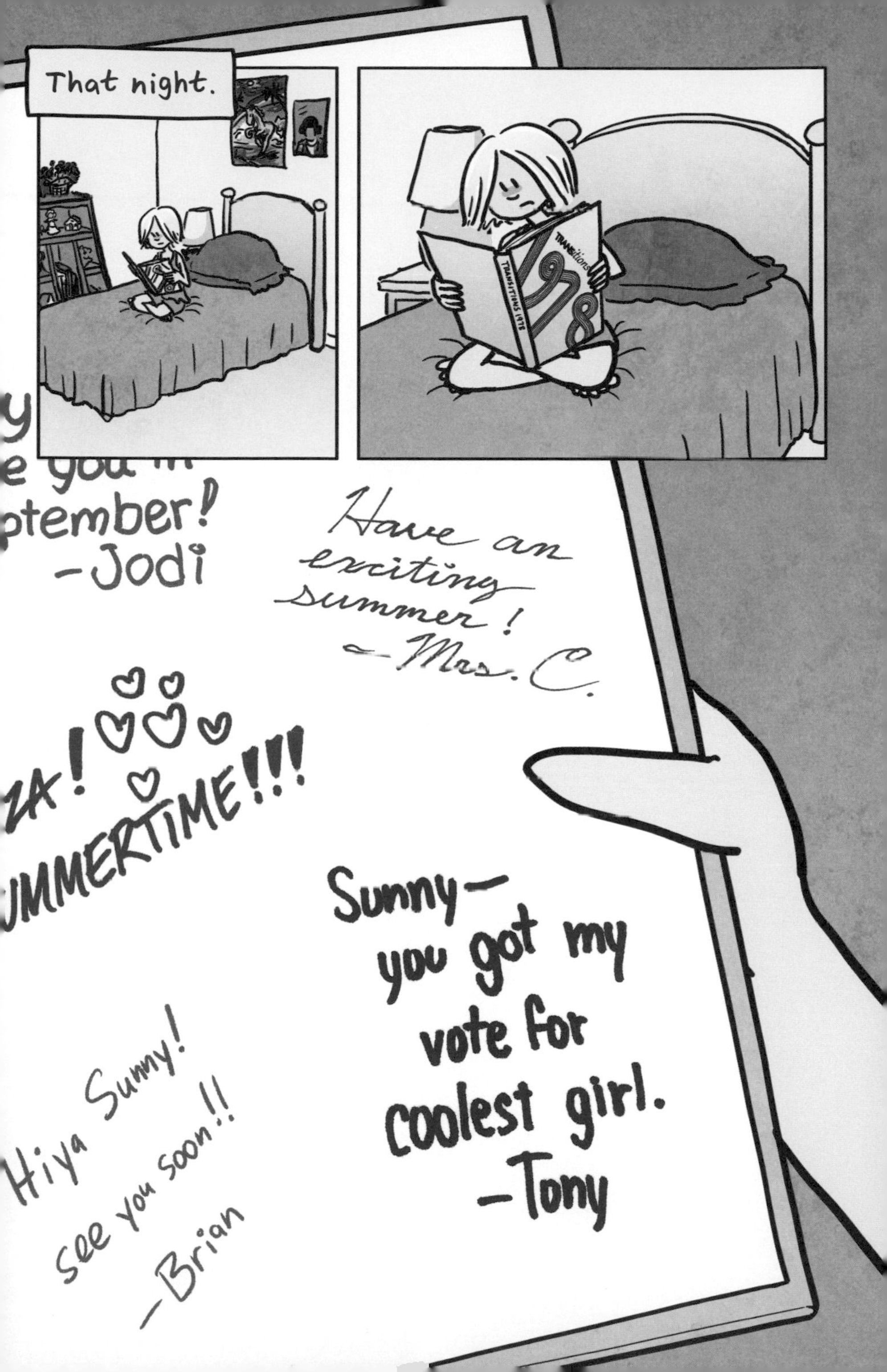
That night.
TRANSITIONS 1978
y
e you in
ptember!
-Jodi
Have an exciting summer!
-Mrs. C.
ZA!
UMMERTIME!!!
Sunny—
you got my
vote for
coolest girl.
-Tony
Hiya Sunny!
see you soon!!
-Brian

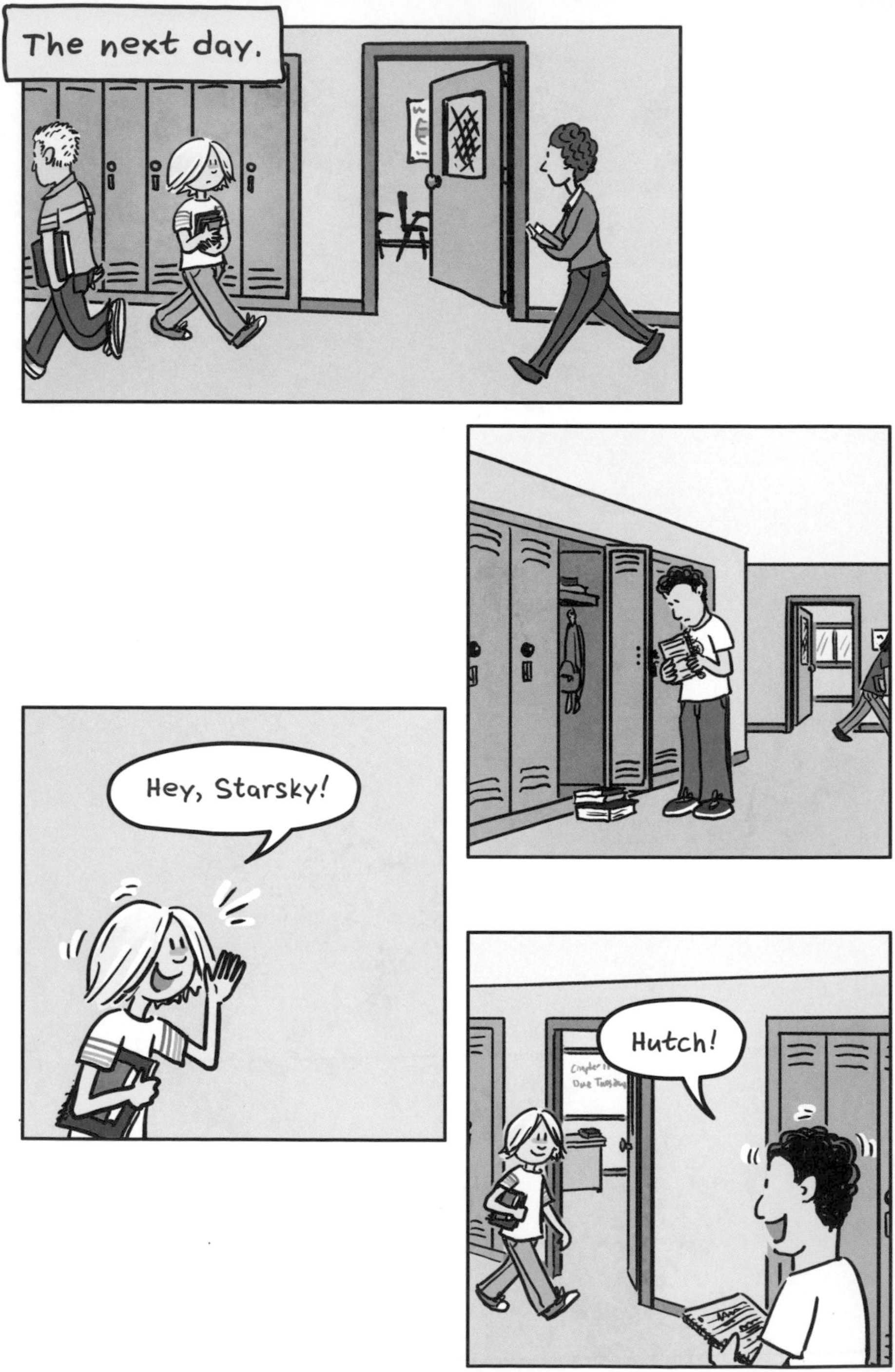
The next day.
Hey, Starsky!
Hutch!

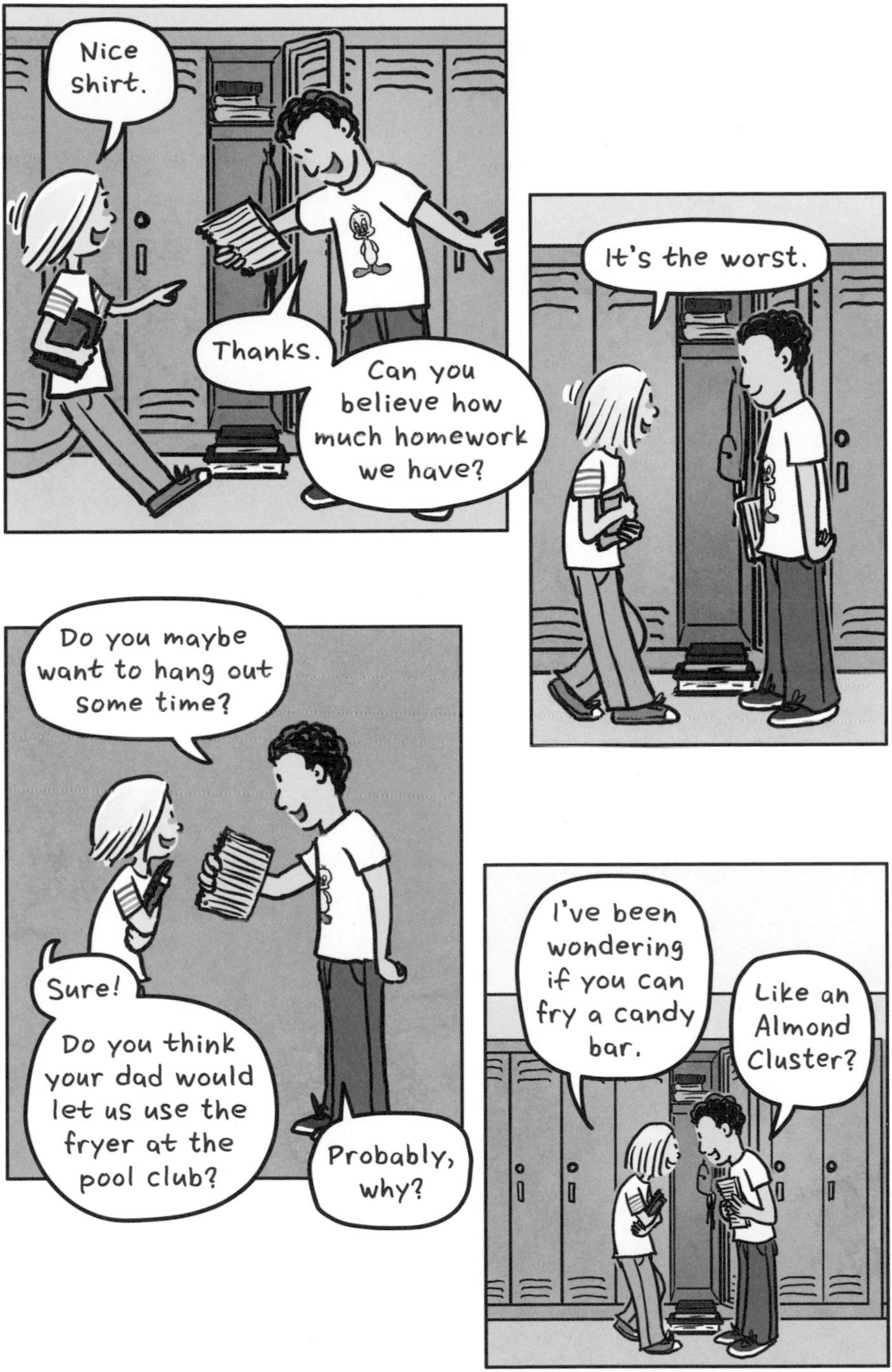

Nice shirt.
Thanks.
Can you believe how much homework we have?
It's the worst.
Do you maybe want to hang out some time?
Sure!
Do you think your dad would let us use the fryer at the pool club?
Probably, why?
I've been wondering if you can fry a candy bar.
Like an Almond Cluster?

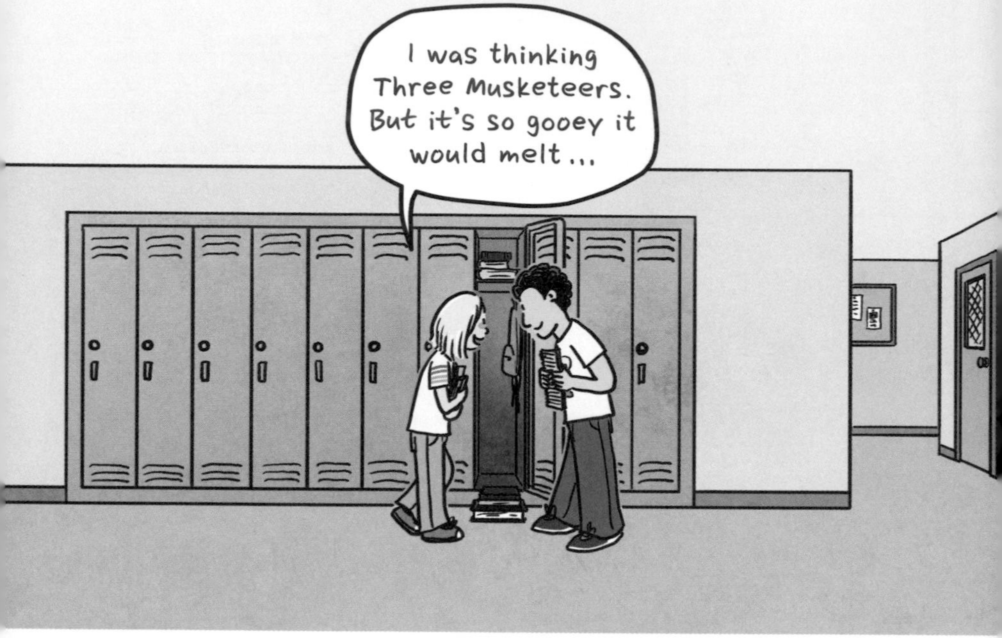
I was thinking Three Musketeers. But it's so gooey it would melt...

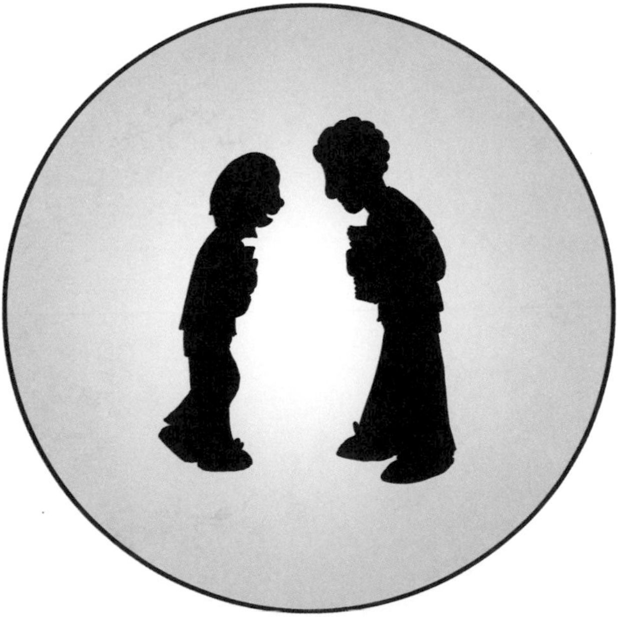

ACKNOWLEDGMENTS

We had many lifeguards who helped Sunny make her Splash! Many thanks to our hardworking crew: Lark Pien and Fawn Lau. The gang at Graphix kept us in top form, especially David Levithan, Phil Falco, and Lauren Donovan. As always, thanks to Cyndi Koon and our lovely agent Jill Grinberg.

Finally, we owe a debt of gratitude to our late grandfather, Michael Hearn, who wrote the poem "Sweet Myrtle." He had the heart of a romantic and the soul of a poet.

A NOTE FROM JENNIFER L. HOLM & MATTHEW HOLM

Sunny's summer adventure was inspired by Jenni's childhood. Her first real job (after babysitting) was working at the snack bar of the local pool. She handed out ice cream and sodas and was a whiz at deep-frying french fries. Eventually, she became a lifeguard at the same pool and spent far too much time telling kids not to run. To this day, if she sees a kid running around a pool, she will shout at them to walk. (Falling on wet concrete is no joke!)

JENNIFER L. HOLM & MATTHEW HOLM are the award-winning brother-sister team behind the Babymouse and Squish series. Jennifer is also the author of many acclaimed novels, including three Newbery Honor books and the NEW YORK TIMES bestseller THE FOURTEENTH GOLDFISH.

LARK PIEN, the colorist of SUNNY MAKES A SPLASH, is an indie cartoonist from Oakland, California. She has published many comics and is the colorist for Printz Award winner AMERICAN BORN CHINESE and BOXERS & SAINTS. Her characters Long Tail Kitty and Mr. Elephanter have been adapted into children's books. You can follow her on Twitter @larkpien.